ONE WEEK IN LINCOLN

BOOK 5 IN THE BACK TO BILLY SAGA

2ND EDITION

A novel by:
Michael Anthony Giudicissi

Mankind Productions, LLC
Albuquerque, NM

2nd Edition

Mankind Productions, LLC
Albuquerque, NM
billythekidridesagain@gmail.com

Book Design & Layout: Mary Dolan
Copy Editor: Ann Lokey

Retail: $20.00

WEDNESDAY 8 PM

It happened, if it happened at all, in such a split-second as to be almost immemorable. In one instant, Rosita Luna, a woman whom Martin Teebs had never met, but who was integral to an extensive story within his now-addled brain, was barreling toward him on the lone street of Lincoln, New Mexico. This woman was in lust, no, in *love* with him - apparently from beyond her grave, since Martin existed in the year 2021 and Rosita in the time of the Lincoln County War, circa 1878. Depending on what one believes, Martin had either spent some forty years of his life in this weird shadow-world between the past and present, or he'd spent a mere thirty seconds there while unconscious, after choking on some green-chile enchiladas made by his host and hostess, Dallas and Darlene Jones, at the Patron House Bed & Breakfast in Lincoln. Martin was unable to determine which was true, so lucid and clear was every detail of his incredibly derailed life in his mind at that moment.

Just as the beautiful woman leapt into his arms and her lips began to graze his, the entire scene disappeared, as if one were watching a movie in a theater and the projector bulb blew out: everyone groans, and a teenaged assistant manager comes out to explain that they're 'working on it,' and the entire audience can go avail themselves of a free small soda and popcorn refill. In the seconds before he saw the great beauty, Martin wouldn't have even remembered her, having lost all but the tiniest slivers of memories of the extraordinary journey that he now decided must have been his brain's last-ditch attempt to fire during his death throes. Luckily for him, Lilly Teebs, his pretty wife of twenty years, had forcefully pounded on Martin's chest, hard enough to dislodge the choking hazard after what amounted to (or so he was told) less than a minute.

Upon coming to, Martin was left with a vaguely unsatisfied feeling that he'd been ripped from some reality that was at once both incredible and unbearable. His decision to take a walk in the night air hadn't done a thing to help fill in the mostly blank spots in his mental canvas - until he'd fallen ill by the side of the road. About to regurgitate what was left of his dinner, he'd tumbled into a roadside depression and then awoke, seemingly in another time and in the very brief company of Ms Luna. At the first sight of her, the entirety of his story flooded his brain like an angry tsunami, and each detail filed neatly into place.

Martin Teebs was the best friend of none other than Billy the Kid, with whom he'd become somewhat obsessed over the past eight months. After a late-night rendezvous with the film *Young Guns*, Martin began researching the life of the young outlaw by watching every film and reading every book he could find. Upon winning a work-sponsored contest for two plane tickets to wherever he and Lilly wanted to fly, they both enthusiastically agreed that New Mexico would make a fine destination for their late summer journey. In preparation for immersion into the lore of William H. Bonney, Martin and Lilly watched *Young Guns* and its sequel more than once. While Mrs. Teebs was not the historian that her husband had become, she was quite the fan of actor Keifer Sutherland, who in both films played a tragically romantic character named 'Doc Scurlock.' While wondering if the real Doc had been able to turn a phrase like the actor, Lilly became intrigued by the entire cast of characters of the real Lincoln County War and decided that tiny Lincoln, NM, would indeed be an ideal spot for her and Martin to rekindle the flame of their somewhat stagnant relationship.

Not only had Martin been friends with the Kid - at least in his wildly complex fantasy ('The Dream,' as Martin decided it should be called) - but he'd written some four books about his experiences of being pulled back and forth through time. Great joy and overwhelming tragedy had befallen Martin, and those around him, as he was thrust into the center of the Lincoln County War. He'd seen men killed, and he'd killed a man or two on his own. His repeated slingshots back and forth in time had created tension and drama in his otherwise unspectacular life. The books he'd written (or maybe some other shadowy figure had authored) told, in great detail, the bittersweet tale of one Martin Teebs. However, his writings had been panned as pure fantasy and fiction. His heartbreak over his beloved Rosita's ultimate end was ridiculed by internet bullies far and wide, as was his professed 'best-friend' relationship with Billy the Kid.

So here Martin stood, on the outskirts of nowhere, on a vacant street in a town that most of the world could not care any less about, staring to the west in hopes that Rosita Luna, the great beauty and love of his life - at least The Dream version - would return.

In short, Martin felt like a fool.

"You just had a dream," he explained to himself, as darkness fell on Lincoln. "You almost died. Be happy you're alive."

Martin breathed in a brace of the increasingly cool night air and scanned the town. This was what he and Lilly had waited for. They'd carefully planned this trip to coincide with Old Lincoln Days, a pageant of sorts celebrating the life and times of the Kid and the Lincoln County War. He couldn't let a fat chunk of enchiladas ruin the entire thing for them. Shaking his head, he turned back toward the Patron House, as night encroached upon the remnants of the day.

Martin proceeded carefully because he clearly remembered his numerous clumsy falls in The Dream, accidents that somehow propelled him forward and backward through the fabric of time. Although by now he'd explained himself to himself enough to know that what was in his brain didn't *really* happen, the vivid colors of The Dream achingly haunted him still. As he approached the Patron House, he was taken aback by his memories of the place, and how he eventually came to own it and seal it up for all time - at least in The Dream. This place, and the magic it somehow contained, seemed to endow The Dream version of Martin Teebs with the ability to flip back and forth to a time and place with which he had fallen in love. He'd ridden as a Lincoln County Regulator. He'd made some wrongs right, and he'd made some wrongs even more wrong.

Martin couldn't help but feel that somehow the wrong life had flashed before his eyes when he had lost consciousness earlier in the evening. The tale his mind was telling him was fantastical, to say the least, but it wasn't the kind of thing that happened to a middling, quality-control manager from Waldwick, NJ. With so many ghosts of times gone by probably lurking in this historical town, Martin imagined that somehow his death throes had been mixed in with those of someone else in the town's archives, and that short circuit had given him access to a life he had never lived.

"That's gotta be it," he finally told himself, as he walked across the crunchy gravel parking lot toward his *casita*. He allowed the memories to begin to drift away, like a pile of feathers in a warm summer breeze. One by one, they left Martin alone, at least for the time being - except for one that stubbornly refused to cede its ground.

Rosita

Martin had never heard or read about any 'Rosita Luna' during the era of Billy the Kid and the Lincoln County War. She certainly *could* have existed on the fringe of history, but the woman in his mind's eye was so perfect, so incredible, and so sought after that Martin would have expected at least a mention of her *somewhere* in accounts of Lincoln County's violent past. That he could have conjured her out of thin air as

he lay dying seemed impossible. His dream girl was Lilly, his long-suffering wife of twenty-plus years. He knew that having a woman like Lilly agree to spend her life with him was a once-in-a-million shot, a fact he was reminded of just about every time he looked at her.
So what of this Rosita?

Even if she were conjured up from some subconscious recess of his mind, how could he have created every detail of the woman's tragic story arc with such precision? How, in fact, could he have seen her bearing down on him in the street just a few minutes ago? He hesitated to ask himself, but how could a woman like her fall in love with a guy like him? He finally decided that focusing on The Dream, while fascinating, was going to ruin much of the here-and-now he planned to enjoy with Lilly, starting early the next morning. Focusing on Rosita - a non-existent girlfriend of the type Martin used to imagine as a young boy - might ruin more than just his trip to Lincoln. Pushing aside all thoughts of anything but his lovely wife, he climbed the porch steps to his *casita* and turned the door handle. Martin stepped across the threshold to find a smiling Lilly waiting for him on the sofa, eager to plan their next day's activities. As he did so, somewhere in Lincoln, the ghosts of the past flitted back and forth, before spinning away like so many tiny dust devils, until they were all long gone.

THURSDAY 6 AM

With a mighty yawn, Martin stretched his arms wide and peered through sleepy eyes at the morning's light streaming into the windows of his *casita*. He pushed his arm farther left, searching for Lilly, but her presence was not apparent. Taking a deep breath, he could smell the aroma of freshly brewing coffee, and he surmised that she must have already awakened and prepared the magical elixir. Sliding slowly out of bed, he carefully padded down the steps of the loft to the life waiting for him below.

"Morning, hon," Lilly greeted, as she took her first sip of steaming coffee. "How'd you sleep?"

Martin took another deep, bracing breath to wake himself up before answering. "Really well. I'm not sure I moved at all last night. How about you?"

Lilly smiled and raised her glass to Martin as if toasting him. "Okay. I've been excited to get out and see some sights, so I guess my brain got the better of me!"

As Martin walked over to the coffee pot, he marveled at how lucky he'd gotten. Not only did he have an incredible wife who was far more beautiful than he probably deserved, but she'd actually fallen into the same mania as he had: an obsession with Billy the Kid. To be fair, Lilly was much less 'into' the Kid than her husband; but her curiosity about history, coupled with her affinity for '80s and '90s brat-pack stars, swayed her to agree to *this* trip over a number of other, more desirable destinations. In fact, when Martin had suggested Lincoln subsequent to winning the airline tickets, it took Lilly only a second or two to agree. After pouring himself a steaming mug of coffee, he joined his wife on the couch.

"So, Captain, what are we going to do first?" she asked.

"Well, Lil, I mean…the town is right here. We should go see all the buildings and museums today. It's going to start getting pretty crowded tonight, I'll bet, with people coming in for the pageant." Martin imagined an influx of Billy 'newbies' for the annual Old Lincoln Days, people who would have a passing interest in the Kid and stop because it 'seemed like something fun to do.' To Martin, this town was like his church. He held the buildings and history of the place sacred. He imagined himself annoyed, walking through town tomorrow with a bunch of people quoting *Young Guns* and misidentifying buildings and key spots in the Lincoln County War. While he knew he couldn't stop the sacrilege, he could avoid the experience by getting out into town early and having some real time to connect with some real history.

The other thing gnawing at Martin on this warm August morning was the recollections of The Dream he'd had the day before. Although already dismissed as resulting from his frantic brain spraying its excess energy into the world while he lay dying, he still couldn't get past the realism and intricate detail of the thing. He'd not mentioned a word of it to Lilly as she was represented in it - and not at all favorably. He did wish he had someone to talk to about it; however, his friend Colin was two thousand miles away, and his father Arlo was living the quiet life of a widower in Rhode Island.

"Okay!" Lilly broke in, tearing the silent thoughts from Martin's mind. "As long as you're up for it, hon? After last night, I was a little worried about you."

"No, no…I'm fine, Lil," Martin declared. "It was a wild ride there for a few seconds, I guess, but I'm good."

Martin's dismissal was meant to make Lilly feel better, but his description of the event piqued her curiosity to the point that she was forced to ask, "What do you mean 'a wild ride'?"
Martin quickly tried to defend his innocent statement. "Oh, I mean…you know. It was just...ummm...well, I imagine that it was scary for everyone. Yeah, it just...oh, ummm…felt weird, I guess."

If Martin's broken answer was intended to put Lilly at ease, it worked in just the opposite way. More intrigued than ever, she pressed on, rubbing the back of his head with her hand as she spoke. "Did you feel something, Martin? Did you see something…like a bright light?"

Venturing into a territory he didn't want to visit, Martin tried to joke the whole conversation away. "Bright light? Me? No. I just felt a sledgehammer on my chest when I was coming out of it. How could I know my pretty wife could hit so hard!"

Lilly feigned a little smile but persisted. "Yeah, but I mean you were almost gone, at least for a few seconds. Oh my God, Martin, did you have a near-death experience? What was it like?"

What was it like? thought Martin. At the time he came to, he wouldn't have been able to tell Lilly much of anything. It had felt like being ripped from a dream so forcefully that the fabric of it shredded into a million pieces. Only when Martin had walked out onto the street last night had the memories - if that's what they were - come back. It was as if all of the water that just went down the drain suddenly refilled the entire sink in the blink of an eye, such was the volume of the story that he was sure he had concocted in his brain.

What could Martin possibly tell Lilly about 'what it was like'? Could he tell her that she'd been sleeping with the guy who probably built the *casita* they were sitting in right now? Should he tell her that they'd gotten divorced when that guy got Lilly pregnant with a little boy she'd name Austin? How about her buying her way back into Martin's life by purchasing the very bed and breakfast in which they were now ensconced? There were a hundred more horrible ways in which The Dream portrayed Lilly, yet none that Martin could articulate. It wasn't real. Those things didn't happen. This was the year 2021, and he and his lovely wife were enjoying their first real vacation in years. If Martin was going to confess this...dream, this...fantasy, then it should be to someone else at another time. To bring it up today would only ruin the wonderful experiences he planned to have with his wife.

"It wasn't like anything, really, Lil," Martin lied, "it was just like I was asleep or something, and when you hit me, you woke me up."

"Oh," said Lilly, in what could be considered a dejected voice, "I thought maybe you would see something cool, or maybe know what comes next?"

By 'next,' Martin understood his wife meant *after* you die. If indeed Martin had had some insight into a past or future life while he lay choking, he wasn't sure he wanted any part of it at all. The feeling of heavy dread still hung over him, laced though it was with moments of sheer unbridled love and adventure. Pushing those thoughts as far as he could from his consciousness, he leaned over and gave his wife a big kiss on the cheek before speaking. "What comes next, Mrs. Teebs, is we have some breakfast. After that, we should get dressed and get out to meet the Kid. There are so many things to see here, and I don't want to waste a minute."

Lilly smiled warmly back at her man and batted her eyes. Pushing her head onto his chest, she attempted to clarify the last few items on their itinerary. "Sounds good. Now, when is that buddy of yours speaking? That Sergio guy?"

"Ha!" Martin laughed at the thought that he was actually friends with a famous author. "Sergio Bachaca and I are not buddies, Lil. I mean, we've traded a couple of emails and all, but I don't think that qualifies me as his buddy." While Martin was flattered by his wife believing that the author of the seminal book on the life of Billy the Kid was his friend, he wanted to make sure that Lilly didn't view him in the same way that she was bound to see a hundred or so losers, all who'd crowd Mr. Bachaca's table that weekend, all greedily seeking the author's autograph and hoping to get even a few words in with 'Serge,' so they too could consider him their 'friend.'

"Hmmm, okay, then. When does your email-trading author of that Billy the Kid book you're always reading speak?" asked Lilly, with tongue planted firmly in cheek.

"Saturday night!" Martin proclaimed joyously. "I've already got us tickets so we don't miss out." Martin had planned the events of the trip down to the letter, not wanting to miss out on any important Billy-related events. "Tomorrow night is the Lincoln After Dark tour with Brandon, Bachaca on Saturday night, and then the big pageant and reenactment on Sunday. In between, we can head to Ruidoso for some shopping, maybe?" offered Martin.

"Umm, sure, hon," said Lilly. "That's fine. I don't want us to miss anything here just to go shopping for some touristy stuff, though."

What a keeper! thought Martin. Most other women would run for the hills when faced with a weekend of middle-America hayseeds chasing down the legend of a long-lost outlaw in a dusty town on the verge of nowhere. Here was his wife, actually immersing herself in it! Martin made a mental note that the next vacation they took would be somewhere more tropical, more fitting to what he supposed Lilly's tastes to be. After being such a trooper here in New Mexico, she deserved at least that.

With the previous night's bad feelings receding, Martin reframed himself and eagerly started looking forward to the day. He rose to refresh his rapidly diminishing supply of coffee. Setting the mug down, he peered out the front door to find a bountiful tray of breakfast goodies waiting for him, just as hosts Darlene and Dallas had promised. Martin scooped up the tray, shut the door, and set their breakfast down on the dining table.

"Breakfast is served, my dear," he offered with a flourish. "Let's eat, dress, and get out there!"

Lilly smiled once again and walked over to the chair that Martin was holding out for her. "Thank you, Mr. Teebs," she said.

"You're most welcome, Mrs. Teebs," he responded brightly. "After we eat, we'll head out and start chasing the real Billy the Kid. Not like that stuff you've been seeing in the movies, Lil."

Lilly popped a grape into her mouth and pondered the upcoming day. Seeing her husband so full of life would be fun, she thought. It had been a long time since Martin had been this lively. "Okay, then, let's get this trip kicked off," she announced, before adding, "Hey, do you think we'll see Kiefer or Emilio here?"

Thursday - 7 am

Carl Farber had been saving for this trip for the better part of three years. The mild-mannered teacher from Waldwick, NJ, always had a love of the past, and US history was his weakness. As a young boy, he'd been placed in front of the television when his parents had other matters to attend to; and he was immersed in the western worlds of *Gunsmoke, Bonanza,* and *Tales of Wells Fargo*. When he was old enough to seek out such knowledge, he began to devour every book he could find on the Old Wild West and its many characters. Foremost among his favorites was, of course, Billy the Kid. Little Carl could imagine the Kid fighting for justice against the likes of the villainous Murphy-Dolan clan and standing up for those unfortunate, impoverished farmers and ranchers who bore the brunt of evils of The House. In Farber's mind, Billy stood for everything good and pure in the Old West, notwithstanding his need to kill a man or twenty-one in the process; therefore, the young outlaw was revered by those who loved him and feared by those who didn't. As Carl grew, he carried the spirit of the Kid with him, hoping one day to visit the haunts of Lincoln County so he too could walk in the footsteps of William H. Bonney.

Now an eleventh-grade history teacher, Farber's salary was small, but his dreams were big. He'd finally put together enough money for a full week's journey to New Mexico to coincide with Old Lincoln Days and, as last, get his fill of Billy and the Lincoln County War. On this morning, he stood patiently in line at Newark Liberty International Airport, waiting to board his big silver bird, nonstop to the great American southwest. As the line slowly moved along, Farber reviewed his itinerary in his head. He hoped to arrive in Lincoln (a three-hour drive from his wheels-down destination of the Albuquerque Sunport) late in the afternoon so that he'd have some time to explore before the throngs of other tourists flooded the small village.

Carl had booked a Lincoln After Dark tour for Friday night and would attend the Last Escape of Billy the Kid reenactment on Sunday. That left the big event, Saturday night. On Saturday, he had reserved himself a seat at the book talk by the esteemed Sergio Bachaca, author of *The True Life of Billy the Kid*, which Farber considered to be among the best books on the life of the outlaw. Secretly, Carl was hoping to get a few minutes with Sergio, enamored as he was with the man. If he could get a word in with his idol, he planned to press into Bachaca's hand a thumb drive containing Farber's own Billy book. Carl had spent a good part of the last five years researching and writing an academic history of the House of Murphy, the rise of Tunstall, and the origins of the Lincoln County War. He hoped that perhaps 'Serge' would think enough of it to send it to his own publisher, with a favorable recommendation. Farber didn't dare let himself dream - but perhaps one day, *he* could be the one giving the important book talks about Billy-related events around the country. Why not? he figured. Didn't Bachaca have to start somewhere, too?

"Sir?" The voice shocked Farber out of his daydreams and back into the present as a pleasant-looking gate agent implored him to show his boarding pass or scan a digital copy on his phone.

Embarrassed, Carl smiled, said, "Oh, I'm sorry," and handed over the crumpled paper. Walking down the jetway in the super-refrigerated air, he felt chills coming on, both from the ice-cold air and the excitement at his impending journey. Finally, after so many years of wanting and waiting, he was heading to New Mexico.

Carl Farber, the mild-mannered history teacher from New Jersey, was going to Lincoln County and, for the first time ever, was going to meet the real, historical Billy the Kid.

Thursday – 8 am

"Come on, Martin, everything's opening now," pleaded Lilly. At the stroke of 8 am, the entire town of Lincoln would come to life, and Lilly wanted to avoid standing in a lengthy line to buy a day pass to all of the historical buildings.

"Coming, coming," Martin huffed down the stairs, "just wanted to get my camera. Sorry, Lil." For the occasion of their trip, Martin had invested in a new digital SLR camera, surmising that the camera on his iPhone was good, but not good enough to capture every detail of the town. Martin assumed this would be his one-and-only chance to make the long trek to Lincoln and so didn't want to miss a thing to remember it by. Lilly held forth the screen door as he exited, and they made their way out toward the street.

"Let me go fill up water bottles, okay?" suggested Lilly. "I saw that Darlene has a water filter in the main house."

Just as Lilly crested the three stairs to the top of the porch, Dallas Jones bounded from the front door, nearly colliding with her. "Whoa! Sorry, Mrs. Teebs!" said the jovial host. "You're so tiny, I didn't see you there."

Lilly sidestepped the door and walked inside with a smile, saying quickly, "Just going to get some water."

Martin eyed his host carefully. He was absolutely prepared not to like the man, owing to the fact that in The Dream, Dallas had been screwing Lilly, both here in Lincoln and then back in New Jersey. One of their couplings had resulted in Lilly's pregnancy and a new little life named Austin to be welcomed into the world. With no other recourse, Martin and Lilly had divorced, and his life had spun helplessly out of control from that point forward. However, Martin knew that everything he was feeling toward the man was anger resulting from a situation that had never actually happened, so he pushed back hard on his feelings until they released him.

"Hey, Dallas, how're you doing?"

"Good morning, Martin. I'm doing spectacular. Are you okay?" Dallas ventured carefully, alluding to Martin's near death the evening before.
"Oh, you mean last night?" Martin acknowledged. "Yeah, fine…fine. I even went out for a little walk last night, I was feeling so good."

Dallas looked relieved, not sure what a guest choking to death on his wife's cooking would do to his insurance rates. While the two men chatted, the street behind them came to life with a slow but steady stream of tourists beginning to infiltrate the site of the infamous Lincoln County War, just as Lilly had predicted.

"So, are you one of those hardcores?" asked the pearly smiled Dallas Jones of his guest. "I mean, like a real serious Billy the Kid historian? Or are you more of a casual fan?"

Martin pondered the question before answering. Six months ago, he'd have had to admit he was a casual *Young-Guns*-type fan, but that had changed. After ordering and reading book after book, Martin felt he knew enough details about the War to host his own lectures. Of course, he never did since no one else he knew (other than Lilly) had anything more than a passing interest in Billy the Kid. So many details had he absorbed that Martin almost felt like he could have been part of the Lincoln County War. Even so, he yearned to know still more, even one additional fragment of information that would place him closer to the Kid. Martin had stared endlessly at the one commonly known picture of Billy; but he wanted to talk to the boy, listen to his voice, ask him mundane questions about what kind of dessert he liked, and so much more. Try as he might, Martin was unable to bridge the divide. In the end, he was just a serious amateur historian, who'd made the trek to Lincoln like thousands before him had. While he would probably know more about Billy than most of the people in the crowd this weekend, there would be others who would eclipse even Martin's knowledge bank. They were all chasing the same thing: to know a young man who had died one hundred forty years ago and would never be heard from again. Maybe just being in the presence of experts would be enough for Martin to feel like he had achieved his goal.

"Well, I guess I'm pretty serious, Dallas," Martin ventured. "A lot of people know more, but I've studied up on him quite a bit. I know I'm really looking forward to this weekend."

Dallas smiled back at Martin, just as he had a hundred or more times at the middle-aged men who paraded through the village. They all wanted the same thing, it seemed, and they all would spend money in order to obtain it. For what it was worth, Dallas Jones existed on the very edge of Billy the Kid knowledge. He knew enough to keep up the conversation with his guests, but his interests were in the here and *now*, not the here and *then*.

"That's awesome, Martin," Dallas began. "I hope it's everything you thought it would be. New Mexico puts on a pretty good show every year. I don't know nearly as much as you do, and I live here!" he admitted.

Martin could only laugh modestly at what he perceived was a small compliment. "Everyone appreciates the Kid in his own way, Dallas. I'll bet you know plenty of the real inside stuff. You'd have to, living here." Teebs looked around in wonderment, as if he were in heaven.

"No, seriously, I don't, Martin," replied Dallas. "These guys come in and sit around the table and talk 'Billy,' and I can't keep up. Most of what they talk about are movie quotes anyway. I can't tell you how many times in my day I've heard 'I'll make ya famous' or 'You remember me, I'm Travers, from Tularosa.' I just laugh it off and let them go on with themselves."

Martin made a mental note to not use any movie quotes this weekend as that obviously had the red, flashing 'rookie mistake' sign painted all over it. He'd have to tell Lilly, too, being that she'd watched the movies almost as many times as Martin had. Both men took a deep breath of the morning air, and Lilly and Darlene made an appearance on the porch.

"Looks like you're all ready for a big day in Lincoln!" announced Darlene, then looking at Martin. "I'm so glad you're okay. You had us worried sick last night, Martin. Tonight, we'll have something maybe a little less spicy."

Martin could only shrug and laugh it off. He didn't want to be known as the picky child who would only eat peanut butter and jelly. He was sure that whatever happened last night was merely an unfortunate accident. "No worries, Darlene, it was just bad luck. Anything is fine. Really," he assured her, as he turned toward Lilly. "Ready?"

"I'm ready," announced Lilly, with some verve in her voice. "Let's go see if we can't find Billy the Kid." With a grin, they walked off the porch toward the village's one street, now more crowded than Martin had hoped for.

Just before husband and wife got out of earshot of their hosts, Darlene called out, "Have a great time, you two!"

Lilly nudged Martin in the ribs with a smile before turning back and yelling, "I'll make ya famous!"

Thursday – 8:20 am

At the stroke of 8 am, it was as if all of the Billy-philes from all over the world had wound up in the same line to purchase a day pass to the village's historic buildings. Had Martin been a bit quicker out the door, the Teebs might have been somewhere around twentieth in line, rather than back the fifty or so spots currently spacing them from the overburdened employee selling tickets one at a time.

"Well, at least, it's a nice morning, huh, hon?" chirped Lilly.

"Yeah, I guess," said Martin uneasily. It wasn't the line that was making him squirm, it was *something* about the spot on which they were standing. The line snaked its way out of the Visitor Center and Museum and up toward the road. So many people had shown up that it stretched around the corner of one of the monument buildings and along Route 380 to the east. Standing at the corner of the roadside building, everything felt wrong to Martin, and he knew exactly why: This building didn't belong here - at least not during The Dream. What should have been there, historically preserved for all to see, was the tiny hut of Rosita Luna, with its turquoise-blue door.

In The Dream, Martin had stood in this exact spot many times over. He'd had dinner, kissed the beautiful young woman, undressed her slowly, and made love to her, all within a few feet of where he now stood with his wife Lilly. Of course, none of that

had actually happened in real life; but the more time he spent in Lincoln, the more real The Dream seemed. How could his memories (or complete fabrications) be so vivid that Martin could even remember what kind of candle Rosita lit on her dining table? It made no sense. The combination of the incredible sadness he felt toward a woman who had never existed, along with the guilt of having such love-making thoughts while in the presence of his wife, repelled Martin from the locale.
"Lil, I need some air. I'm just going to walk down by the creek," he said quickly. "Okay? I'll be back before you get to the ticket counter."

Lilly was at least a little surprised that Martin 'needed some air' since they were standing outside, and she raised her voice to be heard as he scooted away. "Are you okay, Martin?"

Martin just nodded and raised a hand in assent as he hastily tried to leave behind him Rosita Luna, Lilly Teebs, and a hundred hungry and cranky tourists. Walking along the parking lot, he finally escaped the asphalt and made the trees, where he began to castigate himself. "Pull it together, genius! You've been planning this trip for months, and you're going to ruin it over a dream?"

Rubbing his head in his hands, Martin tried to shake away the lingering sadness. Everything in his real world was topsy-turvy to what he had experienced in The Dream - Dallas was a decent guy, Lilly was psyched about learning about Billy the Kid, and Darlene hadn't so much as looked at Martin's ass even once (that he knew about, anyway). All this insanity had started because he was shoveling food into his mouth way too quickly, in hopes of getting done with dinner and gaining a chance to explore Lincoln. "Oh, you explored Lincoln, Martin," he said ruefully to himself. "You explored it and good!"

Peering back toward the line, he could see Lilly was making good time and was only a few minutes from reaching the ticket counter. Determining that he was giving no credence to his memories of The Dream for the rest of their stay, he turned to head back, just as a voice shocked him from his thoughts.

"Crowd's too much for you, huh? Same here," said a tall young man, arms covered in tattoos.

"Oh, you surprised me there," Martin responded tentatively.

The young man thrust his hand out toward Martin, who shook it gingerly. "Name's Brandon. I run the Lincoln After Dark tour. I love it here 'cause it's usually real quiet, but on days like this…" Brandon swept his hand across the parking lot, with a wry expression on his face, reinforcing the throngs of tourists that both broke the fabric of quietness of the small town, yet provided his income.

"I get it," replied Martin. "I'm Martin. Teebs. We're actually going to be taking your tour tomorrow night, Brandon. Nice to meet you."

The young man visibly brightened upon hearing that his new friend was also a paying customer. "Martin and Lilly Teebs! From…," he hesitated as he scanned his memory banks, "New Jersey, right?"

Martin was impressed. How many people must come through this town taking tours, and here the area's premiere tour guide not only knew their names, but where they were from! "That's pretty good, Brandon, wow! Yes. Lilly and I just got in yesterday from New Jersey."

"Well, cool, Martin," the tour guide said enthusiastically. "That'll make three of you from the Garden State."

Martin was doubly surprised that anyone else from New Jersey would be in Lincoln ever, but most especially during the pageant. "Really, huh? Who would have guessed!"

"Yep. Lemme see how the old brain is working," considered Brandon, as he squinted his eyes and turned his head. "Ummm...Farber, I think. Yeah, Carl Farber. Yep, that's it."

Farber! Martin saw red at the mere mention of a man he hadn't even known really existed up until this point. In The Dream, Farber was a scumbag, Dolan man who'd raped the great love of Martin's life and somehow lived to tell about it. Farber, the balding history teacher from Martin's own town of Waldwick, Martin's one-time friend, who had started a chain of events resulting in the death of Rosita Luna. Martin began to breathe heavily, and his eyes twitched at the mention of the man. Even though he knew

The Dream wasn't real, the coincidence of a man named Carl Farber from New Jersey, heading to Lincoln at the same time Martin and his wife would be there, was just too much. Somehow, this thing, this Dream, had taken on a life of its own. Martin's jaw tensed, and his fists balled up reflexively.

"Umm, Martin, you okay?" asked the tour guide, sensing his client's sudden dismay. "Do you know this guy? You have some kind of history with him?"

Motherfucker, thought Martin, do I have some kind of history with him! Where do I begin? He wanted to tell Brandon the sordid details. Of course, right after he informed Brandon that Farber was a part of some elaborate near-death dream he'd had, and that he'd traveled from the future to take part in the Lincoln County War, Brandon would tell the Lincoln County Psychiatric Hospital to come and fetch one of their residents who'd clearly gotten off the reservation. Martin let the tension wash away for a second before he answered.

"No," he responded, shaking his head gently. "No. I was...I was just thinking about waiting in lines all day. Sorry about that, Brandon."

Unsure of whether he believed the man or not, Brandon clapped him on the shoulder as he prepared to leave. "Okay, then. Hey, no lines tomorrow night! Meet at the *Torreon* at 8:30 pm sharp. You're going to love walking in the footsteps of Billy the Kid! See ya, Martin." With that, the tour guide walked back toward the Rio Bonito and disappeared into the trees.

Martin looked toward the Visitor Center and saw that Lilly was waving to get his attention, inching closer to the ticket booth all the time. He forcefully exhaled all of the negative energy from his body and began to walk toward her. The very fact that a Carl Farber was breathing was bad enough, but the idea that the man would be in Lincoln (or maybe was already here!) was too eerie for Martin. Reasoning that everything in The Dream had been the opposite of reality gave him some hope that perhaps Farber was a nice, mild-mannered guy, who loved the history of Billy the Kid as much as Martin did. As he crunched through the tall, brown grass toward the parking lot, Martin set the odds at a thousand to one that his premonition could be true.

"Farber a nice guy? Yeah, right," Martin grumbled to himself through gritted teeth.

"Fucking scumbag is what he is." Making his way back to Lilly, Martin forced a big, fake grin on his face, hiding the disturbing secrets he'd been holding in since death had come last night, but had failed to claim him..

Thursday – 11 am

Carl Farber shuffled up the jetway into the Albuquerque Sunport. He'd have moved faster if traffic would allow, but these people in front of him showed none of the alacrity that he did for being in the land of Billy the Kid. Once clear of the waddling throngs, Carl shifted into high gear and made his way to the rental car counter. He would be making the three-hour drive to Lincoln just as soon as he could secure his ride. Estimating that he'd arrive by mid-afternoon, Farber gleefully imagined himself watching the sun set in the small village on his first-ever night there.

Driving south on I-25 with the air conditioner humming along, the history teacher was taken with the breathtaking beauty of his surroundings. Born and raised in New Jersey, he'd never experienced the wide-open vistas and multicolored hues that The Land of Enchantment provided.

After fifty or so miles of the non-stop technicolor landscape, Farber began wondering if he could get a job as a teacher in New Mexico. He had years of experience and impeccable references, he reasoned, so why wouldn't a local school scoop up the chance to get a teacher like himself? However, that thought inevitably led to Carl remembering the research he'd done prior to his trip. The disadvantaged state ranked dead last, or near enough to it, in almost every educational measure, as well as in child welfare. Farber had built his career teaching the well-to-do children of Bergen County, who might view school differently than some of the hardscrabble kids of the deserts of New Mexico. He imagined that salaries would be a lot less, too, and even on his current teaching stipend, he was far from the financial comfort attained by most of the parents of his students. No, he concluded, New Mexico wouldn't be his next home…or any home, short of him winning the Powerball lottery. This trip, this deep dive into his hero Billy the Kid's life and legacy, would have to be it.

As the car began the long pull through the upper reaches of the White Sands Missile Range, Farber decided that he'd make the most of every single moment in Lincoln. To leave anything unseen, anything unexperienced, anything undone, and to never have that chance again, would almost be committing a crime.

Thursday - Noon

Martin wheezed a bit in the high mountain air as he and Lilly traipsed back to the Patron House for lunch. After finally scoring an all-access ticket to the monument museums, they had spent the better part of the morning at the Visitor Center and Museum, seeing photos and artifacts of days gone by and watching a film about the violent history of Lincoln. Then, the two shopped at a couple of the village's small stores, which threatened to remove from your pockets just about all of your Billy the Kid money, if you let them. Martin had come across a number of books and cool 'gee whiz' trinkets that would look great in cubicle #31 back at work, but like a gambler arriving in Las Vegas for the first time, he cautioned himself to take it slow in order not to blow his bankroll on the very first day.

Typically, lunch would not have been included in the offerings of their hosts, but knowing how busy Lincoln would be on the eve of Old Lincoln Days, and how crowded its few eateries were likely to become, the Joneses saw fit to remind their guests to return for a delicious, home-cooked meal. Lilly was a few steps ahead of Martin as they made their way toward the main house.

"Hey, hon, I'm just going to put these packages in the *casita*," said Lilly, looking back over her shoulder. "I'll meet you inside, okay?"

Martin smiled an "Of course," as Lilly disappeared around the side of the building. After walking tiredly up the three steps into the main house, he cracked open the screen door to hear a number of voices laughing at some joke of which he was not a part.

"Come on in!" yelled Darlene from the kitchen, not even knowing who was breaching the threshold of her home. Martin stepped through the cool living room toward the kitchen and saw the origin of the laughs. Two other couples - Martin was sure he'd seen both walking out on the street - were seated around the table while Darlene cooked and Dallas held forth on some funny anecdote of guests gone by. "Hey, Martin! Welcome back," said an obviously jovial Darlene upon seeing her guest. "Where's Lilly?"

The other couples looked at Martin with anticipation, as if he might be someone of importance to the festivities; he answered, "Oh, she just went to drop off some bags in the *casita*. There's an awful lot of things out there you can spend your money on." The two male guests nodded knowingly at Martin, while the women simply laughed. Just then, Lilly made her way through the front door and into the kitchen. After introductions to the Reeds and Fosters of Texas, Lilly fell into an easy conversation with the women, while the men, minus Martin, talked Dallas Cowboys football, which was set to start its season in just a few weeks.

Martin scored an ice-cold glass of fresh-squeezed lemonade and excused himself to the living room. He'd been wanting to see something since the previous evening, and he wanted to do it alone. As the conversation grew dimmer in his ears, he moved toward the wall over the sofa, which was festooned with photos of the various personalities of the Lincoln County War. Naggingly, the blank spot on the wall caught Martin's eye and called him forth. In The Dream, this was where the picture of Rosita Luna and Martin Junior hung. So important had that picture become to Martin in his Dream that he reasoned it *must* exist in real life. He wondered why that one photo had been removed, while all the others, including the Blazer's Mill photo, were allowed to remain.

Walking softly to the hallway, Martin once again examined the picture of Billy and his Regulator pals following the gunfight at Blazer's Mill. In his Dream, or whatever the hell had happened to him, Teebs had lost Sergio Bachaca's book during the Regulator's assassination of Sheriff Brady. When Martin had returned to the Patron House, apparently in The Dream, he had looked closely at the photo; there, in black and white (with a hint of sepia), and in Billy's hand, was that very book. Today, however, in Martin's real world and real life, there was no such revelation. Billy grinned in the photo as if he hadn't a care in the world, but the Kid certainly had never received any divine intervention in the form of a book written in 2014 and dropped by a clumsy man from the future.

So the whole thing clearly was an invention of his own mind, thought Martin. What he couldn't rectify was how he knew the name 'Carl Farber,' a man he assumed he'd never met. He also couldn't shed the thought that Rosita's picture should be hanging on that lonely finishing nail on the west wall of the Patron House living room. Whatever once had been in that spot, Martin had to know what had become of it.

"Hey, Dallas, could you come out here for a sec?" he asked, as he poked his head back into the kitchen. Dallas, in the middle of another sure-to-be side-splitting story, held up a single finger to the men, indicating that they should wait for the punchline, and smiled as he made his way toward Martin. "Sure, buddy, what's up?"

"Well, I've been looking at all of these great photos," Martin began, "and noticed that this one spot on the wall is empty. I was just wondering what photo was here, and why it's gone?"

"Ah! You've found me out, Martin!" exclaimed Dallas, so convincingly that Martin half-expected Doc, Billy, and Rosita to burst through the door in some sort of nineteenth-century Candid Camera moment.

"What? I did?" stammered Martin, in breathless anticipation of what he was about to learn.

"Yeah, man. We rearranged those photos when we dusted everything off. That one was a picture of a woman from the Lincoln County War era, but damned if I didn't drop it and break the glass." Dallas looked toward the kitchen as he spoke, as if Darlene might scold him for his carelessness. "The local historians told us it was the only known picture of her, so I have it in the back until I can get some new glass for it."

Martin's heart began to race at the news. So it was Rosita in the picture. Whether or not The Dream was real, Martin had somehow found out about the Belle of Lincoln, whom no historian had ever documented. If Rosita was real, then was his Dream real also? Was Martin Junior in the photo, too? If so, that had to prove that he hadn't somehow dreamt this all up and that it had actually happened, right? Martin was almost afraid to ask, but finally got up the courage. "Dallas, would you mind if I just saw the photo?"

Martin knew the slippery slope he was going down at the moment. Seeing Rosita would confirm something that he already knew: Martin was an adulterer. It would also confirm that he had a son somewhere in time; it would confirm that he was a murderer; and it would confirm that somehow, he and the famous outlaw Billy the Kid were indeed best of friends. Every emotion he'd been feeling since being saved from choking last night was coursing through Martin's brain and his veins. It was about to happen, and even if Martin could stop it, he steadfastly refused to.

"Sure, Martin, it's in our bedroom. Come on back," said Dallas, with a wave of his hand.

If Martin thought that The Dream was on the verge of being proven real, then he expected that Dallas and Darlene's bedroom would be an orgiastic pleasure palace, designed less for show and more for go. Would there be whips and handcuffs on the bedposts? Would the ceiling be mirrored so they could enjoy the rear view of their latest conquests? So curious was Martin about his hosts that for a second, he almost forgot about his impending reunion with his soulmate and the great love of his life.

As they walked into the bedroom, Martin's eyes went wide with wonder at what he saw.

Nothing.

As in, nothing that would indicate that his hosts were sex-crazed lunatics who'd bed down any willing guest. The room was simple, with plain furniture, a sensible queen-sized bed, and a 'probably-from-Target,' southwest-patterned comforter on the bed. Once again, nothing in Martin's topsy-turvy world was as expected, which only amped up his desire to see Rosita's photo one more time.

"Here it is, Martin," offered Dallas, as he scooped up a manila folder and handed it to his guest. Martin fingertips went wild with electricity pulsing through them. He gently grabbed the corner of the folder and lifted it slowly away, his heart beating a drum-roll introduction. As the cover folded back and revealed the mystery woman behind it, Martin's heart sank. Dressed in a high-necked Victorian dress - which could fit three Rositas inside of its grand proportions - and smiling at the camera was a matronly woman with a spot of flour on her forehead and a rolling pin in her hand.

"That's Monica Mills," said Dallas proudly, "wife of Ham Mills. They tell me he was the sheriff just before the War got started."

Martin suddenly felt very nauseous and handed the folder back to Dallas. What the hell was he doing? he asked himself. Chasing ghosts of people long gone, and some that never even existed? This was counterproductive. He had his dream girl just in the other room. Lilly was everything Martin had ever hoped for in a wife, and then some by a lot. Miracle of miracles, she was also into Billy the Kid and the history of Lincoln. What more could he possibly ask for?

Suddenly, he felt absolutely silly, standing there staring at a picture of a chubby old lady he'd hoped was the woman for whom he'd somehow traveled back in time to engage in a torrid affair. For the tenth time that day, Martin pushed thoughts of The Dream to the back of his mind and committed to focusing on the here and now. Lilly was his wife. Lilly, the only dream girl Martin needed, was in the next room, and he vowed to spend the rest of his time in Lincoln parading around like the luckiest bastard in New Mexico for having such an incredible partner. This nonsense had to stop, for it was robbing Martin of the joy he had expected to feel, walking in the footsteps of Billy the Kid.

"That's enough," he said to himself, before realizing that Dallas was still there.

"Yeah, I agree with you, buddy. I've heard she was supposedly sweet on the Kid, but I can't see Billy going for a woman like her," said Dallas, through his pearly white teeth. "But, hey, not everyone has beautiful wives like we do, huh?" Dallas gave Martin a little tap on the chest and smirked at him. Smiling back, Martin followed him out of the room and back toward the kitchen. As they walked, Martin vowed that lunch would be the beginning of his Lincoln trip version 2.0. Version 1 had been an unmitigated disaster, and he was ready to do whatever it took to get their trip back on track.

Thursday – 2:25 pm

Carl Farber rolled into Lincoln just as he expected. As he cornered around the last outcrop of the tiny village, he saw throngs of tourists of every shape and size milling about. Pushing firmly on the brakes, he slowed to make sure that no one on the street had to scatter to avoid him. 'Awestruck' was about the right word to describe his initial reaction to Lincoln and the historical splendor it represented.

The first building on his right was the most recognizable in all of the town: the old Murphy/Dolan store known as 'The House.' Upon the demise of The House of Murphy, the county had purchased the building and turned it into a courthouse and sheriff's office. From the rooms upstairs, thought Farber, Billy the Kid had gunned his way out of Lincoln after Governor Lew Wallace reneged on his promise to pardon the young outlaw. While the scene was less threatening today, Farber still looked on the building with a reverence usually reserved for a church, or maybe even a famous grave.

Employees of the state's Monuments Division enthusiastically waved at incoming cars, guided tourists, and managed the large parking area behind the courthouse. Easily recognizing their uniforms of green polo shirts and khaki pants, Carl waved back to the three or four young people who were managing to keep control of the burgeoning temporary population of the town.

Farber wasn't staying in Lincoln, as every available room had been booked months in advance. He had settled on a much-less-expensive room in the neighboring small town of Capitan, which he'd passed some ten miles ago. Right now, he was simply looking for a place to park so he could stretch his legs and, hopefully, find somewhere and something to eat. Slowly weaving his way east on Route 380, he kept a keen eye out for anything resembling an open parking spot. Finally, just near the old Montano store, he found a place into which he could shoehorn his tiny rental car, and he escaped its seat for the first time in over three hours.

"Arrrrhhhhgggg," he said satisfactorily, as he unleashed a mighty arm and leg stretch. Just breathing in the high-desert air made him feel more awake, more alive. Farber slowly turned 360 degrees, taking in the sights and sounds of the village. While it was a bit too busy to imagine he was back in old Lincoln, he hoped that early next week, after the rest of the tourists left, he'd be able to get a real sense of what Billy and the Regulators had felt during the War. Right now, though, the next order of business was some food, as he hadn't eaten anything since the two bags of peanuts on his economy coach cabin flight. With no options in sight, however, he simply began to walk back to the west to see what he could find.

Everywhere he looked, he saw various Billy the Kids and all sorts of Lincoln County warriors. From somewhere behind him, he heard a voice yell, "Kelly!" and right in front of Carl, Sheriff Pat Garrett turned around, nearly stepping on Farber's foot. He looked up at the tall man and had to admit that the likeness was pretty good. With a serious face, 'Garrett' tipped his hat, said "Excuse me," and whisked out of sight to attend to some sure-to-be-important sheriffy kind of task.

Pressing on, Farber found the aptly-named Lincoln County Brewery, which also appeared to have a menu of some sort. Luckily for Carl, he was late enough in the afternoon that most people had already eaten lunch but hadn't yet thought about dinner, so he slipped inside and found a seat at the bar. Scooping up the menu, he quickly zeroed in on a few choices, including something called a 'green-chile cheeseburger.' Just then, a pretty bartender slid down the length of the bar, with a big smile and an order pad at the ready.

"What can I get for ya, cowboy?" she asked happily. This was a far cry from the very few restaurants where Carl ate in New Jersey. Often the servers there seemed to feel they were doing you a favor by taking your order and, of course, your money.

"Ummm," stuttered Farber, hoping for a few more seconds and a few more smiles. "How's this green-chile-cheeseburger thing? I've never had one."

"Oh, hon! It'll give you religion," his server gushed. "You've got to try one. If you don't like it, it's on me!"

"Oh, that's…I mean, you don't have to do that…," stumbled Farber, "I'm sure I'll love it. Medium, please."

"Gotcha, love, now what to drink?"

"How about any light beer you've got on tap?" asked Farber, as he prepared to show his ID. Jane (now he could see his server's name tag) just laughed it off with a wave of her hand, and she flitted to the tap and to put in his order.

"Man, this place is as far away from New Jersey as you can get," he said to himself. "The people are *so* much nicer. A guy could definitely get used to this." Instinctively, Carl knew that it was Jane's job to be nice to him, and probably a good idea to maximize her tip; but still, he lived a relatively lonely life and to have someone be that nice, that outgoing, to him was like a gift one didn't expect and might never get again. Carl thought about it and decided that the world needed more Janes and less cranky, depressed, soulless, soccer moms who were chasing the perfect nose job, boob job, and antidepressant cocktail, just to stay sane in the wilds of northern New Jersey.

A few minutes later, Jane scurried right back down the bar with a heaping plate of food and an ice-cold beer. “Here ya go, honey, enjoy it…and let me know what you think!”

Farber wasn’t lying when he replied, “It smells incredible! Thanks, Jane,” giving her a warm smile.

Jane leaned over the bar and pointed her index finger, tapping Carl on the tip of his nose, adding, “You make sure you come back and see me again!” And with that, like a frenetic ball of energy, she was off.
Farber dug into a bite of an immense burger and, with the juices dripping down his chin, he said to himself, “I think I’ll just do that, Miss Jane.”

Thursday - 3:30 pm

In the hot August sun, Martin and Lilly stood just off the porch of the Tunstall store. Like almost everything else that day, they wound up waiting in line to see anything of any historical value. Still, both of their spirits were high, and Martin was not-so-secretly thrilled that Lilly seemed to be having a better time than he was. It was apparent that Lilly had studied both *Young Guns* and some of Martin’s books before leaving on their trip. At the *Torreon* - a round, rock tower built to allow the residents of Lincoln to defend themselves against Indian attack - she wandered in circles with curiosity, before exclaiming “Why wasn’t this in *Young Guns*? It’s so cool!” And when they walked the now-vacant lot where the McSween house had once stood, Martin was surprised (and a little embarrassed) at Lilly pretending to load her rifle while shouting, “Yeah, Charlie! Yeah, Charlie!” over and over. Although Lilly had supported her husband’s interest in Billy the Kid, as well as his voluminous purchases of Kid-related books, Martin had never thought that she’d take her interest this far.

“So, this is it, huh?” asked Lilly eagerly. “This is the thing that started the whole War?”

Martin looked around at the Tunstall store and the line of people waiting to enter, judging it would take at least another fifteen minutes before they were inside. “Well, yeah. I mean, kind of, Lil, “ stammered Martin, doing his best to explain the intricacies of the government beef contracts and the loans that The House of Murphy offered anyone in need - basically everyone in Lincoln County - at prices and terms that brought nearly everyone to the point of bankruptcy. “There’s more to it than that, but sure…Tunstall opening his store right here, right near Murphy’s place, really lit the fuse.” With some disdain, Martin looked up the road to the old courthouse. Any Billy fan automatically had to hate Murphy and Dolan and most likely Brady as well. It was kind of like how Martin hated the Philadelphia Eagles, being that they were the sworn rivals of his beloved New York football Giants. Checking his watch again, he began to get jumpy, and Lilly leaned in to kiss him on the cheek.

“What’s the matter, Martin? Why so nervous?” she asked.

“I’m not nervous, Lil, but if we don’t get in here soon, we’re not going to have time for the courthouse. Everything closes at five, you know.” Martin looked expectantly at the line that stubbornly refused to move.

“Don’t worry, hon,” Lilly said brightly. “We’ve got an entire week to see everything. If we don’t get to the courthouse today, we’ll get there tomorrow.”

To Martin, that sounded like the worst idea he’d heard all day. If Lincoln was such a zoo today, a day before the pageant started, it would be positively Disneyworld-like over the weekend. He couldn’t imagine fighting these crowds for three more days. “Umm hmm,” was all he could muster in return.

Finally, after some twenty more minutes, the two adventurers made it past the front door and into the relative coolness of the thickly walled, adobe structure. While Martin had seen a number of pictures of the store online, it wasn’t the same as actually standing inside it. Defying his promise, Martin allowed his memories of The Dream to creep into his psyche, remembering the very serious conversation he’d had with Billy about his lost Bachaca book, right in Tunstall’s personal chambers. As he and Lilly oohed and aahed over a number of period items in the store’s showcases, they inevitably made their way to the small doorway in the back that represented the living space of the now-long-dead John Henry Tunstall.

Lilly pushed forward to see the space in all of its Victorian glory, but Martin had a hard time stepping across the threshold. He’d accepted his Dream as just that, a dream, but the realism and sharp edges of his memory made it seem more than that. In his Dream, he'd changed clothes in this store on two occasions. He'd defended the store, along with Doc, Jose Chavez y Chavez, Billy, and Big Jim French. He'd had a real honest-to-goodness conversation with Tunstall about getting some work to pay off a debt Martin owed the Englishman, right in the place he was standing now. It was all a bit much for Martin, but Lilly beckoned him to come closer to see something. "Look! Look at the hole in the floor! Isn't this where Billy was hiding that one time? After they shot Brady?" asked Lilly excitedly.

Martin wasn't at all sure that the hole was genuine; someone probably cut the floor-boards later, after the story became legend. Still, he couldn't say for sure it wasn't legit, although to his memory, it was French who'd hidden under that floor. Rather than a long discussion about Sheriff Brady's murder and such, though, Martin decided to just agree. "Yep, I think you're right, Lil." Lilly beamed as if she was ready to start giving her own tours in the tiny town.

With his wife studying every minute corner of Tunstall's bedroom, Martin receded into the store. Notwithstanding his promise to forget The Dream, nothing about this felt right. He decided to step outside onto the porch for some fresh air, but was greeted with the superheated New Mexico desert sun instead. Finally, he slumped against the front wall and just held it up until Lilly had her fill of the sights and sounds of the Tunstall mercantile.

As his eyes drifted to the left, he couldn't help but remember the first time Rosita Luna had launched herself out of an alleyway, seeing Martin talking to his Regulator pals. Like a heat-seeking missile, she had jumped into his arms - although, at the time, he'd never seen the woman before in his own life. It was all terribly confusing, and Martin hadn't made a good show by mentioning he had to get back to his wife.

The irony of the situation wasn't lost on him as he dripped sweat waiting for Lilly to rejoin him. Here he was, at the fictitious site of his first meeting with his lover from another time. During that meeting, he'd slipped and told Rosita he was married (which had earned him a slap in the face); now, his real wife was just a few feet away from the spot that had shifted the course of his Dream life. At that moment, Martin was glad that The Dream was not real. His performance in front of the Regulators, his ridiculously modern clothes, and his faux pas with Rosita were all bad enough as part of a dream, much less having to endure them in real life.

Shortly, Lilly exited the building to find Martin still holding forth against the front wall. "What happened?" she asked him, concerned he might be suffering some aftereffects of his near-death experience.

"Oh, nothing, Lil. Just wanted to get some air. Pretty crowded in there," Martin offered, with a weak smile.

"So cool Martin. Imagine shopping there a hundred years ago! I guess this was the Target or Wal-Mart of the day, huh?" Lilly suggested.

Martin glanced around the town and mentally agreed that yes, Tunstall's store, the Montano store, and even The House served to meet any need a old-time Lincolnite might come up against. There certainly wasn't anywhere else to go in those days. Martin laughed to himself that there wasn't really anywhere else to go in the area these days, either. Lincoln had been born and remained a distant outpost on the western frontier, and nothing was likely to change that. People didn't come to Lincoln for shopping or convenience, they came for the past…and maybe for the quiet of the present. If you were a thrill-a-minute kind of person, you'd head to Phoenix, Albuquerque, or Denver, but not to Lincoln. The reason the town was so well preserved, thought Martin, was that nobody, except a small fraction of locals, wanted to live here anymore. There simply wasn't enough traffic to warrant the kind of development that would ruin the place.

"It's 4:20 now. Let's go to the courthouse, okay?" Lilly proposed, glad that they would have enough time for Martin to see everything he'd been fantasizing about for months.

Martin checked his watch and craned his neck to see how long the line was to enter. As the end of the day was nearing, a number of people had called it quits, and it actually looked like there was no line at all. "Okay, let's do it! No waiting, this time," said an unusually spry Martin Teebs; and they headed west to the imposing, two-story structure. As they approached, Martin was able to single out the window from where Billy had shot Olinger. Lilly couldn't resist a quick, "Keep the change, Bob!" for some redneck family that was lying on the ground around the stone marking Olinger's demise.

The Teebs dutifully climbed the steps onto the upper balcony, joining a brace of tourists who also thought it a great idea to take pictures of Billy's final vantage point of the village following his escape. After pointing out as many buildings of interest as he could from their perch, Martin and Lilly clomped back down the stairs and headed to the glass-paned front door. Swinging it open, they were met with a blast of refrigerated air that threatened to blow them back out onto the street. The Teebs stepped in line behind an elderly couple showing their passes, and, as the couple slowly shuffled away, Martin's heart fell to his feet; he simply stared at the ticket counter - dumbfounded and lost for words.

The woman behind it, smiling with a radiance Martin had seen a thousand times, was none other than Rosita Luna.

Thursday – 4:25 pm

Before Martin's brain could stop them, his lips poured forth a breathless, "Rosita!" at the great beauty of Lincoln County.

The woman's smile didn't change one iota, but she slightly cocked her head to the side in confusion. So desperate did her husband sound that Lilly joined the pretty young woman in a confused stare.

"I'm sorry?" the woman said. "What did you say, sir?"

Martin swallowed hard as he felt four eyes burning into him, wondering what he was going to say next. "I…ummm," began Martin, unsure how to proceed.

"Do you know this young lady, Martin?" asked Lilly, in a tone with way more formality than Martin had heard during their entire trip.

By now, Martin had been able to focus enough to read the woman's name tag and saw that she was going by the name 'Trisha.' "I...eeee...is...your...." For the life of himself, Martin could not put together a coherent sentence, as Trisha looked on in what seemed to be some amusement.

Embarrassed at her husband's gawking and fawning over a woman he didn't even know, Lilly jumped in. "I'm sorry. It's been a long day, and he's been out in the hot sun," justified Lilly, as she handed their passes to be punched for admittance. "We just want to see where Billy escaped."

Trisha took the passes in her graceful hand, punched each with the official Monuments Division hole punch, and handed them back to Lilly with a smile. "You two enjoy yourself, and just step over to your left to enter the museum."

If Martin had heard this exchange or knew he was now supposed to leave his current spot, it seemed that his feet had grown roots. Letting her words pass him by unacknowledged, Martin gaped at Trisha, full of wonder and awe, as one might feel while looking at a rare beautiful animal in a cage. Finally, he was able to find his voice, this time much softer and less fragmented than before. "Rosita? Rosita Luna? Is that you?" Martin asked hopefully.

With a smile, Trisha shook her head. "I'm sorry, no, sir. I think maybe you have the wrong person?" Although Martin somehow felt that he and Trisha were the only two people in the world at that moment, she did not. She continued to glance over his shoulder at other ticket holders who were eager to get into the courthouse before it closed for the day.

"Martin!" Lilly barked to bring her husband back from whatever beyond he was lost in. "Come on, people are waiting!"

Still Martin could not move, locking eyes with the beautiful woman in the hope of seeing some tiny sliver of recognition of what they'd both been through. He slowly turned his head toward Lilly but almost seemed to be looking through her, captured as he was by the pretty employee of the State of New Mexico's Monuments Division. "I'm sorry," Martin said in almost a whisper. "It's just that you look so much like someone I...knew, well, didn't know...*per se*...but know about."

Trisha smiled with her eyes, even as she looked worriedly at the line of people now stretching out the door. Unsure how to move this middle-aged man along so that the rest of her visitors could get into the museum, she spoke. "So I look like this 'Rosita,' is it? I think," she said, rubbing her hand to the side of her head, "that my great-great-grandmother's name was Rosita? I think I'm remembering that right."

Martin was floored. Had he inadvertently walked into a spitting image relative of the Belle of Lincoln? If so, the resemblance was uncanny. The two women were virtual twins. How could the DNA of Rosita have passed through four other generations and stayed so untainted as to produce the beauty he now saw in front of him?

Eager to know more, he asked, "Really? So she was from here? In Lincoln?"

Trisha laughed, answering with an accent that Martin could tell was not from New Mexico. "Nooo. My family is from California. I just came to work here for the summer. I'm finishing up my MBA at UCLA."

Now annoyed that Martin couldn't seem to break free from the twenty-something woman in his gaze, Lilly became more insistent. "Martin, let's go!" she said, as she grabbed him by the sleeve. "People are waiting!" Still staring dumbly at the woman, Martin allowed himself to be led a few steps to the left, while a family from the midwest shot him an evil glare for wasting their museum time.

Trisha took the midwesterners' tickets and punched them quickly, even as Teebs continued to stare at her from a few feet away. Handing the tickets back to the small family, she looked over at Martin with pursed lips, as if wondering what to say to release the man. "Nice to meet you folks," the young woman finally said, with a friendly wave. "I hope you find who you're looking for, sir." With that, she looked away, turning back to the swollen line of grouchy people who only wanted to hang out the upstairs window and pretend to shred Bob Olinger with his own shotgun. The corn-fed family had just made the jump in front of the Teebs and was in no hurry to move along, captivated as they were at each of them taking a picture with a life-sized cutout of the Kid.

Lilly tapped her foot impatiently at both the family and her husband, trying to figure out just what kind of spectacle he had created back there. For his part, Martin continued to glance back occasionally - without Lilly noticing - still struck by the woman who wore the face, but not the name, of the great love of his life…or at least The Dream version of it.

As the chorus of grumbling and 'what's holding up the line?' grew, Trisha decided, in the best interests of customer service, she should call in some aid. "Kevin!" she yelled over the din, "can you come and help in-process these people?"

A few moments later, from the far office, someone stepped into the throngs of semi-angry tourists, pushing his way through the crowd. A few cheers of 'Yay!' and 'Finally!' were heard as the sandy-haired young man made his way toward the check-in desk. At the last second, he looked up and met eyes with Martin, who this time came close to passing out and collapsing on the spot.

It was Billy the Kid.

Thursday – 4:26 pm

Carl Farber checked his watch again as he peered to the left and right. Whatever had happened inside the courthouse was grinding the check-in line to a halt. Worried he'd miss seeing the famous window from which the Kid shot Olinger, he began asking people around him, "What's going on up there? Why are we stopped?"

No one seemed to have an answer; men grumbled, women told the men to calm down, and kids joined in with the familiar refrain of 'I'm bored.' Even though Carl had a full week in the old town, he didn't want to miss any of the highlights so early in his trip.

After what seemed to him like forever, Farber heard a chorus of 'Yay!' and 'Finally!' from inside the building, and the line soon began inching forward again. By the time he had cleared the front door, a beautiful young woman was conferring with a young man about whether she could be released to head upstairs to answer questions from the multitude of visitors packing the courthouse in the final minutes before it closed for the day. With a nod and smile, the young man waved her off, and she pushed through the crowd toward the famous stairwell where Deputy J.W. Bell was shot by the Kid during his spectacular escape.

As Farber approached the ticket counter, he thrust his hand into his pocket to produce his pass, which the young man then took with a grin. "First time here?" he asked Carl.

"Oh, yeah," Farber responded, "I've been waiting a long time to visit. This is really great!"

The young man called 'Kevin' - as Farber could now tell from his name badge - handed back the punched pass. "Well, we just got you in, sir." Kevin checked his watch and continued, "You've got a half hour. Plenty of time to see all of the good stuff!"

Farber nodded a thank you to the man and prepared to shuffle off, before turning back. "Gosh, Kevin, you look really familiar. Have we met somewhere before?"

A big smile came upon the young man's face, betraying his slightly bucked two front teeth before he spoke. "I don't think so, but I seem to get that a lot around here!"

Farber tilted his head quizzically to the side before nodding and walking off into the museum. As he approached a large cutout of Billy the Kid, he wondered who might take a picture of him with the boy bandit? Never much of a social butterfly, Carl didn't want to impose upon the other tourists, who had much to see and probably too little time left in the day to see it. About to bail out on the photo op, Carl saw the pretty young woman from the ticket counter, pushing back through the crowd. She wore the green polo shirt and khaki pants of the Monuments Division and would probably, Farber reasoned, be happy to snap a photo for him.

"Umm, excuse me, miss?" called Farber loudly, to be heard over the din, "Would you mind?" Farber reached out to grab her shoulder as he said it, holding up his phone with a questioning look in his eyes.

Despite the chaos around her, the woman - 'Trisha,' now that Farber could see her nametag - smiled broadly and nodded her head. Carl handed her his phone and sidled over to the cardboard cutout. Feeling a bit foolish, he put his arm behind the picture and rested it on the cutout's other shoulder. "Ok, ready?" Trisha said, opening her brown eyes wide.

"Let's do it," replied Carl, as he put on as much of a smile as he thought Billy would have allowed. "Did you get it?" he asked eagerly, after a couple of snapshots. Trisha reviewed the photos on his phone to confirm that she did indeed 'get it' and nodded approvingly before handing the phone back to its owner. "Thanks so much, Trisha, I appreciate that."

"Of course!" she replied brightly. "Everyone should get a picture with Billy at least once."

Suddenly, it dawned on Farber why the young man at the front desk had looked so familiar: Kevin was the spitting image of Billy the Kid! "That's who he looks like!" he said out loud, to no one but himself.

About to leave the room, Trisha turned back out of curiosity to ask the man, "Excuse me? That's who *who* looks like?"

Farber's head snapped around, unaware that the pretty woman was still there. "Oh, the guy up front...at the ticket counter. He looks like Billy the Kid!"

A broad grin broke out on Trisha's beautiful face, and she laughed a little as she responded, "Yes he does! In fact, Kevin plays Billy in the Last Escape reenactment on Sunday. And keep your eyes open. You never know where else he'll pop up this weekend!" With a broad grin, Trisha pushed off through the crowd, making her way to the stairwell to answer the sure-to-be-dozens of questions from the packed house just upstairs.

Farber watched her go away and rubbed his head as he thought to himself, "Man, people are really nice here. I kinda wish I *could* stay here forever."

Thursday – 4:28 pm

Martin's mouth hung agape, staring into the eyes of his long-lost pal, Billy Bonney. If Billy - or whoever this young man was pretending to be - recognized Martin, he must have hidden it well, as he practically looked through him to the gathering crowd trying to muscle its way upstairs. Scooting behind the ticket booth, Kevin deftly picked up a hole punch and started allowing guests in.

There they stood, side-by-side, his love and his friend for all eternity: Rosita Luna and William H. Bonney, perfectly presented in twenty-first-century format. How in the hell this was all happening was too much for Martin to comprehend. It seemed that around every corner in Lincoln, he'd had to fight off the memories of The Dream, knowing that it existed only in his mind. That had worked well enough - right up until two of its main characters showed up, live and in the flesh. Martin stared at the two figures, until Lilly's urging and the crowd's inertia moved him farther into the recesses of the museum.

"What was that about?" Lilly whispered sternly to her seemingly dazed husband, "and who is 'Rosita'?"

Even in his addle-pated state of mind, Martin knew to take his time and answer the question cautiously. One wrong move here could spoil the rest of the trip - and his chances of finding out just what the hell was going on with his life. "Sorry, Lil," Martin apologized. "She just looked so much like an old picture that I've seen. Like…the spitting image. It was just kind of shocking when we walked in, and I saw her."

"Old *picture*?" questioned Lilly. "It looked more like an old *lover*, the way you were going on and on, Martin!"

Shit, thought Martin, was it that apparent? Was he so transparent that he couldn't hide what his mind told him he was feeling, even for a few seconds? His next words needed to be chosen with great care and great precision. "Oh, come on, Lil! She's a *kid*. She could be our daughter. I was just surprised that someone looked so much like this woman I'd seen from Lincoln's past."

Lilly looked sideways at Martin as the crowd surged and pushed again, moving them along and to the base of the stairway. While she wasn't sure whether to believe Martin, she didn't want to ruin the rest of the day, or their trip, over petty jealousy. Patting him on the chest, she gave a tight smile and said simply, "Okay."

Martin was greatly relieved that he'd dodged a bullet, and they prepared to climb the steps to the second floor. It struck him that Rosita/Trisha *could* have been their daughter if his wife had gotten pregnant while Martin and Lilly were in college. As that realization sunk into his brain, his entire fantasy came crumbling down. How would forty-five-year-old Martin Teebs romance a twenty-five-year-old beauty in 2021? Martin was happy to settle in and watch TV at 8 pm most nights, and he imagined that by then, Trisha hadn't even started putting on her makeup to go out. He visualized himself puking his guts up at a rave after too many shots, while she danced the night away with every handsome boy who asked her. Martin probably couldn't name even two songs that Trisha knew and liked, and she most likely couldn't name any of his. With her MBA, she'd get a job at a high-priced ad agency in LA, while Martin lived a quiet suburban life in New Jersey, considering it a success to have the greenest lawn on the block.

The Dream, as it were, fell like a heavy load of bricks. Whatever recesses of his mind the images had come from, it surely wasn't from some other life or alternate reality that Martin had experienced. No amazingly beautiful, twenty-five-year-old woman was falling in love with a slightly overweight and very married, quality-control manager from New Jersey. Martin was not best friends with Billy the Kid. He had *not* ridden bravely with the Regulators. And he certainly had not fathered a son who was lost in time, never to meet his own father until the very day of that son's death. No, none of that happened. Martin Teebs was the most ordinary of men, and things like that simply didn't happen to him. Hell, he reasoned, they probably didn't happen to anyone.

As he glanced back, he saw Trisha pushing forward through the crowd. Where could he have seen her before his NDE? he wondered. Then it occurred to him: Trish and most of the Monuments Division staff had been out on the street, greeting visitors, as he and Lilly drove into Lincoln. Kevin must have been there, too. *That's* where he got the mental pictures that filled out his Dream. Of course, he'd notice a pretty girl and a boy that looked kind of like Billy Bonney. It only took the few seconds they had been in his field of vision to imprint on his memory, only to be used later while his brain was in the death throes of oxygen deprivation. Martin scolded himself for wasting an entire day on his mental gymnastics over something so stupid. What a stupid investment, he thought, to ruin an entire day with his incredible wife because of a thirty-second dream! Once more, he vowed not to let it happen again.

Martin urged Lilly forward by putting his hand on her ass, to which she didn't take kindly and shot him a death stare. Released from his troubling thoughts, he just laughed it off and grinned back at her. As he put his foot up on the first step, one final thought occurred to him.

Farber

Everything else about how The Dream had come together had been explained. But how could he possibly have dreamt of a guy named Carl Farber from New Jersey, only to find out that said guy was going to be in Lincoln the following evening, on the same tour as Martin and Lilly? Maybe he'd heard the name somewhere in the local papers? he guessed. Or maybe Farber could have been at Shoopman's grocery one day when a friend yelled out his name, within earshot of Martin as he checked out his ice cream purchases? Whatever it was that made the name stick, it couldn't be all that important since Martin had no recollection of it. The guy in his Dream probably didn't look anything like the real Carl Farber anyway. *This* Carl Farber was just a name of a local somebody that Martin had never met, and his dying brain had thrown it onto a rapidly balding, nobody of a history teacher from Waldwick, NJ. Case closed. Martin began to walk up the stairs, glancing back to give Trisha one more farewell look as she pushed her way through the crowd, when he saw it.

Farber!

In an instant, Martin's blood again began to boil. The satisfying thud of Farber's sickly skull being bashed to bits on Pete Maxwell's floor resonated in his mind. Carl's stupid dying face reflecting on how on earth both Billy and Martin had gotten the best of him. Everything in Martin wanted to go kill the man, even as *this* Farber laid his hand gently on Trisha's shoulder to get her attention. Any second now, Martin expected Rosita to scream in horror; but this time, Martin would be ready. This time, he'd be the man she needed when she needed him most. This time, the only person who'd be dead and gone would be the filthy rapist Carl Farber. Martin started marching toward his soulmate, ready to save the day, when he saw the oddest thing -

She smiled at Farber.

"What?" questioned Martin's brain, as he stopped dead in his tracks.

Then she took Farber's phone and posed him for a picture beside the Billy the Kid cutout.

Then she smiled at him again, and they both looked at the pictures, like two friends taking selfies for their Instagram account.

Martin stared, dumbfounded, completely at a loss as to what to do.

Rosita...no...Trisha handed the phone back to Farber with a pat on the arm and turned toward Martin. As she walked toward him, she beamed a smile that would light up the entire town. Perhaps this was her way of saying that it was all right, that she was finally going to be all right. Martin couldn't help but smile back as she approached, and he began to lift his arms to embrace her - the great love of his life.

And then she walked right on by. She'd never even noticed him.

Martin quickly lowered his arms and pushed his way back to Lilly, who was now peering around the corner, wondering what had become of her husband. Without making eye contact, he jogged up a few stairs to catch her, while forcing out a tight smile. On his left, Trisha quickly scooted in front of the couple, around the landing, and out of sight, leaving a trail of her sweet scent in her wake.

Martin inhaled deeply as the building blocks of The Dream - crumbled to bits just minutes ago - began to rebuild themselves even stronger, despite their owner's fervent wishes that they not do so.

Thursday – 8 pm

Settled back in their *casita* after dinner - this time, without a side helping of near death - Martin and Lilly sat on the sofa, while the radio whined on about the big Capitan pig roast or some such event.

Lilly was hesitant to speak, but finally felt she had no choice. "Martin, are you okay? I mean, are you really okay?" Lilly was worried that her husband's brush with death might have changed him somehow. She'd read all sorts of books and seen movies on the subject, and she wondered if Martin's odd behavior today might be a result of his momentary death yesterday.

"What do you mean? Sure, I'm okay, Lil," Martin reassured her.

Lilly took a deep breath before continuing. "It's just that you were kind of in a dark mood all day. And then, at the courthouse, what was that all about? The Rosita thing?"

Martin realized he'd reached a crossroads. He could either confess to Lilly about his Dream and Rosita's brief appearance in the street last night, or he could play it off as nothing and tell her not to worry. He couldn't do both, and the time to pick one was now. At the last moment, though, before he opened his mouth to speak, he decided upon an amended plan that would admit to Lilly what had happened, but spare her the details so that she wouldn't be watching him like a hawk for the rest of their trip.

"Well, Lil, you always know me so well," he began, "and you're right. I wasn't in the best of moods today." Martin looked at Lilly, whose face studied him with intent. "Last night, I had some kind of, I don't know…what to call it. A…dream, maybe? It happened when I was out."

"You did see something!" said Lilly, half in surprise and half in curiosity. "I knew it! Was it a light? Did you see God? What does He look like?"

This, thought Martin, was the conversation he didn't want to have. As Lilly peppered him with questions, he wondered if he should start laughing and play it off as a joke. At least, that would get him out of this spin cycle, allowing him to process what happened on his own. Lilly was his wife, though, and she was the person he should be able to trust the most with this information. If he couldn't tell her, who could he talk to? He'd never seen a shrink and didn't think he'd find one in tiny Lincoln, NM, either. With no better options, he just plowed ahead, trusting Lilly with his story.

"It wasn't like that at all, Lil," he began. "I don't think I was dead *per se*, I think I was just unconscious. You know how people say they saw their lives flash before their eyes?" Lilly enthusiastically nodded. All she needed was a tub of popcorn, so focused was she on watching the Martin Teebs show. "Well, I kind of saw that…except it wasn't really *my* life." Lilly cast a confused glance at Martin, encouraging him to continue. "It was *like* me…but I don't know…in the *past* or something. These characters from here, like Billy the Kid, were in it. It was all just...weird, but it felt very real. That's all."

Lilly pondered what she'd just heard and judged that Martin probably hadn't had an after-death experience after all. He probably had his head filled up with all sorts of Billy the Kid and Lincoln County War images, and they just created some kind of dream for the short time he was out. For his part, Martin was glad that Lilly wasn't questioning him about any details, for if she did, they could spend the rest of their vacation right on the couch they currently occupied and still not finish the story.

"So who's Rosita?" Lilly asked out of the blue. Martin's veins filled with ice water, and he had to look away from his faithful wife. He pretended to cough into his hand in a desperate bid to buy a few precious seconds to decide how to respond.

"Oh, nobody. In my dream, or whatever it was, she was Billy's girlfriend," he lied, "and I got to know her and Billy. When I saw that girl today, she just reminded me of her, and I was kind of shocked."

"Hmmph," snorted Lilly, while looking at her husband. "Billy had pretty good taste in women, then. That girl was beautiful, huh?"

Martin had been married long enough not to fall into the trap that Lilly set for him, so he quickly responded, "She's okay. She's no Lilly Teebs, though."

Lilly laughed out loud and gave Martin a good, hard kiss on the lips. She let her hand fall between his thighs and brushed up to just below his belt. Kissing his ear, she whispered, "Let's just make sure you don't forget that, Mr. Teebs," as she slid off of him and climbed the steps to the bed in the loft. Martin rearranged himself as best he could, turned out the lights, and slowly climbed upstairs as well, finding Lilly laid out on top of the sheets, naked as the day is long. She pushed her chin out and said simply, "Ride em, cowboy."

Had anyone walked by several minutes later, they might have heard the breathless voice of Lilly Teebs yell out, "Regulators! Let's mount up!"

FRIDAY 7 AM

In his tiny Capitan motel room, Carl Farber rubbed the sleep from his eyes.. The high-desert air, plus the extra beer or three he'd had last night, hoping that Jane might swing around to his end of the bar one more time, conspired to have him sleep more soundly than he had in years. As he stared at the ceiling and wondered what options he might have for breakfast, he mentally began planning his day in Lincoln. Lunch at the Brewery was an automatic. Realistically, he knew that a pretty young lady like Jane would have no real interest in an aging history teacher like himself, but he enjoyed play-acting that she might. Wasn't that the same mentality that guys used at Hooters or in strip clubs? It didn't matter whether the women *were* into you, it only mattered that you believed they *might* be. For a guy who lived near the boundaries of loneliness like Carl did, he would take whatever he could get.

The other order of business for the day was going to be this evening's Lincoln After Dark tour. Farber relished the opportunity to see all the cool spots in town, shorn of the multitudes of tourists packing them during daylight hours. For weeks now, he had been listing all of his questions for the tour guide, Brandon. While Carl still hoped to publish his own book someday, he realized that he could never know all the ins and outs of the Lincoln County War while living in New Jersey. The people who lived *here*, who breathed the same air that Billy had every day, had an advantage that he could never overcome. If anything, Carl hoped that his book would give an outsider's point of view of the tenuous beginnings of the War. Maybe a fresh perspective would excite people, and, hey, he could just have a bestseller on his hands!

"Fat chance," admitted Farber ruefully. "I'd be happy if I only sold a hundred copies." With that, he slid out of bed and into a warm shower to get ready for what he was sure was going to be an eventful day.

Friday – 7:15 am

Stiffly, Martin stood up from the couch he'd been planted on for the better part of an hour and quietly padded over to the kitchen for another cup of coffee. Lilly, having been the recipient of Martin's best lovemaking performance in years, was still out cold upstairs in the loft, and Martin was treasuring the peaceful silence the morning provided. The prior night's conversation with Lilly about his Dream seemed to free him, if only for a time, from its grasp. Sinking deeper into the cushions as the blazing-hot coffee warmed his soul, Martin pondered the upcoming day. Today would actually serve as the opening of Old Lincoln Days and the festivities within it. If people thought yesterday was a zoo, this day would be positively insane. Martin was glad that he and Lilly had been able to see so much of the town the day prior, knowing there was no way he'd venture into the miasma of humanity again today.

That Lilly hadn't laughed or made fun of last night's confession spoke to how much she loved Martin, and he her. He'd seen all too many couples that relished breaking each other down, especially in public. He was proud that he and Lilly hadn't become 'that couple.' Thinking back on their decision to take this trip - how Lilly had thrown herself into Billy the Kid (well, mostly via *Young Guns*, anyway), and how terrified she had looked when he came back from the brink of death - he was filled with warm, fuzzy feelings for the woman whom he could hear breathing just above where he sat. While Martin's heart led the way, other parts of his body quickly joined in; and he set his coffee cup down, softly climbed the stairs, and slid into bed. As he spooned his wife awake, Lilly felt an urgency behind her that obviously needed some attention. Smiling as she rolled over, she reached down to check its pulse and said, "What's this all about?"

Had anyone walked by a few minutes later, this time, they would have heard Martin Teebs's breathless voice yelling, "Regulators! Let's mount up!"

Friday 7:30 am

"You ready for today? It's going to be crazy, brother."

Brandon Evans, the tour guide for Lincoln After Dark, sat next to Kevin Barrow on the ancient front porch of the Murphy store. While the monument buildings wouldn't officially open for another thirty minutes, people were already scattered about town, looking for something to eat or something to buy before the madness of the morning set in.

"Yeah, man, I'm ready," replied Kevin. "Is it really that bad?" Barrow had only been employed for a few weeks before the pageant and so had no frame of reference for just how completely Billy-mania would set in over the next three days.

This wasn't the life Barrow had expected. He'd been a junior at Boulder Community College in Colorado and a member of the triathlon team. Although he wasn't the fastest, he had the grit to outwork his teammates and most of his competitors, and he scored podium finishes in nearly all of his races. However, one day, while mountain biking on one of the many single-track trails near school, he had hit a nasty slot in some tree roots and went down hard. His right knee was destroyed; even after extensive reconstruction, his surgeon told him he'd never again be able to run at such a high level. Scratching the itch to stay in motion, he took up hiking around the southwest to keep himself fit. On one such trip to New Mexico, he came across the tiny hamlet of Lincoln and was fascinated by the history of a young man about his own age, about whom he knew nothing.

Everywhere he wandered in Lincoln, people would stop and stare, so much did he looked like the boy outlaw. When one of the monument employees did a double take, Kevin knew his looks had to be legit. Bumping around town, he found that the Monuments Division was looking for summer employees; with no better plans, he decided to apply. Kevin always felt he got the job more for the way he looked than for his resume. 'Injured Triathlete' didn't offer much in the way of customer service or maintenance of the town, so his skills might have been limited to walking around and greeting every surprised, middle-aged guy who came along. Such thoughts, however, were pushed to the back of his mind on this morning as he prepared for what Brandon had labeled "an onslaught" in just a half-hour's time.

"Yeah, bro, it's that bad...and it's that good. Everybody here will be talking 'Billy' today," the tour guide stated, with some reverence in his voice. "You better bring your autograph pen 'cause you'll be signing and taking selfies with people all day!"

Barrow laughed a little to himself. When he took the job, he hadn't had any idea about posing as a long-dead outlaw for this three-day event; however, the reenactment group out of Texas that relived the Kid's final flight got word about him. After the group saw his pictures, leader Kelly Childs, who portrayed Pat Garrett, called Kevin personally, with a plea to join in for Billy's Last Escape, three times over on Sunday. So persuasive was the 'sheriff' that Kevin couldn't say no.

Once the young man was onboard for that mission, Brandon cooked up an idea for his nighttime tour that would delight his guests...or scare the crap out of them...proposing that Kevin join that endeavor as well. “I’ll bring the shotgun and blanks tonight, but we gotta meet behind the courthouse by 7:45, okay?” asked Brandon excitedly. His idea, one that Kevin bought into, was that at the end of the tour - which finished exactly where the men were sitting now - ‘Billy’ would crash out of the upstairs window and pop off two blank rounds from a 10-gauge shotgun. He’d yell the familiar, “Hello, Bob!” as he did so, then disappear into the night. Brandon could imagine his guests ducking for cover as he was just about to thank them for joining his tour. To avoid any problems with the authorities, he’d cleared his plan with the Lincoln County Sheriff’s Office: prior to the event, there would be a police car nearby to calm anyone whose nerves got *too* frazzled.

“Got it, 7:45. Hey, since they won’t see me, do I need to be in costume?” Kevin asked, reasonably.

“Heck, yeah! If you come down afterwards, you’ll be the star of the evening. Take some pictures, mingle a little. Hell, I’ll bet some of those people even tip you,” said Brandon with a wink. “And remember, don’t aim that thing at anybody. Make sure we’re all in front of the building before you pop those rounds off. Blanks *can* kill, you know.”

Kevin rolled his eyes and wagged his head. “Dude, I’ve shot a gun before. A lot of times, in fact. I know what I’m doing.”

“Good,” stressed Brandon seriously, “because I’ve been on the wrong side of one more times than I care to remember...and it ain’t fun.”

Kevin Barrow sighed and nodded his head, understanding exactly what his buddy was talking about. He patted him on the shoulder and rose from the porch. “I gotta get to work. See you tonight.” And with that, the boy who looked so much like Billy the Kid scurried off into the old courthouse - which, of course, was the last place anyone in Lincoln had ever seen the real Billy run out of.

Friday - 7:45 am

"Up? Down? Up? Down?" Several times, Trisha Davis ran through her two options for how to wear her hair, before deciding that today's workload would definitely call for a ponytail. Pulling her hair back off her freshly scrubbed face, she examined the twenty-four years of sun, surf, and fun that had taken root on her face. "Okay, big day," she said to her reflection. "Smile, be helpful, and don't let the stress get to you."

With one semester left at UCLA in pursuit of her MBA in International Management, she had taken the summer off to explore the west. Her friend Jane had landed a job tending bar at a brewery in someplace called Lincoln, New Mexico, and excitedly told Trisha that she should join her for the season in the little mountain town. Having grown up in a privileged household in Pacific Palisades, California, a mostly deserted Old West town didn't sound all that exciting at first; but Jane assured her that there was an undercurrent, a nightlife among the town's younger workers, that would keep both women occupied. With the choice between another summer at the beach or trying something new, Trisha opted for 'new' and packed her car for Lincoln.

Jane made quick work of introducing her around town and scoring her an interview with the Monuments Division, which ran all of the historic buildings and museums. Trisha won a summer job designed to handle the influx of tourists from all over, each chasing the legend of Billy the Kid. The best part of the job was meeting people from around the globe who were coming to the tiny hamlet to pay homage to the boy bandit. Trisha had done some modeling in college and always enjoyed her trips abroad to exotic locales, meeting friendly people with whom she'd otherwise never have interacted.

The most challenging part of *this* job was learning anything about Lincoln and Billy the Kid. Trisha didn't need to feign ignorance on the subject, as she truly knew nothing about it. The men, always the men, came to town and started spouting off about government beef contracts, Tunstall's death wish in starting a ranch and opening a store, and how they'd 'make ya famous!' - a line that she soon found out was from a movie made long before she was even born. With history not ever appearing at the top of her favorite classes list, she had to force herself to learn some facts in order to keep up. By the time August rolled around, Trisha was happy to report that she could lead a very decent tour of the town and its buildings, sprinkling in some historical nuggets along the way to keep her charges interested.

Checking her watch, she realized she needed to be moving through town right now. She had been renting a room from a homeowner on the far eastern edge of town, a man who only visited Lincoln every other month or so. While she had just a mile to go, there was no way she was going to drive her car, and the Division employees had been discouraged from bringing their trucks into town to save space for as many visitors' cars as possible.

Pulling her green polo shirt down over a lacy, coral-colored bra, she laughed a bit at the sight. Who was she wearing this frilly thing for, anyway? It's not like anyone was going to see it. She tucked the too-long tails of the shirt into her standard-issue khaki pants, slipped on a belt and boots, and was out the door. The street was already alive with people clamoring to walk in the footsteps of a twenty-one-year-old outlaw. Trisha strode quickly past the Patron House, Visitor Center and Museum, and Torreon on her way to an already long line snaking out in front of the courthouse. As she passed the Brewery, she wondered how crazy Jane's day would wind up being?

If Trisha could just make it until closing time, all would be fine. She'd head back to her place, shower and eat, and maybe even catch a nap. Friday night in Lincoln was usually a pretty quiet affair, but tonight was going to be different. Tonight, there'd be music and dancing in the street to coincide with the festival. It had been so long since she'd been dancing that Trisha could barely contain herself. A night to cut loose, dance with a few of the local boys, and catch up on her drinking with Jane was just about what the doctor ordered. As she smiled at the line of middle-aged men ogling her every time their wives looked away, she slipped up the steps and unlocked the courthouse door, letting the mass of humanity start to make its way inside.

"5 pm," she said to herself, "just make it to 5 pm, and then it'll be a night to remember."

Friday – 2 pm

By early afternoon, Martin had had his fill of shopping in Ruidoso and, surprisingly, so had Lilly. They'd made it back to the *casita* to relax in some refrigerated air, and Lilly had drifted over to the main house to talk to Darlene about other potential shopping excursions. Martin had given his wife advance warning that he might take a stroll down Lincoln's lone street to burn off his lunch, and, with sleep evading him, he decided to do just that. Shuffling out the front door into the afternoon heat, he looked disdainfully at the large number of people milling about. Martin instinctively knew that he wouldn't be coming back to Lincoln anytime, but he did wish for a trip when the town was quiet. He figured that, aside from the War, the small village would have been a pretty good and peaceful spot to set down roots, and his imagination wanted that experience for at least a day or two. The Teebs' limited travel budget wasn't going to allow for any extra vacations, though, so Martin plodded to the street to join the huddled masses waiting for Billy.

While yesterday's crowd had been busy, today's was positively unreal. On every bare patch of land sat either someone's car or a vendor's table. Only the middle of the town's only street was bare of anything except slow-moving tourists. Martin began feeling claustrophobic and edged his way toward the side of the road to avoid his feet being stepped on for the fifteenth time since he'd left the B&B.

Some sure-to-be-unpopular Kid fan had brought an RV into town prior to the road being closed and now needed to escape the packed village because of some sort of emergency. It would be hard enough to find room to ride a *bicycle* down the street, but pulling an RV onto the congested road seemed on the verge of an impossibility. Nevertheless, the driver made progress, inch-by-inch, as a kindly tourist would step a foot or two to the side. After watching five minutes of this, Martin was ready to move on, except for the fact that his way was now blocked by the wallowing RV. Martin shifted uneasily from foot to foot, trying to figure out just how long he'd be stuck at this showdown of one driver versus a thousand pedestrians. Suddenly, a horn blared behind him, scaring him almost to the point of falling. As he whipped his head around, he was shocked yet again to see his friend Billy Bonney, this time exiting a silver pickup truck.

"Hey, everyone! Can we make way for this guy, please?" yelled Billy to the uncooperative crowd. Getting little response, he went back to the driver's side door, beeped the horn loudly a few more times, and then got on the truck's PA system.

"People! Please! This man needs to get out of Lincoln for a medical emergency. Can you PLEASE make way so he can pull out onto the street?!" Hearing the sharp blasts of the horn and the young man's firmly put plea, people grudgingly began to vacate space, allowing the behemoth RV to edge farther out. With a thumbs up to Billy, the driver made the final swing down the street, inching his way slowly toward the boundaries of the closed road. Billy got back on the mic one last time. "Thank you! That's some real Lincoln hospitality! Have a great day!"

With that, the Billy the Kid look alike slid back into his driver's seat as Martin could only stand and stare. With everyone flowing back onto the road like Moses reconnecting the Red Sea, the young man was now stuck, at least for a while. Looking around at Lincoln's visitors, he was suddenly confronted by a large man staring directly at him, seemingly surprised to see him. Billy cracked a knowing grin and waved. "Howdy, sir. Having a good time?" he asked Martin.

Shocked out of his mental paralysis, Martin simply pointed to himself as if to ask, "Are you talking to me?" Still grinning, the boy nodded as Teebs approached. With a look of wonder in his eyes, Martin leaned into the window and whispered, "Billy?"

The Kid reenactor laughed with good feelings and replied, "Nope, but I get that a lot. My name is Kevin Barrow," he said, as he offered his right hand to Martin.

Unwilling to accept that this was not his long-lost friend, Martin grabbed the young man's hand and pulled him in closer and whispered, "It's okay, Billy. No one else will know. How'd you get here?"

Kevin just smiled again, deciding to play along, at least a little bit. Still holding Martin's hand in his own, he pulled the big man in even closer and looked him directly in the eye. "It wasn't easy, sir. Took me the better part of an entire day in my old Jeep… but you're right, I wouldn't want anyone to know that!" The boy finished off with a laugh, while Martin stared at him in confusion.

"You mean, you're not him?" Martin asked sadly.

"I'll tell you what, Mr…," Kevin paused to allow Martin to fill in the blank.

"Oh, it's Martin Teebs."

"I'll tell you what, Mr. Martin Teebs," the boy began mysteriously, "if you want me to be Billy the Kid, I'll admit I'm him."

Martin's eyes went wide; he was on the verge of receiving the confession he knew would be coming.

"I'll admit I'm him at 11 am, 1 pm, and 3 pm on Sunday, at the Last Escape reenactment. How's that for you, sir?"

Martin stood dumbly for a moment before looking back at the young reenactor. "I'm sorry. This whole thing, the people, everything. It just kind of got to me. You just look so much like him."

"That's what this event is for, Mr Teebs," said Kevin brightly, "to get lost in it. There's no shame in that. Come on by the Escape on Sunday, and we'll take a picture together, okay? I can't give you the *real* Billy, but hopefully this will do for you!"

Martin smiled a sad little smile, missing his friend so badly. His 'friend,' he thought - Billy the Kid wasn't Martin's *friend.* He was just the character in an elaborate dream and nothing more. The closest Martin was going to get to being friends with Billy the Kid was by taking a picture with Kevin Barrow in full Kid costume. Martin stuck his hand out to thank the young man. "I'll do that, Kevin. Looking forward to it."

With a quick shake of the hand, Barrow put his full attention on driving through the crowd without another killing on the Deadliest Street in America. Watching Kevin drive away, Martin decided to just pack it in for the afternoon and wait for the tour that evening. As he turned to walk away, he thought he heard a faint but very familiar voice say - over the din of the crowd - "See ya, Teebsie." Snapping his head around, expecting to spot Billy grinning behind him, Martin saw only Kevin's truck making its way up the road, clearly too far away to have said anything that Martin might have thought he heard.

Friday 2:30 pm

As the giant RV creaked and groaned out of sight, there went up a great cheer from those sitting inside and outside the Lincoln County Brewery. In the last few minutes, an impromptu betting pool had sprung up about how long it would take for the vehicle to find freedom, and now good-natured tourists and locals paid off their bets or collected their winnings. Carl Farber hadn't placed a bet, but he'd truly enjoyed the show, as schools of tourists dashed back and forth like baitfish being chased by a bass while the giant home-on-wheels struggled to escape Lincoln. Finding his seat at the end of the bar, he waited patiently until Jane noticed the empty space on the bar in front of him and glided down with a grin.

"Heya, cowboy!" she greeted him, almost as if she remembered him. "How's your day going?"

A slight smile spread on Farber's face. "Hi, Jane. I was, uh, in here...yesterday."

"I know that, silly!" she joked with him. "Green-chile cheeseburger and three light beers. If you muscle up and have a real man's beer today, you might only need two!"

They both laughed at the joke, and Farber let the afternoon's happiness wash over him. Here he was, talking to a real, live woman - young as she may be - who actually seemed to want to talk to him. He'd expected to learn a lot by coming to Lincoln, but he hadn't expected he was going to make many new friends.

"What'll it be today?" Jane asked, as she wiped off the bar in front of him.

"Hmmmm," considered Farber, putting his hand to his chin in mock thought, "let's go for one of those 'real man's' beers you were talking about. I'm at your mercy, you pick."

"Well, all right!" said Jane, as she began to shimmy away. A step or two later, she stopped and turned around. "Now don't go too deep in the well this afternoon. You gotta come by tonight for the party, *comprende, amigo*?"

Party? Carl hadn't heard of any party. "What party? I don't know anything about it."

"Well, now you do! Live band, dancing, lots of drinking. It'll go until the sheriff chases us all home…which he won't, since he'll be drunk and dancing, too!" announced Jane, with what looked almost like a fond remembrance of a previous party. With that, Jane danced her way up the bar, shaking her ass to a song she heard only in her head, before grabbing a tall glass and tapping something that might make Carl's already good afternoon get even better.

Friday - 8:30 pm

Martin and Lilly ambled down the street, which had been in turmoil during the day but took on a peaceful air this evening. As the sun sprayed its last bit of color against the sky, the couple made its way toward the Torreon tower, as instructed, to meet the guide for the Lincoln After Dark tour. While Lilly practically skipped along, happy at the thought of a night out to learn more about the Kid, Martin trudged onward apprehensively. If Brandon were correct, that damn Carl Farber would be part of the tour, and Martin was having a hard time deciding how to handle himself.

From Martin's time yesterday at the courthouse, he knew that Trisha and Farber had met face to face, and they'd seemed to be in great spirits. Martin reasonably assumed - although he hadn't seen Kevin - that the boy had also been aware of Farber as he entered the building and hadn't had an issue with the man. To Martin, that left several possibilities. The first was that Farber was a lying scumbag, just like he'd been in Martin's Dream, but Trisha and Kevin were not Rosita and Billy. The second option was that Trisha and Kevin actually *were* Rosita and Billy, but *Farber* was just a mild-mannered history teacher from New Jersey, and Martin had somehow conjured up the version of the man on whom he was currently hating. The third option was the one that worried Martin the most.

Option number three was that Martin Teebs was going insane.

If Martin had been a betting man, he'd have wagered a year's salary on option number three. The things he was seeing, the people he was running into, were all so real to him, yet in completely different identities. This, he thought, must be the first touch of madness. He took real people and his warped mind was twisting them into something they were not. That seemed about as close to losing a grip on reality as Martin dared to imagine. While his talk with Lilly the night before had offered him some temporary absolution, he knew that coming face to face with Carl Farber was going to make The Dream all the more real yet again. Every five steps or so, Martin told himself not to make a scene.

A small group of people, including a few children, had already gathered at the meeting spot, and Brandon held forth with some introductions and a few jokes to break the ice. Dressed in a blue-and-white gingham-checked shirt, grey trousers, black boots, and with a Colt resting firmly in cross-draw fashion on his left hip, he looked every bit the type who would have inhabited Lincoln, and perhaps fought and died during the famous War. Seeing more guests approaching, he grinned broadly. "Martin and Lilly Teebs," he said, pointing his finger at them with each word to emphasize that he'd gotten their names correctly. "Did I get that right?"

Lilly smiled and reached her hand out to the young man. "Yes, Lilly Teebs, and this is my husband, Martin," she offered, as though the tour guide might be someone who couldn't tell which Teebs was which.

"I'm Brandon. I'll be your tour guide tonight!" he said enthusiastically. "Good to see you again, Martin."

Again? thought Lilly. Where had Martin seen this man before? Rather than question her husband, who seemed to be trapped within some of his own thoughts, she simply assumed the two men must have run into each other during Martin's walk earlier in the afternoon.

Not seeing Farber anywhere around, Martin hoped that perhaps he'd lucked out and the sniveling coward had decided to bail. "Hey, Brandon," said Martin, as he glanced around nervously. "Everyone here? Let's get this show on the road, huh?"

Lilly scowled at her husband's out-of-character behavior. "What's the rush, Martin? Let's meet some of these nice people." Lilly melted into the small crowd, talking animatedly about the tour and her husband's obsession with Billy the Kid. Martin stepped off to the side and rested his back against the cool rocks of the tower.

“I’m here, sorry!” came a voice from the darkness as Carl Farber himself jogged onto the scene. “I had to run back to Capitan to change. Sorry,” he said again, offering an apology to Brandon.

“Okay, then,” the tour guide spoke up to get everyone’s attention, “looks like we’re all here and looks like Lincoln has gone dark. It’s just about time to head back in time to the Lincoln County War!”

If only! thought Martin. Then he’d have his Colt, and he could dispatch this piece-of-shit history teacher right here and now.

To Martin’s horror, upon seeing Teebs standing alone, Farber made his way over with a tentative smile. “Hi. I’m Carl. Carl Farber,” he said, while offering his hand.

This was the moment Martin had dreaded. The stupid face he’d seen a hundred times now hovered directly in front of him, as if daring Martin to punch it. He had nothing but seething animosity for this man, whom common sense told him he’d never even met. Martin’s decision on what to do, whatever it might be, would have to come now. Sticking his own hand out, he grabbed Farber’s and gave it a good, hard squeeze. “Nice to meet you, Farber. Name’s Teebs. Martin Teebs,” said Martin tersely, giving his best Clint Eastwood impersonation.

The strength of the handshake surprised Carl, but he laughed it off by saying, “That’s some grip! Hey, you’re the other folks from New Jersey? I’m from Waldwick myself.”

Hearing the familiar name of her town, Lilly spun her head around to see her husband in conversation with another middle-aged man who was obviously fascinated by the lore of the Kid. “Waldwick? Who’s your friend, Martin?” she asked innocently. Martin almost vomited the remains of his supper at the mention of the word ‘*friend*’ in conjunction with his arch enemy.

Before Martin could answer, Carl jumped in. “Hi, there. My name’s Carl Farber. Yes, I teach history at Waldwick High.”

“Small world, Carl!” said Lilly, gratefully shaking his hand. “I’m Lilly Teebs, and I guess you’ve already met Martin. We’re from Waldwick, too. How crazy is this!”

Lilly's mouth hung open, and her eyes danced between the two men. While the history teacher seemed in good spirits, however, her husband's already odd mood seemed to have soured even more. Lilly didn't understand Martin's issue: Here they were, in Lincoln, practically his church due to his reverence for Billy Bonney, and all he could do was scowl. Martin raised the corner of his mouth in a sneer and nodded his head toward his wife, as Brandon jumped back in.

"Okay, everyone! Welcome to Lincoln After Dark!" announced Brandon, and a small cheer went up from the fifteen or so people gathered around. "Tonight, we're going to see Lincoln in an entirely different way. Without cars on the street and without the sun shining on everything modern, we'll take a trip back in time to 1878, on the eve of the Lincoln County War. You'll experience the town the way that Billy and the Regulators did. Feel free to take as many pictures as you like, and ask any questions as they come up…don't hold 'em all until the end."

A general murmur of 'okay' went up from the group. Lilly raised her hand. "Umm, Brandon?"

"Yes," he said, pointing in her direction, "Lilly Teebs from New Jersey."

"*Young Guns*," she began, "pretty accurate or no?"

Brandon rolled his eyes back a bit and threw his head to the side. He'd have bet this question would have come up at least three times tonight, but not before they'd even set off on the tour. Smiling at Lilly and then the group, he gave his canned answer, "Soooo...the movie itself took a lot of liberties with history; but as a way to get more people into the Kid, it did a great job."

Brandon began shepherding his charges so they could walk to the east before Lilly cut in again. "Yeah, because this place doesn't look at all like Lincoln in the movie, you know."

This time, Brandon could only let out a laugh before he replied, "No, it sure doesn't. Let's go see what the *real* Lincoln looked like, shall we?" With that, Brandon and his little troupe moved off from the Torreon and headed toward the old cemetery where, by flashlight, he'd point out a number of luminaries of the Lincoln County War era.

As they walked along, he was peppered by questions from his guests, not the least of whom was Lilly, who continued to compare everything in real Lincoln to everything she'd seen in the movies. Farther to the back, Martin lagged a bit behind, lost as he was in his thoughts about Farber and his memories (if that's what they even were) of his Dream.

Still trying to make friends, Carl drifted to the back of the pack. "Who'd have thought that two guys from Jersey would be here in Lincoln, huh?"

"Yeah," said Martin, with a steely resolve to his voice, "what a coincidence."

Carl was unsure what he'd done to anger the man - or perhaps that was just who he was - but if his efforts with Jane had proved anything, persistence usually paid off. "How long have you been into the Kid, Martin?"

Martin only wished to be left alone, and for this night to be over. Still, the question was valid enough to make Martin ask himself, how long had it been? "I don't know, Farber, let's say...a hundred forty years, give or take," he offered.

Farber laughed, immediately getting the joke. "Ah, you must be a time traveler then!"

The accusation cut Martin right to the core and made him snap, "Takes one to know one, doesn't it, Farber!"

Martin's voice had risen so loud that everyone took notice, and Brandon stopped the tour. A veteran of three combat tours of duty in Iraq, and the recipient of three Bronze Stars and a Purple Heart, he was not a man to be trifled with. "What's going on back here? Do we have some sort of problem?" he asked, as he stared first at Martin, then at Carl.

Lilly rushed up behind Brandon to intervene, if needed. "Martin! Why are you yelling at this man? What's wrong?" she demanded.

Carl looked genuinely hurt, or maybe he was just concerned, as he waved his hand a little toward Martin before speaking. "I'm sorry. I didn't mean to cross any boundaries, Martin. I was just making conversation."

With no other options, Martin let his anger dissipate in a mighty sigh. "No problem here, Brandon. I'm sorry, Carl. I've had a lot of stuff on my mind since we got here, and I shouldn't have taken it out on you." Martin offered his hand - not because he wanted to, but because he was afraid that Brandon might kick both of their asses if he didn't.

Farber nodded with a smile and accepted the apology. "No worries. All is forgotten."

Satisfied that peace was restored, Brandon made his way up to the front of the group to set off again while Lilly grabbed Martin's sleeve and pulled him closer to her. Farber's words kept ringing in Martin's brain.

"All is forgotten."

While the cascade of emotions he was feeling threatened to overwhelm him, Martin only wished that those words could somehow, some way, be true.

Friday – 8:45 pm

As the tour group made its way toward the cemetery, it came upon the not-so-quiet Lincoln County Brewery, where the party was just starting to rev up. While Brandon kept his charges across the street so that he didn't lose any of them to music and booze, Martin couldn't help looking over to see what was going on. With the band warming up, a few people were up and swaying in time to whatever fragments of music were being made. Immediately, his eyes were drawn to a raven-haired beauty, wearing a cropped top with her perfectly flat stomach exposed, and jeans tight enough to allow no room for father, son, or holy ghost. Trisha!

At the sight of her, Martin experienced a stabbing pain where his heart used to be. The feelings he had - or was it hormones? - for her were so real as to be painful because the two were apart. What made it worse was that this incredible creature was totally unaware that she was madly, passionately in love with Martin - at least in his own subconscious. He saw her swaying next to the stage, drink in hand, and laughing with a woman who looked as though she might be a bartender there. Just two pretty, young

American girls, with their entire lives in front of them, and no use for a middle-aged nobody like Martin Teebs.

What Martin had first thought was pain now evolved into something else: sadness. His feelings were made even worse because he was in the company of his beloved wife but could only be whimpering for another woman. Martin felt like he'd been shown the trailer for an incredible film, only to be forced to leave once the real movie started. Downward, he spiraled into a funk that he just couldn't shake. Suddenly, going to some old graveyard seemed perfectly appropriate to him. Why not spend his evening with a bunch of people who had lost everything...just like he had?

"Nice night, huh, hon?" asked Lilly, as she turned her head to catch Martin's gaze.

Shocked out of his self-pity, Martin snapped to attention. "Huh? Oh…yeah. Great. Not so hot, like earlier," he responded simply.

If Lilly were waiting for more from her husband, the wait could be substantial since he seemed to retreat right back into his own thoughts. With no one else to talk to, Lilly piped up to ask another question of their tour guide. "Brandon, where's that big tree that Billy shot Murphy under at the end of the movie?"

Friday – 8:46 pm

Carl Farber looked longingly across the street at Jane. Standing there in her tight black jeans and barely-holding-everything-in tank top, she seemed to be having a ripping good time with the dark-haired woman from the museum. There was a band about to start playing, and the two women laughed and joked with the guitar player.

"Should have learned guitar rather than the damn recorder," Farber mumbled to himself, picturing himself on stage with pretty women lining up to talk to him before he strummed the opening chords of *Smoke on the Water* or some other love-it-when-you're-drunk party hit. Since the blowup by the other guy from New Jersey, Farber had stayed at the back of the pack to not risk irritating the big man again. Whatever issue the guy had with him, it had to be some sort of mistaken identity as Carl was sure they'd never met before. He'd never experienced someone having such disdain for him without even knowing who he was.

As excited as he was about the tour, Carl was even more thrilled with his plan to head to the Brewery once the trek concluded. He reminded himself again and again that Jane was being professionally nice to him, but with that tiny fraction of a percent chance that maybe it might be real, he just had to be there to see her again.

While the tour moved down the road away from the Brewery, the big guy's wife asked another inane question about *Young Guns*, and Farber secretly laughed to himself. Maybe if he'd been married to that woman, with all of her misconceptions about Billy the Kid, Carl might have been pretty grouchy, too.

Friday – 9 pm

The cemetery was positively spooky on this barely moonlit night. Over the years, the graves had been pushed and pulled by the sands of time so that a visitor could easily trip on them, and maybe even get hurt badly enough to need one as well. Luckily, Brandon had asked each person to bring his or her own flashlight and helpfully brought a few extras, just in case. As the small group crunched through the darkened tombstones, their guide offered a running commentary on some of the more famous inhabitants. "This right here is Yginio Salazar's grave. He was a Regulator, as you probably know, and a real good friend of Billy's," lectured Brandon, as iPhones came to life and photos were snapped. "A lot of the old-timers from the War wanted to be buried here, even after they'd moved away. I guess this place felt more like home than anywhere they went later on."

Brandon let that thought - the thought of being 'home' - hang in the air, while his guests stared in reverence.

Martin stood near the top of the grave, out of the line of sight of photos, but close enough to remember (or so he thought) Yginio lining up behind Doc Scurlock, ready to run from the burning McSween house, fear written on his face, as they rushed out the back door. He could almost feel the heat from the inferno tickling his feet and see McSween's desperate eyes imploring him to figure out what to do.

Until now, everything in this trip to Lincoln had been about Martin. Selfishly, he had stewed about how sad and angry he was because he wasn't living in the world of his Dream, but now he was face to face with the grave of a man who'd truly suffered greatly. Salazar was shot twice in the…

"Back and shoulder," said Brandon, as Martin's psyche snapped back to reality. "He laid there in the backyard, near that burning house, for hours. People say that some of the Dolan men even came by and kicked him, just to make sure he really was dead. Can't imagine the pain he must have endured until they all left, and he crawled a half mile to his sister-in-law's house to finally get some help with his wounds."

Contrary to Brandon's statement that he couldn't imagine how Salazar had suffered, Martin knew that his tour guide had been awarded a Purple Heart, which was given only to those wounded or killed in battle. He surmised that Brandon knew *exactly* how Yginio had felt on that fateful night.

Martin had joined that fraternity in The Dream, after being gut-shot in December 1880 by Pat Garrett and his posse in Fort Sumner. Struggling to crawl away from the battle, Martin was tracked by that sniveling Carl Farber. The coward had seen his own good fortune in his rival being shot, and he went to gloat over Martin's dying body. Martin could still see Farber's misshapen face, stringy hair, and yellow teeth malevolently smiling over him, while the life flowed from Martin's body. Instinctively, his hand went to his abdomen, where the ugly scar would remind him for the rest of his days just how close he'd come to death - and just how much he wanted to take part in Farber's. The only rub to the current situation was...

There was no scar. Martin had never been shot. He touched his abdomen, and, although it was victim to too many cinnamon rolls, no bullet had ever broken the sanctity of his flesh. His mind vacillated between the past he'd never had, but could remember clearly, and the present he was having, in which none of these incredible events had ever happened. If Martin wanted to somehow escape from all this, where would he go? The Patron House wasn't going to allay his memories, nor would any other place in this tiny town. He doubted he could convince Lilly that they should up and drive all the way to Albuquerque, or El Paso, or the moon, this late at night. Even if he could snap his fingers and be back in New Jersey, he'd still be haunted by the specter of what he remembered from his Dream and which was tormenting him within his present.

“You okay, hon?” asked Lilly gently. Having noticed Martin’s sour mood since they arrived at the *Torreon*, she didn’t want to push him too far and risk another meltdown. “You seem kind of quiet.”

The tension in Martin’s neck and shoulders seemed to melt with Lilly’s presence. He pulled her in for a hug and inhaled the scent of her thick, black hair. More tightly than before, he pressed her against him, feeling her full breasts and strong shoulders fitting perfectly against his chest. Here, in her arms, he felt finally safe. Standing in the darkened cemetery, he let his anguish and heartbreak wash away, leaving him strong and clean. How could he let her know how much she truly meant to him? How much he needed her to pull himself away from the darkness that had enveloped him since arriving in Lincoln? How much his very existence depended on the love that she had unconditionally given him? Before he pulled her back for a passionate kiss, he let a single word escape from his hungry lips…

“Rosita.”

Friday – 9:01 pm

“What?!” demanded Lilly, at the same time surprised, embarrassed, and furious.

“What?” responded Martin frantically, as he snapped back to reality.

“What?!” repeated Lilly, now confused about just what was happening. “You just called me ‘Rosita’!”

Martin looked wildly back and forth, hoping someone from the tour might somehow save him - or maybe just kill him. Most everyone stared at first, then awkwardly looked and stepped away to allow the couple to work out their issue. “No! I didn’t, Lil,” Martin finally protested. “I was asking Brandon about…well, about that person I was telling you about. I just thought she might be buried here.”

Brandon looked more surprised than anyone, due to the fact that Martin had been nowhere near him and definitely wasn’t asking him any question. Still, he didn’t want his tour to crumble just as it was getting started, so he jumped in to save the hapless man. "What was that name again, Martin? 'Rosita'? You have a last name?"

Martin looked carefully at Lilly, seeing that she still wasn't happy, but at least the focus had been shifted from romantic to historical. "It was, uh...," pondered Martin for a moment, as if he couldn't quite remember, and as if the woman's identity wasn't all that important to him anyway. "Luna. Yeah, that's it. 'Rosita Luna'."

Brandon scrunched up his eyes, sorting through his mental library of Lincoln County historical figures. "Mmmppphhh, 'Luna,' huh?" he queried. The pause went on longer than he liked because he wanted his guests to feel secure that, as a historian, his knowledge was complete. But this name threw him. "I don't think I've ever heard of a 'Rosita Luna' in Lincoln County. Where'd you hear about her?"

Reaching for the best lie he could manage under the circumstances, Martin looked at Lilly, who tilted her head and opened her eyes wide as if to say, "*Now* what are you going to tell him?"

"Umm, it was just a webpage on the internet, I think," Martin offered. "I just thought she was maybe one of Billy's girls or something?" Lilly just shook her head and walked off a few steps, and the others resumed their picture taking.

As he prepared to lead his group out of the cemetery, Brandon shot back, "I don't think so, Martin, but I've got some books back at my place. I'll see what I can dig up."

At the mention of Rosita's name - and the thought of digging up anything - Martin's head began to pound, and he broke out into a cold sweat in the midst of the warm evening desert air.

Somewhere from what seemed like a great distance away, Martin heard Lilly's voice. "Brandon, where was this Salazar when they threw Billy down the stairs in that trunk?"

Friday – 9:05 pm

Carl Farber had watched with interest the discussion between Martin and Brandon. That Teebs was such a fanatical researcher as to find a reference to one of Billy's girlfriends - about whom even their tour guide was unaware - impressed him greatly. While Farber himself had never run across a 'Rosita Luna' in his own research, he was enough of a historian to know that failing to find easily accessible information about someone did *not* mean that person hadn't existed. It just meant he or she hadn't been discovered *yet*. Maybe it was the mystery of being in Lincoln, or the fact they were both from the same town, or maybe even the affinity that Farber felt for someone else who pored through reams of internet data to try to understand just one iota more about Billy the Kid; but something in him told Farber to try one more time to connect with the dismayed man. As the group tramped out of the cemetery gate on its way back to Lincoln proper, Farber drifted to the side of the group, waiting until Martin made his way to the gate.
"Hey, I'm really sorry again, Martin," said the history teacher in his most conciliatory tone. "Sometimes I just don't know when to keep my mouth shut."

Martin looked at the man he was somehow programmed to hate, but he failed to raise enough emotion to even care at the moment. With Lilly still sore at him, and walking on thin ice with Brandon, Martin reasoned that having an ally, even if it happened to be Carl Farber, wouldn't be the worst thing to get him through the rest of this night.

"Eh, no worries, Carl. It's more my fault than yours," offered Martin, as they shuffled up the hill, just clinging to the tail end of the group. The two men walked in silence for a few moments before Farber decided it was safe to continue the conversation.

"You do a lot of research on Billy, it sounds like?" inquired Farber, as politely as he could.

Martin's defenses were down, exhausted by all of the mental energy he'd expended over the past two days. "Yeah, I guess," he admitted. "Coming here was going to be the *coup de grace* of it all."

Farber smiled ruefully. "Yeah, same here. You don't get many vacations on a teacher's salary, and I've been saving for this one for a while."

Martin sighed. "Well, I guess I'm glad we both made it here, finally."

Farber clapped Martin on the shoulder in friendly fashion, and judging by the fact that he didn't get hit back, he shared, "I wanted to experience this, but also want to gather some final information for the book I'm writing."

At the mention of Farber writing a book, another chill shot through Martin's being. He distinctly remembered the book that his Dream version of Farber had been writing, calling out Billy as the coward of Lincoln County. That book also seemed to be Farber's portal to travel back through time at his leisure to precisely the period he wanted. All of it made Martin shudder, and he almost didn't want an answer to the question he was about to ask.

"A book, huh? What's it going to be about?" he inquired, with more determination in his voice than he'd wanted to betray.

Now at ease in his academic world, Farber explained, "It's a critical analysis of the rise of The House of Murphy. I haven't seen much written about how Murphy became Murphy, and I thought it would help other Billy-buffs to understand the forces that Tunstall, McSween, and their Regulators faced."

Martin ventured carefully into what could be a minefield if this Farber actually turned out to be The Dream's Farber, trying to hide in plain sight. "What's your take on Murphy, then?"

"He was a scumbag! That's what I think of him," Farber stated emphatically. "He didn't just take advantage of the people of Lincoln, he pressed that advantage until they popped. I only wish his real end was as dramatic as they showed in *Young Guns*!"

Martin could only laugh to himself. This man was about as different from Dream Farber as two men could be. Whatever mistrust he held in reserve for Farber was put aside for the time being. The two men marched down Lincoln's street, quickly catching up to the group. Martin glanced over at Farber and said, "Amen to that."

As the chatter of Brandon telling the story of how some local musicians came to serenade Billy while he was under guard at the Patron House drifted back to them, Farber looked at Martin and asked, “Hey, you wanna grab a beer at the Brewery when this thing is over?”

Friday – 9:45 pm

Having seen all there was to see and heard all the stories there were to hear during a one-mile-long town, Brandon’s tour was winding down as he led his group toward the courthouse. He imagined that many (or all) of these people would attend the pageant on Sunday, but he didn’t want them to go without reviewing the history of the most famous building in the whole village. The entire legend of Billy the Kid, and most probably of the Lincoln County War, would have been forgotten to history if not for Billy’s daring escape from this very building. Although it was closed for the evening, Brandon walked his clients around the back of the courthouse, pointing out such key historical spots as the location of the old outhouse, Deputy Bell’s death marker, the staircase where he took his final walk, and finally around the corner and back toward the street to see where Bob Olinger died, a victim of his own shotgun in the hands of William H. Bonney.

“So, Bell staggers out the back door and falls into the hands of old Godfrey Gauss,” continued Brandon, “almost at the same time Olinger is making a run for the courthouse from the Wortley Hotel, where he’s marched six prisoners for a meal.” Brandon held his hands up to signify that his group shouldn’t follow him as he walked into the street toward the Wortley.

Now speaking louder, he played the part of Olinger, gun drawn and eerily stalking ghosts in the moonlight. “Olinger closes in on the corner of the building,” reflected Brandon, as he crept closer to his group, “and when he gets here, he hears Billy saying, ‘Hello, Bob!’ from that window up there.” As he pointed toward the window, everyone could feel at least a bit of the hopelessness of Olinger in that moment. With both barrels of his own shotgun aimed at him, it would take only a split-second for the Kid to pull one trigger and shred Olinger’s upper torso. “Kid fires and Olinger falls, cut to pieces, right here at this stone,” said Brandon, now pointing at Olinger’s famous death marker. “And despite what you may have heard, no one reported Olinger saying a thing before he died. Probably didn’t have any time.”

His history lesson went on to explain that Billy then made his way to the front balcony and unloaded the second barrel into Olinger's face and breast, probably so that he couldn't have an open coffin. Most adults in the group winced at the description of the earthly remains of 'Pecos' Bob Olinger being reduced to so-much hamburger. Brandon allowed the silence to descend upon his group for a moment, before a voice from the crowd - Lilly's - cackled, "Best dollar and eighty I ever spent!"

Both Martin and Farber looked with pained expressions at their tour guide, who took it all in stride. "That didn't really happen, Lilly, but good on you for remembering so many lines from the movie. It's usually just the guys who go around saying them," he said truthfully. "Come on, all, let's go around to the front and answer any last questions."

With the group seated on the porch and steps of the courthouse, Brandon graciously thanked his guests for attending, requested that they please tell their friends to take the tour when they visited Lincoln, and asked for any remaining questions.

"So, like…do you think Billy made it to Old Mexico?" asked a middle-aged man, who'd been corralling his wife and three kids around for the better part of ninety minutes.

"The truth, sir, is that we just don't know. It's probable that Pat Garrett killed Billy in Fort Sumner, but there's always the possibility that history wasn't exactly the way it was written. For my money, I'd say he died in 1881."

Another woman in the group, obviously possessing romantic notions, raised her hand to ask, "Billy and Paulita Maxwell were an item, don't you think? I mean, the kiss at Christmas, him being shot in her brother's house? Her being so coy later on in life to deny it so strongly?"

Brandon thought for a few seconds before answering. "I do think there was more going on there than that they were just friends. Paulita herself never denied that long kiss with him. My guess is they probably fooled around a bit. But Billy was in demand by a lot of women, and I doubt Paulita was going to put up with that for very long."

After a few more questions, the conversation wound down; and Brandon spoke loudly, as if someone out of range might need to hear him. "Ok, folks, that concludes our tour. Be careful walking back to your hotel, this still is the Most Dangerous Street in America!"

Precisely at that moment, a voice from the second-floor window - around the corner and out of sight - yelled, "Hello, Bob!" immediately followed by the thunderous blast of a double-barreled, 10-gauge shotgun. Everyone in Brandon's group screamed, hit the deck, or began running away into the night, as they heard faint laughter coming from somewhere up above.

"Wait! It's okay!" shouted Brandon to his confused and frightened guests. "It's just part of the tour!"

With children crying, men checking their pulses, and women becoming furious, a chorus of 'What?' and 'Are you fucking kidding me?' came raining down upon the tour guide.

"No, no," Brandon reassured everyone, waving his hands toward the ground as if to minimize the risk. "Just a little something for you to remember Lincoln by. I wanted to put y'all in that mindset of the people here in Lincoln, hearing the Kid kill Bell and Olinger." The tour guide put on a big grin to hopefully win the group back over as he called upstairs, "Hey, Kid, come on down!"

With a heavy thud of boots on the darkened balcony above them, the group was able to trace the sound of a man walking down the stairs and slowly coming into the light in front of the building. Silence held forth and trepidation ruled as into Martin's field of vision walked the best friend he'd ever had...

William H. Bonney.

Friday – 9:55 pm

To his new pal Martin's "Holy shit," Carl Farber couldn't help but add, "Looks just like him, huh?" Martin seemed transfixed by the young man. The rest of the tour group, now either recovered or dead from the shock, gave the Billy the Kid pretender a round of applause. Even Lilly clucked her tongue in approval of the boy, who looked nothing like Emilio Estevez, to her, anyway.

"Ladies and gentlemen, I present to you Mr. William H. Bonney!" announced Brandon, as if he were master showman P.T. Barnum. People went up to talk to 'Billy,' some going so far as to touch his clothes and hat. With tempers abated, a number of jokes were told; before long, the boy bandit was signing autographs, taking photos, and even leaving an "I'll make ya famous" voicemail greeting on someone's phone. Even Farber was so impressed at the likeness that he had to have his picture taken with the Kid, asking Lilly to snap the photo for posterity.

Only Martin hung back, unable to approach the young man. It was as if his mind was caught on a sandbar in the ocean, with the tide rising. Eventually, he'd have to jump off and go one way or the other, but he just couldn't seem to make himself do it. As people shook hands, laughed, and said goodbye to Brandon, the crowd around Billy began to thin. Lilly and Farber were chatting up something about New Jersey - probably the latest episode of *The Real Housewives*, thought Martin. Brandon walked over and relieved the Kid of the shotgun, carefully unloading it and getting its case, which had been hidden on the porch.

Finally, Billy stood alone.

With his heart racing and trying not to betray his nervousness with his facial expressions, Martin walked directly up to the man and said simply, "Billy."
The familiar grin that Martin had seen hundreds of times lit up the night as Billy cocked his head and offered a genuine "Hey" in return. It was him! Martin had seen through the veneer - which Billy had had to put on for everyone else - to find the real man hiding underneath. He had a thousand questions to ask his friend. How did he get here? What did Martin's Dream mean? Did it all really happen? Was Trisha really Rosita? Why wasn't he trying to kill Farber right now? So many things rushed through Martin's brain that he was having trouble focusing at all.

Martin understood that Billy couldn't talk to him here or he'd risk giving himself away. Who knows what Farber would do if he found out the truth? No, they'd need to find a quiet place where he and Billy would be undisturbed so that Martin could be caught up on the whole thing, and then plan for what would happen next. If Teebs was thrilled to see his friend, the implication was that he soon would be reunited with Rosita, too! His heart soared at the prospect of pulling her to him and holding her like the entire world could pass them by before they'd let go.

Billy was just about to say something, but Martin already knew what it would be. "I know, Billy. We've got to find someplace to talk." The big man looked around wildly as Farber and Lilly's conversation was drawing to a close. Whatever he and Billy decided, it would have to happen right now.

"I was just thinking the same thing," said Billy. "How about we all head to the Brewery? There's a band and beer. Hey, Brandon! Are you going to come with us to get a beer?"

Martin's eyes went slack, unable to quite comprehend what was happening. Billy looked back at him and announced, "I've just gotta get changed out of these ridiculous things. I'll be wearing them enough on Sunday," he added, with a chuckle.

Martin began short circuiting. Was this Billy or wasn't it? A moment ago, he had been sure; now Billy was calling his own clothes 'ridiculous.' Was this Billy so bold as to invite his sworn enemy Farber to have a beer with him? It all made no sense to Martin, and his hopes plummeted.

"Hey," Kevin announced, "I'm gonna get changed, and I'll meet y'all at the dance. I left my iPhone upstairs, and I need it for the alarm to get up for work tomorrow."

An iPhone? So forlorn did Martin look that one might be forgiven for thinking that someone had stolen all his birthday presents. "Mr. Teebs? That's it, right...Teebs? You okay, sir?" asked Kevin.

Martin had no words and could only shake his head sadly and slowly from side to side.

Friday – 10 pm

"Babe, what did you think of the tour?" asked a very chipper Lilly, as she, Martin, and Farber wandered east on the quiet street.

"Oh, it was fine. Good, I mean," mumbled Martin in response, but never looking up from watching his feet swing in front of him.

Lilly had been worried about her husband all evening. His mood had been lousy for the first half of the tour, then he and Carl had seemed to have a discussion and hit it off; but now, after that shotgun stunt, Martin seemed in a funk he couldn't escape. Wanting to do whatever would be the best wifely thing she could, Lilly encouraged him to hang out with his new buddies. "Carl tells me you guys are going to have a couple beers? I think I heard Brandon and Kevin are going to join you?"

At that moment, Martin had no desire to go anywhere except crawl into bed to get this disturbing day behind him. "Well, I should walk you back to the *casita* first, then I'll see how I feel," said Martin glumly.

Lilly knew that once Martin walked past the bar, there was no way he'd be going back. She thought it would be good for him to spend some time with the guys, especially if those guys happened to be into Billy the Kid as much as her husband was. "No, I'm fine, Martin. It's so quiet out here. You go and have some fun with your friends, really," Lilly insisted.

Dammit, Martin thought to himself. If only Lilly had wanted him to stay with her, he would never go back out to meet Farber. However, Lilly knew him better than anyone else, and so she had maneuvered him to a place where he couldn't wriggle away. Then the thought hit him: Did *Lilly* really know him better than anyone else, or was it *Rosita* who claimed that title? Of course, currently, Rosita didn't even exist, so even if she won the competition, she wouldn't be there to stand on the podium. Martin settled on that thought for a moment, before another struck him between the eyes.

Rosita! or...*Trisha*!

Trisha had been at the Brewery earlier, and she might just still be there. While Martin knew he wasn't getting anywhere with a mid-twenties, co-ed MBA candidate, he also knew that *looking* didn't hurt anything; and maybe, just maybe, he could capture enough memories to dream about *Rosita* one more time. What the hell, he reasoned, if the place sucked or Farber turned out to be a total bore - which Martin figured the smart money was on - then he could just up and pay his tab and head back to his life with Lilly. Screw it, he thought to himself, he didn't get many chances to cut loose, and this one seemed to be wife-condoned.

"Are you sure, Lil? If you're okay, I guess I'll have one beer and be back soon."

"Don't rush, hon, I'm going to take a bath and read a magazine or something. Take your time and enjoy!" she said enthusiastically. "And hey, Carl, nice to meet you!"

Farber turned toward Martin with a grin on his face. "Man, you scored big time, Martin. A pretty wife who wants you to go out drinking without her, and on top of that, she's into Billy the Kid! Leave some luck for the rest of us, huh!" Martin grinned out of the side of his mouth as Lilly walked off into the darkness, and the two men stepped off the lone street and into the middle of the biggest party of the year in Lincoln, New Mexico.

Friday – 10:05 pm

"You made it!" said Jane enthusiastically, as she moved quickly down the bar toward Farber. Arriving, she offered a wide smile and leaned over to give him a big kiss on the cheek. Whether Martin or Carl was more surprised by the action was up for debate because both men sat in wide-eyed shock, and the pretty young lady backed off with a grin. "Cat got your tongue?" asked the woman through a mischievous smirk.

"Uh, no. No. Hi, Jane," offered Farber, still woozy from the physical contact. "Good to see you, too." Farber smiled to let her know his statement was intended to be humorous, and the three of them laughed a bit.

"Who's the Regulator here with you?" questioned Jane, motioning at Martin. Martin's blood froze again for a second. *Regulator*? Was this the proof he had been looking for - the proof of his secret past in Old West history? Farber seemed not to notice any underlying intent, if there even had been any.

"This is Martin Teebs, also from New Jersey," said Farber, with a feigned look of surprise on his face. "What are the odds, huh?"

Unable to wait any longer, Martin jumped in. "Did you say 'Regulator'? Why would you say that?"

Jane looked him up and down with an approving eye before responding, "Dunno. You just look like the big, strong type who would have been one. That's all. Sure didn't mean it as an insult, stranger." Jane flashed another big grin to let Martin know she didn't really give a damn how he took the compliment.

"Oh, no…no," stumbled Martin, "I didn't take it that...you know…oh, forget it. Thank you."

With no one needing to explain any actions or words, Jane scanned the busy brewery and asked, "What are you cowboys drinking tonight?"

Farber looked over at Martin and began, "Couple of…" - wagging his finger between himself and Martin - "...beers. That good with you?" Still stung by the Regulator comment and wondering if Jane had some portal to a mysterious past life, Martin just nodded.

"Great! Coming right up, boys! Get yourself on outside, 'cause the band's kicking, and there's a lot of pretty girls needing someone to dance with." Before Farber could tell her that none was nearly as pretty as she, Jane flitted off as yet another man approached the bar behind her. Seeing him, she shouted, "You made it!" and bent over to give him a big, fat kiss on his cheek.

Friday - 10:10 pm

Martin and Carl had made their way outside just in time for the band to strike up the Marshall Tucker Band hit *Can't You See*? The two men searched in vain for any place to sit down, finally accepting that resting against the railing on the near side of the small stage was as comfy as they could get. After the first salvos of the song hit the ears of the mix of tourists and locals, a great murmur was heard from the crowd, the type of din arising anytime a band plays *Freebird* or some other great crowd-pleaser. A few laughing couples headed to the dance floor; and, not to be outdone, a handful of women, who simply wouldn't wait to be asked to dance, strolled in time with the music as they, too, joined the commotion.

"Well, here's to a good night, huh, Martin?" Farber toasted, raising his glass.

Martin grinned and raised his in return, and they each took a generous swig of the Lincoln County Brewery's finest. The scene that evening had a certain air of *hippiness* and wouldn't have been out of place in SoCal or Haight-Ashbury in the late sixties. Far from the violence that had wracked this street for many of its years of existence, tonight felt downright full of peace, love, and understanding. Martin allowed himself to relax after the events of the past two hours, gazing upon the shiny, happy people. He had to admit that the band wasn't half bad, as the lead singer crooned his way through the chorus of the song.

Just then, as an obviously drunken couple decided to sit this one out and returned to its table, into Martin's field of vision came Rosita. Hands in the air, eyes closed, hips swaying in time with the music, she looked as perfect as Martin had ever seen her. She was wearing a tank top, or what was supposed to be one, cut as it was halfway up her midriff. Her full breasts fought and swayed underneath, clearly not bound by a bra of any sort. She wore the kind of jeans that looked as though they'd been poured on, so tight that Martin often wondered how women could even breathe in them. At some point, her movements hampered by the strappy heels she wore, she simply kicked them off and danced, barefooted and with an invisible partner. So plainly beautiful while completely unadorned was this woman that Martin was having a hard time catching his breath.

A flood of memories of his intimate times with her - or with someone like her, or maybe with someone he had completely made up in his own mind - coursed through his brain. Both love and lust alternately rose in Martin, like the sap from a mature maple tree, so much so that he adjusted his body slightly to the side to avoid alarming any perv police who might be watching him. As she spun with her back toward him, he traced her spine with his eyes to the area just above the waist of her jeans. Martin was secretly happy that this Rosita wasn't adorned by a tramp stamp and that her skin appeared to be undisturbed by a tattooist's needle. Just before her spine ducked under her jeans, he caught the merest glimpse of a bright-red thong peeking back at him. Although Martin wished the show could go on forever, he was also hammered by the loneliness and isolation he was feeling. So many of these people - Farber, Kevin, Trisha, and probably more - had meant so much to him in some other reality; and here he was, unable to share even a bit of it with any of them.

As the band played through the refrain a few more times, Martin was struck by how appropriate the song was for him. Anyone who cared to look could see exactly what this woman had been doing to him. Yes, he thought. He decided that if the earth could just swallow him up at that moment, he'd gladly go without putting up any fight. With the last note still hanging in the air, the crowd applauded wildly, people went to reclaim their seats, and someone did indeed actually scream out "*Freebird!*" much to the delight of every other drunken Lincolnite.

While Trisha was carefully slipping her heels back on, she looked over directly at Martin and Farber. As she did, a huge smile broke out on her face, and she began quickly walking in their direction.

Oh my God, thought Martin, this is it! Trisha had finally seen through the fog of the present and recognized him for the man with whom she'd pledged to live her entire life. Thankfully, Martin's earlier erection had subsided enough that he wouldn't put her on alert, but he didn't have much time to think of what to say before she would launch herself into his arms. What would he tell Farber? What would Farber tell Lilly? In an instant, this scenario was going to happen; so, whatever his decision, he'd have to figure out how to deal with the fallout later.

"Hey!" said Trisha brightly, as she pointed and made great haste toward the men, "I've been looking for you!"

For his part, Farber could only point a questioning finger at himself, as if to say, "*Me*? Are you sure?"
Martin stood up straight, with a welcoming smile on his face, and wondered if putting his arms out for her might be too forward. With just two steps to go until he was reunited with the soulmate he'd chased throughout time and back, both he and Farber were immediately surprised by a quick kiss on Trisha's cheek from someone coming behind them, saying, "Girl, you looked *way* too sexy out there!"

Friday – 10:15 pm

"Who are your friends?" Trisha asked Jane, who'd slipped behind Farber and Martin while on a short break. In her hands were two frosty beers that she'd decided to comp the men.

"Here you go, boys, this round's on me," Jane exclaimed, with the gusto of a woman who was going to get to dance for the next fifteen minutes. "These boys are…" and then stopped. Jane had only met Martin a few minutes ago and had never even gotten Farber's name. Both men looked vaguely familiar to Trisha, but she'd had well over a thousand tourists come and go over the previous two days, and she couldn't place this tiny percentage of them.

"Well, boys, as often happens, I don't have the slightest idea what your names are. This one," she said, throwing her thumb out at Farber, "has had about every meal here for the last couple days, but damned if I ever got his name." Jane smiled to let Farber know he should probably answer - but shouldn't expect her to remember his name five minutes from now.

"It's Carl," he said over the band, which was just firing up another song. "And this is Martin. We actually just met tonight, for the first time, on the Lincoln After Dark tour." Martin was confused about whom he was being introduced to; Farber had been talking to Jane, but Trisha stood right there, taking it all in. In the end, Martin just offered a sheepish wave of his hand somewhere between both women.

Before the silence between them could grow uncomfortable, Jane piped in. "So, are we gonna dance or what? I've got fifteen freaking minutes!" With that, she hurdled the rail behind the men, grabbed Trisha's hand, and the two women scurried out onto the dance floor as a solid two-step beat took hold of the crowd. If Martin and Carl were being invited to join in, it wasn't clear to either of them. Their best course of action seemed to be to just stand there and smile in the women's direction whenever their eyes met.

"Wow," said Martin simply, "that Jane is a firecracker! You got a thing for her?"

Farber quickly turned his head away as if to show the absurdity of Martin's comment. "Noooo, come on. She could be my daughter. She's just being friendly to me is all. It's nice to have someone so pretty pay attention to you, you know?" Martin did indeed know how it was to have a great beauty pay him attention - and a whole lot more.

As he absorbed Farber's answer, Teebs gazed again at Trisha. She moved in a way that was so much more than sensual, it was almost animalistic. So natural was her vibe that Martin could do nothing but stand and stare, his mouth agape. Trisha looked over at him and just laughed, as she leaned in to Jane to say something that was clearly about him. He saw the two young women giggle, high five, and point in his direction.

"Great," Martin muttered out loud, but to himself, in disgust. "Now they're laughing at me. This was a huge mistake."

"What? What did you say, Martin?" asked Farber, who'd been lost in a trance of his own watching Jane dance.

Martin just shook his head and replied, "Nothing. Nothing. I think I need to get going, Carl. Thanks for the invite and take care…."

Martin took a last swill of his beer, put the glass down, and began to walk off the deck without looking back, furious at himself for even getting his hopes up. He reached the bottom of the stairs before he heard a voice behind him calling, "Hey! Where are you going?"

Turning around, he saw Trisha's bright smile as she reached to grab his arm. "We haven't even danced yet, you know," she purred, clearly at least a little drunk.

Although Martin was flattered, and his heart jumped a number of beats per minute, he

knew this was a dead-end road; and he didn't want to prolong his agony any longer. "I need to get back to the Patron House. It's been a long day."
Trisha frowned at the news, but whether it was real or play acting, Martin couldn't tell. Like a petulant child, she wouldn't let go of his wrist, even stomping her foot a time or two. "Come on back, Martin. One dance, okay?" she demanded, while gazing at his wedding ring. "I'm sure your wife won't mind one dance?"

Now Martin knew without question: *This wasn't Rosita, it was Trisha.* Rosita had been fiercely loyal to her man and expected the same in return. In The Dream, Martin had slipped during his first meeting with the Belle of Lincoln County by mentioning his wife. That mistake had cost him a hard slap in the face - which he could almost feel all over again - as well as days of groveling to win his way back into her heart. Rosita wouldn't take well the news of Martin being married; to Trisha, however, it was merely a challenge to see if she could get a married man to dance with her. Suddenly, rather than standing there trying to bridge a hundred forty years of time to be together again with Rosita, Martin was just standing with a pretty young woman who wouldn't even remember she met him when she woke up the next day. The magic, if it had ever existed, was gone.

"I'm sorry, but I really need to get going," he said, as he extricated his arm and grinned in her direction. "Have a great night, Trisha." And with that, Martin turned and walked away.

"You mean *Rosita*."

The hair on the back of Martin's neck stood up on end at the mention of that name. He slowly turned around, half expecting Lincoln to have been reset to its 1878 glory. "What did you say?" he asked very slowly of the now-not-smiling woman.

"You said, 'Goodnight, *Trisha*,' but what you really wanted to say was 'Goodnight, *Rosita*.' Am I right?"

Martin was unsure what to say. If he answered yes, would Trisha magically transform into Rosita? If he denied it, would she know anyway? The back and forth of this whole ordeal had him barely hanging onto the edge of his sanity. He finally decided he'd answer with exactly what he was feeling and thinking: "If you were Rosita, I wouldn't want to say goodnight at all. I'd never want to leave you…I mean, her."

Trisha's face softened at Martin's words. Just in the last moments, she'd remembered why this man looked so familiar. He was the one who'd held up the ticket line, insisting that her name was Rosita - or at least that she was the spitting image of her. She was intrigued enough to find out more about this mystery woman to chase down a middle-aged man and entice him with a dance so she might learn. Now, the guy - who earlier had stood before her with his pretty wife begging him to move on - had stripped his heart bare over the name of another woman that he clearly loved, probably more so than his own wife. Trisha just *had* to learn more.

"Martin, please? Come back, let's talk. I'd like to know more about this woman I look so much like. Please?"

The softness of her voice disarmed Martin. He checked his watch for no reason, since Lilly wasn't expecting him at any certain time. After glancing nervously to the left and right, he sighed deeply and nodded his head. "Okay. Just for a bit, though."

Trisha grabbed his hand and led him back up on the deck, as Farber and Jane stepped out for a dance. While Farber wouldn't be winning any dance contests, he looked a lot better than Teebs had figured he would. Now, if Martin could just get this conversation behind him, he might be able to exorcise the ghost of Rosita Luna from his mind once…and for all.

Friday - 10:25 pm

Brandon packed up the last few tour items into his truck and waited while Kevin locked up the balcony doors on the courthouse and shuffled quickly down the steps. "You want to go get a beer?" he asked the Billy the Kid look alike. "You earned it with that performance!"

Kevin blushed a little as he tossed his backpack over his shoulder. "Sure do. Might just get lucky and have more than a beer tonight!" Brandon just laughed, and the men had started walking toward the Brewery when Kevin suddenly stopped. "Oh, shoot, wait. I forgot something upstairs." Brandon wagged his head from side to side impatiently while the young man ran back up the stairs. The sound of keys jingling was heard, along with the squeak of the dry hinges. Boots stomped quickly and heavily on the floor. Kevin made his way toward the back of the courtroom and shined his iPhone flashlight at the judge's desk. He reached for a book that looked like it had been around for a hundred years. The pages were ragged, the cover was torn, and the binding was doing its best in a losing effort to keep the pages in numerical order.

The well-worn book he slipped into his backpack was a first edition of Sergio Bachaca's *The True Life of Billy the Kid*, which looked like it itself had somehow lived through the great battles of the Lincoln County War.

Friday – 10:30 pm

"So, tell me about her. Rosita, I mean," Trisha asked earnestly, as she had pulled Martin to the back patio of the Brewery. With all of the action inside and out front, this was the quietest spot they were going to find on this night.

Martin didn't really know what to say. As far as he could tell, there was no real Rosita Luna, only a version that had been born from his oxygen-deprived brain. To lie and make up some ridiculous story about his soulmate didn't feel right, but neither did telling Trisha the truth. She'd probably get a great laugh from a middle-aged loser in love with a woman who never even existed.

"Well, this is hard to explain," he began. "I mean, I almost died the other night…choking…"

"Oh my God, Martin! Are you okay?" Trisha interrupted, with what seemed to be genuine concern.

"Oh yeah, yeah. Fine," he replied. "It's just that I guess I had one of those, what do you call it, near-death experiences?"

Trisha looked strangely at Martin, wondering how this Rosita woman played into all of that. Furthermore, the young woman wasn't completely sure about NDEs or the afterlife, despite having grown up in a relatively strict Catholic household. She wondered if their conversation might be about to go off the deep end, enough so that she considered just standing up and walking back to the dance floor; but something about the honesty in Martin's eyes wouldn't allow it.

"What was it like? Was it a white light or something?" she asked, as she softened her eyes to let Martin know she wasn't mocking him.

Martin sighed a little before answering, now determined to tell this woman the truth so that he might be released from his misery. "It wasn't like that. People say that your life flashes before your eyes, right? Well, a life flashed before my eyes - but it wasn't *my* life, at least not that I remember." Trisha seemed captivated by Martin's admission and looked quizzically into his eyes to see if there was any hint that he might be lying to her. Martin took the pause to mean he should continue. "And in that…thing…whatever it was, was Rosita Luna, from right here in Lincoln.

"And you love her, Martin," she stated directly, "I can see it all over your face."

In that moment, Martin felt like crying, so completely did he release all of his emotions over The Dream. With tears starting to stain the corners of his eyes and his nose running, he stammered out, "I…I think I do, but I can never reach her." Allowing his tears to fall freely, Martin put his head in his hands and laid them down on the table in front of him.

Trisha felt horrible for bringing Martin this far into the depths of his emotions. She thought they'd have a conversation about an old high-school flame or some such thing, but this was...real. Wanting to provide some comfort to the man, she reached her hand across the small table and touched his shoulder, which generated an electric shock to run down Martin's spine but seemed only to cause Trisha to recoil as if she'd hurt him. "I'm sorry! I didn't mean to startle you, Martin. I'm sorry."

Martin raised his head with his red, puffy eyes, once again studying the spitting image of the woman he was prepared to love for all eternity. Trisha returned Martin's look with compassion and a soft smile. "So I look like her, huh? I guess that could freak anybody out."

Martin swallowed hard before answering. "You don't just *look* like her, Trisha. You're her *twin*. I remember enough...a lot, really, from that…Dream, that I know every curve of her face and every expression on it. When I saw you, I just…." He stopped, unable or unwilling to go on.

"So, why can't you reach her? You said that a minute ago," Trisha asked softly.

Martin inhaled deeply and let his head fall back onto his shoulders, wondering if he should continue. He assumed that this woman already believed he was deranged, but telling her that his great love existed over a hundred years ago would probably be the last straw before she called for reinforcements. Still, he'd come this far, and she hadn't run yet; and just maybe, if he told her everything - all the things he couldn't say even to Lilly - the visions might just let him go from their grasp.

"You're going to think I'm nuts, Trisha, if I tell you why."

Trisha's face relaxed into the welcoming smile that Martin knew so well from Rosita. In that look, he felt alive, safe, and warm. When she opened her mouth to speak, she said simply, "Oh, Martin, I already think you're nuts. How much worse could it get?"

It was the perfect landing for Martin, and he laughed enough for his shoulders to jump a couple of times. "Fine," he replied, "then here it is. Anytime you want to make a run for it, go on. I wouldn't blame you."

Trisha slipped her heels off and held them up so Martin could see. "Okay, I'm ready. Just in case." She and her new friend dissolved into laughter, and Martin Teebs began to tell the long, sad tale of how he won and lost the Belle of Lincoln.

Friday – 10:40 pm

Arriving at the Brewery, Brandon and Kevin settled in on the last two chairs they could find on the deck. The band's music roared across the tiny town, and the voices of the party goers intermingled with the clink of glasses being served and then being picked up to be pressed into service again.

"What's your plan for tomorrow night?" asked Brandon, as the men sat there in the warm, summer breeze.

Kevin glanced in the air and rolled his eyes back a bit to collect his thoughts. "Well, I'm gonna go to that book-talk thing. That Sergio guy? I'm supposed to work it, anyway, so I don't have to pay to get in."

"Cool, cool. Serge is a great guy. Knows tons about Lincoln and the Kid. I'd go, but my girl wants to get out of town for the night." Kevin just nodded in response as the music swelled a bit. Brandon peered out on the dance floor. "Hey, look! It's that guy from the tour. Carl…."

Kevin snapped his head to the left, and there indeed was the man from New Jersey who had spent five minutes telling him about the book he was working on about L.G. Murphy. "Damn!" said Kevin, "and he's got a pretty girl to dance with, too. What the hell am I doing wrong?"

Brandon couldn't resist. "Lots, but that's another story," he said, as he grinned back at his new buddy.

From behind the building, two figures approached; when they got closer, both men were able to identify them as Martin Teebs and Trisha. Kevin cast a quick, curious glance at Brandon, as if to ask why the duo had been alone, behind the Brewery; but before any discussion could be had, Martin and Trisha had joined them.

"Hey, guys," greeted Martin, "you finally made it!" Trisha patted Kevin on the shoulder and sat on the arm of his chair.

"Yeah, sure did. Having a good time?" asked Brandon, only semi-ironically.

Trisha took control of the conversation, understanding where it might be going. "Martin tells me I look like some woman he used to know a while ago. I wanted to hear more about her, so we found a quiet spot to talk."

"Okay, okay," said Brandon, putting his hands up to show he was only joking. "Glad you two are getting along."

Trisha smiled at Martin and said, "Famously. Now come and dance with me, Brandon, I love this song." Trisha rose, grabbed the tour guide by the sleeve, and whisked him away to the dance floor, alongside Farber and Jane.

Martin slipped heavily into the seat that Brandon had just vacated.

"How'd you like the tour, Mr. Teebs?" asked Kevin.
Having just unburdened himself to Trisha, Martin felt better than he had in days; so he pasted on a smile and said, "It's Martin, okay? Just call me Martin. I'm not even sure my father is Mr. Teebs."

With a laugh, Kevin replied, "Okay, Martin, what did you think?"

Martin pondered his thoughts. He'd been in such a lousy mood for most of the tour that he had failed to really appreciate how much Brandon knew. However, he assumed a little white lie couldn't hurt all that badly. "It was great. I learned a ton of details about the Kid that I never knew. I wish we had time to take it again."

"Yeah, cool. Sorry about that shotgun thing. That was his idea," Kevin said, pointing to the dance floor, where Brandon was moving around awkwardly as Jane and Trisha danced closely together.

Martin grinned and laughed, remembering how scared everyone (including himself) had been.

"Damn, when that thing went off, it was like…BOOM!" said Kevin, as he flung his arms to the sides to emphasize his point. In doing so, he knocked loose his backpack that had been hanging over the back of his chair, scattering its contents on the deck. "See?" he said. "Just like that."

Both men laughed, and Martin stood up to help the boy gather his things. Immediately, he froze in his tracks with fear - or was it anger? Looking down in front of his feet, he saw a terribly weathered version of Sergio Bachaca's book, with the cover almost completely faded and the dog-eared pages nearly falling out of the binding. The last time Martin had seen this book was on the porch of Billy Bonney's house in Magdalena as he cradled the dying outlaw - or at least he did in his mind.

"Where did you get that!" Martin demanded, pointing at the book.

"What? The book?" asked Kevin, clearly confused about what had agitated the older man so quickly.

Martin's voice got low and threatening. "I said, where did you get that damn book?" Kevin looked around to see who might help him should the older man completely snap. "Mr. Teebs, I mean, it's just a book from that guy that's coming here tomorr…" "Where did you get it?!" Martin roared over the volume of the band, loudly enough for people to begin looking over to see what the commotion was.

While Kevin didn't want to fight, he also didn't want to be continually dressed down in public like this. Finally, he just told Martin what he wanted to know: "A guy came through a couple weeks back. Lives nearby. Said I looked so much like the Kid, I should learn more about him. Had this old book in his truck, so he gave it to me to read. That's it. What's the problem?"

His suspicions raging at who the mystery "guy" might be, Martin demanded more: "Who's the guy?"

"His name is Steve," protested Kevin. "He lives over in..."

"Capitan," Martin cut in, knowing all he needed to know about the origin of the now-ancient tome.

Friday – 10:45 pm

Martin shuffled slowly to the east on Lincoln's only street, the music receding into the background. All alone, he unspooled his tortured mind. This, all of this, was like some giant game. Someone was playing him. Someone was pulling the strings. How could all of these people, names, and faces all be in the same place at the same time? Somebody must have put this concerted effort together to fuck with him.

But how? And…why?

Who in the hell is Martin Teebs, he thought to himself, to be worthy of such a far-reaching charade? If some vast, Old West conspiracy theory were in play, why on earth would someone pick *Martin* as its focus, not someone more famous or with more money? Maybe his entire life, ever since he was born, had been a Truman Show-esque play that people watched on TV? Perhaps this was just an episode that some junior writer threw out there to try to make a name for himself? Martin really couldn't see how what he currently was existing in was any sort of reality. Steve from Capitan?

"You've got to be kidding me!" Martin announced to the desolate street. "That guy is the puppet master here?" Of course, the rub for Martin was that he'd never even met Steve, at least not in real life. He'd probably seen the man from Capitan as one of the talking heads on some historical documentary, but was that enough to plant the seed for Martin's brain to concoct an entire story around Steve? Hardly, thought Martin, but he at least had to entertain all possibilities.

Martin's next and darker thought was that he somehow hadn't survived the choking incident, and he was, in fact, *dead.* Of course, if that were the case, then why didn't his first "death" rule over this one? How many times could you die in your near-death experience? Martin wondered if, at this very moment, he was actually choking on green-chile enchiladas, with Lilly frantically pounding his chest, trying to save him. It certainly seemed like an incredible waste of time for God, or whoever ran the show, to make him go through this exercise a second time, just to finally kill him off. Maybe death was kind of like your driver's ed test? Maybe you get to keep doing it until you get it right? Martin laughed at the thought of himself living fifty lifetimes between past and present, and every time waking up to Lilly hammering him on the chest as he regurgitated spicy New Mexican food. Perhaps by the fiftieth time, he'd figure out the one small thing he was doing wrong, and he could finally just leave the world behind!

With the Patron House in sight, Martin resolved that, dead or alive, he was going to get some answers on this trip. The next day would give him a good opportunity as he might be able to steal a few precious seconds with Sergio Bachaca to ask him about the possibility of a Rosita Luna in Lincoln during the War. Maybe Bachaca's research did point to a minor character who hadn't played enough of a role (or any role at all) to merit mention in his book? Either way, Martin was determined to get to the bottom of this mystery. Martin could just imagine Kevin and Trisha laughing over a beer at this very moment, slapping their knees about how they had this middle-aged fool in a twist over some long-lost girlfriend who never even existed.

Wearily, Teebs climbed the steps to the *casita*, entering to find Lilly asleep on the couch, an open magazine draped over her chest and a rapidly cooling cup of tea on the table next to her. He gently folded the magazine, placing it on the coffee table, and touched her shoulder. “Lil. Wake up. Let’s go up to bed.”

Lilly’s sleepy eyes slowly opened as she tried to blink away the fog. “Hey, hon. How was it? Did you have fun?”

Martin snorted to himself. Fun? No. Rather than go into all of the reasons that he didn’t, however, he simply decided to whitewash the truth. “It was fine. Lots of young people. Not my scene, you know? I’m happy to be here with you.”

Lilly smiled and rose slightly to give Martin a kiss. Rising from the couch, the couple turned out the lights and had begun the march up the stairs to the loft when Lilly remembered something: “Oh, how about Carl? Do you think you’ll see him again?”

Martin stopped halfway up the stairs and allowed Lilly to go on. Would he see Farber again?

“You know, Lil,” Martin finally answered, in a more sinister voice than he’d planned, “I’m pretty sure that I’ll see him at least one more time.”

SATURDAY 7 AM

“Ugghh,” groaned Jane, as she rolled over in bed to avoid the rising sun, “I’m hung the hell over.” Too drunk to drive home to Ruidoso after work, she had walked noisily down the street with Trisha to her place to crash until sunup. Now that sunup had actually occurred, it didn’t seem like such a great idea to Jane’s pounding head. Finally staggering out of the bedroom, she heard the shower running and knew that her friend was probably getting ready for work.

“How are you up already?” Jane moaned, sticking her head into the steamy bathroom. “You drank as much as I did.”

A laugh emitted from the shower area as Trisha responded, “*No one* drank as much as you did!”
Jane stood at the bathroom door, doing some mental gymnastics. She and Trisha had arrived home at some point before it got light out, and the sun now had probably been up for almost an hour, so she could safely say that she’d gotten at least ninety minutes of sleep. That might be enough for her to be able to walk to get her car, drive to her own home, and then pass out, just in time to have to wake up, shower, and go to work herself. As the warm steam entered her nostrils, she heard the shower shut off; and the curtain slid back, revealing the very naked Trisha.

“Damn, girl,” Jane exclaimed, looking at her friend. “Stop hogging all the perfect and save some for the rest of us.”

Trisha laughed. “Stop! It’s just a body.” That was the same phrase she’d repeated most of her college days, when boys would pledge their willingness to kill or die to sleep with her, so perfect was her body. “Besides,” she added, “have you looked in a mirror lately? You’re pretty kickin’ yourself. You had that Carl guy following you around like a lost puppy.”

“Haha! I love older guys. They’ll do anything for you and are usually too afraid to ask for anything in return. He was cool, though...fun to talk to, in a history-teacher sort of way.” As the pain in Jane’s head started to subside, she rummaged around for her clothes, which seemed to have been dropped in a trail leading from the landing of the stairs all the way to the bedroom. “What in the hell was I doing without my clothes?”

she exclaimed. "Did you take advantage of me?!"
Trisha laughed heartily as she wrapped a towel around herself and stepped into the hallway. "You know it, baby!" she joked. "Actually, you just kept saying how hot it was, and you started pulling clothes off back in town. But luckily, you held out most of them til we got home. You were so drunk, you didn't even know what you were doing."

Jane just snorted and shook her head at her own behavior. It had been some time since she'd tied one on like that, and she didn't plan on doing it again for the foreseeable future. "What was with you and that big guy, Martin? He's married, you know."

Trisha frowned at her friend to let her know she wouldn't do anything with a married man. "I know that, silly. He's just a guy who mistook me, or something like that, for someone else. He was really hurting about something, so I just listened to him talk. That's all."

"Yeah, 'mistook' you," responded Jane, using air quotes to emphasize her point.

Upset that her motives with a married man were being questioned, Trisha fired back. "Yes. *Mistook*. Seriously. I'm not into older guys, and if I were, I wouldn't be into *that* older guy. Sometimes you just need someone to listen to you. That's all he wanted. Okay?"

"Okay, okay. Sorry, sister. Didn't mean to get your panties in a bunch." Then, after a pause, Jane added, "But he did!!" Trisha just shook her head and walked back into the bathroom to get ready for another long day of tours and tourists at the old courthouse. Struggling to get her boots on, Jane finally felt that she looked presentable enough to walk back to the Brewery to get her car. "Hey, girl, thanks for putting me up. I'll see you later tonight, maybe?"

Trisha weaved her thick, black hair into a long braid while she thought through her schedule. "Umm, maybe. I'm working that book-talk thing tonight at the Visitor Center. Depends on how tired I am after that."

Jane clomped across the floor, back to the threshold of the bathroom door. Sticking her head in, she teased, "And what if your friend Martin is there? He must be a Billy-head like the rest of them. You gonna ask him to introduce you to his wife?"

His wife, Trisha thought, that was the least of what Martin had told her about last night. In his Dream, or whatever it was, he'd had an entire life with this great beauty Rosita. He'd been back and forth in time so many times that it became routine. He was ready to give up on his entire existence in the present to travel and stay, back in time, with her forever. That kind of love, thought Trisha, was what she wanted someday. A man who would march through the gates of hell to be with her, and never leave. Just hearing about it made her jealous of this Rosita. Even if she hadn't ever existed, she *should* have, so she could have been the recipient of that kind of pure, loving commitment.

On two occasions, the older man had stopped himself short of telling her what had eventually happened to Rosita; but when the name 'Carl Farber' came up, Martin's face clouded over with something akin to a murderous rage. Whatever happened in his Dream, or his NDE, Farber hadn't been the buddy to Martin that he had appeared to be last night.

Once Martin had finally finished telling her all that he was comfortable with, he had seemed relieved, drained almost. It was as if the secret that he had been holding had been choking him and that just by telling it to someone, he could finally breathe again. Trisha was glad she was some help to the man, but now she also felt some sort of sad connection to his story. That she looked like what seemed to be a tragic beauty in Martin's world didn't make her feel good. She almost wished she hadn't asked about Rosita, but it was far too late. It seemed that Martin had transferred a portion of the story, and some of his pain and confusion had gone along with it.

Trisha couldn't forget Martin's eyes when he had mentioned Carl Farber. It was disconcerting enough that she couldn't let it go. She cautioned her friend: "Stop, okay, Jane? He's a nice guy. But, hey, do me a favor…just be careful around that Carl guy."

Jane smiled in confusion, believing Farber was as harmless as a puppy dog. "What? Why? Do you know something?"

Trisha sighed deeply before replying. "No, but I just have a feeling. Just - be careful."

"Okay, girl," agreed Jane as she kissed her friend on the cheek. "Have a great day, sunshine. See ya!" And like that, she was gone.

The dark feeling that had enveloped Trisha would not abate. She put on a small amount of makeup - enough to make herself look awake - and got dressed. Sitting in the kitchen a few minutes later, munching on breakfast, she wondered what it was that Martin wouldn't tell her. She was part of the story now, he'd made sure of that by confiding in her. She just couldn't leave it alone. Trisha vowed that, by the end of this day, she'd find Martin Teebs and make him come clean on just what kind of tragic events were tied to Carl Farber and to the Belle of Lincoln, Rosita Luna.

Saturday - 7:45 am

Carl Farber's tired and desert-dry eyes cracked open far sooner than he had hoped they would. After a rip-roaring time the evening prior, he'd limped back to his Capitan motel sometime around 3 am. Farber was prepared to say he hadn't had that good a time in a long while…until he realized he'd *never* had that much fun on an evening out in his *entire* life. Not only did the bartender Jane dance with him whenever she could sneak away for a few minutes, but he also felt like one of the guys for the first time since, probably, grade school. Tour guide Brandon and Kevin, that kid from the Monuments Division, eagerly included him in their guy-talk while they drank beer after beer. Farber had hoped that Trisha, the pretty girl from the courthouse, would be a little more friendly; but according to Jane, her friend had gotten into some sort of argument with his new buddy Martin, who'd wound up storming off early for some reason. Carl didn't have any way to contact Martin, so he hoped he'd run into him in Lincoln today - if the man and his wife were even still there.

Then Farber's thoughts settled back on Jane. If you'd asked him at 9 pm last night whether that sexy twenty-something bartender had any interest in him - other than getting a bigger tip - he'd have had to say no. After the night they'd all had, however, he wasn't so sure. Jane had bought him at least a couple of the too-many beers he'd been drinking, and she seemed to make a beeline for him every time she had a few spare minutes. They'd danced to a handful of songs, and every time he made eye contact with her, she seemed to be greatly enjoying herself. Not wanting to pull the wool over his own eyes, though, Carl did consider that he was just 'safe' and that, by hanging out with him and the guys, she'd be protected from the advances of other 'I'd-kill-or-die-to-sleep-with-you' tourists in attendance at the party last night. Still, Jane could have latched onto any number of middle-aged, Old West buffs, most with fatter wallets than he had. He resolved not to question too much, lest he pop the bubble he'd built in his mind about her possible interest in him.

Farber was forced to speculate: Would he kill or die to sleep with Jane? Killing seemed pretty extreme for a mild-mannered, high-school history teacher, but dying? There were days when Carl wondered what was the point of his existence. He had no family left, having been an only child. He'd never been married, although he had been on the verge of getting engaged in college, after dating a girl named Theresa for only a month. He'd never before had a woman pay that much attention to him, so he resolved to put a ring on it as soon as he could. Saving what he could scrape up from his job bussing tables, he'd bought a tiny gold ring. One fateful night, Carl got down on one knee; however, before that knee even hit the floor, he knew it wasn't going to end well. Theresa's goal during that night's meeting was to let Farber know she was breaking up with him in order to sleep with one of the football players, who had a much bigger dick than Carl. Before the rejected man could even push out enough words to make his pitch for marriage, Theresa was shaking her head sadly and walking out of the room.

The only thing that Farber could identify as the point of his seemingly pointless existence was teaching. Through him, kids would learn the past; and because of that, they would not be condemned to repeat it, as the famous saying went. Such thoughts were heavy for a Saturday morning during the first proper vacation he'd had in years. These were happy times - or at least they were supposed to be - so Farber pushed those bleak musings from his mind, groaning and creaking his way out of bed, with a few good pops thrown in for good measure.

Tonight, Carl remembered, he was going to meet writer Serge Bachaca. Farber had always loved meeting authors and historians, people who took an interest in the past more seriously than your average man on the street. Maybe, just maybe, he could interest Bachaca enough in his own book to get an introduction to the man's publisher? Farber could picture it now: jet-setting to all sorts of luxurious book conferences around the globe, waxing poetic on Murphy, Dolan, and Sheriff Brady. Carl glanced around his sparse motel room and imagined that he'd never again be forced to stay in a place like this. He'd probably score a Hampton Inn, with their free breakfast and ever-flowing, 24 hours of coffee. "That's living," he said to the motel room walls, "all the coffee I can drink and limitless powdered eggs." In the meantime, though, Farber would need to make due with what he had, so he switched on the ancient coffee maker and made his way toward the bathroom.

"And Jane," Carl said to himself, hoping he might spend a few more minutes in her presence - and maybe a lot more than that.

Had Farber known that Jane's car was speeding past his motel at that very minute in a desperate attempt to make it home for some much-needed sleep before her next shift started, he would probably have shoved himself back into his boxers and chased her down U.S. Route 380, just as fast as his spindly legs could carry him.

Saturday – 8 am

Martin and Lilly sat contentedly on the porch of their little *casita*, munching on granola, fruit, and some of the best banana bread that Martin had ever tasted. A full night of sleep had done wonders to improve Martin's mood, and, for the moment, he was in a good place.

"Who else was there last night? Did Brandon ever show up?" asked Lilly innocently. Martin measured just how innocent Lilly's question really was. Was he being coaxed into talking about Trisha so that Lilly could go off on him, or was it really just her curiosity. He figured that with the current good feelings between them, he might as well tell the truth. "He and that kid Kevin did come by later on. Farber was dancing up a storm with that barmaid…uh, Jane."

Lilly's face broke out into a smile at the thought of that history teacher dancing with a probably-twenty-years-younger woman. She imagined him thrusting out his limbs at odd angles, mostly off-time with the music. "Really?" she said. "Is he, like...any good?" She couldn't help laughing at the thought.

Martin was unable to stifle a smile of his own as he replied, "You know, for an old guy just like me, he wasn't half bad. I was surprised."

The sounds of the town coming to life filtered through the trees to reach their ears, while Martin plucked another slice of banana bread from the loaf. "And that girl from the museum was there. The one that looked like...uh, Rosita." As soon as Martin said the words, he regretted it. Lilly hadn't asked him about anyone else and probably wouldn't have. All he did was needlessly introduce another complicating factor into an equation that had no business being there.

"Oh yeah, that pretty one," Lilly began. "Were you dancing with her?"

"No!" responded Martin, instinctively and truthfully. "Not at all. She was asking who this 'Rosita' was, and I told her about my - I don't know - dream?"
"I don't know, Martin," said Lilly, looking out the side of her eyes. "She's an awfully pretty girl. Maybe you have a thing for her?"

Martin stopped himself from responding right away, knowing that this conversation demanded the *right* answer, not just the quick one. After considering his options for a moment, he looked directly at his wife of twenty years. "Lil, I have a thing for *you*. Some pretty girl who could be my daughter isn't going to change that. Besides, *you* were the one who told me to go out last night, remember?" He had learned the art of transference well: Now that the burden of Martin even having been in the same vicinity as Trisha was placed in Lilly's lap, he could just sit back and wait for her to volley it back to him.

For her part, Lilly just smirked and replied, "Right. I know. I'm glad you had some fun! Now, what's on tap for today?"

Bullet dodged, Martin leaned into his chair and tossed back a mini-blueberry muffin. He wasn't sure how the day would start, but he knew that it would end sitting in the presence of the greatest Billy the Kid historian the world had ever known - the one and only Sergio Bachaca.

Saturday – 8:01 am

As the throng of Billy tourists pushed its way into the courthouse, Kevin stepped back gingerly to avoid being trampled. Amid a chorus of 'Keep the change, Bob!' and 'Best dollar and eighty I ever spent!' he tried to stave off the pounding in his head, an aftereffect of the partying he had done last night. While the masses bunched up at the check-in desk, he glanced across at Trisha to see if she was faring as badly as he, but she looked none the worse for the wear from their extended fiesta.

Just then, a matronly woman - who had to be pushing sixty years old - stepped up to him. "Young man, has anyone ever told you that you look just like Billy the Kid?!" With her husband enthusiastically raising both thumbs to add his vote, it was all Kevin could do not to roll his eyes. But these people might have saved their entire lives to be here, he reminded himself; hangover or not, it was his job to show them a good time.

"I've heard it a few times, ma'am," he responded with a warm smile, before leaning in closer to her, "but never from a woman as pretty as you." He finished with a wink, and the woman blushed and batted her eyes at him. Her husband, for his part, didn't seem to be upset and indeed looked as if he wouldn't mind at all his wife banging a doppelganger of Billy the Kid, providing he got to be in the room to take pictures.

As the tidal wave of humanity subsided, Kevin made his way over to the ticket desk. "Some night, huh? Ugghh…my head is killing me." Trisha gave him a big laugh and grin, looking at him with pitying eyes. "It was fun, but you boys dance too little and drink too much."

Kevin looked at her in mock disgust, asking, "You're fine? You're telling me you're not tired or anything?"

"I never said that," offered Trisha. "I could have used another hour or six of sleep, but I'm not hungover. Jane, on the other hand, did the walk of shame out of my place only an hour ago. It'll be interesting to see if she makes it through work today!" She watched the young man rub his head a few more times as a few stray tourists made their way into the courthouse. Determined to find out more about the unbelievable story she'd been told the night before, she finally queried, "What happened between you and Martin…uh, Mr. Teebs, last night? It looked like you guys were arguing?"

Kevin just shook his head at the memory. "I have no idea. That's the truth. I dropped a book out of my backpack, and he freaked out, wanting to know where I got it.

"What was the book?" Trisha inquired, her curiosity piqued.

“Some Billy the Kid book, from that guy who’s gonna be here tonight,” Kevin remembered. “I didn’t even read the thing! That old cowboy Steve who comes by here gave it to me. I just had it so I could maybe get the writer to sign it.”

A book, thought Trisha. Martin had briefly mentioned a book or books several times while talking about his travels. She guessed that the book Kevin had must have reminded Martin of something in his vision and thus had probably set him off. After all, how could a simple book account for everything that he had told her last night? She decided there was no great revelation here, believing that Kevin and his magic book were a dead end.

“Okay, then. Why don’t you go lie down in the back or something, Kevin?” she suggested. “You really don’t look good.”

Feeling green around the gills, the young man gratefully accepted the offer and walked toward the office to put his head down. Just before he left, he turned back to say, “If that Mr. Teebs or Steve comes looking for me, tell them I took the day off! I only signed up to play Billy the Kid in this pageant, not to be pushed around by a couple of old guys wanting to argue about some outlaw who’s been dead a hundred years!” And with that, Kevin quietly closed the door behind him.

The words he left behind hung in the air while the last few tourists climbed the stairs to the second floor. Trisha had taken this job on a whim, knowing nothing about Billy the Kid or the mania that surrounded him. Why would a grown man get so worked up about Billy as to lose his handle on reality? After all, this Kid and Rosita - if she had ever existed - had both been dead and buried for over a century. Was it possible that Martin Teebs was insane? Trisha didn’t think so, but her college psych classes told her that perhaps he was. Many people with mental or delusionary illnesses can seem totally normal until they come across their trigger. Maybe Martin was like that? Maybe he lived a completely normal life with his wife, and only when it came to Billy and Rosita did he lose his grip? Still, he seemed totally normal. He had prefaced every single thing he told Trisha with a disclaimer that he had no idea where the memories came from or how they were so crystal clear to him. If he was nuts, he was the most sane insane person that anyone could ever meet.

Trisha had heard Martin mention that he was staying at the Patron House, and she had half a mind to walk down there on her lunch break to ask him all of the questions swirling in her head. Then she thought of his wife and decided that perhaps her plan was too aggressive. If she were married, she wouldn't want some young woman coming around for her husband to question him about an old love of his. As much as she wanted to learn all she could about the mysterious Rosita, she knew that trying to learn it from Martin wasn't in the cards, at least not today. She'd have to come up with something else. What that 'something else' might be was eluding her at the moment as yet another surge of happy tourists came barging into the courthouse, ready for one more full day of imbibing the long shadow of William H. Bonney.

Saturday – 5 pm

By closing time on Saturday, the town of Lincoln had seen its highest single-day visitor count in the history of Old Lincoln Days. Exhausted vendors and Monuments employees wearily locked up, packed up, and got themselves in front of either a cold drink or a cold air conditioner. Jane had spent the better part of the afternoon nursing her own hangover, while contributing to the numerous future ones that she was spawning among those who beat the afternoon heat in the Brewery.

By 5 pm, Carl Farber had glided into town and found a parking space for his rental ride. There never really was any doubt that he'd stop by the Brewery to see Jane, even as he spent the day driving to some other Billy-related sites, just to avoid the crushing masses in Lincoln. He picked his way up the steps and past the remnants of last night's stage, entering the super-chilled air as he breached the front door.

"Howdy," came the greeting from a pretty blonde bartender before he could even get a seat at the bar. "What'll you have?"

Carl didn't want to offend the young lady, but he did have designs on Jane tapping his beer and maybe laying one of those platonic cheek kisses on him. He saw her at the other end of the bar, talking animatedly with a good-looking man, and the history teacher felt a tinge of jealousy shoot through him. With the young blonde still staring at him, he figured if Jane could 'cheat' on him, then there was nothing wrong with having another woman pour his drink. "I'll have a Tunstall Pale Englishman Ale," he requested, and the girl bounced off to get it while he settled into his seat.

Although he attempted to look cool sitting there, glancing around the place so as not to be staring at Jane, he couldn't help but continually check back to see if she might be approaching. Last night had been the best time he'd probably ever had. Even hanging out with his tour guide and the other kid from the courthouse had made Carl feel like he belonged, which was a feeling sorely lacking in his life. He was pretty certain that nothing was going to happen between him and Jane, owing to the fact that he was easily twenty years older than she was, and she was beautiful, and she could have her pick of guys; but having a friend like that made him walk taller and feel better about himself. If that's the only thing he got from this trip, it would be more than enough. Staring blankly at a baseball game on the screen across from the bar, he was nudged back to reality by Jane herself, standing there with a grin and holding his beer.

"What's this? Having Ashley get you a beer? Are you cheating on me, Carl?" she asked with a laugh and a smile.

Farber was caught so off guard that he fumbled his answer. "Uh, no…she just, when I came in, you know…you were…." He finally stopped when he realized he wasn't making a point, he was just making himself look foolish.

"Dude, I'm messing with you!" she said through a sly grin and offered him her knuckles to tap. "Come on, give it up, dance partner." Carl slowly made a fist and touched knuckles with her, wondering what had happened to the kiss he'd spent all day dreaming about? Too shy to ask - and definitely not forward enough to offer one on his own - he had to be satisfied with the brief connection.

"So,what are you up to today, Mr. Farber?" asked Jane in mock formality.

"Uh, you know. I drove around to some Billy the Kid sites. Did a little sightseeing. Now I'm here, talking to you, and then later, I'm going to that book signing and talk."

Jane nodded her head and batted her eyes at the much older man, "Well, la di da, look at you, all busy and shit. I'm just glad that our little Brewery fit into your plans." Farber could only laugh at the knowledge that he'd basically been killing time all day, just so that he wouldn't arrive at Jane's too early and seem too eager. "You coming back over here after the book thing is over?" she continued.

Now Carl was pleased. Even if it was a total put on, he didn't see Jane asking anyone else if he was coming back to see her tonight. He decided to take a little risk with his response. "Well, yeah, I mean…if you want me to?"

The silence in the moment after he asked the question was tortuous, but Jane didn't let it hang too long before responding. "Of course I do! Who's my favorite customer and dance partner, huh?" Although Farber might have been happier being labeled a boyfriend, love interest, lover, or some such thing, 'dance partner' seemed like the best he was going to get on this day. Before he could formulate any decent response, however, Jane added, "Bring your friend Martin, too, if you see him. He kinda stormed off last night. You guys are still friends, aren't you?"

"Uh, yeah. Why wouldn't we be?" inquired Farber, as if he lacked some vital piece of information.

"Oh, I don't know. I crashed with Trisha last night, and Martin said something to her about you guys not getting along? I don't know…it's probably nothing." Jane shook her head and grinned at a patron at the other end of the bar, banging his empty glass. "Hey, gotta go. Enjoy the…thing. See ya later, gator!" said Jane, and she was off again.

Carl sat there, wondering what Martin could have told Trisha about him. They barely knew each other and had only met for an hour before heading to the Brewery last night. If this guy was spreading rumors about him, he wanted to know why? Farber checked his watch: 5:15 pm. The book talk started at 7, so he had another hour and change before he needed to walk to the Visitor Center to get his seat. He decided that he'd go down the street a bit early. Maybe he'd see Martin in line and find out just what issue the guy had with a harmless school teacher he'd never known at all before last night.

Saturday – 5:45 pm

If there was a heaven, and it was full of water, then God must have opened the floodgates on Lincoln County this night. A hellacious thunderstorm raced across the mountains and deluged tiny Lincoln to the point that the lone street ran in shin-deep water at the same speed and rhythm as the nearby Rio Bonito. For those unlucky enough to be caught outside, a thorough soaking took only seconds. For those waiting to traipse over to the Visitor Center for Sergio Bachaca's meet-and-greet, even the stoutest of umbrellas wouldn't be of help. However, that was all to the good, since, at this moment, Bachaca himself was trapped behind a torrent of water flowing across Route 380, just to the east of Carrizozo. Until the storm let up, no one was going anywhere; and at present, the entire event was in question.

Lilly peeked at the torrent out of their *casita*'s window and exclaimed, "I've never seen rain like this! This is insane, Martin." For his part, Martin sat patiently on the sofa, sure that nothing was moving forward in Lincoln until the storm abated. He did have some pointed questions for Bachaca, questions he wanted to ask alone; but he assumed those could come at the conclusion of the author's talk, after most people had moved on for the night. The receiving-line book signing, which was supposed to begin right now, probably wouldn't be the forum for Martin's discussion with the writer. "Do you think they'll cancel the talk, hon? We can't go out in this," said Lilly, more concerned for Martin than herself, due to how much he spoke about this particular author and his book.

"Don't know, Lil," he answered nonchalantly, "I'm not sure how long these things last here."

Lilly plopped down on the couch next to him and talked, just to break the silence. "Tell me about this guy. Why is his book so great?"

Martin mused on his answer for a moment before responding. "Well, it's written in plain English. Very easy to follow. The great thing about Bachaca's book is that it's well researched, and whenever he states his opinion, he lets you know. Some of these other clowns fill an entire book with opinion and hearsay and then sell it as fact."

Lilly was suitably impressed with Martin's answer and added, "So he's the best?"

Happy that his explanation had gotten Lilly quickly to the point she was at, he replied, "If there's someone better, I haven't read that book yet. Bachaca's is as close as you can get to being back there during the War."

The sound of rain pummeling the tin roof slowly began to subside and, over the course of five minutes or so, eventually stopped. Lilly went back to the window to peek out again and was awestruck. "Look at this, Martin. It's gone. There's not a cloud in the sky. What the heck!"

Martin checked his watch: 6:15 pm. He decided if they were going, they should go during this break in the action, just in case the floodgates opened once more. Hopping off the couch with more energy that he usually had available, he said, "Let's go, Lil! Before it rains again." Grabbing an umbrella and their jackets, Martin and Lilly headed out of the door, through the rivers of water washing off the mountain behind them, and onto the street that once again had become inhabited by all sorts of book-talk goers having the exact same idea as the Teebs.

Maybe tonight, thought the big man, just maybe tonight, he'd get some answers from the guy who wrote the book that changed everything - at least in Martin's very strange, very lucid Dream.

Saturday – 6:30 pm

Martin and Lilly stood in a very slowly moving queue, waiting for their turn to get seated. As the theater in the Visitor Center was so tiny, the line snaked out the door, into the lobby, and across the covered porch, where people had taken refuge in case the rains came again. Looking around, Martin began to wonder how many of these people he'd ever know or be friends with if not for their mutual fascination with the Kid. He didn't have an exact number, but he pegged it as being a low one. Lilly seemed excited to be in such company and continued to converse with a very stout woman wearing a Harley-Davidson T-shirt and some pants that must have shrunk mightily in the rain on her way here. Trying to will the line into moving faster, Martin glanced toward the street and spotted Carl Farber, making his way onto the tail end.

Martin was torn on how to feel about Farber. From The Dream, he knew that the man was his mortal enemy and must be vanquished. From his real-life experience of the previous evening, though, he saw Farber as a milquetoast, who probably didn't have the balls to harm a flea, even if he wanted to. He almost felt sorry for the man, who apparently had little to talk about except his book, his trip to Lincoln, and his infatuation with the young female bartender. It seemed as if Farber didn't even have a life before arriving in Lincoln, like he'd been hatched in some petri dish and raised solely for the sake of being dropped into this event. Not wanting to disturb his own thoughts with any actual discussions with the man, Martin did his best to blend into the stucco wall behind him.

As the line started chugging along again, Lilly finally ended her conversation with the Harley-Davidson woman and moved alongside her husband. "This is kind of exciting!" she gushed. "I can't wait to learn more about Billy from this friend of yours."

Martin puffed out a little air once more as he explained, "Lil, remember, he's not my friend. He won't know me from Adam. I only sent him a couple of emails that he was nice enough to respond to." Martin looked into Lilly's eyes to make sure she'd heard him and quickly added, "And no *Young Guns* questions! That's the kind of stuff they'll throw you out of here for."

Lilly just shrugged and said, "Oh phooey, Martin. Everybody loves *Young Guns*."

Someone inside the building must have really taken charge because the line suddenly took on a distinctly different speed, and everyone moved steadily toward the theater. Just as Martin and Lilly were about to get inside the lobby, a great cheer went up - Sergio Bachaca himself exited a pickup truck that had been dispatched to save him from the flood waters. He looked nothing like a celebrity in a pair of blue jeans, a snap-front western shirt, and a brown leather belt reining in his belly. In fact, he looked more like a guy who might be fixing street lights in anyone's neighborhood, but who, in this small town, was being treated like Hollywood royalty. Women (and men) ooh'd and aah'd him as he flashed his thousand-dollar smile and waved to the packed crowd.

"Better late than never they say!" he jubilantly offered as he was swept inside.

Just as Lilly was about to follow the author inside, a shadow appeared behind her, and a huge boot nearly stepped on her foot. "Sorry, ma'am," apologized a big cowboy, "didn't see you there. After you," he said, with a sweep of his hand.

It was Steve from Capitan.

Steve looked directly at the woman's husband. Martin waited for the 'gotcha' moment, but the big man seemed to have no recognition that they'd ever met before. With a tip of his hat, he whisked by and into the theater. Martin's heart was racing, wondering just what the hell had happened, as he and Lilly finally reached the entry doors. Minding those doors was Kevin, who smiled warily at Martin when they walked in. "Kevin," said Martin curtly to the young man. Lilly just offered a thin smile, anxious as she was to be seated.

"Hello, Mr. Teebs, Mrs. Teebs. Please follow these people to the main aisle to be seated."

Martin glanced back at the boy once more before the couple followed the herd of tourists, each hoping to secure a good spot. As he and Lilly approached their own row, a woman asked to see their tickets to direct them to their seats.

It was Trisha. Martin's heart, racing just a minute ago, now threatened to stop completely. He hoped that the young woman didn't say anything to Lilly about their previous evening's conversation since Martin had played off his entire talk with Trisha as virtually nothing. Lilly handed over their tickets and turned to Martin, with a wry smile.

"Hi, uh, Mr. and Mrs. Teebs," Trisha stammered. "You're in seats six and seven, right this way." While she longed for a private conversation with Martin to get answers to the growing dismay in her mind, she knew now would not be the time. With the look his wife had just given her, it might *never* be the time…but now was most certainly out.

Lilly nodded and walked down the row, while Martin's eyes locked for a few seconds with the beautiful girl before he too found his seat. Lilly sat and smoothed out her jeans before she spoke. "Well, there's your little friend, Martin. Did you say 'hi'?"

Lilly had no idea how much stress Martin had been under and how little he wanted to do this right now. He inhaled and exhaled deeply before answering. "Come on, Lil. She's not my friend. She just works here. Give me a break, huh?"

Lilly rarely heard Martin angry or even off center with his temper, and so his snappish response surprised her. Either he was hiding something, which she didn't believe, or he was tired of her sniping at him, which she figured was most likely the case. She decided to let it be and grabbed his hand tightly. "Sorry, hon, I was just kidding."

Martin gave her hand a squeeze back, knowing that Lilly had just lied to him. She wasn't kidding, she was jealous - although she had nothing *tangible* to be jealous of.

As the last of the guests filed in and were seated, Martin craned his head around to see if Farber had made it inside. There, in the next-to-last row, sat the simple-looking man, who happened to glance Martin's way at that exact moment. Farber raised his hand to wave and tried to motion to Martin that they should meet up later, but the gesture just looked like he was mixing up the batter for a birthday cake. Martin only lifted his head in recognition and turned back toward the stage.

As Bachaca made his way out, he was flanked by two men in enormous cowboy hats. One was the sheriff of Lincoln County, and the other was Steve. Martin guessed them to be security for the big-fish author in the small pond of Lincoln. Just before Bachaca stepped forward to speak, he whispered something to Steve, and they both had a mighty laugh as they looked up to where Kevin stood by the entrance doors. Shaking Steve's hand, Sergio turned back toward his audience.

"Well, my friends, so good to see you all here," he began to a thunderous ovation. "For a while, it didn't look like I'd make it at all. Perhaps the spirits of Murphy and Dolan would rather I didn't tell you what really happened in 1877!" More laughs and cheers were heard as 'Serge' sat down on the lone stool on the stage.

"I'm terribly sorry for those who signed up for the meet-and-greet. The weather simply wouldn't cooperate. What we're going to do instead is that I'll present my talk right now, we'll take all questions at the end, and then Sheriff Hamlin and Mr. Steve have assured me that some of you ruffians would be happy to head to the Lincoln County Brewery later on this evening, where I'll be happy to sit, sign your books, and take photos. Anyone who paid for the meet-and-greet will, of course, have that portion of the fee refunded."

A series of general murmurs went up from the crowd as Bachaca stood up to begin.

"William H. Bonney, yes? He's the reason we are all here. And by 'here,' I don't mean in this room, I mean the thousands and thousands of tourists who have visited Lincoln over this weekend. Let's face it, the Lincoln County War was an important range war, but it would most likely be forgotten but for a teenaged boy who played a small and relatively insignificant part in it. We've come to know the Kid through books like mine, TV shows, and, of course, movies. What, though, was Billy really like? Well, unless one of you can travel back in time, maybe even bring him back for us, we'll never know for sure!"

The joke sparked the audience to laughter - and Martin to feel sick to his stomach. He peered around to see Kevin still standing behind him, without any emotion betrayed on his face.

"The Kid was at once a complicated and very simple fellow. Brave and loyal to his friends, deadly to his enemies. In that way, he was perhaps like a rattlesnake that only wishes to be left alone but, when provoked, will strike with deadly force and accuracy."

People in the room quietly agreed, nodding their heads.

"And to the ladies," Bachaca continued, to a series of hoots and howls from both women and men, "he proved to be…simply irresistible. Billy could count any number of *queridas* up and down the Rio Bonito and beyond. In Fort Sumner alone, he had a handful of women at his beck and call, some who would even have up and left their spouses, had the Kid requested it! What we know of Billy's *looks* makes us wonder how much of a ladie's man he could possibly have been, but what we know of his *charm* assures us that if the Kid slept alone, it was because he chose to."

The room broke out into a rapturous applause, and Martin was sure that if he were selling Billy the Kid baseball jerseys right now, he could probably retire from working by evening's end. Bachaca smiled widely, knowing he had the audience in his grasp. The author was a pro and had done this enough to know when to amp up the Billy praise and when to get down to brass tacks. With his intro just about done, the crowd began to quiet while Bachaca held the beat of silence for a second or two more, to build some suspense. Suddenly, before he could begin the meat of his lecture, a strong but soft voice from the corner of the room called out, "Who was Rosita Luna?"

Heads snapped to the side, knowing that questions were to be reserved until the end. Bachaca swiveled his head and peered into the darkness to try to find the source of the interruption. "I'm sorry? Rosita who?

"Luna," came the forceful reply, "known as the Belle of Lincoln."

Instantly, Martin recognized the voice - Trisha! He sat bolt upright and stared straight ahead so that he didn't give Lilly even the slightest reason to believe he had anything to do with this outburst. Lilly - with the name that had become so familiar now ringing in her ears - turned first toward the voice and then toward Bachaca to see what he might say. Martin's breath was coming in such shallow little bursts that he feared he might hyperventilate. He focused his eyes ahead but his ears on Trisha.

"Well, as noted, we'd like to answer questions at the end, but," began Bachaca, as Martin braced for the news that would either confirm his sanity or deny it, "in all of my research, and I've done a lot, young lady, I've never come across that name. Where did you hear it?"

For just a moment, Trisha looked over in the direction where she knew Martin was seated before she responded. "From a very reliable source, handed down through the years. You could almost say this person knew her personally."
"Oh, fuck me," thought Martin. This was not going to end well at all. While he dared not look, he could feel Lilly's eyes piercing him from her seat just a few inches away. She was going to demand answers, Martin realized, and this wasn't going to go easily. Finally understanding that he was making it worse by not looking, he casually glanced over at his wife, with as innocent an expression as possible. Lilly peered at him the way a detective would while interrogating a suspect, trying to see if the eyes might tell the truth while the mouth was lying.

"What?" Martin shrugged his shoulders. Lilly just tilted her head to let Martin know they would finish this one-sided conversation later.

"Well, my dear, if anyone rose to the level of the Belle of Lincoln during Billy's day, don't you imagine she might have been one of his sweethearts?" asked Bachaca, to the giggles of the crowd.

Trisha, having been consumed all day by the thought of Martin's disclosures to her, wanted answers, and she found nothing humorous about Bachaca's response. "No, she wouldn't. She wanted more than an outlaw who was going to die young. She wanted true love, lasting love. The kind you read about in books. She wanted the kind of man who would stand by her, no matter the consequences, and would love her until her dying breath!" There were a few gasps from the crowd as Trisha shook her head gingerly.

Where had all that come from? Martin hadn't said a word about anything like that to her. Was Trisha channeling some thread from the long-gone woman - if indeed she had ever even existed?! For his part, Sergio Bachaca sat on his stool, mouth agape, at the testimony of a woman he could still not see in the dark theater. The author wondered to himself if the mysterious speaker could perhaps be correct, and he'd had a major blind spot in his years of research. It didn't make sense that he could have missed someone so important, but the urgency of the woman's words made him question himself.

"Well, she sounds lovely, really. I must take up my research materials when I get back to my office and see if I can find anything," said Bachaca seriously, and then added a final thought: "Do you know what happened to her? When she died, exactly?"

Silence hung over the room for an uncomfortable amount of time. Just the mention of Rosita dying felt to Martin like the theater's ceiling was falling in on him. He had a hard time breathing, such were the visions in his mind, and seemingly right before his eyes. Before she could answer the author, Trisha looked again in Martin's direction, longing for him to jump in and finish the story he'd begun telling her the night before. She knew she was making things bad for the man, based upon the way his wife was staring at him, but he had invited her into his private world; now she had to know everything.

"I don't know that…but I think she died young. I have a feeling things didn't end well for her."

The audience, now dragged into the back and forth, sighed as if sad for a real person, not knowing that the woman being discussed was most likely the figment of the vivid imagination belonging to one member of the attendees.

Sergio Bachaca wrestled back control of his lecture and began to speak brightly about

Billy the Kid's younger days, and the thought of a 'Rosita Luna' faded from almost everyone's mind. Lilly gave Martin a sideways look and stood up to visit the ladies room; Kevin held the door for her. At last, Martin cast a glance at Trisha, whose eyes cut through the darkness to connect with his. In them, he saw a longing that he hadn't seen in a long time. It wasn't a longing for love, however, but for information about the woman she presumably looked so much like.

At the back of the stage, Steve from Capitan adjusted his cowboy hat and leaned back against the wall. He wasn't quite sure what he had just witnessed, but he was sure it demanded an investigation of the type the old cowboy really loved to take on.

Saturday – 8 pm

Carl Farber stood and stretched out his legs, finally escaping from his tiny chair at the back of the theater. He had to admit, Bachaca had a way with words and had held the audience rapt for the better part of seventy-five minutes. During the usual flood of questions at the end, Farber listened intently for any new information, but all he heard were the same old questions and answers, rephrased for a new generation.

He'd been as surprised as everyone else at the early question about some 'Rosita Luna,' especially since he realized it actually had come from that Trisha girl, one of the Monument's employees. She was the one who'd disappeared with Martin the previous evening to 'talk,' as he heard later, and he wondered what was so important that the two had had to find a secret spot in which to converse. In any event, Farber believed that from that conversation must have come some inkling - through Trisha to Jane - that Martin Teebs had some sort of issue with him, and Carl wanted to find out what it was. He'd seen Martin and his wife seated a handful of rows ahead of him, and he decided that as they exited, he'd grab a few minutes with the man. He scooted out of his row and stationed himself near the door to catch Teebs as he left.

"Hey, Martin. Martin!" Farber called over the crowd noise. "Hey, can we talk for a sec?" The big man didn't look in the mood for talking, and his wife looked even less so. Not knowing what was transpiring, Carl pressed his request. "Just for a minute. I need to talk to you about something, okay?" Lilly looked up at Martin and motioned with her eyes for him to go ahead, but not to be long about it.

"What's up, Carl? This really isn't a great time," Martin said, glancing back in Lilly's direction.

"No, no…I know," rushed Farber, trying to get right to the point. "It's just that Jane talked to Trisha or something, and she's under the impression that you have a problem with me? I mean, what have I done, Martin? We just met!"

Martin rubbed his fingers with his thumb so hard it caused him to look down and see that he'd balled his hand up into a fist, a fact that also didn't escape Farber. Shaking his momentary anger away, Teebs unfurled his fingers. "Listen, Carl, you're fine, okay? It's just this thing that happened to me the other night. I don't really have the time to explain it. There was a guy in it, like you, maybe he *was* you." And then Martin suddenly took a different tack and wagged his finger at Farber. "Hey, have we ever met before? Somewhere around Waldwick? Anywhere?"

Farber just shook his head with a questioning expression as he couldn't remember any interaction with or knowledge of the man in front of him. He shrugged his shoulders and replied, "Not that I know of?"

Martin balanced his need to fix things with Lilly versus the man in front of him deserving at least some kind of answer for what he'd heard. He decided on a very abridged version of his Dream.

"The other night I almost died, choking to death," began Martin. "I had what I guess was a near-death experience, except it wasn't really *my* life that I saw flash before my eyes. It was…well, something else. Anyway, Carl, you - or someone a lot like you - were in it and were doing some really bad things. That's the reason we got off to such a rough start at the tour. I don't know what to make of any of it, but it seemed incredibly real," Martin finished and stared at Farber to see whether he'd delivered enough so that the man might move on.

Carl looked dumbfounded and searched for the right words. "How is that even possible? We just met last night. You said that event was a few days ago." Martin just shook his head to show he had no explanation. "What did I do that was so bad anyway? Steal something? Cheat?" Farber asked with some urgency. "What? Rape someone, kill?"

Martin's eyes grew stone cold as Carl announced the final two sins, so much so that his intent was perfectly clear. However, rather than withdraw and apologize to Martin for ruining his Dream, Farber got mad…really mad. "Are you kidding me?! You think I'd do something like that? You don't even know who the hell I am, Martin Teebs, and shame on you for spreading that shit around here! Do me a favor, huh? If you ever do see me back in Jersey, look the other way!" He cast a hard glance at a very surprised-looking Lilly Teebs and stormed off.

Dropping his head, Martin began to rub his eyes. A number of other guests had seen and heard the exchange and were slowly returning to what they had been doing before the outburst. Lilly stepped over quickly, asking, "What was that? What just happened between you two?"

Martin desperately wished he were in the middle of an NDE right now, one from which he could quickly wake up, so badly had this night gone. His only silver lining was that if he played this right, Lilly might forget about the whole Trisha/Rosita thing…at least until tomorrow.

"I must have said some things to him last night, I don't know. He was in my Dream, Lil. I know it's crazy, but when I saw everything I saw while I was choking, Carl Farber was right there - and he was *not* a nice man. He confronted me tonight about what I'd seen, and I told him."

Lilly shook her head and looked sideways yet again at Martin. "You guys were fighting like that over what - a dream? Maybe you'd better tell me everything that went on in this dream."

Oh hell, no, thought Martin, that wasn't going to happen…ever. Was he going to tell Lilly about her affair with Dallas Jones? Her out-of-wedlock pregnancy? Her divorce from Martin? Every other mistake she'd made along the way? How about he threw in a helping of Martin meeting his soulmate a century before Lilly was even born? Maybe he should tell her again that his great love Rosita looked exactly like Trisha! Why not implode his entire life right here and right now?!

"How you folks doin'? Enjoy the show?" came a booming voice from behind them. Martin didn't need to turn around to know it was Steve from Capitan.

Lilly smiled and answered, “Yes, thanks, it was very informative.”

Martin slowly turned around, expecting to see Steve’s twinkling eyes and wry smile, showing he knew everything that had gone on in their mutual past. Instead, the big cowboy looked at him rather blankly and stuck his hand out. “Name’s Steve. I used to be the mayor of Capitan. Retired out here when I left the force.”

Unless Steve was up for an Academy Award for acting, he clearly felt no connection at all to Martin. It was as if the two men were meeting for the very first time. Still on guard, Martin reached his hand out and said slowly, “Martin Teebs. This is my wife, Lilly.”

With a slight smile, Steve tipped his giant cowboy hat at Lilly and said simply, “Ma’am.” Suddenly, there was a murmur through what was left of the crowd as Sergio Bachaca made his way out of the theater. People yelled his name and held out books for him to sign while the throng closed in on him. Seeing he was needed, the big cowboy stepped away and guided the writer through the crowd, as if parting the Red Sea. “Sergio’ll be up at the Brewery if you want stuff signed. Come on by and buy me a beer!” yelled Steve jovially to the crowd, which broke out in laughter. The two men pressed on toward the street and out of sight.

“Well, do you want to go get your book signed? I could sure use a drink,” said Lilly drolly. Martin thought about it for about half a second before saying yes. If Lilly could put a few drinks in her, she might get tipsy enough to forget about *voir dire*-ing him later on about The Dream. For sure, he thought, this was a better idea than heading right back to the *casita* and getting the third degree.

“You bet!” he agreed. “Let’s go now before it gets too packed.” Husband and wife exited the theater and made their way toward the street. Just at the corner of the monument building, Martin spotted two figures deep in discussion. He immediately recognized the voluptuous figure of Trisha but was shocked and revulsed to see her talking to Carl Farber. When they got close enough to see some detail, Martin observed that Farber seemed angry and was continually pointed back toward the theater. Trisha shook her head sadly. As the Teebs approached, Farber shot Martin a stone-cold death stare, and Trisha looked at the big man with eyes that were either of compassion - or maybe of someone who desperately needed to be saved.

Saturday - 8:30 pm

Having closed up the Visitor Center, Kevin punched out for the night and made his way to the Brewery, the ancient copy of Bachaca's book stuffed securely in his backpack. For as old as the book looked, the publication date was merely 2014, so Kevin assumed that the previous owner, whoever that person might have been, 'rode it hard and put it away wet.' Although this night offered neither band nor live music, the crowd seemed to be even greater than the night before, undoubtedly owing to the celebrity author now holding court at a seat in the middle of the deck. Climbing the steps up, Kevin met Trisha on her way down.

"Hey," the young man asked, "are you leaving? Already?"

Trisha didn't look happy, and some sort of emotion clouded her face, although Kevin couldn't quite make out what it was. "Yeah, I think so. I'm not really up for this to-night. It's been a long day," she replied, with as friendly a tone in her voice as she could manage.

Tired as Kevin was, he could empathize, and he figured he'd get a signature and a beer, then call it a night himself. "All right, Trish, get some rest. One more big day tomor-row, huh?"

Trisha just sighed at the thought and walked quickly inside to tell Jane she'd be leav-ing. The place was packed with book-talk goers who'd been thirsting for something cold and were hell-bent on getting it before joining the ever-lengthening line to get their books signed - or to ask 'Serge' a question that surely he'd never heard before. Getting bumped back and forth, Trisha finally came within shouting distance of Jane, and she waved her hand wildly to get her attention. Eventually looking up, Jane con-nected with her friend and gave her a look of panic, so busy was the bar. She held up a single finger to ask Trisha to wait just a minute. Glancing around at the full tables, Jane scanned all the way across the room and saw Martin Teebs' wife Lilly, sitting and doing something with her phone.

"For you and the little lady!" yelled Jane over the din, sliding two beers to the man in front of Trisha. "And how are you doing, girl?" she asked Trisha.

Stepping back to let the gentleman leave with his drinks, Trisha suddenly realized that it was Martin Teebs. Their eyes met in some sort of understanding that, while they needed to talk, this wasn't the time nor place. "Hi," Martin said quietly and with a sheepish look on his face.

"Hi, Martin," was her businesslike reply.

Martin wanted to say so many things in this moment - about Rosita, Farber, Billy, and the other swirling cast of characters dancing in his mind - but one look across the room at Lilly impatiently waiting for her drink, and he knew his time was short. "Listen, uh…I'd like to talk. I saw you talking to Farber and, well, just be careful, okay?"

Trisha gazed around the room and finally said, "Your wife is waiting. Go. Maybe we can talk tomorrow." With that, she waved a quick goodbye to Jane and walked out of the Brewery into the night. Jane looked up at Martin to see his reaction, and all he could offer in return was a shrug and shake of the head.

Martin pushed his way back through the crowd and set the two beers down in front of Lilly, who was freshening up her lipstick. She looked up at her husband with a smirk and said, "So, do you want to get in line now, or do you need to talk to your little girl-friend Trisha some more?"

Saturday – 8:45 pm

Farber inched his way forward in the line the six inches or so that the big biker dude in front of him had managed to move and sighed mightily. Following his discussion with Martin - during which the man had fabricated a version of Carl as a rapist and murderer - his night had gone significantly downhill. The sour mood that enveloped him continued to thicken, and he considered bailing out of the line and heading back to his lonely motel. However, he'd not yet even had a chance to see Jane, and missing out on that would make his lousy night downright sucky.

A couple of spots ahead of Farber was the boy Kevin from the tour last night. While the real Billy the Kid hadn't given people much to go on, what with only one verified photo, Farber had to admit that this young man looked a lot like Billy. Had he not known who he was, he surely would do a double take if finding the boy standing in front of or before him almost anywhere in New Mexico. For some reason, it bothered Farber that Kevin would be before him in line. Maybe it was the boy's youth, plus the fact that he would have more years left to stand in lines, whereas Farber might be getting his first and only chance to talk to Bachaca. Even the thought of meeting the author was starting to weigh on Farber. While the lecture had been fine, he had been hoping for more insight and some new information on the Kid and the Lincoln County War. That Sergio had seemed to just mail in his answers didn't sit well with Carl, being that he'd spent most of his savings to take this trip.

As the line crawled inexorably forward, Farber watched Kevin slip off his backpack, lift out either a very old or very abused book, and start to thumb through it. What would the boy want with Bachaca signing that old relic? Farber wondered. There was no way that book could be a copy of Sergio's, or so Farber thought, unless someone had specifically misused or aged it - maybe as a movie prop? In any event, Carl couldn't imagine what a waste of time it was to have an author sign a book that would probably fall completely apart by next week.

Farber saw that big cowboy, the bodyguard, shoo away a family who apparently wanted to take its Christmas-card picture with the famous writer, in seemingly one hundred different poses. Now only one couple stood between Kevin and the man that Farber hoped would help him launch his own writing career. The woman and her husband greedily handed over four copies of the book, with apologies, explaining that they were planning to give them as gifts. Bachaca rolled his eyes and looked at Steve, who simply shrugged his shoulders as if to say, "What are you going to do?"

Finally, the book whores cleared the table, and Kevin prepared to step up to get signed the book that Steve had given him. Steve's blue eyes twinkled, spotting the gift he'd bestowed upon the young man only a week before. Just as Farber saw the cowboy wave the kid forward, however, another man appeared on the deck, heading to get his own place in line. Within seconds of seeing *the* book once more, Martin Teebs yelled, screamed, and tried to wrestle it away from Kevin, so forcefully that Steve from Capitan had to fulfill his duties as bodyguard for the first time that night.

Saturday – 9 pm

"Whoa! Whoa, big boy! What the hell is going on?" yelled Steve, over the protestations of a man he'd never met.

"Where did you get it, Kevin? Where, goddammit?" screamed Martin, who had lost all control over his faculties upon once again spotting the horribly worn book. Kevin recoiled at the sight of the man charging him, apparently still upset over seeing that book the evening prior. The young man jumped behind Steve and cowered with Bachaca, who'd never had an incident like this in his twenty years of writing and book signings.

"Calm down, now!" admonished Steve, as he grabbed Martin by the collar and yanked him to the side. While Martin was no shrinking violet, Steve had him by three or four inches and twenty or thirty pounds. The crowd scattered, thinking that the Most Dangerous Street in America might once again be living up to its name. Martin tried anew to lunge at Kevin, mostly to grab the book; but the old cop's skills were better, and Teebs only succeeded in sending several glasses flying toward the crowd of people, shattering at their feet. Getting his footing under him, Steve leaned into Martin and threw him back against the rail, which stunned the crazed man enough to stop him charging forward.

"Listen up, son. One more move, and you're gonna get something broken. What the hell is this all about?" demanded Steve.

Martin's wild eyes calmed a bit, knowing in an ass-kicking contest with Steve, he was sure to finish in second place. Sweat poured from his brow as Lilly came storming out from the Brewery, having heard the commotion. "Martin, what the hell have you done? Have you gone insane?!" she shrieked upon seeing the scene.

Martin quickly glanced in every direction, like a caged animal. How the hell did I get here? he asked himself silently. How did things get so far off the rails that I'm fighting a twenty-year-old kid over a piece-of-crap book? For the life of him, Martin could not understand what had happened or even the source of his current rage. With everyone staring at him, apparently waiting for enlightenment about what had caused this entire event, Teebs breathed heavily out of his nose, not confident in opening his mouth lest something emerge that would make a bad situation even worse.

Seeing the man calming before him, Steve took the opportunity to try to further diffuse the situation. "Come on now, hoss, let me take you inside for a beer, and we can put this behind us." He moved toward Martin, firmly grabbing him at the elbow.

As much as Martin wanted to pull away, he knew that it would only reignite the flames of a fire he had no chance of putting out. Instead, he decided on some verbal sparring with the big cowboy. "I want to know where that book came from? That's it."

Steve looked behind him at Bachaca and Kevin as he tried to understand what book Martin was talking about. "*That* book? *That* old-ass, beat-up book of Serge's?" Martin flicked his eyes from focusing on his feet to the book still in Kevin's hands. Finally, he nodded at Steve.

"Damn, son, I found that book up in Magdalena while doing an investigation a couple of weeks ago. Gave it to this kid since he looks so much like *the* Kid. It ain't nothing but a beat-up copy of the book you've got."

The hair on the back of Martin's neck went up at the mention of Magdalena. How many coincidences could this weekend hold? Realizing that Kevin was most probably an innocent in this fiasco, he determined that a conversation with Steve would be in order. His chest still heaving from excitement, he looked over at Lilly. "Why don't you go back now? Everything's okay here. I need to have a talk with Steve." Martin didn't even pretend to put on a happy face. Whatever he and the retired cop were going to talk about, it wasn't going to be fun.
Lilly, disarmed by Martin's resoluteness, looked around at the crowd staring at her and said simply, "Fine. Don't be too long," and turned to walk away.

Crisis averted, most people went back to their discussions, and Kevin finally was able to hand his book to Sergio for the long-awaited signature. First, though, Bachaca opened the back cover, as if looking for something. With a slight shake of his head, perhaps at not finding what he sought, he closed and then opened the front cover to affix his signature.

Meanwhile, Steve guided Martin by the arm toward the Brewery so they could indeed sit and discuss what was so special about that ratty book. As the two approached the door, Martin turned and said, with a menacing undertone, "And don't think I don't know who you are, too."

Saturday - 9:05 pm

Carl Farber was stunned, to say the least. Seeing his new friend-turned-enemy Martin Teebs crashing the book-signing party in such a violent fashion was the most unexpected outcome he could have imagined that night. To Farber, it was interesting that in 'The Dream,' - or whatever Teebs had conjured up about him - Carl had been the bad guy. Now here was Farber peacefully waiting his turn in line, while the supposed hero of 'The Dream' was maniacally throwing his weight around, bellowing about that old book that Kevin had been holding. Farber wondered what kind of threat that Teebs actually was? Would he take action against Farber just because he'd dreamt about him? The guy sure seemed like a loose cannon, and Carl didn't want to be around the next time he went off. "Tell me *I'm* trouble," Farber whispered to himself, under his breath. "Look in the mirror, you jerk!"

Next, Carl turned his gaze to Kevin, who was in the midst of getting a signature on whatever the old book was that had so incensed Teebs. The way that young man had run from danger annoyed Farber. How could someone who looked so much like Billy be such a coward? With derision, Farber sneered in the direction of the author and his young fan. As Kevin finally moved on, the biker family in front of Carl approached Bachaca with open arms, as if greeting a close friend. "Won't be long now," Farber said to himself, grabbing the thumb drive in his pocket and holding it tightly. "Just wait'll you get a load of this, Mr. Bachaca."

Saturday – 9:10 pm

Lilly, steeped in both her anger and amazement at Martin's unexpected eruption, walked down the quiet street toward the Patron House. She and Martin had been planning this trip for months, and she'd really pushed herself to have some interest in Billy the Kid in order to be closer to her husband. Sure, the trip hadn't started out well, what with Martin nearly dying; but once clear of that scare, she'd assumed they'd have a grand old time parading about Lincoln. But Martin's mood and his fascination with his life flashing before his eyes had somehow changed him. He could hold things together for an hour or two, but he kept coming back to whatever the hell had happened in his mind.

When Lilly had shrieked at him, asking if he'd gone insane, she'd actually meant it. From what she'd read, when people nearly died, they usually came back from the experience with some peace and tranquility. They were nicer and more caring, even if they seemed a little nuts. However, that wasn't Martin at all. He'd come back surly and angry at people he didn't even know. He was even sneaking around, talking to pretty young women, women who could never have any interest in a soft-around-the-middle, middling-ad-agency, quality-control manager like him.

Was Martin having some kind of midlife crisis? Lilly wondered. Of course, since he had nearly died, maybe he was considering it an end-of-life crisis, or maybe even a second-chance-at-life crisis? Regardless, Lilly felt it incumbent upon herself to find out what was going on in Martin's head. He'd brushed off his Dream as 'nothing,' but she (and everyone at the Brewery) could clearly see that was not the truth. How exactly was she going to get him to 'fess up to whatever was the problem? Martin had already decided to keep to himself whatever memories were roiling in his head. Lilly could demand that he come clean, but that was likely to make him retreat further. No, she'd have to coax it out of him. She'd need to create a safe space where Martin wouldn't feel foolish or judged if she truly wanted him to unburden himself. She'd have to put the pretty girl, the mean-spirited anger toward Farber, and the events of the night all behind her if she was going to help her husband get back to the person he had been just days ago.

As she passed the Visitor Center and spied the Patron House just ahead, Lilly got the shock of her life when, from out of the darkness, a voice called, "Mrs. Teebs. Can I talk to you for a second?" Lilly snapped her head to the left as a jolt of fear shot through her body. Slowly from out of the shadows, a beautiful young woman appeared, a troubled look on her face. From the margins of the street, Trisha walked slowly toward Lilly, with her hands held slightly up so as not to alarm the woman any further.

"Hi, I'm sorry to startle you. My name is Trisha," she offered.

Lilly didn't extend her hand but nodded her head slightly. "Hello, Trisha. I'm Lilly

Teebs."

Trisha took a deep breath. She didn't want to upset this woman any more than she appeared to have already done. "Mrs. Teebs, first, I want to say I'm sorry. You might think that there's something between your husband and me, and there's not. Absolutely not."

Lilly, in no mood for more drama on this night, asked, "Then why are you apologizing?"

"Because I saw the way you looked at me at the book talk, and the Brewery earlier, and I don't want you to be upset with me over something that isn't happening. My job is important to me, and I don't want to lose it over something like this."

Tired and wanting to put this issue to rest, Lilly shot straight: "What are you doing, talking to my husband? And what does this Rosita character have to do with it…and with you?"

Not knowing how much Martin had told his wife about his…vision, or whatever it was, Trisha trod carefully. "Well, you know, Mr. Teebs thought I looked like this woman. I don't know who she is, or even *if* she is. That's the reason I asked about her earlier. When we talked last night, he told me a lot about her, but there were some things he held back."

Lilly raised her eyes. "You talked last night…is that so?"

Too far into it to backtrack now, Trisha pressed on. "We did, at the Brewery. He looked so sad about something, I just asked him what was wrong. He spilled this whole history of Rosita Luna - well, at least, until he wouldn't tell me any more. I can't explain it, Mrs. Teebs, but it's like whatever was making him sad is now transferred to me...I don't know." Trisha hung her head, knowing she was being judged, most likely as a homewrecker, at this very moment.

"Okay, so what did he tell you about her? Please, enlighten me."

Now Trisha was at a significant crossroad. If she told Lilly everything that Martin had explained to her, it would be bad for *everyone* involved. But if she didn't, the woman would surely be able to tell she was lying, which would make it bad for herself and probably for Martin. She decided to just come clean with everything she remembered. "Look, I don't know what happened to Martin. He doesn't know if this was some dream, vision, past life regression, or what; but to him, it seemed very real. He told me that Rosita Luna was the great love of his life. She lived here, right here in Lincoln, during the time of Billy the Kid. Martin couldn't explain how he was in that time period to be with her, he seemed really confused on that part, but I guess when he saw me, and saw that I guess I look like her, it impacted him. I didn't do or say anything, but whatever that memory is, it's pretty strong. When I saw him last night, and we talked, it was almost as if he wanted to cry over her."

"So," Lilly sneered, "you comforted him. Is that it? Trisha?"

"No!" protested Trisha immediately. "I did not! He didn't even want that from me. Mrs. Teebs, your husband never said or did a thing to me that you would be upset with. I never had any sense that he was coming onto me at all. I think I reminded him of her, and so he wanted to unburden all of his sadness with someone who might understand. That's it."

Lilly's head began to pound in the thin mountain air. If this was a preview of what she wanted Martin to divulge to her, perhaps she really *didn't* want to hear any of it. She reached back to rub some of the tension out of her neck and asked, "Which parts wouldn't he tell you?"

Trisha's eyes got misty, which surprised even her. "When he got to Rosita's - I don't know - end, he couldn't go on. There was something with that teacher, Carl Farber, too, but he wouldn't say what it was. I'm sorry. I wish I knew more."

"You were talking to Carl earlier? After that blowup with Martin in that building? What was that about?" Lilly inquired, as the pain from her head began to throb behind her eyes.

"Farber came up to me, asking if I'd said anything to Mr. Teebs about him," Trisha admitted. "How could I say anything about anyone!" she protested. "I don't even *know* these men. How did I get trapped in this?!"

With that, Trisha broke down, crying so genuinely that Lilly knew the woman was telling the truth. Feeling guilty for making her so sad, Lilly walked over and placed her hand on Trisha's shoulder. "Hey. Hey…it's okay. I'm sorry for the way I looked at you. This isn't your issue, it's mine and Martin's." Trisha looked up thankfully through teary eyes. "Don't worry about this. I'm going to talk to Martin when he gets back and see if we can work this out. It'll be fine, and I'm sorry you got dragged into it," Lilly concluded. She turned to go, adding, "Goodnight, Trisha, get home safe. I'll make sure Martin doesn't bother you with this again."

Lilly walked into the darkness while Trisha stood there, rubbing the sight back into her eyes. While she was thankful that Lilly had absolved her of any blame, she knew that her part in this mystery was far from done. The questions about Rosita, Martin, and everyone else implicated in his Dream swirled like giant storm clouds, just waiting for the chance to wreak havoc on anyone who got too close.

Saturday - 9:12 pm

Finally at the front of the line, Carl Farber put on a big, welcoming smile as he approached the author extraordinaire. In his right hand, he held tight to Bachaca's book, while firmly in his left hand was nestled the thumb drive containing his almost-completed manuscript of *The Rise of The House of Murphy*. Farber had copyrighted the book months ago, so he held no fear of Sergio stealing it from him, but he desperately wanted the man's help in getting it published. On his own, Farber was a nobody, with no contacts, few friends, and no way to drag himself up from his current station. From the time he was a boy, he had always felt he was cut out for something special in life, needing only to be discovered in order to prove it. As he stepped up to the author's table, he whispered to himself, "Prove it."

"Wonderful presentation tonight, Sergio!" exclaimed Farber, trying to get off on the right foot. "Just great info - and that delivery, wow!" Carl knew he was laying it on a bit thick, but, between the sheer number of people that Bachaca was talking to and the fuss that Martin had caused, the history teacher wanted to make sure he had the man's full attention.

"Well, thank you, Mr...?" Bachaca left the question open for the man to fill in the blank.

"Oh yes! Farber. Carl Farber, pleasure to meet you." He dropped the book on the table and stuck his hand out. Bachaca tersely shook his hand and picked up the man's book to sign it. "We have something in common, we're both authors," Farber said brightly, hoping to put himself on a level playing field.

"Is that so?" questioned Bachaca curiously. "What have you written, Mr. Farber?"

This was it, the moment that Carl had been waiting for. His years of research and late-night writing sessions all boiled down to what would happen during the next few seconds. He took a deep breath and dove right in. "Funny you should ask," he said, holding up the thumb drive. "I've got here the first-draft manuscript of my new book, *The Rise of The House of Murphy*. It's a detailed chronology of how Murphy and Dolan came to power prior to the War." Farber was ecstatic at his performance. He couldn't have aced it any better than that, he thought. Now all he had to wait for was Sergio to show enough interest so that Carl could offer him the thumb drive to review.

As the published author finished signing his autograph, he handed the book back to Farber, with some delight dancing in his eyes. "That," he began, "is an incredible book idea, sir." A chill went down Carl's spine as he envisioned the moment for which he'd been waiting - for what seemed an eternity - about to happen. "So much so," Bachaca continued, "that I myself have been working on a book on the very same topic for almost two years now! It looks like we'll have competing books out when mine is published next month!"

Farber's brain slowed down as he tried to process what he had just heard. If his ears were to be believed, Sergio had just told him that in one month, a mere thirty days, Bachaca's own book on the exact same subject as Carl's would be released by the man's publishing house. Said book would get tons of promotion and have a built-in audience, based upon the tens of thousands of Billy the Kid books he'd already sold, one of which Farber held in his trembling hand at that very moment. While the line behind him grew restless, the history teacher put into words what he'd heard, to assure himself that he'd heard correctly.

"You're saying that you already wrote a book on this subject, and it's going to be released next month?"

"That's right!" said Bachaca happily. "I've spent two years on it. I even got proprietary access to sources that no one else has ever seen. It's going to be great for all of these Lincoln County War enthusiasts!"

Farber's heart slowed like his blood was suddenly made of molasses. His head was spinning, and he felt dizzy. This one thing, this one quest of his, was what he'd planned to put himself over the top. It was supposed to take him from being life's also-ran to leader of the pack. And now all he had to show for his pipe dream was a half-finished manuscript that everyone would think was produced solely to copy the much more successful book written by the writer currently preening in front of him. Carl was unable to speak any further and just shook his head at Bachaca. As he turned to walk away, returning to his nondescript life, Sergio called him back. "Mr. Farber, good luck with your book. I look forward to reading it!" And with that, another middle-aged man stepped up to the table, and Carl Farber became not even a memory to the famous author.

Farber stepped off to the side, to a relatively quiet area of the deck, and tried to control his rapid, shallow breathing. Between the smashing of his dream of becoming a famous author and the smearing of his name and character by that asshole Teebs, the distraught writer was desperately trying to hold himself together. Calming down, he focused on the one good thing that this trip had provided: Jane. He decided to stuff what was left of his ego into his pocket, go to the bar, and see if Jane would be as happy to see him as he surely would be to see her.

Saturday – 9:15 pm

"Let's us clear something up first, yeah?" began Steve. "You say you know me? Know about me? How in the hell do you know anything about me?

Martin gave Steve an exasperated look before commencing, "Come on! The jig is up, Steve. You don't know me? You didn't wait for me at that damned convenience store every single time I came through town? You didn't take me to urgent care when I passed out? You didn't plant that book by Farber - what the hell was it called - *Lincoln*

County Days, just to fuck with me? How about that quitclaim deed on the damned courthouse, Steve? How the hell *could* I know about all of this stuff, and yet you say you've never met me?!" By the end of his soliloquy, Martin was practically screaming at Steve, much to the dismay of the other patrons inside the Brewery.

Steve stared straight into Martin's eyes, the way he used to as a beat cop, trying to determine the exact level of crazy with which he was about to deal. His years of detective work hadn't gone to waste, however, as he maneuvered his way into a better position in the conversation.

"So, Martin…it is Martin, right?" Getting a nod, Steve proceeded, "How many times is it that you've been here to Lincoln, again?"

Martin sneered and looked down the end of his nose at the big cowboy. "It's my *first* time here, okay?"

Steve let loose a broad smile, picked up his beer and downed a huge gulp, then set the glass loudly on the table in front of him. "Okay then, hoss, tell me again how it was that I was 'waiting for you at the convenience store' and 'took you to urgent care'?"

Martin's eyes darted around the room as if looking for an escape. How did he get so easily trapped into a question that he was now unable to answer? Steve folded his arms in front of him and said, "Hell, I can't wait to hear this."

Martin felt the blood rush from his head to all parts south, and his world started to spin. So weak did he become, it was as if he were hypoglycemic and there wasn't a sugar cube around for a thousand miles. He swooned in his chair for a few seconds before gathering himself enough to answer. "Look, Steve," he started, "I'm not even sure *what's* going on here. I just know that I know things about this place, about Billy, and about that book that I shouldn't know. My whole world has been thrown upside down since I got here. You're right, we've never met - except that in this Dream, or vision, or some damn thing, we have…and more than once."

The big cowboy looked at Martin with a friendly grin. This wasn't the first guy to come to Lincoln chasing the Kid and lose a little bit of his mind. While this nut seemed kookier than most, the one thing that nagged at Steve was that quitclaim deed on the courthouse. Just the day before, he'd talked to a lawyer about filing it and transferring title. The state had screwed up the title so badly over the years, and Steve wanted to have a little fun with the officials. Unless Martin was bugging his office, or Steve's lawyer ratted him out to a complete stranger, there was no way this big lunk from New Jersey could have, should have, known.

"Tell me about that book, about Magdalena. Please?" asked Martin.

Steve allowed the thought of the quitclaim deed, and his questions around it, to fade for the time being. He figured sharing some information with this distressed man might help him figure out just what the hell was going on. "What do you want to know?"

Martin dipped into his bag of memories and began. "That book, that *exact* copy, has been haunting me for a few days - or maybe years, I'm not sure anymore. It would have wound up in Magdalena, based upon what I know - or what I think I know." Martin shook his head with frustration at trying to explain himself. The fact that he couldn't tell what was real and what wasn't made communicating with Steve, Trisha, Kevin, and Farber all the more challenging. "Let me ask you this," he continued, "were you investigating 887 Kelly Road out there? Is that where you found the book?"

Steve stared at Martin, puzzled. "Kelly Road? No. I'm not even sure where that is. I've been looking for Ira Leonard's old papers, to see if that letter from Wallace to the Kid was in them. Leonard retired in Socorro, but apparently his wife moved to Magdalena after he died."

Ira Leonard? If that was the case, then where did Steve come across the book? Just as Martin was about to inquire further, the big cowboy added, "When I was at city hall, looking through some papers, that book had been shoved into a box of stuff labeled '1949,' which don't make a damn bit of sense, since Serge wrote it just a few years back."

The year '1949' struck Martin - in The Dream, that would have been the year that Maria Hidalgo passed away. Martin tried hard to understand whether what he was hearing was real, or if he just wanted it to be. "Where do you think the book came from? Why was it so beat up?" asked Martin innocently.

"Damned if I know, Martin," replied Steve. "I figured maybe it was a movie prop or something. I sent a picture of it to Serge when I found it. He seemed pretty surprised at what it looked like. Asked me to check inside the back cover for some list or something."

A list! Martin couldn't believe it! A list of the people that Billy planned on visiting after escaping from Garrett in 1881! "Was the list there? What was on it?" he asked eagerly.

Steve just shook his head. "Nope, no list. I'm not sure what Serge was looking for, but he sure thought I'd found it. Guess not. After that, I just threw the book in the truck and wound up giving it to the kid Kevin to read over. Figured it'd give him some inside juice on how to play Billy in the pageant tomorrow."

Martin's shoulders slumped a little bit at the news. If Billy's list wasn't in the book, then it wasn't Billy's book. If there was no list, then maybe there was no Billy after 1881, and maybe Martin's entire Dream was just that: a dream.

Never one to let a lead go without his further investigation, Steve had to ask: "Why'd you get so crazy over that old book? Maybe you know more about it than I do?"

Suddenly realizing his hair was unkempt from the earlier altercation, Martin pushed it back into place while he tried to figure out where to start. "I can't explain it very well, Steve, but I have reason to believe that Billy didn't die in Fort Sumner in '81. I think he married, went to Magdalena, and lived out his life there," Martin stated with enough authority that Steve's ears perked up. "Now I can't tell you how, and I know this sounds batshit crazy, but I think Billy had *that* book. His wife Maria would have died in 1949, and that's probably how it wound up in that box."

From the thousands of arrests that Steve had made in his career, he'd heard hundreds of crazy stories. This one wasn't any crazier than what some of the loons he'd locked up would tell. The difference was, this guy Martin wasn't trying to avoid being arrested or going to jail. He seemed sane, save for his outburst outside over an old book. But 'crazy' often *looked* sane, right up until it didn't. Steve wanted to let the man off easy, and with as little embarrassment as possible.

"Well, if you're right about the Kid, you're gonna kill Sumner's tourist money. They ain't gonna like that. As far as the book and all, I think we'll just agree it's a mystery that probably ain't gonna be solved." Steve looked seriously at Martin, trying to find the slightest recollection of ever meeting him before, but none was forthcoming. "Now, are we okay for you to go back out there? We're not gonna have any more fireworks, right, Martin?"

All of the fight had gone out of Martin anyway, even if he did still want to get his hands on that book. He nodded slowly to Steve and answered, "We're good. I apologize for all that."

"Good," responded Steve. He took his last swig of beer and stood up. "Nice meeting you, Martin. You take it easy tonight." And then he walked back out the door.
Martin also stood, prepared to leave as well. Seeing Farber coming in the front door, and wanting to avoid any further arguments, he headed out of the side door and down the steps. He hit the darkened street and walked east for a meeting with Lilly that he would give almost anything not to have to have.

Saturday – 9:25 pm

Carl Farber's disappointment at his debacle as a budding author washed over him like some sort of baptism of failure. Pressing through the Brewery crowd, he searched in vain for a spot at the bar where he could check in with his new friend Jane. While getting a few minutes to talk to her might not make anything better, it certainly wouldn't make it worse. The problem was, there were so many book-talk people here that those seats anywhere near the bar came at a premium. After a minute or two of walking back and forth, Carl almost decided to call it a night, but something told him that it would be worth it to stay.

With no better option, he determined to press forward to the bar and muscle his way into a beer, then sit patiently at one of the far tables until the place cleared out a bit. Wedging himself between a very-well-fed midwestern couple and three men who were probably old enough to have fought in the Lincoln County War, he waited patiently until Jane made her inevitable trip down the bar. As she did, he stuck his hand out with a grin on his face and much hope in his eyes.

Under extreme duress from the sheer number of people wanting to drink their cares away, the best Jane could manage was a tight smile as she flew by. It wasn't so much that she didn't say anything that bothered Farber, it was the *way* she didn't say anything that got under his skin. She certainly was finding a way to talk to other people spread out along the bar, even in her haste to tap beer and deliver drinks. Why just him? His bitter mood kept expanding, and he knew that spending any more time in this hopeless crowd wasn't going to help it improve. He finally decided that this crappy night just needed to end, so he turned away from the bar, trying to pick his way toward the door, when he felt a slap on his shoulder,

"We close at 2, meet me then!" said Jane, as she whisked away without another word. At that momentary reprieve from his disappointment, Carl checked his watch: 9:30 pm. There was no way he was going to hang around here for another four and a half hours. Weighing his options, he figured he could drive back to his motel, maybe even get a few hours of sleep, then return. He quickly nixed that plan, realizing if he fell asleep, at his age, there was very little likelihood that he was going out again in the middle of the night. If Farber knew anyone else in town, it would be easier, since at least he'd have someone to hang out with. As it was, the only person he knew was Martin Teebs, and the two had recently devolved into bitter enemies.

Finally, Carl decided that he'd walk up to the courthouse. Maybe he could catch some sleep on one of the long benches out front. It seemed fitting, really, that this night might end at the very symbol of the vaunted House of Murphy, the focus of his not-yet-completed book, which would now be shitcanned for eternity. As Farber stretched out on the bench, using his jacket as a pillow, he stared up at the underside of the balcony. The same balcony that the Kid had pranced and preened on after killing his guards Bell and Olinger.

For some reason, Farber suddenly felt anger. Two deputies just doing their jobs and then murdered in cold blood. Why did Billy Bonney think his life was somehow worth more than theirs? Lying here, just a few feet from where it all happened, Carl's attitude started to change. Maybe it was the shit with Martin, or maybe Bachaca stealing his book idea. Maybe even Jane's dismissal at the Brewery set him off. But for the first time, Carl Farber began to see a different side of the legend, Billy the Kid. No longer would he blindly lap up the 'Billy fought corruption' pablum that virtually every fan of the Kid believed. No, thought the history teacher, some of what Billy did was noble, but some of it was downright cowardly. Killing Brady from ambush, assassinating Morton and Baker, stealing horses and cattle just because he wanted them. Here, under the portal of the mighty House that Murphy and Dolan had built, Farber could finally see the truth about the young outlaw whom all of these people came to worship over this long weekend.

Billy the Kid was no noble Robin Hood. No...Billy the Kid...was a coward.

Saturday – 9:30 pm

"Don't worry none," bellowed Steve, as he approached Bachaca's table. "That guy just had an extreme case of mistaken identity with that book of yours, Kevin." The boy looked up at the much taller man and nodded with appreciation. He'd had just about enough of being confronted by some psycho tourist who couldn't distinguish between fantasy and reality.
"Thanks, Steve," the younger man said, "that guy's losing his grip. He called me 'Billy' at least a couple of times. I guess some of these people get down here and get lost in all this." Kevin waved his hand around the crowd, which was still lining up to get autographs on Bachaca's book.

"You know, son, that's some stone-cold truth," admitted Steve. "I've seen it before. These men - hell, women, too - come down after watching *Young Guns* too many times, and they can't get clear of what they seen on the screen. You try to tell 'em some truth, and they get all testy about it. The further they dig in, the more they believe whatever the hell they want to. I guess that old boy just wants to believe so bad in some story that don't exist, he's willing to look past good old common sense."

Kevin opened his book to view Bachaca's signature and grinned. It almost felt like a victory to still have the book in hand, signed by the author, after Martin's repeated efforts to get it away from him. The boy thumbed through the water-stained pages and figured that someday he should actually read the book. To this point, he'd absorbed whatever people in town told him about Billy. To portray the Kid at the Last Escape pageant tomorrow felt a little fraudulent to him since he really didn't know much about the real Billy. Checking his watch, he knew it was too late tonight to do any real reading or studying, so he resolved to read the book sometime over the next couple of weeks, before he left Lincoln and went back to Colorado.

Colorado, thought Kevin, what was he going to do back there? He'd graduated in the spring and bummed around hiking for a couple of months, before landing this gig. While he didn't see any future in tiny Lincoln, NM, he also struggled to see one in much-larger Boulder, CO. The housing prices there were outrageous, and the jobs that he could get fresh out of school wouldn't come close to allowing him to support himself. He'd toyed with the idea of becoming a professional poker player since he'd paid much of his way through school by playing online. 'Professional Gambler' seemed like the kind of thing that would interest women, were they to ask. "I can't solve this all tonight," he mumbled to himself, as he walked over to retrieve his backpack. Besides, Kevin didn't need to figure it out all on his own - he had plans to meet his younger brother Joseph in Denver at the end of the summer, and they would both plan their next moves.

Saturday - 9:40 pm

Martin carefully walked up the steps to the *casita's* portal. His secret hope was that Lilly had fallen asleep, and he might be able to bed down on the sofa so as not to wake her up. While there would still be hell to pay in the morning, at least he could pay it on a solid night's rest. However, his hopes were quickly dashed by the sight of Lilly sitting patiently on the couch, with a cup of tea, waiting for him to arrive. Needing to come up with a plan of attack, Martin decided that his best defense would be a good offense. "Listen, Lil, I'm really sorry about what ha…"

"Stop," she said quickly, not allowing him to finish his thought. "I spoke to Trisha tonight." Martin closed his eyes and stopped breathing for a moment, awaiting the opening salvo that would start the War Between the Teebs.

"She told me everything, Martin," said Lilly, with not enough emotion to betray what 'everything' actually meant.

Martin decided to wade back in before Lilly's reinforcements came to flanking positions. "Look, Lil, all we did was talk. I swear it. All I wan…"

"I know nothing happened. I know there's nothing there between you two, Martin. She told me that. She said she wanted nothing to do with this rift between you and Carl and just wanted to be left alone."

Martin tried to hide the sting of hurt in his eyes at Lilly's summation. Had Trisha really said that? She wanted to be left alone? Earlier this evening, she'd told him she wanted to talk. Her question about Rosita at the book talk made it plain that she also wanted to know more about the mysterious beauty. How could things change so quickly? Martin wondered. Just the previous night, he'd been able to unpack so many memories of the woman who was her spitting image. Trisha had been warm and understanding. To-night, she'd clearly wanted to know more, and now - that was all over? Martin's heart sank at the realization that he'd been creating Trisha into something to satisfy himself, but that the young woman wanted nothing to do with him or his crazy story.

"Yeah, I know," he finally responded in a dejected voice. "It was just that she looked exactly like the person I saw…that's all. There's nothing more to it."

Lilly patted the seat next to her on the sofa. "Martin, come here. Sit down, please." Figuring he'd dodged a bullet with Trisha, he decided that complying would be the best course of action. "Listen, hon, I didn't realize how this choking thing impacted you. I guess…I don't know, I figured it would just be over when you were okay, but I see that's not the case."

As much as Martin would like to have argued the point, he really couldn't. Something was going on in his head that he could neither explain nor control. If someone had asked him five minutes after he'd been saved from choking to death, he'd have said he was fine. Now he wasn't so sure.

"I think we need to get you to talk to someone. A professional who deals with these kinds of things," Lilly proposed reassuringly, "and I think we should probably leave tomorrow so we can do that."

Immediately, the calculator in Martin's head began to figure out how much this trip had cost, the expenses that would be incurred because of the change of flights, and what the chances were of him ever coming back to Lincoln again. While he accepted on some level that Lilly was right about Martin needing someone to talk to, he didn't feel the weight of urgency like she did. He'd at least like to complete the trip so he wouldn't have to wonder what all he'd missed while he was sitting and reading a Billy the Kid book, years from now.

"You're right, Lil. That thing messed me up more than I realized. I'm not even sure what's been making me act the way I have for the past couple of days." Lilly reached her hand into his and held it tightly. He continued, "But it's not something urgent where we have to leave tomorrow, okay? I'm good to stay and finish our trip. I really want to see that Escape thing tomorrow, and maybe have Monday to relax without all the crowds." Martin looked directly at his wife while saying this, in the hope of assuring her he'd be fine.

"But, Martin, you were like a madman before! I've never seen that side of you in twenty years! I can't have you just snap like that on innocent strangers."

Martin breathed a very deep sigh, not only for himself, but also to show Lilly how calm he was in the face of her implication. "I know. That was awful. Total case of mistaken identity, and I'm completely to blame. I talked to that big guy, Steve, and we worked it all out. He's pretty nice, actually. Lil, I promise you it's not going to happen again. Tomorrow, we'll see a few sights, watch the show, and then come back here for a quiet dinner. Just you and me. What do you say?"

Lilly looked at her husband with a mix of worry and skepticism, but she had to admit that he sounded like he was in control. She figured if he could pass two simple tests, then she could be convinced that he'd hold it together for another couple of days. "Okay then, but tomorrow, I want you to apologize to both Carl and that boy Kevin. You were completely out of line with both of them. All right?"

An immediate disdain at even hearing Farber's name shot through Martin's body like an electrical shock. He tried not to pull his hand away from Lilly's, lest he let on how badly he was taking the news. If he did want to stay, however, those were the ground rules, and he concluded it was better to eat a little crow than to waste a bunch more money to avoid them.

"Okay, Lil, that's fair. I know Kevin is in that Escape thing, so I'll make sure to find him. I don't know much about where Carl is staying, but if he's there, I'll do the same."

Happy that her old reliable Martin seemed to be back, Lilly kissed him on the cheek and rested her head on his shoulder. Martin was glad that from her vantage point, she couldn't see his visage roiling with disgust at having to face Farber.

If he could just get through tomorrow with nothing bad happening, he just might be able to save this trip. One day, no drama, no surprises.

How hard could that be?

Saturday – 10 pm

"Hey, you can't sleep here," said Kevin, with as much authority as he could muster at the prone figure on a bench outside of the courthouse. Walking back to retrieve his car and drive to his two-room rental in Capitan, the youth had spotted what might have been a drunk tourist snoozing under the portal. The man - it appeared to be a man - didn't stir, and Kevin began to wonder whether this night was about to go even farther south than it already had.

"Mister, you can't sleep here," Kevin repeated, gently shaking the tourist awake. As he stirred, the sleeping man removed from his face the hat with which he'd been blocking the light. "Mr. Farber?" asked Kevin, surprised. "Are you okay?"

Farber tried to shake the sleep from his eyes. He was having trouble understanding where he was, and how long he'd been asleep, when the twisted little face of Billy Bonney appeared before him. "*You,*" he growled at the young man, "what are *you* doing here?"

"What? I work here, sir." responded a puzzled Kevin, wondering if he was going to again get into it with yet another old Billy the Kid nut on this night.

Farber seemed even more confused about where he was, as well as the identity of the young man who'd awakened him from a sound slumber. "Where am I? How long was I out?" he asked.

Kevin looked around for any backup, just in case the man was on drugs, but finally replied, "You're at the courthouse, but you can't sleep here, Mr. Farber. I don't know how long you've been here. It's ten o'clock."

Farber's irrational disdain for the young man puzzled Carl, but he didn't fight it. Whatever anger he had held inside from the events of the night washed out right there on the porch. "You woke me up already? For what? Who am I bothering out here, Bil…I mean, Kevin?"

Kevin sighed again. What the hell was with these old guys? Here he was, just a kid doing his job, and he was getting crap for it from two doughy dolts who probably couldn't get laid in a room full of whores, with a mountain of cash. Finally, after two nights of abuse, he snapped: "Listen! The monument is closed, get it? Now, you can sleep anywhere else you want, where someone won't call the sheriff, but you cannot sleep here! Is that clear, Mr. Farber?"

Farber's eyes went wide as the mild-mannered kid changed before his eyes. The volume of his missive was enough that Farber was concerned a neighbor might indeed call the sheriff, and rather than spending the night in his motel or on the courthouse bench, he might spend it in the current Lincoln County jail. Annoyed, he scowled at the boy. "All right, all right! Don't get in a tizzy. I'm leaving," Farber grumbled, as he put on his hat and jacket and strode off the porch.

Kevin's heartbeat was still racing from the confrontation, and he eased his grip on the book in his backpack. He had decided that if the older man attacked him, he might use the book as a weapon of sorts. Farber glared at the boy one more time and then slipped into his rental ride, threw up a shower of gravel while making a u-turn, and floored the tiny, four-cylinder engine on his way back to Capitan.

Finally, Kevin could breathe easier, and he let the book slip back to the bottom of his bag. He did wonder how effective a book would be as a weapon, especially this frail book, and especially against a man like Carl Farber.

Saturday – 10:03 pm

"Damn kid!" screamed Farber into the tiny void of his rental. "Messing up my plans with Jane!" Reasoning that his night definitely was over, Farber pointed the car right toward his Capitan motel. Although he had no idea what the night (or early morning) with Jane would have held, he didn't have it in him to sit around for another four hours.

As he drove on the twisting road the ten miles to his destination, he reflected on how badly the weekend had gone. Just the night before, he was taking the Lincoln After Dark tour, making new friends, and getting all sorts of unexpected attention from a beautiful barmaid. Here he was, some twenty-four hours later, his book dreams were shattered, his burgeoning friendship with fellow New Jersian Martin Teebs had disappeared, he'd missed his chance for some real quality time with Jane, and, for some inexplicable reason, dark thoughts of Billy the Kid continued to cloud his brain. If this trip was supposed to be the pinnacle of something wonderful, all it turned out to be was the culminating destruction of his admiration of the Kid. With every passing mile, Farber's thoughts grew darker, wondering how many times that little coward Billy Bonney had ridden this road, tail between his legs, running from the *real* powers of Lincoln County.

Farber had one more day, Sunday, to experience Lincoln before his flight home on Monday. All that was left for him now was to watch the Kid's Last Escape played out three times over. He held out little hope that he'd enjoy any of it, but wondered whether maybe fate would intervene, and somebody would flip the script.

"Imagine that, huh?" he said in the quiet car. "Maybe tomorrow will be the one time that Billy *doesn't* get away." Farber pictured the reenactment going in a far different way than most people were expecting to see. In his vision, Bell bravely fights off the Kid, and a stray gunshot alerts Olinger. Running across the street, Olinger scoops up his shotgun, tells Bell to move, and puts both barrels into Bonney. The two deputies clap each other on the back over the body of the lifeless coward, and Olinger quips, "Look there, I just saved the county the cost of a good piece of hemp! Maybe Garrett'll give me a raise!"

SUNDAY 6 AM

Rolling and thrashing in her bedsheets, Trisha finally determined to just get up. She'd been tossing and turning for over two hours, and the possibility of sleep had long since faded away. On a desperately needed day off, she had planned to sleep in and practice some self-care, but the stubborn morning sun was already peeking into the valley, commanding her to rise. For hours, she'd rehashed last night's conversation on the street with Lilly Teebs. While Trisha felt better that the woman didn't think she was trying to steal her husband, Martin Teebs had dragged her into a quagmire that she couldn't seem to escape. She'd planned to ask the man a number of pointed questions about his 'dream' and his 'Rosita,' when the coast was clear. The only problem was, the coast had never gotten clearer, and so Trisha had wound up leaving. Assuming that the tourists would be heading out of town tomorrow - the day after the pageant ended - today would be her only chance to learn more about the nagging doubts that Martin had planted in her head. If she saw him with his wife, all bets were off. Trisha wasn't going down *that* road again. If, however, she could grab a few minutes alone, she absolutely intended to do it.

Her fall-back plan was not as immediate, but might still help her accomplish her goal. She knew the Teebs were staying at the Patron House. While Trisha didn't know the owners well, she'd seen Darlene and Dallas Jones enough times around town to be on a 'wave and smile' basis with them. In fact, Trisha was reasonably sure that Dallas had made a pass at her when she'd first arrived in town - and might even have implied that his wife also would be into a rendezvous. That type of behavior, coming from so deep in the middle of nowhere, was shocking to her, and it held no appeal.

Trisha knew that a simple batting of her eyes, or a quick, "Let's go," would be enough for her to get the attention of any man. Her beauty had been a staple throughout her short life, and she was aware that it could bring the kind of temptations that could spoil her life. To that end, she'd only ever really dated two boys - one in high school and one during her sophomore year at UCLA. After each relationship had ended, she had gone on a few dates, but found that the men who were available to her were not the type of marrying material that she longed to meet someday. In any event, she felt she could safely sweet-talk Dallas into providing an email address for Martin Teebs, or maybe even a cell phone number. There was no need for her and Martin to have this Rosita/ dream conversation in person. Getting answers via a text message would suit Trisha just fine.

With nothing better to do until the rest of the village woke up, Trisha slipped into a pair of running shorts and a sports bra, tied her hair back, and pulled on her running shoes. From her house to the courthouse and back was just about two and half miles, so she decided to run it twice. Five miles to get the day started. Five miles to kill some time until she could get some answers. Five miles directly through the heart of the Lincoln County War, and the chance to save her doppelganger from a historical exile that Trisha was sure the woman didn't deserve.

Stepping into the coolness of the morning air, the sun just peeking over the mountaintops, Trisha was invigorated. While the feeling wasn't the same as breathing in the salty breeze from the beach at Santa Monica, it was clean and fresh, and it gave her hope that this day would work out exactly as she wished. She started running an easy pace into town, quickly coming upon the Patron House. She allowed herself to look left, just in case either Martin or perhaps Dallas might be up and about. Not only was there no sight of either man, but there didn't seem to be a single soul stirring in town on this early Sunday morning.

Her pace increasing, Trisha scooted along the street that she'd come to know so well. Passing by buildings that held more history than most people could imagine, she wondered: If this Rosita had actually existed, where had she lived? Which stores had she shopped in? Where was she during the War? Somehow, her conversation with Martin had awakened her curiosity about Rosita Luna, and now she wanted to learn everything she could. If Sergio Bachaca had never heard of the young woman, though, it didn't seem probable that she had ever lived. That guy had forgotten more about the Lincoln County War than Trisha would ever know.

Trisha's thoughts carried her all the way to the courthouse, and before she knew it, she was flying back toward her own house. Still no one broke the veil of silence that had descended upon Lincoln. Trisha ran ever faster, her lungs screaming in the thin mountain air, and her imagination on fire for what this day might bring.

Sunday – 6:30 am

Lilly stepped out onto the portal, having fetched one of the thick bathrobes that Darlene and Dallas thoughtfully supplied for their guests to ward off the chill. While she had slept peacefully after her conversation with Martin, he reported that he'd tossed and turned all night. Eventually, sleep no longer an option, he arose and retrieved the tray of breakfast goodies that Darlene must have left just a few minutes prior. With the cool morning air beginning to stimulate his brain, Martin smiled at his wife and poured her a steaming cup of coffee.

"Thanks, hon," Lilly said. "Sorry you didn't sleep well. Too much on your mind?"

If Lilly only knew, thought Martin. His mind had been working overtime since the evening they'd arrived in Lincoln. The nights he slept well were out of pure exhaustion, and the nights he didn't were in spite of it.

"Yeah, but you know all about that. Nothing new or different," he said, through his narrowed eyes.

Lilly just smiled and raised her coffee cup in a toast. "Here's to a great day and to putting the bad stuff behind us, eh, Martin?"

Martin raised his glass weakly and took a sip to show he was on board with the concept of this being a much better day than the three previous had been. "Cheers," he said, "and here's to Billy's final Escape, played out in live action three times today." Lilly laughed at the joke, as Martin continued, "Run, Kid, run, and don't let them catch you this time."

Sunday – 6:35 am

Carl Farber resembled nothing if not a giant burrito, wrapped as he was in the sheets and thin blanket at his Capitan motel. Last night, he'd turned the air conditioner to its polar-ice-cap setting; by early morning, the room could be forgiven if it had been covered in frost. Every time Farber awoke, he'd spin further into his cocoon, hoping at some point the chill would be abated. By now, he knew that wouldn't work, so he finally unencumbered himself, dashed over to the wall unit, and turned it off. Diving back into the warmish bed, he made some mental plans for the upcoming day. He was in no rush to get back to Lincoln, early as it was. Carl absolutely did intend to watch Billy's Last Escape, if for no other reason than to cement into his own mind his new image of the Kid. The show ran three times that day: 11 am, 1 pm, and 3 pm. Farber assumed the last show would be the most lightly attended, as a number of these tourists probably needed to get back to wherever they had come from in order to be ready for work on Monday morning.

Once having selected the 3 pm Escape, Carl went about calculating how to fill the rest of his morning, now that he didn't have anyone to fill it with. Eventually, he opted to rise, shower, and get himself some breakfast in town. There were a couple of restaurants along the main road, and he was sure that their coffee was better than the dingy brown water that his ancient, hotel-room coffee maker continued to offer him.

Sunday – 6:40 am

Kevin opened his eyes once - or, more accurately, *attempted* to open them - before allowing them to fall tightly closed again. For the first day in a week, he didn't need to be up early for work; yet for some reason, a good night's sleep had evaded him. Today, his only responsibility was to portray the young outlaw Billy Bonney three times in The Last Escape of Billy the Kid. He'd been studying the script, as it were, for the better part of two weeks. He knew people were serious about this stuff, and he wanted to step up and represent the Kid in the light that his fans would expect. Still, he didn't need to be in Lincoln for hours, and another block of sleep would be welcomed. As he lay there, hoping the sandman would reclaim him, his phone on the bedside table buzzed. At first, he just scrunched his eyes more tightly closed, until it happened again and again. Realizing that whoever thought it was so important to be texting him at this ungodly hour probably was not about to give up, he reached over and grabbed his phone.

Brandon: Dude, you awake?

Kevin: Ugh…I am now.

Brandon: You ready for the show? You can't screw this up.

Kevin: I'm NOT going to screw up!

Brandon: Let's meet at that breakfast place on Main. 7 am. I'm buying.

Kevin: I'm not hungry.

Brandon: Well, I am! And I want to go over the script with you.

Kevin: Bro, I got this. What's with the full-court press?

Brandon: Dude, if you screw up, people don't come back. That affects my business.

Kevin: Ye of little faith.

Brandon: Ye of little Billy knowledge.

Kevin: Fine, but give me til 7:15.

Brandon: Cool, I'll let Steve know, too.

Kevin: Steve? The cowboy?

Brandon: Yeah. He knows more about Billy than anyone around here.

Kevin: Whatever. See you in a few.

Brandon: Late….

Kevin rolled out of bed and turned on the shower, which seemed to take a ridiculously long time to offer any hot water. He looked over at the chair with his wardrobe draped over it. Each piece had been either selected or created to match what Billy had worn in the famous photograph taken in front of Beaver Smith's saloon. Even if his acting sucked, at least he'd look like the Kid, he thought. For half a second, he considered wearing his costume to the restaurant. Amused, he imagined how Brandon, Steve, and whoever else was there having breakfast would react when the real, live Billy the Kid strode in, ready to kill Bell and Olinger all over again.

Sunday – 6:55 am

"Good morning, Teebs family!" enthusiastically chirped Darlene Jones, as she spied her guests enjoying their breakfast out on the portal.

If Martin truly remembered anything about The Dream, he definitely recollected the hypersexual behavior of the hosts of the B&B in which he and Lilly were staying. To this point, though, he'd not seen any such conduct - in fact, Dallas and Darlene had been a non-factor for most of the weekend, busy as they were with a full house of guests.

Lilly raised her cup of coffee in appreciation, declaring, "Excellent breakfast…thank you, Darlene!" to which, their hostess grinned happily.

As she approached the portal, Darlene jogged up the three stairs, which made it clear to Martin that her breasts were free of any restraint except the thin silk T-shirt she wore. "Hey, Lilly," she said breathlessly, "what do you and this big guy have planned for tomorrow?"

Due to Martin's uncertain mental state, Lilly hadn't even considered making any plans, so sure she had been that the couple would already be on its way home to New Jersey. "Well," she said, glancing at her husband, "I don't know that we planned anything… yet?" Martin just smiled and shrugged his shoulders, an encouragement for Darlene to proceed.

"Tomorrow, two of the ladies in the main house and I are going to Ruidoso for a lunch-cooking-type thing. It's from some American-Asian fusion chef who just opened a place down there. Would you like to join us? It'll be fun, and there's wine!" Darlene hopped and clapped a little on the tail end of her sales pitch, which generously provided Martin yet another glimpse at her unbound breasts, celebrating the occasion.

With some concern, Lilly gazed over at Martin. Would he be okay on his own? she wondered. Of course, if he held true to his promise to apologize today to all concerned, things would likely be fine. Although Lilly was indeed looking forward to the day's

Escape reenactment, she figured that by the conclusion of that event, she'd already have had enough of Billy the Kid to last her for some time. A jaunt out with the ladies, drinking wine, learning to cook a fusion lunch, maybe even a little shopping not from a touristy curio shop - it all sounded pretty good to Lilly.

"Well, I…" Lilly began, before Martin jumped in.

"She'd love to. Go, Lil. Have some fun that's outside of tiny old Lincoln. I'll be fine here, and the crowds will be all gone."

Lilly smiled gratefully at her husband, and, with a twinkle in her eyes, she nodded to Darlene. "Okay then," said Darlene frantically, "we need to get you signed up right now! Here, we can do it online. Do you have your phone?"

While Darlene and Lilly began pecking away at a website to register for the class, Martin felt enough of a reprieve to excuse himself to walk off his breakfast. Lilly glanced up only long enough to say, "Bye, hon," before she went back to talking excitedly with Darlene about their big day out.

Sunday – 7 am

Martin Teebs shuffled his way down to the only road, still peaceful as many of the more spiritual types were either at church service or preparing to attend. With no plan other than to walk and clear his mind, he headed west, toward the main part of Lincoln, treading just on the edge of the paved street. *This* was the village he had been hoping to see when he first booked the trip. Martin had badly misjudged just how crowded the tiny town would become during Old Lincoln Days, and he felt that he'd barely gotten to 'know' anything about it since arriving. The closest he'd had to experiencing some quiet contemplative time had been those few minutes he went walking after nearly choking to death on Darlene's enchiladas. And even those few minutes were marred by a rampaging truck, and then…

Then, of course, Rosita had come to him, like out of a dream. As far as Martin had figured out so far, it actually *was* a dream; but in that moment, everything had seemed entirely real. A bittersweet feeling welled up inside him as he remembered the moment when Rosita had thrown her arms around him, and they'd tumbled to the ground. Her eyes sparkled like diamonds; he saw the love in them reflected back at him.

His Dream, cloudy and fragmented until then, came into sharp focus. Every single detail of what seemed like a years-long adventure raced to line up in his mind, all in perfect order. His faithful friend Billy, his great love Rosita, his Regulator buddies, and, of course, that piece-of-crap Farber. What most amused and bemused Martin was that the real-life people he'd met during this trip to Lincoln actually bore little resemblance to The Dream versions. Trisha was a gorgeous young woman, kind and friendly, but with zero interest in Martin. Kevin knew next to nothing about Billy the Kid and seemed to shrink from any kind of confrontation. Farber was a mild-mannered school teacher and hadn't called Martin 'cupcake' or any other silly name in the days since they met. And Steve…

Steve. The man didn't seem to recognize Martin at all. The big cowboy wasn't creepy and didn't seem to be hiding any secrets. If anything, during their talk at the bar last night, Martin had felt as if *he* was the secretive one, while Steve was just doing his job, bodyguarding author Sergio Bachaca.

Not one of the people he had met had lived up to The Dream version, and for some reason, that made Martin sad. As crazy and dangerous as his life in The Dream had been, it was full and robust. There were challenges to overcome, new skills to learn, and death to be defied nearly every day. *Martin Teebs, bland middle manager,* became *Martin Teebs, Regulator* - now, a successful sales rep and, most importantly, a guy who could be counted on when the chips were down. Martin sighed heavily and accepted the fact that his lot in life had already been drawn, and this, his current life, was it.

If Martin was honest with himself, the thing he missed most was, of course, Rosita. Even during the earliest days of their relationship Lilly had never looked at him the way Rosita did. Although he and Lilly were in love, he couldn't remember a time when his breath left his body and his heart threatened to follow, like it did when he saw Rosita Luna. Perhaps it was because, in real life, Lilly had had options. Dozens of men had wanted to date her when she met Martin. However, Rosita, at least The Dream version, only waited for one man with whom to spend the rest of her life. The chance that somehow that one man would arrive in tiny Lincoln was incredibly small. But then one day, there he was. The single-minded purpose of Rosita - only to be happy with

Martin and make him happy in return - was a crushing depression on him, knowing that in his real world, she'd never exist.

As he neared the Visitor Center, his dejection worsened. In his Dream, this building near the street would not have been here. Instead, this was the very spot where two small shacks had stood, and the one with the blue door had held a fascination for Martin that would have lasted him the rest of his days.

While walking here on Wednesday night, Martin had begun to feel sick from what he thought was the enchiladas; now, he suspected it was sadness. After being blown into a ditch by the truck, Martin rose and, well - his entire world changed. In the split-second that their lips had touched, Martin hadn't been able to even utter her name, but he longed to hear Rosita once more call out…

"Martin!"

Martin jerked his head around in surprise, trying to find the source of the sound.

"Martin! Hey, Martin!"

For a moment, Martin was caught between fantasy and reality: a beautiful woman was approaching him rapidly, with a big grin on her face. He wanted to pretend that it was Rosita who was running up Lincoln's lone street to jump into his arms forever, but the SoCal accent pierced his Dream world, aided by the running shorts and sports bra. This...was Trisha.

"Hey," huffed the young woman, out of breath from her run, "what are you doing out here all alone?"

The sudden pivot from Martin's Dream to his real world shook him, and it took a moment for him to respond. "Oh, Lilly's just doing something with Darlene, so I thought I'd take a walk while it's quiet.

"Okay, I don't want to bother you if you're..."

"No. No bother at all, Trisha, what's up?" Martin interjected quickly.

Trisha pointed her hand back down the street, from the direction she just arrived. "Well, can we walk?" The two near-strangers set off, heading to the west.

"I talked to Lilly last night. You probably know that, huh?" Trisha asked, hoping that Martin hadn't been on the receiving end of a jealous wife all night.

"Yeah," he began slowly, "she told me about it. Look, Trisha, I didn't mean to get you involved in my issue. I'm really sorry for that. I know you don't want or need to be a part of this, and you should just forget about what I said. It's all just, well, kind of silly."

"No, Martin," the young woman stated resolutely, "it's *not* silly, and like it or not, I *am* a part of it now." Martin swallowed hard and looked at her, wondering exactly what she meant. "That stuff you told me, about Rosita, about Farber…all of it. I can't let it go now. I tried. I haven't been sleeping. I need to know who this woman was and what happened to her. You heard Bachaca last night, he's never even heard of her - but something tells me you're right, and he's wrong."

Martin was nearly blown away by her admission. Up until now, he'd been alone on an island of lunacy. Everyone who *should* have known *something* about the story didn't, and even Martin's own wife questioned his sanity. Suddenly, Martin felt he had an ally. Someone who didn't believe he was nuts and who actually wanted to help him process the incredible Dream he'd had. Still, he didn't feel right, dragging her into something that he couldn't be sure was even real. "Listen, Trisha, I appreciate that. I told you as much as I could or…should. Anyway, this is my thing to deal with, whatever it is. This really doesn't concern you."

"Doesn't it?" demanded the beautiful young woman. "Really, Martin? Look at me! I'm here in Lincoln fucking New Mexico! What am I doing here? I'm a California girl. I spend my summers on Huntington Beach and in LA. That's what I do, Martin. Two months ago, I would never have known this place existed, and all of a sudden…poof... here I am. Oh, and at the exact time as some guy from New Jersey almost chokes to death and dreams that I'm the great love of his life. So much so that when he sees me for the first time, he calls me Rosita! Who the hell is Rosita, Martin?! Who is she, and why am I here?!"

Martin was stunned by the outburst. Hoping that no one around was in earshot, he studied Trisha's defiant face. She demanded answers, but Martin didn't have them. He figured he'd try to lie his way out of it. "I could have just made that name up? You know, you're really pretty, Trisha. Maybe when I walked into that museum, I just saw this hot girl and wanted to make some small talk, so I just picked a name out of thin air. How about that? You wanted the truth about Rosita? Well, there it is…"

"That's a lie, Martin, and we both know it," interrupted Trisha, now having regained her composure. "I saw your eyes when you looked at me. I saw the emotion in them. You're in love, Martin, so deeply that you can't possibly hide it. No one is that good an actor. *You're* certainly not."

Martin stood there, heart beating nearly out of his chest. He was in love, but certainly not with *Trisha*. The fact that she so easily saw through him either meant that they had some special connection - or that Lilly would soon see the same things that the young woman did, and all the counseling in the world wouldn't save him.

"You're right," Martin sadly agreed, "you're right."

Trisha's eyes started to tear at Martin's admission. He looked so sad, so fragile, that she thought he might break. "What can I do to help you, Martin?"

Martin just shook his head and replied, "You can't. I'm lost here. I'm alone. I'm in love with someone who isn't even real, and I can't bridge the gap. You can't help *that*, Trisha." Martin looked into her big, brown eyes, so much like Rosita's that it was scary. "You asked why you're here? Probably to torture me. Whatever sins I've committed to deserve this, whoever did this to me, probably put you here to remind me of what I'm never, ever going to have."

Trisha wiped the sting of tears from her eyes and gently reached up to touch Martin's cheek, causing him to jump. "Martin. I'm not a curse, and I'm not here to torture you. I want to help. Please, let me help you find this woman. You need to find her, and now I do too…."

Sunday – 7:30 am

Already seated with a steaming cup of coffee in front of him, Steve let his eyes wander around the restaurant to see who was who. Most of the faces he recognized, but there were a few who were clearly tourists, here for Old Lincoln Days, and who would most likely be moving on after today. Steve would be happy for his quiet little town to become quiet again. Capitan was famous for being the home and burial site of Smokey Bear, but not much else.

Other than when an event in Lincoln drew a crowd overlapping into Capitan, the sleepy small town where everyone knew everyone's name was Steve's idea of paradise. The old cowboy loved the history of the area and, even more so, loved the mystery of it. Totally unconvinced that Pat Garrett had shot and killed BIlly the Kid in 1881, Steve kept an open mind, as researchers, authors, and TV talking heads introduced new information to explain the various ending stories of William H. Bonney. That guy from last night, Teebs, had told him a doozy: the Kid had lived in Magdalena, of all places, and died there sometime in the '40s. While Steve wished that tale were true - owing to his own proximity to the tiny town and the chance to be first on the scene of a major investigative breakthrough - he tended to think that Teebs was just losing his grip on reality. The cowboy had seen it so many times that it didn't even surprise him anymore. One of these middle-aged dolts latched on to some 'alternative facts' about Billy and then went running off on a wild tangent about what eventually happened to the Kid. Steve knew that if you told yourself a lie often enough, it would eventually become 'the truth,' and he surmised that Teebs was suffering from this same affliction. However, he couldn't completely write off the guy for one single, solitary reason...

The courthouse.

Not two days ago, Steve had sat in his office with an attorney, signing a quitclaim deed on the building in a complicated legal maneuver that would allow someone in his family to claim title on it. For the cowboy, it was all in fun, and something in which to rub the Santa Fe politician's noses. Eventually, of course, he'd deed it back to the State of New Mexico, where it belonged; and maybe the state would be a little more forthcoming in supporting some of his own investigations. The problem with all of this was: No one, not a soul outside of himself and his lawyer Albert Bretz, knew about his plan or the cloudy title to the courthouse.

Immediately after talking to Teebs, Steve had texted Bretz: Who did you tell? The answer came back as expected: No one. So how the hell could this middle-aged maniac from New Jersey know anything about any of this? The question had so tormented the former cop that he hadn't slept a wink last night. He was on edge, like someone was watching him and using the information gleaned to get the better of him. He'd spent his entire career knowing more than the guy he was chasing, and this Teebs had turned the tables on him. It didn't sit well with Steve, and he was determined to figure out how it had happened.

The bells hanging on the restaurant's old leaded-glass door rang out as two young men entered the place, scouring the tables for Steve. Spotting him, Brandon and Kevin slid into the opposite side of the booth and greeted the old cowboy. "Brandon," said Steve, offering the man his knuckles. "And what's up with you, young gun?" Kevin smiled and stuck his hand out for a shake, and the three men settled down into a pleasant conversation.

"Kevin here needs a few tips to really capture what Billy was like, you think you can help? Brandon asked Steve, the resident Billy the Kid expert.

"Well, hell," sighed Steve, looking at the young man who'd need to channel the Kid three times today. "If you go by what his friends wrote, he was a happy-go-lucky kid who liked to sing, dance, and joke around. Now, if you go by what his enemies wrote, well…there ain't much of that since most of 'em wound up dead."

The three men laughed in unison, so loudly that they spurred the curiosity of another man, who'd been enjoying his breakfast at the other side of the room. Looking up from his runny eggs, Carl Farber spied the giant cowboy hat that could only belong to Steve, and then noticed that the man wasn't alone. At the sight of Kevin, a feeling of disgust shot through Farber. However, today was a new day, and he decided to give the little dweeb another chance.

"Hey, guys, heard you laughing and thought I'd come say hello," said Farber, having crossed the room to stand over the booth.

Brandon rolled his head to the side and recognized his tour client. "Hey, Carl! How ya doing, man? Want to sit down?" Although Steve hadn't invited any company to sit next to him, he looked up to see what the balding man was going to do.

"Nooo, noooo," said Farber, "I don't want to intrude. Besides, I'm almost done with my breakfast, anyway." Then, turning to Steve, he continued, "That was something last night, with that dope Martin, huh? What the hell was his problem?"

Steve looked up at Farber and wondered how the man knew about Teebs. He must have been somewhere in line to have seen all the commotion. "Yeah, just a little confusion," offered Steve, "and a 'case of mistaken identity' is all," using air quotes to punctuate the phrase.

"Yeah, well. I've seen and heard enough about Martin Teebs in the past few days to know that nothing is a 'mistake' with him. He's an ass and doesn't care who he hurts with his bullshit stories."

Something in Carl's speech struck Kevin. Who the hell was this guy to talk down about Martin when Farber himself had been skulking around Lincoln for hours the night before and had to be shown out of town? Kevin couldn't resist just a little dig. "Did you get back to your motel okay? That bench you were sleeping on didn't seem too comfortable," he offered, with a big, fake grin.

Carl sneered as Brandon and Steve looked on, puzzled by the two men's apparent antagonism. "I got back just fine, thank you," retorted Farber.

Wanting to break the tension, Brandon jumped into the fray. "So, Carl, you going to watch Kevin in the Last Escape today? It's gonna be great, and I'm playing Bell."

Farber scratched at his neck as he pondered his answer. Of course, he was going to go to the reenactment. He was two thousand miles from home for the first time ever, and he wanted to see everything he could. On the other hand, he didn't want to give that sniveling little Kevin the satisfaction of letting him know that, yes, Carl would indeed be in attendance.

"Yeah," said Farber offhandedly. "I didn't know you were going to be in it, Brandon. It'll be worth it just for that." Kevin rolled his eyes, and Brandon laughed. Farber started to leave, but quickly turned back, as if he'd suddenly had a brilliant idea. "You know, Brandon, everybody already knows how this thing ends. Why not have *Bell* kill the *Kid*, just once, huh? Now that would make some headlines!" With that, Farber walked away. Kevin just looked at the other two men and shook his head.

Sunday – 8 am

With Lincoln coming to life and Trisha having run off to her own home, Martin ambled back toward the Patron House, trying to make sense of what had just happened. He almost felt bad, like he'd sentenced the young woman to the same game of 'is it real?' that he was now forced to play. To Martin, trading phone numbers with Trisha felt like cheating because he had no intention of telling Lilly. This was no passionate tryst between Martin and Trisha - it was a quest, a quest for truth, if such truth even existed. Once the boundaries of communication had been breached, there was no need for the two to make any plans about what would come next. Martin could simply text Trisha anytime with remembrances, discoveries, or insights that might solve the one-hundred-forty-year-old puzzle of Rosita Luna.

As he approached a flock of tourists, Martin walked with a certain swagger. *He* had the phone number of the most beautiful girl in Lincoln in his cell; did anyone else? It wasn't lost on Martin that he'd now scored the Belle of Lincoln in both past and present - although the 'present' version wasn't anywhere near the relationship he'd had with Rosita.

Entering their *casita*, he saw Lilly flitting about, picking up things with an energy he hadn't seen in days.

"Hey!" she called upon seeing her husband. "Where'd you go?"

Martin determined that he could tell the truth without telling the *whole* truth, so help him God. 'I just walked the main drag and back. It was pretty quiet out there for once…it was pleasant."

"Great. I'm so excited about tomorrow. It'll be a fun change of pace from being here in Lincoln. What will you do all day, Martin?" asked Lilly.

Truthfully, Martin hadn't thought that far ahead, so satisfied was he in having formed an alliance with Trisha. His real focus was to enjoy today's festivities and try to make enough amends to Farber and Kevin for Lilly to back off from watching him like a hawk.

"I'm not sure, Lil. The down time will probably be nice, after all of these tourists clear out," Martin mused. "Maybe I'll go to the gym with Dallas and work on my pecs!" If the joke had been intended to make Lilly laugh, it fell well wide of the mark. In fact, she seemed almost annoyed by it, casting Martin a sideways glance that made him uncomfortable enough not to ask why he was its recipient. "Anyway, I'll be just fine here. I want you to go and have fun with the ladies. Take as much time as you need!"

"I will," said Lilly. "What time do you want to go see that show thingy today?"

From people around town, Martin had heard that the first two shows of the day - 11 am and 1 pm - would be the most crowded, with many folks coming early and sitting around in the hot sun for almost an hour, just to guarantee themselves a seat. By 3 pm, the majority of the day-trippers would be heading out, and seats would be easier to come by. Bursting as he was with excitement over the morning's activities, however, he wasn't at all sure he could sit still for another seven hours.

"Let's plan on the one at three o'clock, Lil. The crowds will be lighter, and we won't have to stand around in the hot sun, waiting for a seat. Sound good?" Martin asked.

Over the past few days, Lilly had had her fill of Billy the Kid, and she welcomed some time to focus on other things before spending an hour watching some actors pretend to be heroic warriors of the Lincoln County War. "Sure, that sounds fine, Martin," she replied. "I'm going to head over to the main house for a while. Darlene wants to introduce me to the ladies we'll be going with tomorrow. That okay with you?"

"Uh, sure. Of course, I mean," said Martin, as he tried to both answer and figure out what to do with himself at the same time. "Maybe I'll just go down and watch the early show to see how it goes. I can apologize to Kevin, too - just like I said I would."

If Lilly remembered anything about her command that Martin apologize to the men he'd wronged, it had been vanquished by her delight at being able to get out of Lincoln for a day. At the current moment, she really didn't care to whom Martin apologized or whatever he did this morning, just so long as he was happy and otherwise occupied. "Sounds great, hon, have fun. I'm going to jump in the shower!"

Martin's head bobbed up and down, congratulating himself on earning some small amount of freedom. When Lilly was done, he'd shower and dress, and then hit the lone street of Lincoln. A smile spread across his face at the thought of having some hours where no one was watching him nor expecting him to be somewhere. Martin felt... well, *light*, for the first time in days. Grabbing a mug and pouring himself a last cup of coffee, he sensed a vibration in his pocket as he sat down. Pulling his phone out, he saw the green icon of a text message and a single line:

"Can you come to my house for a few minutes this morning?"

It was marked from contact 'T' - from Trisha.

Sunday – 8:30 am

"So you're all set, then?" Steve asked his breakfast mates. "Better go git this show on the road."

Brandon slammed down a last piece of bacon and sip of coffee, while Kevin fought a losing battle with the remnants of pancake syrup on his fingers. Still scrubbing with a napkin to clear the goop, Kevin agreed on his preparedness. "Yep, I've got it down. As long as there's no drama like last night, I'll be fine."

Steve took the last corner of toast and dunked it in his now-cold coffee. "Don't you worry about that. I let old Kelly know that I'll be there for security. That Martin guy might be the craziest egg in the carton, but he for damn sure ain't the only one." Brandon and Kevin looked at each other and simply laughed. Everyone from these parts knew that Steve had a way with words. The men said their goodbyes and planned to join up later for a pre-show meeting. Steve watched the two reenactors climb into their truck and head east for Lincoln. Craning his neck behind him, he spotted that Farber guy, still sitting in a booth against the wall, almost appearing to be having a conversation - except there was no one sitting across from him.

"Billy brings out the crazy in everybody," Steve mumbled, "especially that guy...."

Sunday – 9 am

Lilly finally left the *casita* just before 9 am. While she had planned to 'run over' to the main house, Martin didn't understand that in woman-time that meant a shower, complete outfit coordination, makeup, and doing her hair. Of course, Lilly wanted to make a good impression on the other two women, who, Martin figured, had simply rolled out of bed in their Snoopy pajamas and hadn't even bothered to brush their teeth. With his wife in the rearview mirror, he nonchalantly ambled past the main house and out to the street. He'd been able to sneak off a couple of texts to Trisha, first letting her know that he'd be there as soon as Lilly left, and then asking where 'there' actually was. As it turned out, Trisha was at a residence just a few hundred yards down the road from the Patron House.

Unsure that he'd know exactly which building it was - and not wanting to be shot for trespassing - Martin texted Trisha to please wait outside for him. It didn't take him long to see a beautiful woman in a thin, filmy sundress standing barefoot by the road, the wind waving her thick, black hair. Martin stopped short when he saw her. *Rosita*! Transfixed, he couldn't get his feet to move an inch and only hoped the woman would notice him and run down the road into his arms. Finally, after what seemed like an eternity, her face shifted in his direction, and the smile that could light up an entire town centered upon him.

"Martin!" she called, waving her arms. "Here! You made it!" Something in the voice didn't fit the moment, and it took only a few steps forward for him to realize his wishful thinking. This woman was beautiful, but she was not in love with him and definitely was not his soulmate. It was Trisha.

"Hey!" she said, as he approached. "Is this okay? Are you going to be in trouble?" She glanced around as if there might be someone watching them, which seemed preposterous to her on this remote edge of a town in which barely anyone lived.

"No, it's fine," responded Martin. "Lilly is meeting with some women about a cooking class or something they're taking tomorrow. She'll be at it for an hour, at least."

Trisha looked relieved and grabbed Martin's hand to pull him toward the front door. "Come on," she said urgently, "you're not going to believe this!" After they quickly entered an impressive home, Trisha slammed the door shut and drew Martin down the hall.

Trying to take it all in, Martin was blown away by what he was seeing. This place belonged to Trisha? He knew her family must have money if she came from Pacific Palisades, but this remote mansion was millionaire-many-times-over money!

"This is your place?" he said, as she rushed him further into the home. "Like, you own it?"

"No, silly! I'm housesitting for someone this summer. I couldn't afford a place like this!" Finally, Trisha stopped short at two giant oak doors, which she swung open to reveal an incredibly large home library and reading room. Martin's modest collection of Billy the Kid books looked like the starter set for this impressive layout.

"Ummm, wow?" Martin said, not understanding exactly what emergency had brought him here.
Trisha made a complete circle to show Martin just how expansive the library truly was. "So, the reason I asked you here is…," Trisha built a little suspense before continuing, "every one of these books, every last one, is about Billy the Kid and the War. Look at this place!"

Martin was forced to do a double take around the room. There were hundreds of books here, thousands even. How could every single one be about the Kid? He went to investigate the book spines, finding titles both common and extremely rare. Some were compilations of Old West stories and characters, and there was even a section for magazines in which the Kid had been written about. If Martin had had to guess how many books were ever written that mentioned Billy the Kid, he would have guessed a hundred, maybe two? Never in his wildest dreams did he think the young outlaw was memorialized in *thousands* of printed pieces.

“This library is pretty incredible, I have to admit, Trisha. How long have you known about it?”

“That’s just it!” she beamed. “I never even opened this door! For all I knew, it went to a guest room or the garage. This place is so big, I’ve kind of just been in my bedroom and the kitchen.”

Wondering what made her decide to open it today, but not wanting to pry, Martin just moved forward in the conversation. “But what am I doing here? This is great and all, but…?” Martin couldn’t even guess what was expected of him.

Trisha rolled her eyes a bit and cocked her head. “Martin, if there ever was a Rosita Luna, one of these books must talk about her. This is every single thing ever written about Lincoln. I need your help to scan through them to find Rosita!”

Martin looked hopelessly at the bulging shelves full of books. It would take months to read all of these, and he had an hour, two tops. The chance of finding that needle in this haystack was ridiculously low. “Trisha, look at this place,” he protested, waving his hands around the room. “We don’t have time for this. How are we going to…”

“Come on, Martin!” she implored. “Stop wasting time and start pulling books. Maybe we won’t find it if we look, but we damn sure won’t if we don’t at least try.”
Martin just blew a big puff of air out of his mouth, knowing that arguing would be futile. He walked over to one wall and began reading the spines and authors, his head tilted sideways at the chore. Trisha pulled out book after book, checking the index to see if the name *Luna, Rosita* was mentioned anywhere. Book after book went back on the shelf, her quest unsuccessful. Martin’s plan was different. He knew enough about the popular history of the Kid and the War to avoid the well-known tomes; he selected only the ones he’d never seen or heard of, but so far, to no avail.

“Martin,” cooed Trisha, in a much softer voice, “I’m sorry for snapping at you. Really. I just know that you know all about Rosita and if anyone can find her in here, you can.”

Martin smiled and chuckled to himself. If he’d just allow himself, he could find Rosita in Trisha, or at least a close-enough version for him to pretend he had. Trisha caught his smile and said, “You’re laughing at me…why?”

Normally tongue-tied in situations such as this, Martin easily answered, "I wasn't laughing at you. I was laughing at *me*. How impossible this whole thing is! Here I am, searching for Rosita, sitting right next to a woman who looks exactly like her. I can't figure out how I got here!"

"Neither can I, Martin," she said even more softly, "But I know she's here somewhere, and we've got to find her."

Martin nodded and went back to scanning titles. He checked his watch often and calculated how long he could stay here before having to split fifty percent of all of his property with Lilly when she divorced him. Every shelf had at least one book that he'd had never seen before. Some of these were clearly manuscripts that had never been published. Martin imagined that whoever owned the house was such an avid collector that he purchased unpublished books, just to have something that no one else did.

After another fifteen minutes, he checked his watch again and informed Trisha that he'd need to get going. "Lilly's going to be looking for me soon. I can't imagine she's staying with those women all morning."

Trisha looked defeated, surrounded by books that said not a word about the Belle of Lincoln. She let her head fall back, her hair cascading past her shoulders, and she let out a deep sigh. "Okay. I know. I know. I don't want to get you in trouble again." Trisha looked at the scattering of books around her. "I really thought we'd find something."

Martin felt terrible for the young woman, being as he'd brought her into all this. "Listen, Trisha. If you have more time, check out these manuscripts. The rest of these books just tell the same history that everyone knows," Martin suggested, pulling another thick, paperclipped stack of pages from the shelf. "One like this might have something on Rosita that no one's ever seen."

Trisha nodded, smiling enough to let Martin know that she'd try. "But there's nothing in any so far, right? Nothing in that one in your hand, Martin?"

Martin smirked a bit and lowered the cover page so he could read it. The second he did, the papers flew from his hand as he lost all control over his senses. Alarmed, Trisha jumped up to see the cover page float down to earth on top of Martin's shoes. Reading it, she was at least as shocked as Martin was.

Billy the Kid, The Coward of Lincoln County

by

Carl Farber

Sunday - 10:00 am

Farber drove rapidly east on Route 380 toward Lincoln, hoping he'd find an acceptable parking spot not too far from the pageant grounds. With his trip ending tomorrow, he wanted to soak up whatever else he could of the town, knowing he most likely would never return. His ire was still up over last night's run-in with Kevin, and this morning, he'd already decided he'd play the role of both critic and heckler when that young man invariably blew his lines during the reenactment. "Screw him," said Farber to his dashboard. "Silver-spoon little weasel." As promising as the weekend had started, in truth, Carl could really only count Brandon as a 'friend' - and even that was laced with a substantial amount of wishful thinking. If Farber had designs on forging some lifelong relationships with others having his same interests, it seemed he'd need to ramp up his efforts quickly - or else fail miserably.

Soon Farber's meditations turned to Jane. In a fit of misdirected anger, he'd foolishly blown her off last night. He had no idea where she lived or how to contact her. Probably the way she wanted it, he thought to himself. As foolish as he felt every time he imagined her being into him, he couldn't lose the feeling that somehow she was. Without even knowing whether she'd be working today, Carl had no idea if he'd ever see her again. He expected to rise early tomorrow and make his way to Albuquerque Sunport to catch his midday flight back to Newark. If he didn't see Jane today, the likelihood was that he'd never see her again.

Of course, he could always ask Trisha, provided he could find her. She and his favorite bartender were friends, so he could probably get a message to Jane via her pal. After their discussion following the book talk last night, Farber was convinced that Trisha was in his corner, both of them being charter members of the Martin Teebs Haters Club. While Farber had regaled her with tales of Teebs' filthy accusations and character assassinations, Trisha had ooh'd and aah'd in all the right places, enough to make him believe that she agreed with him.

So it was settled: Carl would search for his girl Jane, but lacking her appearance would then entrust his other new friend Trisha with passing along his contact info to *her* friend. Farber imagined the text-message exchanges he and Jane would have as their relationship grew, with her sending the occasional nude photo to keep him interested in only her. Finally, he'd invite her to the big city of Waldwick, NJ - Jane would need to pay her own way, of course - to romance her properly and let her see the glory of Carl Farber in his natural environment. He could look further into the future, seeing how attached the woman would be to him, even as he kept enough distance to play the field with the other groups of women who would surely flock to him, once they saw that his shirts were made of boyfriend material.

As he approached Lincoln proper, the history teacher was finally breathing easy. He had a plan, and he was in demand, at least in his own mind. He rolled down the window to take a deep breath of mountain air and exclaimed, "Jane! Trisha! I'm here! And don't worry, there's enough of Carl Farber to go around!"

Sunday - 10:05 am

"What the fuck?!" hissed Trisha, upon seeing the crudely typed cover page. "Did you know about this?" She held the paper bearing Farber's name and waved it accusingly toward Martin.

"Yes, no," he said, and then much more slowly, "yes."

Trisha bent down and began to scoop up the remaining pages, first trying to put them in order, then trying to scan them for any mention of Rosita Luna. "Why didn't you tell me, Martin?"

Martin just looked down, first at his shoes, then at the messy pile of Farber's work. "I only knew about this in my Dream," he responded sadly. "I mean, this is what Farber was in Lincoln for - in The Dream. He hated Billy long before he ever met him. Since I was a friend of Billy's, he hated me, too."

Trisha looked sternly at Martin, trying to make sense of the physical object she held in her hand. This - the first tangible object that had ostensibly jumped from Martin's Dream world to his real one - proved to her that the man had been telling her the truth. It also proved to her that, somehow, either his Dream was real, or he had the prescience to know all of these things about all of these people without even realizing it himself. "So you were right about him," she said slowly. "He's not the nice guy he's pretending to be?"

Truthfully, Martin did not have an answer to that question. The Farber he'd met in Lincoln just two days ago seemed like a decent-enough chap. It really was Martin's actions that had forced the man to back away from him. Here, though, resting on his foot, was proof that Farber wasn't decent at all. It was proof that he was a hateful bastard, who lived only to crush the legend of Billy the Kid.

"No, I don't believe he is," Martin stated. "The guy I met in my Dream wrote this and was a total scumbag. I don't see how this Farber can be any different."

Still trying to rearrange the pages of the book, Trisha had a thought explode in her brain: "Is Rosita in *here*? She must be, right? Farber knew her. He…." Trisha stopped as the enormity of what Farber had really done to Rosita settled on her. Here she was, over a century away from the act, and she felt dirty, scared, and broken. A chill coursed through her body, and she peered up sadly at Martin. "He raped her. Did he write about that, too?"

The blood drained from Martin's head, so dejected did the woman before him look. She appeared completely vulnerable, just like Rosita. Martin held back on his instinct to reach out to comfort her, even as the memory left *him* in need of being comforted. Shaking his head, he replied, "No, I don't think so. He finished that book before I ever met him."

With Trisha standing before him trembling, Martin gently bent down to retrieve the rest of the pages. As he scooped up a handful, something solid and heavier than mere paper slipped out onto the floor in front of his astonished eyes. It was a copy of *Lin-*

coln County Days, allegedly written by Juan Panchito Baca…'Dummy,' as Billy liked to call him. Of course, Martin knew that Dummy hadn't written it. This one was also authored by Carl Farber, as a sick joke to taunt him through time. Martin picked up the delicate volume, realizing this copy had all of the pages in it, including the ones that Steve would not allow him to read during his Dream.

Trisha stared downward, trying to see what had Martin so interested. Slowly, he looked up to her, and their eyes engaged again. "Here," he said, handing her the tiny book with his shaking hand. "This one is about Rosita. I think you'll find out everything you want to know about her, and probably a lot that you don't."

Sunday – 10:30 am

"Where the hell is Craswell?" barked Kelly Childs, the Pat Garrett reenactor who would also be the MC of today's events. "Without him, we've got no Olinger!" With only thirty minutes before the first performance of the day, Childs was frantic that 'Billy' would lean out of the courthouse window and have no one to shoot. "How about you, Steve? You could do it, no?"

Steve let a big grin spread across his face, before squashing the idea of getting killed. "Hell, no, Sheriff. I gave up being shot at when I retired from the force! Besides, I'm just here for event security. You can find some other old guy to get blasted into oblivion."

Childs looked around at his cast, wondering whom he might press into double duty as Olinger/Someone Else. The costume change would take some time, and he wasn't sure who would be up for it. Turning to Brandon, who knew everyone in this part of the world, he asked, "Well, got any ideas?"

Brandon's first thought was for himself to play both Bell and Olinger. That way, he'd get shot and stumble down the stairs, dead as a doornail, then reincarnate and run to the Wortley, just so he could be gunned down by the Kid again. The whole concept made him laugh, but he knew he needed a better plan.

"Lemme see who's here, maybe I know someone who can stand in and take a blast."

With that, he strolled outside to see the already mostly full bleachers, loaded with tourists of all types patiently waiting to see the big show. In his full J.W. Bell costume, Brandon got a number of looks from the crowd, staring at him as if he were a celebrity. He scanned the cheap seats to see if anyone could fit the bill of Olinger, pulling off the deputy's one line before being made into hamburger by his own shotgun. Coming up empty, he headed back to the real courthouse, which was adjacent to the set for the show. Just as he was about to walk inside, he heard his name being called.

"Brandon! Wow, you look great, buddy," commented Carl Farber, who'd just parked himself in one of the last spots, back near the bathrooms. "It's a shame that punk kid is going to kill you." Farber chuckled to soften the joke, but Brandon seemed to be occupied with other thoughts.

"Thanks, Carl," he said distractedly, and then a thought occurred to him: "Hey! Would you be willing to help with the show? Our guy who plays Olinger is MIA. Maybe just for this first one? I'm sure he'll be here later."

Farber had come expecting to see a show, not to be part of one. Of course, the role of Olinger would give him a spectacular death to work with, and Carl *had* played Judd Fry in his sixth grade class's production of *Oklahoma*. "Do I have time to learn my lines? Get into wardrobe?" Farber asked seriously.

Brandon just laughed and grabbed his arm, dragging him into the real courthouse to meet the rest of the cast.

Sunday – 10:45 am

Martin walked slowly down the street toward the set where the reenactment would be. Lilly had come back in time to let him know that the ladies were going to have a little shopping excursion in Lincoln, just to practice for the big trip the next day, and would Martin mind if she went along with them? As preoccupied as he was, Martin was glad for the alone time and quickly, almost too quickly, responded that no, he wouldn't mind at all.

He checked his watch, seeing that he had just a few spare minutes to get to the early show. He expected it would be standing room only, which was fine, since he and Lilly still planned on attending the 3 pm performance. As he plugged along, Martin admitted that he had no idea what was happening to him. His weekend was supposed to get better after not dying, but instead, it continued to get worse. Every time he ran into someone from The Dream, the complications grew. At this point, his honest emotion - which he'd admit only to himself - was *fear*. Fear that he'd either gone completely mad, or that someone, some Wizard of Oz, was pulling the strings and spinning the dials on some diabolical human-behavioral experiment, with Martin Teebs as the main study candidate. There was no script for him to follow, no owner's manual for a life gone wrong. Martin felt he was being led around by the nose at the whim and whimsy of a madman (or woman), and it didn't feel good.

Before he left the *casita*, he'd grabbed a small backpack and stowed two things in it. He'd asked Trisha if he could take both Farber's manuscript and *Lincoln County Days* with him. While his promise to Lilly had been to apologize to Carl, his new plan went in a completely different direction. Martin now suspected that Carl Farber, the mild-mannered history teacher, was at the helm of this ship full of crazy. He certainly didn't know how the man had so masterfully woven together all of these fabrics, but every bit of the evidence - including these two books - pointed directly at Farber.

Martin Teebs had decided: If he was going crazy, he was definitely taking a few people with him on the trip.

Sunday – 10:50 am

"No, Carl! It's just that one line: 'Did Bell kill the Kid?' Then, you run to the base of the window," declared Kelly Childs, desperately trying to get his ragtag bunch of actors in line. "This pageant has been going on for eighty years, and *we're* not gonna screw this up, gentlemen!" he raged, as they all peered left and right at each other.

For his part, Farber had attempted to put more drama into his performance. He had devised a dramatic soliloquy, expounding upon the pitfalls of breaking the law and proclaiming that justice should be served to any who didn't follow it. However, with time ticking down on the clock, Childs had stamped his foot down on that plan.

"Ok, Steve, last safety check, and blanks loaded, please?" Child asked the man serving as unofficial armorer for the event.

Steve walked man to man, holding out his hand to take each one's firearms, much like a drill instructor would. As he went, he loaded only the exact amount of shots each man would need to take, while giving them all the standard safety lecture as he moved down the line. "Gentlemen, these are blanks, and blanks can kill!" he threatened. "So do not ever cover a target with your muzzle that you are not willing to destroy. Aim to the side and aim low, as you've been taught. Every gun, and I mean *every* gun, is loaded, no matter what anyone tells you. If you treat them that way, you'll stay alive. All guns stay in holsters until you are ready to fire. Is that clear?"

There was a general, apathetic chorus of 'yes' from the men, and Steve made his way down to Farber, who held out a shiny nickel-plated Colt that should have been on the hip of Earl Craswell. Steve cleared the weapon and handed it back.

"Hey, wait, don't you need to load me up?" Farber asked, with some concern.

"Olinger never fired a shot, so, no, I don't," flatly replied Steve.

Farber seethed a bit, believing that he should at least have the opportunity to defend himself with fake bullets if the fake Billy the Kid was going to fake fire upon him.

"All right, everyone! This is it. Let's make it real!" cheered Childs, as his little band of troubadours moved into position.

Farber looked at Kevin as Billy the Kid, chains already on his feet, hobbling up the stairs. Carl was glad that his gun didn't have blanks in it. "No, I don't want any blanks, Steve," he said to himself, as he moved toward the fake Wortley Hotel, "I want the real things."

Sunday – 10:55 am

Jane picked her way along Lincoln's very quiet street just as the reenactment was about to begin. On the previous two days, the road had been jammed with people doing

Billy stuff, but today, she knew they'd either be on the way home or at the show site. Slowly passing the cemetery and about to roll into Lincoln proper, she saw Trisha up ahead, walking slowly, almost as if in a trance. Gliding up next to her and lowering the passenger window, Jane yelled, "Hey, girl! Where you headed?"

Trisha's head turned to greet Jane, but without her typical million-megawatt grin. "Hey," was all Trisha could offer, along with a tight smile. Knowing something was off, Jane pressed her friend. "What's wrong? Get in," she commanded and stopped the car right next to the young woman. Without the will to decline, Trisha got into the passenger seat and slowly closed the door.

"Girl, you look like you've seen a ghost or something! What the hell is going on with you?" asked Jane. Trisha looked her friend directly in the eyes. Although she seemed extraordinarily calm at the moment, it appeared to Jane that she'd been crying.

"Jane, who am I?" she asked plainly.

Jane stared at her in confusion, wondering if she was asking a serious question. "Say what, honey? Who are you?" responded Jane, with a small laugh.

"Yeah. Tell me who I am. Please?" Trisha begged weakly.

Jane was worried about her friend and her current state of mind. Attempting to shock her out of the funk she seemed to be in, Jane responded briskly, "You are Trisha fucking Davis! You are a goddess with a rocking body and a brain to match. You're going to be an MBA by the end of the year, and every man, *every* man, wants you, but none deserves you. *That's* who you are, sweetie!"

Trisha gulped. "Thanks," she said gratefully. "I'm feeling out of sorts with some stuff that I found out. Martin came by this morning, and we went through a bunch of those old books in the house."

"And? Should I cut this Martin's balls off?" inquired Jane, with enough lilt to make it a joke, but not so much that anyone would think she wouldn't do it if asked.

"No! No, no, Martin's been great. It's not that, it's...," Trisha's voice trailed off. How could she explain the impossible to Jane and have her understand? How could she let her friend know that this man, this Martin, had some near-death dream, and now all of it seemed to be coming true? How could she explain that this Rosita Luna, apparently her twin from a century ago, was raped by Jane's friend, Carl Farber, and then put a gun to her head, taking her own life when she finally saw him again, face to face? How could Trisha explain the feelings of dread she'd been having ever since Martin sat her down two nights ago and began to spin his fantastical tale? It was almost as if she'd been infected by his Dream, and now the disease was spreading through her mind.

"It's *what*, kitten? How can I help?" Jane asked, seeing the struggle that Trisha was having.

"Do me a favor, please? Stay away from Carl Farber, okay?" Trisha beseeched her friend. "Just promise me that. I've seen some stuff. He's not who you think he is. He's..."

"He's *what?*" Jane interrupted, curious.

"He's bad news, Jane. I've seen it. I've seen the books he wrote, and I know what he did. Just promise me you'll stay away from him?"

Jane had never seen her friend this serious before. While the thought of Farber didn't scare Jane, she wanted to be sensitive to Trisha's request, so she simply said "Okay, you got it."

Trisha smiled and opened the car door to get out. With a big sigh, she stepped onto the street and stuck her head back in the window. "If you have time, come by the show at 3 pm. All the tourists should be gone by then, and we can cheer for Brandon and Kevin." Agreeing to see each other later, Jane drove off to the Brewery. She'd only been asked to fill in for an hour or two until someone's hangover subsided, and so she accepted.

Trisha walked to the west, past the old buildings and museums, the history of this place tugging harder and harder at her with every single step.

Sunday - 11:25 am

"Look up, old boy, and see what you git!" shouted Kevin, as he stared down the double barrels of a 10-gauge shotgun with Carl Farber at the other end. When the substitute Olinger dramatically raised his head as if waiting to hear the voice of God, the Billy reenactor cut loose with both barrels. The sound in the small arena was thunderous, and Farber spun around, groaning and pulling at his chest, before finally falling and letting his body go limp. The effect was way overdone and not in the script, but the history teacher wanted to be remembered for *something*, and this might just be it. To his dismay, however, the crowd cheered mightily - but for Billy the Kid, not for Carl's melodramatic death spiral.

Kevin ducked back into the false-fronted courtroom set to grab the stunt gun - that is, the already broken one that he'd fling at Olinger's corpse. Smashing the railing with it, he uttered the line, "Take it, you son of a bitch! You won't round me up again with it!" And threw it down at Farber. The gun rattled off the dirt and landed partially on Farber, infuriating the man. Supposing that bastard Kevin did it on purpose, it was all Carl could do not to move while 'Billy' went on and on about how he regretted killing Bell. Farber made a note to confront the boy about his aim to make sure that the next two shows went off without Farber himself going off.

Sunday - Noon

"Okay, boys! That was a pretty good start," cheered Kelly Childs. "Carl, a little too much drama on the death scene. Just take the hit and fall down next time, savvy?"

"Next time? I thought you told me you only needed me for one show?" objected Farber, although he'd certainly hoped to be asked to stay for the whole day.

"Earl's got food poisoning, ain't gonna make it. I'd be obliged if you could do the other two shows?"

Farber grumbled to himself before answering, "Fine. But listen up, 'Kid,' you watch where the hell you throw that gun next time. Got it?"

Kevin was taken aback, figuring that it had all just been part of the reenactment. He and Farber had had their differences, but he assumed the older man would act professionally today. "Sorry, I didn't mean anything by it," he offered, before turning his eyes away.

"Ok, Steve, clear these guns, please. Let's have something cold to drink and get ready for the next show," ordered the good Sheriff Pat Garrett.

Steve moved his way around the room, again unloading guns and checking for misfired blanks. As he handed 'Olinger' back his unfired weapon, Farber asked, "What's *your* gun for? You're not in the show. You firing blanks, too?"

Steve raised his chin in either disgust or defiance before answering. "You know, I was a cop for thirty years, Carl. I learned a lot, but one thing I learned early on is that the bad guys use real bullets. If I'm putting a gun on my hip, it's to protect me - and maybe even you - from them. So, no, I'm not firing blanks...but I'll just bet you do." Steve laughed right in Farber's face with the last insult, moving away while Farber stewed even more.

Although Carl hadn't been too crazy about the bossy, school-teacher-like Childs, he now counted both Kevin and Steve as two guys he wouldn't piss on if they were on fire. Watching Kevin and Brandon cutting up in the corner, reliving Bell's death, Farber pondered more and more, eventually concluding that the next show might just have a little different ending than history would tell.

Sunday – 12:30 pm

Martin leaned heavily against the bleachers, staying out of the hot sun as much as he could. He'd made it just in time for the first show and had to admit, it wasn't bad at all. Of all the packed house, he seemed to be the only one laughing when Carl Farber spun around time after time in his death throes, portraying Bob Olinger. It seemed that the school teacher had finally gotten his time to shine and wasn't willing to allow his triumphant moment to end. Teebs wondered if the guy running the show would coach Farber to just die and get it over with during the 1 pm show.

Just as the early show had ended, Martin noticed Trisha heading very slowly toward the set. She had almost seemed to be avoiding him while she stared at the history of

Lincoln coming back to life. Although she did acknowledge Martin with a small wave, she wound up walking back toward the trees that fringed the Rio Bonito. While his impulse was to follow her, she didn't look to be someone who wanted company at that moment.

At the present, Martin had a task to fulfill and was looking for the right opportunity to do it. He did sincerely want to apologize to Kevin for his craziness over Bachaca's old book. Although he had also intended to bury the hatchet with Farber, the discovery of Carl's two books nixed that plan. Now he just wanted to confront the man and find out what his part is this entire charade actually was. The problem with accomplishing either of these assignments was that the show's entire cast immediately retreated into the courthouse, which must have been their staging area, and hadn't been seen since. Martin's presence near the bleachers was simply positioning him for when they returned, so he could make a dash to have a word with whomever he saw first. Checking his watch, he knew it couldn't be long, as the next show would be starting shortly.

Finally, a few minutes later, the cast began to stream out of the courthouse via the very stairwell on which J.W. Bell had been killed so many years ago. The tall Pat Garrett guy was barking instructions to everyone, while Steve waved and joked at people in the crowd. Martin's eyes grew narrow as he saw Farber making his way to the mockup of the Wortley Hotel. Martin had almost convinced himself to confront the weasel when Steve went and parked himself nearby, probably as event security, Martin reasoned. The person he didn't see in all of this activity was Kevin, the star of the Escape. Curious, since the show was soon to begin, Martin walked off toward the real courthouse to see if he could catch the young Billy impersonator before he got on-set. As Teebs reached the bottom of the stairwell, he heard heavy footsteps of boots descending his way.

Rounding the corner, Kevin seemed surprised to see Martin waiting for him. "Oh, hello, Mr. Teebs," he said, extending a polite greeting, so as not to attract the big man's ire again.

"Hi, Kevin, great show, by the way," Martin started, to soften the boy up. "Hey, I came by to apologize for last night. I don't know what happened to me, but I never should have taken it out on you. I'm really, really sorry."
Taking the apology better than Martin had expected, Kevin replied, "Aw, don't worry

none. It's fine. Besides, Steve told me that book probably belonged more to you than me, anyway."

Martin was caught off guard by the comment. Why would Steve say that? Martin had spent the better part of thirty minutes last night explaining to Steve that he realized the book wasn't what he thought it was. What would cause the cowboy to tell Kevin that, somehow, it was?

Before Martin could gather himself to ask the young man what Steve had meant, Kevin quickly said, "Hey, come on. I got a few minutes before we start," waving Martin up the stairs behind him. As Kevin's boots retreated back up the narrow stairwell, Martin took a deep breath and followed.

"Here, I want you to have this back, Mr. Teebs." In his hand, Kevin offered the heavily damaged *The True Life of Billy the Kid*. "It's signed and everything. I think I know enough about Billy the Kid to get through today, anyway." Martin held his hands up as if to say "no, I can't," but the young man persisted, "Martin, come on. Take it. I don't need it anymore."

Martin slowly reached out and gently took the volume, its weight seeming much greater than it should for a book that size. Upon its release, Kevin grinned and nodded his head, happy that it had been returned to the rightful owner. The youth stepped to the side and toward the stairs as he added, "Okay, showtime!" leaving Martin alone in the old courthouse, with only the book and his thoughts to keep him company.

Touching the book lightly to avoid inflicting any further damage, Martin peeled open a few of the crinkled pages. There was no need to read it; he'd done that a dozen times over already. What he couldn't get past was how much this copy resembled the one he'd lost in The Dream, only to be found, used, and kept by Billy the Kid until his final moments on earth. The only glaring difference was that *this* volume didn't have the Kid's famous list inside the back cover. Whoever had planted this copy clearly didn't know enough about Billy's planned and actual travels from the time he'd left Sumner in 1881 until he was firmly in his 40s and had visited Martin at his place just up the road from the famous cemetery. Of course, Martin reasoned, all that had actually never happened, had it? It was all a dream. And if someone had found a way to read Martin's thoughts, then that person should have taken notice of the key detail of the list before constructing this fake replica of the infamous book.

Martin could hear the muffled sounds of the PA from the set as Kelly Childs began to recite the scripted intro to the show. Teebs smiled and closed *The True Life of Billy the Kid*, only to notice that one of the last pages had come loose. Opening the back cover, Martin realized that someone had glued a plain sheet inside. Pulling the loose piece away, he nearly dropped to his knees when he saw what was written and obviously intentionally hidden:

~~1. Lew Wallace~~
~~2. Jimmy Dolan~~
~~3. Governor of New Mexico (whoever it might be at that time)~~
~~4. Pat Garrett~~
~~5. Doc Scurlock~~
~~6. Pete Maxwell~~
~~7. Abrana Garcia~~
~~8. John Miller~~
~~9. Brushy Bill Roberts~~
10. Martin Teebs

This *was* it! This was Martin's book, kept by Billy all those years! Martin's first instinct was to race down the stairs to confront Kevin to determine whether he even knew about the list. With the first gunshots from the show already firing to an appreciative audience, though, he thought better of that plan.

Martin was frantic, wanting to learn how *this* book had come to be. This was the third piece of tangible proof turning up in a matter of hours - either The Dream was real; or Martin had been able to decipher an incredible story that he'd been a part of, but had somehow been convinced was just a dream!

With his heart racing, Martin tried to compose himself so he could decide on his next move. "Calm down," he instructed himself out loud. "Calm down, think it through. Who could have done this?" His eyes darted around the room, scanning to see if someone might be watching him go mad, but he definitely seemed to be alone. Curiosity getting the better of him, he edged his way over to Kevin's backpack, which had been left unattended and unzipped. He wondered: If he went through it, would he find the boy's iPhone, chock-full of text messages and laughing emojis about how he and Brandon were driving that old Teebs fellow insane? Martin asked himself whether he really wanted to do this, but he finally pulled back the open flap of the backpack to check what was inside.

Just before he blacked out and hit the floor, Martin spotted the unmistakable orange and yellow cover of the book *Sunset in Sumner,* written by Michael Anthony Giudicissi, also known as - Martin Teebs! His vision returning in spasms as he fought to stay conscious, Martin heard the tread of hefty footsteps crossing the ancient courthouse floor. The feet - whomever they belonged to - walked up to Teebs, reached down for something, sighed deeply, and then walked away. Martin succumbed to the blackness, letting it wash over him like the chilly waters of the Rio Bonito.

Sunday – 1:05 pm

Hearing the gunfire, Jane knew that the 1 pm show had already begun. Since she and Trisha had agreed to go at 3 pm, Jane had some time to wander around town, a treat in rare commodity over the past week. Ambling toward the reenactment set, she saw a gaggle of brightly colored tourists sitting rapt in their seats as the story of Billy's capture and escape played out in front of them.

Interestingly to Jane, she spotted her friend Carl Farber, in full Bob Olinger costume, standing behind the false-fronted set of the Wortley Hotel. Farber was closer to the street than any of the other actors, accompanied only by that big cowboy from Capitan, Steve. Figuring Carl had stood her up last night and might want to avoid her, she almost walked right by him. Trisha's condemnation of the man also was ringing in Jane's ears, but something made her want to say hello. She sidled up to the corner of the building and leaned in to whisper, "Now I got stood up by two men, Bob Olinger *and* Carl Farber." The wicked smile on her face let Farber know her comment was in jest.

"Jane!" he exclaimed, loudly enough for the audience to hear. Childs glared over from his perch across the dirt lot and aggressively held a finger to his lips, reminding Farber to shut the hell up. "Jane," he repeated, this time in a loud whisper, "I didn't expect to see you here."

Never one to let any man get the upper hand, she smirked as she replied, “I’ll bet not, after the way you ditched me last night.”

“Noooo, no, nooo,” he said, shaking his head, “it wasn’t like that. I just didn’t have any place to crash for a few hours and wound up heading back to the motel to get some sleep.” He continued to glance back and forth from the pretty young woman to the set, making sure he didn’t miss his cue.

“Listen, you go back to your little playacting, I’m going to find a seat and see if you have any skills,” said Jane, only semi-joking as she grinned and started to walk off.

Within a few steps, Farber hissed after her, “Hey, wait till you see what I’ve got cooked up for old Billy this time!” Jane just rolled her eyes and walked toward the bleachers, waving her fingers as she went.

Sunday - 1:10 pm

Martin’s buzzing ears started to come around, as light streaming through the windows cracked his eyes open. He worked his hands to his head to see if he might be bleeding, but all seemed secure north of his neck. With no idea how long he’d been out, he groggily pushed himself to his knees and looked around the room. He remembered someone coming into the room as he was blacking out, but there had been no offer of help nor even a check to see if Martin was okay. He could only surmise that it was someone on the inside of the twisted game in which he had found himself.

He peered over to Kevin’s backpack, to the very book that had knocked him to the floor, but saw it was gone. *That* must have been what someone had come to take. Bachaca’s *The True Life of Billy the Kid* was still sitting right on the table where Martin had left it, so whoever took *Sunset in Sumner* knew exactly what he - or she? - was coming for.

By now, Martin realized he was caught in a rather complex situation, way more than he had ever anticipated. Just a few days ago, he was coughing up green-chile enchiladas, glad to be alive and convinced that his entire life in the past was nothing but a fragmented dream. Now, here, the evidence all pointed to the fact that he had badly miscalculated - and that what few had believed to be true, actually was.

Martin's thoughts immediately turned to one person - *Rosita.* If all else were true, then she also would be true. Would he somehow get another chance with her? How would he explain to Lilly that he was escaping to the year 1878, never to return? Did Lilly deserve any less of his love than Rosita did? Then a darker thought occurred to him: Was his history with Billy, Rosita, and the Regulators cast in stone, like seemingly everything else? If this were all real, would Martin be forced yet again to follow Rosita on the heartbreaking journey that ended with her taking her own life? Martin's head immediately felt too heavy for his shoulders to hold up. There was no way he'd survive a repeat performance of the last few years of his life. No. Way.

"Lilly's gonna love this," he said to the empty room. All of the 'might be's' and 'could happens' were pulling him in so many directions, he felt he might just fall apart right there in the courthouse. "I need some air," he spoke into the void and made his way to the stairs. With each step he climbed down, the sound of the performance became more clear. With each step, he also came closer to his destiny, whatever it might wind up being. Martin reached the bottom, opened the door, and walked out into the bright sunlight - and heard the distinctive voice of the best friend he'd ever had, William H. Bonney, better known as Billy the Kid.

Sunday - 1:20 pm

With a thunderous explosion from Garrett's Winchester, poor little Charlie Bowdre was blasted right back into the rock house from where he'd come. The actor portraying him, a local guy from the SASS ranks, looked incredibly like the real Charlie, and it gave Martin the chills to view his death.

From inside the mocked-up house came a voice over the P.A. "They killed ya, Charlie. You kin get revenge. Take some of 'em before you go!" Just as 'Charlie' was about to exit the door, the same voice called him back and, with a familiar cackle, added, "And here, piss on these so Garrett's boys get a taste of ya after yer gone!"

Martin was stunned, as was the audience, the rest of the cast, and especially Kelly Childs. Two times in the same performance, he'd had to admonish his actors to keep quiet and to stay on script. Where the hell did these guys come up with this stuff, anyway?

Martin watched with anticipation, knowing the voice he'd heard did not belong to Kevin; it was Billy's! Something about the look that Kevin had given him when handing over Bachaca's book was different - more confident, more cocky. Martin wasn't sure what had happened, but he waited to see if the boy who exited the rock house was his long-lost pal or just a cheap imitation.

As the surrender played out, and 'Billy' walked from the rock house with his hands held high, the boy smirked at the audience and pointed with his thumb toward Garrett, as if to say, 'get a load of this guy!' The response was a wave of laughter that Billy ate up; Childs rolled his eyes.

Martin felt a rush of emotion while his friend was led away in fake handcuffs and leg irons. In his own mind, Teebs was no longer alone on this crazy journey. How in the hell Billy had made it back here, all of twenty years old in his life, Martin had no idea. Did he come here on purpose? Was Billy controlled, just the same as Martin, by whoever was pulling the strings on this weird trip? He couldn't figure it out at the moment, but he was desperate to talk to Billy just as soon as the show was over.

Martin's chance would be arriving soon, as the young outlaw was now in the courthouse, about to shoot Brandon as J.W. Bell, and then his nemesis Carl Farber as Bob Olinger. With the report of a Colt and Brandon spectacularly falling into the arms of Godfrey Gauss at the bottom of the stairwell, a voice from one of the other actors yelled out, "The Kid's killed Bell!"

The audience was held rapt, knowing one of the most famous shootings of the Old West was about to take place. Farber delivered his next line with a Shakespearian lilt, arms waving toward the crowd, "Yes, and he might just kill me, too!"

Might? What the hell was Farber doing? Childs was enraged and nearly sprinted across the set to shoot Carl himself, while Martin waited for whatever came next, puzzled over what Farber was up to.

Billy looked down from the window and chuckled as he delivered what was to be his final line of the show, "Hello, Bob!" and then let loose with a blast from the 10-gauge Whitney replica. Rather than falling on the spot like he was supposed to, or even twisting and turning like in his overacted first performance of the day, Farber did nothing. He simply stood there, as if Billy's shot had missed. A shocked murmur went through the crowd, which was full well expecting Billy to next come prancing out on the balcony.

Childs could contain himself no more and barely covered his mic in time to scream, "Get down, Farber!" Which only had the effect of making the audience laugh.

For a tense second, Martin wondered what would happen, until Billy, always the showman, came through. "Hell, Bob! Ya got so fat the damn buckshot couldn't reach anything important!" With a wave of laughter echoing through the crowd, he continued, "Guess I'll juss hafta shoot ya again, ya cur!" And with that, Billy pulled the second trigger on the Whitney.

With Childs closing in fast - probably planning to knock Farber flat with his bare hands - and Steve casting a menacing look from behind him, the fake Olinger decided the time to take a dive was at hand; and he quickly fell to the ground, clutching his chest. Billy cackled into his microphone, "Second time's a charm, Bob!" The audience roared in laughter and appreciation at the improvisation.

If Martin had had any doubts, they were no more. Never at a loss for what to say, Billy was cool under pressure, and usually funny, too. Martin stood there, marveling at his young friend and wishing the reenactment could be over so he could let Billy know he was in on the secret.

The show wound down, and the crowd gave a hearty round of applause to the cast members as they all took a bow in the dirt lot in front of the set. Most actors joined hands but, conspicuously, no one reached out to Farber. While some of the tourists made their way down to the actors, hoping to get an autograph or photo, Childs raged at Farber to get his ass upstairs to the real courtroom so they could have a 'little talk.' Farber, seeing Jane approaching, mouthed, "I'll be right back," to her, before following his irate leader up the stairs and out of sight.

Appreciative of Billy's acting performance, members of the audience pressed in to get photos with the young man, who smiled and nodded every time he was asked. One gentleman, an older, middle-aged, white guy, leaned in as his wife was about to snap the shutter and said, "You know, the Kid never said anything like that 'strike-two' thing you did." Billy just clapped the man on the back and laughed, all the while darting his eyes back and forth between the camera and his good friend Martin Teebs.

Sunday - 1:50 pm

"Farber, you stupid son of a bitch!" railed Kelly Childs. "You're ruining a show that's run for eighty years. Eighty years! Every year, Olinger gets shot. Olinger falls. The crowd goes wild. What's so hard to understand about that?"

Carl had a look of disdain on his face, but said nothing. Even though this wasn't the real Pat Garrett, Farber was programmed to dislike the man. Over the course of the last few hours, memories - or maybe wishfully crafted dreams - had been piling up in Farber's brain. His scattered thoughts of both Garrett and the Kid were none too pleasant, and he particularly didn't like being taken to task by the egotistical sheriff. Farber stewed in silence as Childs glared at him.

"So, can you stick to the script for this last show, or do I need to pull some other untalented fat guy from the audience to play Olinger?"

In Farber's mind, he'd already envisioned the last show going, well, *differently* than the first two. The smug look of Kevin firing down upon him, then ad-libbing the fat joke, had set him on edge. He hadn't liked the boy since their run-in last night, and he liked him less every minute that went by. Something had changed in that kid since this morning, and Farber couldn't put his finger on what it was...but he didn't like it. It was as if Farber were a block of cheese and Kevin the metal grater. Every interaction wore Farber down more and made his dislike for the boy more raw. Farber had a plan, but in order to execute it, he needed to be part of the reenactment; so he swallowed what was left of his pride and said simply, "I'll do it Pat, er…Kelly. I'll stick to the script." A promise that Farber knew he could never, ever keep.

Sunday - 1:51 pm

As the crowd began to dissipate, Brandon and Billy turned to walk upstairs to join the rest of the cast. Martin shadowed them at a short distance, not wanting to cause any alarm, but desperate to let his friend know that he was onto him. Just before the men entered the stairwell, Martin shouted out, "Good work, Kevin! Nice performance out there."

With his trademark smirk, Billy turned his head, connected eyes with Martin, and just shook his head slightly, letting Teebs know that now wasn't the time to divulge their secret. With a wink, Billy turned back to the stairs, walking up and out of sight.

Sunday - 1:52 pm

If anyone other than Farber sensed the change in Kevin, he kept it to himself. For his part, Kelly Childs was a frustrated director trying to impress upon his actors how important it was to stay on script. "Look, Kevin, not sure about that pissing line. Let's cut that from the next show, okay?"

Billy's eyes lit up, and he smiled in Child's direction, answering, "Whatever you say, Patsy. It's your show."

Childs took a deep breath, happy that he seemed to have control of his troops again. "But good job on that ad-lib with Farber. I've been assured that *won't* happen again, right, Carl?" Childs asked with some force, in the man's direction.

Farber just waved his hand in acknowledgment and turned away. As the cast tanked up on Gatorade and blueberry muffins, Farber peered out of the window, looking for Jane. "Are we done here?" he asked. "I've got a friend outside."

Childs took a gulp of the orange liquid and nodded. "Yeah, we're done."

Farber hurried over to the stairs and rushed outside to find out what chances, if any, he still had with Jane.

Sunday - 1:53 pm

Martin walked quickly back to the Patron House since he'd been gone far longer than he had expected to be. He assumed Lilly would be waiting to give him the third degree, and he tried to get his story straight in his mind before the questions started flying. He'd tell her that he had apologized to Kevin and had hung around to do the same with Farber; however, in the rush between shows, he hadn't yet been able to. Martin would cast himself as the man who lived up to his word, even if it meant ditching his wife for a few hours to do so. Of course, with Lilly coming to the next show, he'd actually have to apologize to Farber in front of her, which was about as distasteful a thought as he could imagine at the moment.

Approaching the portal, he carefully opened the door and waited for the first salvo of questions to arrive.

Nothing. Not a word.

He walked into the *casita* and saw nothing out of the ordinary, but heard the shower humming in the background. Martin carefully headed toward the sound and knocked on the door. "Lil, is that you?"

Sliding back the shower curtain, Lilly responded, "Hey, hon! Yep, just rinsing off. Wanna join me?"

In any other time or place, Martin would have risen to the occasion and jumped right into the fray. At the moment, though, his mind was scattered in so many directions that he simply wouldn't be able to participate, so he carefully chose his words. "I'd love to! But...we're going to miss the show so how about a raincheck…or shower check... or whatever it might be."

"No problem!" Lilly called happily. "I'll be out in a few."

Bullet dodged, Martin sat on the couch and thought about Lilly's invitation. Did he really want to join her in the shower, or did his libido simply want to do it? He would *really* have wanted to join *Rosita* in the shower, of course, but she was nowhere to be found, other than in the pages of Farber's shitty book. At some point today, or at the latest tomorrow, Martin was going to have to tell Lilly what was going on. If Martin and Billy had experienced some sort of awakening, wouldn't Lilly follow suit? Maybe, he thought, he wouldn't have to explain anything? Perhaps Lilly would simply have all the pieces fall into place just the way they had for Martin? Maybe she'd see her happy life with Michael Roberts and just head back to New Jersey on her own? However, the lack of a little Austin around meant that part of Lilly's life hadn't happened yet, or so Martin assumed.

Time was mixed up, and Martin couldn't seem to fit all the pieces of The Dream together with what was happening in the present. If the past had already been written, then Lilly had already had a son, moved to New Jersey, and divorced Martin years ago. That had happened. Martin had lived it…or at least, he thought he had. Of course, if the past was truly already written, then Rosita was dead, long gone, and buried in Billy's grave. That would explain why she hadn't shown up to attend Martin's 'heading-to-insanity' party with the rest of the gang.

In any event, the chipper lilt in Lilly's voice let Martin know he was most likely off the hook for disappearing for hours. Now he needed to make it through one more show, find his friend Billy, and figure out just what the hell was going on around here.

Sunday – 1:54 pm

Trisha had spent most of the afternoon in her home, contemplating life. The problem for her was that she wasn't quite sure *which* life to contemplate. There was the LA dream-girl life she'd lived for twenty-four years, the child of well-to-do parents, and gifted with incredible genetics. Then, there was the living-in-a-mountain-town girl, who essentially worked for Parks & Rec. Finally, there was the swashbuckling time detective, desperately trying to figure out what had happened to a long-lost woman, whom she just happened to look just like. Glancing at the time on her iPhone, she realized that if she was to meet Jane for the final reenactment performance, she'd need to get ready and head to the other side of town.

That was the rub, however. Since reading the final few pages of *Lincoln County Days* - which seemed to have been written by Carl Farber as some sort of sick joke - Trisha knew what the man's intentions were toward Rosita. More so than even his intentions, she knew exactly what that horrible creep would do. She had to continue reminding herself: *I'm not Rosita, I just look like her*. She wondered: Would Farber perceive enough of a distinction to prevent him from yet another horrific act? Just thinking of the man's stringy hair and cheesy smile made her retch. She was sure that he'd be at the show since Jane planned to be there, too. She hoped her friend had taken her advice to stay clear of the lunatic, but she wasn't sure that Jane was the type to take warnings well.

As the clock ticked over on the precious minutes she'd need to get to the show and find a seat, Trisha realized that she couldn't bear seeing Carl Farber after what she'd learned today. A moment later, however, she realized that she couldn't bear *not* seeing Carl Farber today after what she'd just learned. If what he wrote was true, he was a dangerous man who needed to be put in his place. She wasn't sure why, but she somehow felt it was her responsibility to do that.

Then she thought of Martin. He'd taken those two books this morning with the promise of returning them. What was he planning to do with them? Clearly, he wanted to confront Farber, but had he done so? And had it changed anything? She desperately wanted to speak to Martin to learn what was happening, but she knew he'd be with his wife and didn't want to cause any more trouble than already existed. Trisha finally determined to get dressed and make her way to the show's grounds. She only hoped her conflicted emotions would hold together when she saw Farber, Jane, and, of course, Martin Teebs.

Sunday – 1:55 pm

"There she is!" Farber said, as he walked across the set to greet Jane. "I was hoping you didn't leave."

"That was some improv there, cowboy," she laughed. "I don't think that's exactly the way it actually went down. What did your boss think of it?"

Farber's face clouded over, thinking back to Childs's dress down. Still, he was in the company of a pretty woman and didn't want to waste his time on those losers inside the courthouse. "Well, he wasn't crazy about it, but everyone got a laugh, so that's got to be good."

Jane shrugged her shoulders in amusement and looked around the mostly empty bleachers. "You go on again at 3?" she asked. "You've got an hour, let's get something to drink...it's hot out here!" Farber smiled greatly at the invitation, not sure if she meant an adult libation or something more child friendly. "Across the street, that little place has some damn good lemonade. C'mon 'Olinger,' my treat before Billy shoots you down again." Carl smiled ruefully at the thought as the two left the site of both Billy and Bob's last stand.

Sunday – 2:15 pm

Martin and Lilly strolled hand in hand down the street of the much-less-congested village. As predicted, most of the day tourists had already seen at least one of the earlier reenactments and begun their drive back to wherever they had come from. All that were left now were locals and hardcore Billy fanatics.

"How real is this thing, Martin? Is it exactly like the real thing when Billy escaped?" asked Lilly excitedly. While she'd had her fill of Lincoln, she still had a big day planned tomorrow; and the chance to see a live show, even if it was about Billy the Kid, was a nice change of pace from staring at old pictures in museums.

"Uhhh," stammered Martin, remembering the 1 pm performance, "if they stick to the script, then it's probably pretty close. Things went a little off center at the last one, though."

Lilly cocked her head, puzzled. "What do you mean, 'a little off center'?"

Martin pondered how much to tell Lilly right now. After all, they were about to watch the 3 pm show; and if Farber pulled the same BS he did earlier, she'd see it with her own eyes. That way, Martin wouldn't have to be the bearer of bad news, and Lilly wouldn't have to worry that he held a grudge against the supposedly mild-mannered school teacher. "Well, a couple of the reenactors went off the script. Not sure why. The guy who runs the thing, he's playing Pat Garrett, wasn't very happy with them. That's all."

"I've seen *Young Guns*, so I've kind of seen it all already, huh?" asked Lilly innocently. Had Martin been in a better frame of mind, he'd have reminded her of every historical detail the movie got wrong; under the present circumstances, he just let it pass. "Did you talk to the guys?" she asked, as if an afterthought.

By 'the guys,' Martin knew she meant Kevin and Farber. "I talked to Kevin, everything's good. He's exactly who I thought he'd be..." started Martin, before Lilly interrupted.

"What does that mean, Martin?"

Martin wished he could go back and rephrase his answer, but that time has passed. "I just mean I figured he'd be easygoing and understand. He did, and it's all good."
"And Carl?" Lilly questioned, raising her eyebrows.

"Not yet. Didn't get a chance to talk to him, but I'm sure I will," Martin replied through gritted teeth. He most definitely did intend to speak to Farber, but an apology was not anything even close to what he planned. Martin grabbed the strap of his backpack, still containing the two books with which he would confront the bastard; the feeling of possessing them warmed Teebs.

"Okay, then!" Lilly said, as if not a thing in the world was wrong. Martin understood, in her world, there was not; however, in his, he was in a tsunami shifting time that felt hopelessly like it wouldn't end well, no matter what he did.

Sunday – 2:30 pm

"And so I was going to finish up the book after this trip, but now it seems like a waste of time." Carl Farber sat in the shade of a white-oak tree, talking to Jane in Lincoln's only tiny little park, their lemonades sweating in the heat of a New Mexico summer. He was finally getting the chance to talk about who he really was, not just that guy on the other side of the bar, tipping ridiculously well to keep his bartender happy.

"Well, look, Carl. There's how many books on Lincoln and the Kid? A hundred? A thousand? Like, what's the difference if there's two books on that Murphy thing? If you've put all the work into it already, you might as well finish it up. That's the ultimate cop-out, dude, getting near the finish line and quitting 'cause you might not win."

The last sentence stung Farber a bit, and in his surly mood of the past few days, he'd normally have snapped if anyone else had said it. Furthermore, he knew Jane was right. If his book was any good, he'd find an audience somewhere, and probably over a long period of time. What did Carl Farber have but time? he asked himself. The answer, if he even allowed it to form, was simple: nothing. Carl Farber had nothing but time in his life. His job was at a dead end, and he certainly wasn't going anywhere further up the teaching ladder. His love life had been on life support since having a grand total of three dates in the past decade. Every morning he looked in the mirror, he had less hair and more flab than the day before. His bank account, such as it was, held enough for the bare essentials and a pizza at the end of the week, if all went well. Carl Farber was a nothing man in his own little nothing world. The only time lately he felt like *somebody* was when he was writing his book - and when he'd met Jane, here in Lincoln.

"What happens with you after the tourists leave?" he asked the young woman idly playing with the melting ice in her cup.

"I sling drinks til the end of September, usually," she allowed, "then head for one of the ski towns for the fall and winter. I get by, bartending, waiting tables, sometimes giving snowboard lessons."

Farber wondered why he'd never felt such freedom in his own life. The freedom to just pack up what you owned in your car and light out for a new town. Find a job, find a room, hustle during the day and party all night. Where the hell had his life gone so off the rails that he'd blinked when he was twenty-five and by the time his eyes reopened, another twenty years had gone by? The thought of it, of his mortality, made him sad. "Sounds like a dream life to me." He continued, however: "What's the long-range plan? Do you ever want to settle down? Have a family?"

Jane snorted so hard, lemonade came out of her nose. "Settle down? Are you shitting me, Carl? Do I seem like the type to settle down? Hellllll, no, I don't plan to settle down. And family? My family is so fucked up, they ruined the definition of 'family' for every family that ever exists for the rest of eternity!"

Farber sighed, the question he was going to ask remaining on his lips for the time being. Checking his watch, he noticed he'd shortly need to get ready for the next show. The final show of the day, the one that everyone attending would *never* forget.

Sunday - 2:45 pm

Kelly Childs and his band of reenactors rummaged up whatever they'd need for the day's final performance. Circling up, he had Steve once again clear every weapon and then load each with enough blanks to get through the curtain call. Looking around, Kelly noticed that one of his cast was missing. "Where the hell is Farber?" he said, with some exasperation in his voice. "He needs his weapon cleared!" No one seemed to know where Carl Farber - the day's fly in the ointment - had gone off to, but he hadn't been seen in a good thirty minutes.
"His gun's here, so don't worry," boomed Steve, ricocheting off of the ancient adobe walls. "I'll just clear it and keep it with me."

"No," snapped Childs, wagging his finger. "Screw him. If he can't be here on time, he gets no gun. Let Olinger get shot down without even the chance to defend himself... *jerk*." Kelly threw up his hands and turned away.

With a smile, Brandon approached Billy. "One more time, hey, Kid? You ready to put me down?"

Billy laughed but turned introspective. "Ya know, I ain't wantin' to kill ya, and I still feel bad 'bout it. But, yeah, ya goin' down, Bell."
Brandon screwed up his eyes and asked, "Why are you talking like that all of sudden, dude?"

Billy just smirked and said, "Talkin' like what? This's the way I talk, Bell."

Brandon just shook his head and wrote it off as Kevin getting into character for the final performance. Across the room, Steve watched with interest the exchange between the two young men. Something was different, and he rubbed his chin, trying to figure out what it was. Peering over the rim of his sunglasses, he stared at Kevin, who'd suddenly become the most authentic reenactor of the bunch. Oh, well, thought Steve, he'd either figure it out in the next forty-five minutes or he wouldn't.

"All right, everyone," Childs bellowed. "Let's do this one for Billy! One more time for the Kid to ride free…at least, until I gun his ass down in Sumner!"

Had he looked back as he headed down the stairs, he'd have seen the real William H. Bonney frowning - and definitely not amused.

"And where the hell is Farber?!"

Sunday - 2:46 pm

Arriving early enough to score almost front-row seats, Martin and Lilly Teebs waited, along with a half-full section of bleachers, for the show to start. He noticed the reenactors beginning to file out of the courthouse and excused himself so he could have a word with 'Kevin.' Heading across the dirt set, he was sighted by Steve, who in his capacity as security, walked over to him. "Whatcha doing, hoss?"

Martin smiled his most unthreatening smile. "Hey, Steve, not causing any trouble. Just wanted to wish Kevin good luck on the show. We patched things up earlier today, anyway."

Steve eyed the man up and down and admitted to himself that he didn't look like much of a troublemaker. "Okay, make it quick, show's about to start." And with that, Steve ambled off to his post at the fake Wortley Hotel.

Martin quickly made his way toward the courthouse stairwell, Billy being the last person to descend it. Teebs first saw his boots, then slowly the whole man came into frame, grinning from ear to ear. Making sure no one was around who could hear them, Billy finally said, "Teebsie! Ain't this a sonofabitch?!"

Martin grabbed his friend by the shoulders and shook him slightly, almost as if to see if he was real. "Billy? It's you, right, Billy? Oh my God. What the hell is going on?"

Billy's smirk never left his face as he gazed around at the mountains behind the courthouse. "Well, I was hopin' that's one you could answer fer me, *amigo*. Cause this is some damn fine mess we're in."

Martin's words rushed out of his mouth faster than he could think: "I had this Dream, the books, and then the book that you had, then when you gave it, everything changed, and then today, the other book and the..."

"Whoa, Teebsie, rein that colt in!" exclaimed Billy. "I can't make out what the hell yer sayin', and this ain't the time. I gotta get me up in that building and blow the bejesus out of that piece-of-crap Farber."

Martin's breathing was heavy and labored. He had a hundred questions to ask, but no time to ask them. He could hear the pop of Child's microphone as he tested out the PA system. Finally, Martin steadied himself, looked Billy directly in the eyes, and queried, "Do you remember *any* of it?"

Billy leaned into the big man, wrapping his arm around Martin's shoulder and grinning. "I remember *all* of it, pal. Every damn thing. Now let me git, and we'll figure this out later."

Suddenly, all of the stress Martin had been feeling for the past few days washed away. He felt clean and clear; most of all he felt...*sane*. Martin let his head loll back as a big smile of relief spread across his face.

Just before Billy climbed the set stairs to his position, he turned back and asked, "Teebsie, you got any *real* shells for that damn Whitney? I'd like ta finish this once and for all…and for real."

Martin looked at him, shaking his head, to let him know what a bad idea that would be.

Sunday – 2:50 pm

"Where the hell is he, Brandon? You suggested him!" growled Kelly Childs.

"I looked around everywhere. Can't find him. I'm sure he'll be here for his part. Just start it up, and if we get to where Billy shoots him, I'll run over and take the fall." Childs glared back at the tour guide, knowing this year's pageant would go down in history as being the worst of all time - all due to one Carl Farber.

Sunday – 2:52 pm

"Good talk with Kevin?" Lilly asked, as Martin returned to his seat. She looked at her husband to see him look happier than he had since they'd stepped off the plane in Albuquerque, some five days ago.

"Lil, you have no idea," gushed Martin. "I'm so glad I talked to him again. This is going to be a great show, just you watch." Martin put his arm around his wife, and she scooted closer to him. As pleased as Lilly was that Martin was happy, she was also relieved that maybe, just maybe, he wasn't going to need some expensive psychotherapy that she wasn't at all sure their insurance would cover.

Sunday – 2:55 pm

"Umm, don't you need to go? The show's about to start?" inquired Jane, as she stared at the somber Carl Farber. The man seemed to be wrestling with something, and while she didn't want to rush him, she also didn't want to miss the performance.

"Yeah, yeah…in a minute. I'm not in the first few scenes anyway," he explained. "Jane, did you ever think about leaving New Mexico? I mean, setting up shop in another state?"

Jane lifted one corner of her mouth and cocked her head. "Hmm…well, sure, I guess. Colorado, Nevada, maybe Arizona? I go out and visit Trisha a couple of times a year in LA, but I'm more of a mountain-and-desert girl."

"Well, I mean somewhere more...I don't know…more east of here. Like maybe New Jersey?" Farber asked the question, with a lift to the final word to indicate it was just a question and not a suggestion. He'd desperately hoped that maybe the woman saw more in him than that long-ago, other woman, Theresa, who'd seen nothing in him.

Jane sported a confused look, not truly understanding what Farber was asking. "You mean to live there? I don't know…it's not really my scene."

Farber was expecting this reaction, and he wondered just how far he should push the issue. "Well, you know, it's hard to get started in a new place, I understand. I was thinking, if you wanted to maybe try it out, you could stay for a while at my place? I have an extra bedroom and all."

Jane was careful and deliberate before she answered the question. She now was relatively sure that Carl had just asked her to move in with him. A guy she'd known for all of about three days, who was twice her age, didn't look like he had enough money to support himself, and wasn't her type at all, to say the least. She remembered her conversation with Trisha that she shouldn't lead on this man (or any man), lest he conceive ridiculous scenarios - like inviting her to move in with him!

In her mind, Jane was just being a playful flirt. She meant nothing by her actions, and these men meant nothing to her. She knew if she treated them right and made them feel special, they'd treat her right when it came time to close out their tab, plus they'd come back another time. It had seemed like a very fair and completely obvious arrangement, but this time, at least, her signals had gotten mixed.

"Carl...umm…that's very sweet and all, but no. I mean, just…no," answered Jane flatly. She realized she'd gone over some line with this man. Inviting him to meet her after work last night had been spontaneously stupid, and Jane would never have done it but for the hopeful look on the guy's face - and the five Jack Daniel's shots that a group of Japanese tourists had insisted on buying her. She looked at Farber and knew immediately that he wasn't taking it well. The man was wounded by her words, but if nothing else, Jane's father had taught her to shoot straight and not bullshit anyone.

"So that's it?" asked Farber, "this is over?"

Hearing the words 'this is over' shocked Jane. Just how attached was this guy to her? For God's sake, she thought, I've been around him for what, two hours in total? She knew he was in too deep, so she tried to soften the blow as she made her way out of the park and to the show's grounds "Hey," she said softly, "look at me." Farber raised his eyes with a mixture of sadness and anger. "You're a great guy, Carl, but just not for me. We come from two different worlds. I liked getting to know you, a lot. Not too many guys who come through here can make conversation about anything except Billy the Kid," she said with a laugh.

The plan to let Farber down easy clearly wasn't working very well, however, as he sat mute, staring right past her. The sounds of the show could be heard going in full force, and Jane knew that sooner or later, his character was going to have some lines to say. "Carl, the show? They need you! C'mon, Carl, show me what you've got!"

Somewhere in Farber's currently dark mind, there was a point of light. There *must* be a point of light, so dark were his thoughts at the moment. Here he was, being dumped by a vapid college dropout, who probably didn't know the first thing about the Magna Carta or the Louisiana Purchase. *She* was letting *him* down? *He* should be the one letting *her* down.

Jane bent down to give Farber a final kiss on the cheek, but at the last second, almost beyond his control, he turned his lips toward hers and jammed his tongue in her mouth, while simultaneously grabbing the back of her head and pushing her into him.

"NO!" she screamed, as she pulled her head away. "What the fuck are you doing, you creep?!" Had the reenactment not been proceeding, Jane would have been heard plainly on the street, but Pat Garrett and his posse were gunning down Tom Folliard as it happened, and no one but Farber and Jane was the wiser.

Farber glared at her, the taste of her lemonade still on his tongue. "You tease! You used me all week, for what? To get bigger tips? You don't deserve someone like me!" The tone he used was low and threatening, but Jane hadn't survived three years as a bartender by being a pushover.

"No kidding, I don't deserve you! Have a nice life, Carl!" she snapped and turned to walk away.

An impulse totally foreign to Farber materialized within him. At first, he was confused - the images he saw in his head were sexual, and violent, but he felt no sexual excitement at the time. It was as if he were being shown a 'how to' film and compelled to act on it. It was all about power, and domination, and humiliation. In the final seconds before he jumped up from the picnic table, he realized that for his entire life around women, he had lacked power, was always dominated by them, and frequently humiliated, just like what was happening now. As he rose from his seat, he could clearly see the 'off' button that he should hit and let Jane leave; but in his mind, he simply laughed and said, "Fuck it."

Carl lunged at Jane, tearing at her tight T-shirt. She screamed again, loudly so that anyone near might hear, but no one came. The sound of Garrett's guns killing Charlie Bowdre drowned out the sound of Farber's attack. Jane spun around with a backfist, but just missed connecting with his face; while he pushed her hard against a tree, pawing at her breasts and pressing his mouth to hers. As soon as she could free her mouth, she bit his cheek hard, which caused him to howl in pain. Reflexively, he brought his hand to his face to protect it; and then he hit her as hard as he could, with a backhand across her face. Jane's head slammed into the tree with a sickening thud, and she slid down to the ground, either dead or unconscious.

Instantly, Carl's mind returned to a tiny, candlelit room on this very street, but over one-hundred-forty years ago. He saw the same defiance and fear in the eyes of that beautiful, dark-haired woman. He knew he had to have her, not for the sexual conquest, but so his bitter rival Martin Teebs would know that Carl Farber could have anything that he wanted - nothing, especially not a middling salesman from New Jersey, was going to stop him. In his mind's eye, he saw himself backhanding the woman, who fell to the floor, fighting for her life; but ultimately, she could not stop the inevitable.

Farber looked down at Jane, blood leaking from the corner of her mouth, and he began to panic. If she wasn't dead, then he'd be hunted, tried, and jailed for a long time. If she was, he'd be in jail forever or executed. If he ran, perhaps he could make it to his motel to gather his things, race to Albuquerque, and fly home to New Jersey on the next flight. Of course, he was smart enough to know about extradition rules, and the New Jersey State Police would find him in a matter of minutes.

Farber's breathing escalated, and he began to twitch. He needed a plan. What he needed was an escape. A place to run where no one knew him, and no one would find him. The entirety of his misdeeds in the past came into sharp focus, and he knew where he needed to go: *Lincoln, NM, circa 1878*. If that dumbass Teebs followed him, Farber would take care of him just the way he had the last time. The only person he truly worried about was the one currently prancing about those false-fronted buildings across the street. Farber could run, but he could never hide from Billy the Kid. With every fiber of his being, Carl Farber knew, in that moment, that the boy known as William H. Bonney must die.

Sunday – 3:20 pm

Trisha sat high up on the last row of the bleachers, both to avoid coming into contact with Martin and his wife, whom she could plainly see below, and to keep an eye out for Jane. While Jane was pretty much of a free spirit, she generally appeared when she was expected somewhere and texted if she wasn't going to make it. Trisha checked her phone for the tenth time, but there was still no text from her friend.

The show was reaching its climactic point as Deputy Bell walked Billy up the stairs into the courthouse. Inside, a great scuffle was heard, and a shot rang out. Seconds later, Brandon/Bell fell out of the door, into the arms of Godfrey Gauss, as he'd done twice during the earlier shows. Brandon peered around to see if Carl Farber had ever arrived at his station, being as Billy would momentarily make the window with the Whitney shotgun to blow him to kingdom come. Not seeing Farber, the tour guide began to crawl out of sight so he might run around the buildings and be able to substitute as Olinger.

Sunday – 3:26 pm

Martin had glanced back for at least the twentieth time to see whether Trisha was still sitting in the bleachers behind him. Each time, she seemed to be either lost in thought or checking her phone, so their eyes never connected.

As Deputy Bell fell from Gauss's arms, the recently deceased started crawling away for some reason. Suddenly, the crowd gasped; a man came sprinting across the street at full speed.

Kelly Childs, furious that his show once again was falling apart, waited for Gauss to deliver the seminal line: "The Kid killed Bell!" Just as Childs prepared to recite Olinger's "And he's killed me, too," the director spotted Farber streaking to the set, running toward Steve at full speed. In a split-second, Steve was hit from behind and fell, Farber grabbed the revolver from the retired cop's holster, and Billy came to the window, ready to blast whoever presented himself as Olinger.

Unaware of what had happened only an instant ago, Billy shouted, "Hello, Bob!" and pulled the shotgun's trigger, with a percussive slapback toward the half-empty stands.

Farber jumped up, shrieking, "Hello yourself, you little prick!" and fired Steve's .45.

The round tore into Billy's shoulder, and he cried out in pain. Confused about what had just occurred, the crowd offered a weak, uncertain applause, while Steve shouted over the din, "That's a live gun! Get down!"

At the same moment, Billy struggled onto the balcony, blood soaking his shirt and vest and beginning to drip onto the rail. Those in the audience realized something must have gone horribly wrong and began to scream and scatter, as Billy called out toward the bleachers:

"Teebsie!!!"

Sunday – 3:28 pm

Trisha watched the entire scene unfold before her horrified eyes. The once-gentle school teacher, who had danced with her at the Brewery only two nights ago, had just seized a real gun and shot Kevin, who was now bleeding profusely and apparently calling for Martin to save him. Men, women, and children shrieked and dispersed, some hiding under the bleachers, others dashing for the safety of a line of cars parked just behind. Farber still stood menacingly, pointing the gun alternately at Steve and Billy, and then swinging it toward the crowd.

Running down the metal steps and looking around wildly for some direction, Trisha practically stepped on the Teebs. Martin grabbed her arm with one hand and Lilly's with the other and yelled, “Get out of here! To the cars, go!”

Lilly screamed for him to follow, but Martin knew this was a situation he couldn’t run from. Lilly tried to run back for him, but Trisha grabbed her, shouting, “No! No! Carl will kill us!” and dragged her off, out of the line of fire.

Sunday – 3:28 pm

Farber looked up at the balcony and saw his nemesis groaning and trying to staunch the flow of blood from his shoulder. He heard the boy shout, “*Teebsie*!” and Carl swung the gun around to the stands, intent on putting both of his enemies in the grave at the same time. He saw the big coward running around the corner of the bleachers, pulling two women along as human shields, and decided not to waste a bullet on a target he couldn’t hit. First waving the gun toward Steve and then toward Billy, Farber thought quickly about how to make his escape.

Sunday – 3:28 pm

When the shot went off from Steve’s .45, Brandon knew the show had gone terribly amiss. Seeing Kevin stagger onto the balcony, bleeding, had triggered a mass, frantic exit by the spectators. After Steve yelled out that the gun was live, Brandon began an inexorable low crawl toward his vehicle, sitting in the line behind the bleachers. If he could just make it to the truck, he could retrieve his own sidearm and take Farber out. Brandon had been in a lot more dire shit than this in Iraq, against far-better-trained enemies than a balding, high-school history teacher. He motioned for Kelly Childs and the actor portraying Gauss to stay down and not call attention to themselves. Inch-by-inch, Brandon got closer to the truck; amazingly, Farber hadn’t taken another shot…yet.

Sunday – 3:29 pm

Martin sprinted across the back of the bleachers, which afforded almost no protection but at least disguised him from Farber. When he reached the center walkway, he ran toward the front, just as Billy noticed him. “Teebsie, I’m hit!” the Kid yelled, as Farber swung the barrel toward Martin and fired. The bullet whizzed by Martin's ear, close enough to feel the heat, but barely missing him. Martin sprinted across the open field to the set buildings just as Steve, who had regained his feet, vaulted at Farber.

Sunday – 3:29 pm

Steve, who'd been taken out from behind by the frantic Farber, got to his feet and lunged at the man just after he'd fired the second round. He became aware of Steve's presence a split-second before the cowboy got close enough to tackle him. Swinging the big revolver backhand, Carl laid open a deep and nasty gash along Steve's temple. The big man went down again, and Farber sprinted for the courthouse.

Sunday – 3:29 pm

While Farber raced to the courthouse stairwell, Martin bounded up the steps to where Billy was. "Damn, Teebsie, this hurts," the boy said, smiling weakly. "Git me a gun and lemme finish the job on that bastard." Martin examined the wound, which was serious but didn't appear to be fatal. He helped Billy down the steps, where he hoped medics would be dispatched at any second.

Sunday – 3:30 pm

As he watched Farber run, Brandon was able to reach his truck, get inside, and retrieve his own .45. Although Farber now held the high ground, he wasn't an experienced fighter (or so Brandon believed), and he had limited ammo. Rather than wait for the real Lincoln County sheriff to arrive, Brandon decided the risk to others was too great, and he carefully made his way toward the courthouse. He knew to tread cautiously, lest the stairs he was about to climb become the same death trap they had been for the man he had been portraying, J.W. Bell.

Sunday – 3:30 pm

Steve walked over toward Billy, both men bleeding badly but alive. The hit to his head had knocked a memory into Steve, who suddenly knew *exactly* who Martin Teebs was and what he was doing (and had done) in Lincoln. He nodded at Teebs to let him know they were on the same side.

"Watch him!" Martin yelled to Steve, while gesturing toward Billy. "I'm going to kill that fuck!" Totally unarmed, Teebs ran toward the steps, not caring whether he lived or died, as long as he took Farber with him.

"You ain't armed!" Steve roared after him, but it was too late.

Unwilling to let his friend suffer his fate alone, Billy demanded, "Help me up!" Once he regained his feet, the Kid unsteadily climbed the stairs, pursuing Martin. Arising and going against every bit of tactical training he'd ever received, Steve followed the two men, figuring Farber might kill one of them, but whoever was left could get the son of a bitch in a rush.

Sunday – 3:30 pm

Just near enough to the courthouse to spot Farber in the upstairs windows, frantically rummaging around, Brandon was shocked to see *three* men run up the stairs - all apparently unarmed - after Farber. "Dammit!" the tour guide growled under his breath, as Martin, Kevin, and Steve quickly rushed up. Now Farber had something more powerful than a gun: He had hostages. Not willing to be the catalyst that got the three men killed, Brandon was forced to withdraw behind the nearby privy, where he could keep his eyes on the situation.

Sunday – 3:30 pm

Trisha and Lilly huddled behind a line of cars, along with at least a dozen other frightened people. When Martin had run across the open lot, they'd both viewed and heard Farber fire at him. Lilly screamed, "Martin!" to no avail, while Trisha cried. Now that the gunfire had stopped, none of the men involved in the shooting was anywhere to be seen. Just as Lilly was about to make a dash toward the courthouse, a voice shouted out, "Stay where you are! He's got hostages!"

Sunday - 3:31 pm

Carl Farber frantically searched among backpacks, discarded clothes, and bags, clearly looking for something. His breath came in giant, sucking bursts, the run up the steps having winded him. Throwing things to and fro, he knew he had only seconds before whatever was going to happen to him happened. Hearing the sounds of multiple feet charging up the stairs, he felt like Billy must have during the Kid's escape from the jail in 1881. He knew - act now, or he'd probably be dead. For a brief moment, Farber considered suicide and began to lift the gun to his temple, until he heard the voice of Martin Teebs screaming, "I'll kill you!" echoing off the adobe walls. Farber narrowed his eyes and pointed the gun to the spot where he was sure his enemy would appear just seconds from now.

Sunday - 3:31 pm

Billy, surprisingly considering his blood loss, pushed past Martin at the first landing to the stairs, with Steve hot on his heels. All three men sprinted up the final ten steps, arriving together on top of the bloodstains that belonged to J.W. Bell. Faced with the barrel of Steve's .45 revolver now in Carl Farber's hands, they all stopped as both factions stood, glaring at each other.

Sunday - 3:31 pm

"I don't care if all you assholes die," threatened Farber, "but I'm getting out of here as soon as I find that book." The sound of four men's heavy breathing was the only noise in the now-quiet room. Martin, never having shed his backpack, reached to slide it off. Farber instantly covered him with the gun. "Whoa, there, you bastard! Don't move another inch."

Martin stopped, but looked directly at Farber. "If I had a gun in here, I'd already have used it, you piece of shit. You want books, here they are." With that, Martin reached down into the backpack and retrieved Farber's *Coward of Lincoln County* manuscript and the tiny copy of *Lincoln County Days*, tossing both at the armed man's feet.

"What the hell are these?" queried Farber, cautiously bending over while still covering the men.

"That's what you wanted, right? Open a page, and go to any time you damn well please? Well, go, but know I'm going to follow you to hell if I have to, you son of a bitch," Martin said defiantly.

Billy pressed his neckerchief to his wound, slowing the flow of blood, while Steve used his sleeve to wipe away from his eyes whatever he could of his own blood. Confused, Farber held both books in his hands. "What is this? I never wrote these! Who did this?" he asked, enraged and waving the gun in front of the three men.

Just as Martin was opening his mouth to speak, a soft voice called out from behind Farber: "I did."

All four heads snapped in the direction of the voice; out of the next room walked none other than Sergio Bachaca.

Sunday – 3:32 pm

"You!" exclaimed Farber, backing up against the outside wall to be able to cover all four men. "What the hell did *you* have to do with this?"

Billy was feeling woozy and started to waver. Steve caught him in his big hands and gently sat the boy against the wall.

"Talk!" ordered Farber, urging on Bachaca with the barrel of his gun.

"My book, people called it the best researched of all time, no?" Bachaca began coolly. "There's a reason for that, gentlemen." Martin continued to dart his eyes around the room, still only intent on killing Farber, and looking for a way to accomplish it. "The reason is," continued Bachaca, "that in 2012, while I was finalizing my research, I came to this very town, during this very event, and I wound up falling backwards in time to the year 1878. Imagine my amazement to be walking among the Regulators, Billy the Kid, and, of course, the warriors aligned with Murphy and Dolan. You, young William, must remember seeing me on the street at least a time or two?"

Billy was more concerned at the moment with stopping the blood flowing out of the hole in his shoulder, and his memory was hazy; but he managed, "Hmmpphh, maybe so. Can't remember right now."

"Understandable," said Bachaca, condescendingly. "In any event, I knew about what happened during the Lincoln County War because I lived through it. However and whyever I wound up traveling back through time, I have no idea. One day, when the War was over, I woke up and was simply in the present, with only a day in my real life having passed. Try as I might, I could not will myself back to the past; so I wrote it off as a wonderful research mission and put everything I knew into that book that you have in your backpack, Martin."

Martin was shocked at the story he was hearing - and even more shocked to hear his own name. He reached down again into the backpack, which caused Farber to swing the gun in his direction. Martin slowly withdrew the heavily worn copy of *The True Life of Billy the Kid* and held it up for Bachaca to see. "This book?" Martin questioned.

"Yes," Sergio said, looking at the book as if seeing an offspring who'd just done something to be proud of. "I heard about that copy in Magdalena, and I dispatched Steve to fetch it. When he sent me the photos, Billy's list was not there, and I was most disappointed that we apparently hadn't found my wayward child. I see, however, that this volume is indeed my creation, and I'm most thankful it's back in your possession, Martin." No one in the room could quite believe what they were hearing.

Farber looked nervously out of the window, aware that the sheriff would be arriving any minute. He needed a portal out of this time period if he was going to save his neck.

"And what about *these* books?" Farber demanded. "*I* didn't write these!"

“No, you didn’t, Carl. But every good story needs both a protagonist and, of course, an antagonist. You fit the bill so nicely, almost without me having to do any work.” Bachaca looked straight at Farber.

“This isn’t me!” Farber raged, swinging the gun around wildly. “You made me into a fucking monster! Do you know what I’ve done because of you?!”

Bachaca glanced over at the other three men standing at the top of the stairwell before responding to Farber. “I do indeed, Carl. But remember, I no more ‘made’ you into anything than I did Martin. Your own tendencies and thoughts ‘made’ you who you are. My book simply created a playing field for those traits to come out. So, do I know what you’ve done? Of course! And I’m sorry to say that it cannot continue. That’s why I came up here earlier and secured this.” From behind his back, Bachaca produced a shiny copy of *Sunset in Sumner*, which he’d taken earlier from Kevin’s backpack while Martin lay unconscious at his feet.

Instinctively, Farber knew that book was his only way out. “Give it to me…*now*,” he commanded.

Bachaca sighed and replied, “You know I can’t do that, Carl. Look at the damage done here…and elsewhere. It’s time that y…”
Boom! Steve’s revolver roared as Farber put a slug directly between and just north of Bachaca’s eyes. The stunned author seemed to have a nanosecond of understanding of how badly he’d underestimated Farber before falling flat on the floor, dead as a stone. Farber rushed over and grabbed *Sunset in Sumner*, a few drops of Bachaca’s blood now gracing its slick cover. Sirens wailed in the distance as the noose began to tighten around the former teacher. Carl swung the gun back toward the three men now blocking his path out of the courthouse. He just needed to escape the building. Just needed to get to the trees and read a passage about 1880 or so, and he knew he’d vanish and be free.

“Get out of the way!” he yelled menacingly, as Martin and Steve edged to the side. Farber clearly had no compunction against killing, but he hadn’t the time to waste on this little trio of impotents. As he ran for the stairs, Carl caught Martin’s eyes and said with a devilish smile, “Thanks for writing this one, Martin, I’m *sure* I’m going to enjoy it!” And he fled down the stairs.

Sunday – 3:35 pm

Carl Farber raced from the back door of the Lincoln County courthouse and made his way toward the street, aiming to lose himself in the trees along the river. Hot on his heels was Martin Teebs, determined to chase the man either back to 1880 or, more hopefully, to his grave. As Carl cleared the buildings of the reenactment set, the sound of a semi-automatic handgun firing was heard; a puff of dust went up from Farber's chest, just before he hit the ground, hard. Thirty yards to the side, Jane stood, blood running down the side of her mouth, a wisp of smoke rising from the barrel of her 9 mm, and her nostrils flaring in anger.

A split-second after Jane's shot, another, more powerful round rang out from the other direction, intended to be a headshot to take out Farber once and for all. Unfortunately, Farber fell just before the round arrived; instead, it found a home in the man pursuing him: Martin Teebs.

Sunday – 3:36 pm

"Martin!" Lilly shrieked in terror, seeing him hit the ground after being shot.

"*Martin*!" Trisha yelled at exactly the same moment, but in an accent she'd never had nor heard from herself before.

Both Lilly and Trisha dashed toward the killing zone, where Martin was writhing in agony and Farber not moving at all. Just before the women got there, Farber pried his eyes open, blood pooling on the dirt from a wound to his upper chest. Sounding as if he was drowning in his own blood, he struggled to breathe as he looked around. Ten feet to his left was Steve's gun; ten feet to his right was Martin Teebs, also bleeding profusely; at his feet lay the copy of *Sunset in Sumner*. Two women sprinted at him; the rest of the crowd cried out in shock at the bloodletting. In his final second, Farber had to decide which to reach for.

While Lilly and Trisha converged on Martin, Farber caught the horrified eyes of a beautiful, dark-haired woman staring straight at him. She screamed as if shot herself, while he struggled to reach *Sunset in Sumner*. Gurgling blood from somewhere deep within, he pulled himself along the dirt as Teebs tried to rise to stop him. Farber reached the book a split-second before Martin, gave a ghastly smile to the screaming woman, and opened its pages - disappearing into thin air before the stunned onlookers, leaving behind only Steve's pistol and a bloody puddle.

Anything that was left of Trisha Davis disintegrated into the sand as she rushed to her lover's side. "*Martin! Martin! Regresa a mi*!!" This was Rosita Luna.

Lilly dropped to her knees near Martin's head, shocked at the scene unfolding in front of her. The woman with whom Lilly had spent the last ten minutes, cowering behind a car, looked exactly the same but clearly was no longer the same person. If forced at gunpoint to explain what she was seeing, Lilly wasn't sure she could do it. It was as if a new person had entered the young woman's body.

"It's *you*," Lilly said, in a tense, quiet voice, watching the young woman's heavy tears splatter in the sand.

Martin pushed himself up, pain wracking his left arm. He quickly looked to see the damage and realized the bullet had grazed him deeply, but hadn't actually entered his arm. "I'm okay," he coughed out, starting to realize where he was, "I'm okay."

Rosita closed her eyes, squeezing more tears from them as she then stared sorrowfully at Lilly. Lilly began to cry as well, neither woman able to break the lock of their mutual gaze. Martin reached up for Rosita, still confused but amazed that she was finally with him. Never looking down at his eyes, the young woman began to back away. Hurt and puzzled, Martin tried to reach her, but she stood up, bottom lip trembling, and walked off, fixated on Lilly the entire time. Unable to help himself, Martin cried hoarsely, "Rosita!" but to no avail. Falling back onto the dirt, only then did Martin comprehend that Lilly also was there. He looked up into her sad eyes for a moment, before the pain in his arm gave him the sweet relief of unconsciousness.

Sunday – 3:37 pm

"Code 3! Old Lincoln County courthouse. Multiple gunshot victims. Roll every bus you've got!" cried a Lincoln County deputy sheriff into her mic, hoping that by the time the ambulances arrived, there'd actually be someone alive to need one.

Sunday - 3:38 pm

Having heard the gunshots, Steve struggled down the stairs, with Billy hanging onto his right arm. The boy had lost a lot of blood, and his skin had taken on a disturbing gray pallor.

"Need help!" Steve shouted, ignoring his own injury, "Kid needs help here!" Seeing Martin lying on the ground, and his own gun a short distance away, Steve could only imagine that Farber had figured out some way to escape. He noticed a puddle of blood that clearly didn't belong to Martin and secretly smiled that Farber might be off in the bushes at this very moment, dying a horribly painful death.

"Oh, shit, Kevin!" yelled Brandon, who rushed over to help with the young man. "Oh, shit, don't die! Don't you dare die on me!" They laid out Billy next to Martin, with Lilly still kneeling at her husband's head. Brandon grabbed a bandana from around his own neck and pushed it into Billy's wound. The pressure seemed to help staunch the blood flow, but the Kid looked as bad as anyone can look and still be alive. Glancing up at Steve to see what the hell had just happened, Brandon was shocked to see the severity of the cowboy's wound, having been cut so deeply that the side of his skull glared out from its recesses. "Steve, sit down, man, that's a nasty gash," coaxed Brandon in his calmest voice.

"It's okay, I think," said Steve, dabbing his fingers at the blood still running down his cheek.

Knowing that shock could set in easily if he didn't stabilize Steve's situation, Brandon decided to call it as he saw it. "Steve, I can see your skull, man, sit the fuck down. *Now*!" Wavering, Steve's wobbly legs buckled, and he plopped down at the feet of both Billy and Martin. Brandon pressed firmly on Billy's wound as he surveyed the scene. He'd been in a lot of battles - this much damage from one man, in such a short amount of time, placed this near the top of the list. "What the hell happened here, Steve? Where did that guy go? How did he get all three of you?"

"Four," Steve corrected, as he started to swoon a bit. "Check upstairs. Bachaca's dead."

Sunday – 3:50 pm

With sirens wailing and ambulances loaded, the gruesome convoy turned east and raced for Roswell's trauma center. The young Billy the Kid was the most seriously injured, with a gunshot wound and suffering from hypovolemic shock. The other two men would live, after being patched up and observed overnight.

As the vehicles pulled away, the crowd members - who had managed to stay hidden during the carnage - began to emerge, bearing incredulous stories of the murderer being shot and then disappearing before their very eyes. The sheriff and his deputies questioned everyone they could, trying to piece together some kind of a timeline. Brandon identified the shooter as Carl Farber, a schoolteacher from New Jersey, who had been participating in the reenactment. When they got to the part of determining where this Farber had gotten off to, however, Brandon struggled to explain what he'd seen.

Lilly also was questioned before they would let her leave to follow Martin to the hospital. She offered no great insight, repeating what they'd heard a dozen times before. She certainly wasn't going to tell the cops that her husband had dreamt that something like this would happen with Carl Farber; then she'd also have to tell them that, in some other reality, Farber had raped Rosita Luna, who currently stood twenty paces away, leaning against the bleachers and silently crying about the unbelievable events.

Rosita gave a huge gasp when medics carried Sergio Bachaca's body, on a gurney, out of the back door of the courthouse. As horrible as this day had been, she thought that at least, no one had died…yet. That is, until she saw the man's body being wheeled into an ambulance and driven off in no hurry at all. Rosita had had enough and began to walk east, through town, back toward Trisha's house. She had no idea where she was going or what she was supposed to do, now lost in a time about which she knew nothing. Suddenly, a car came up alongside her, the driver opening the window to speak - it was Lilly Teebs.

"Get in," Lilly commanded.

Sunday – 4 pm.

Fittingly, Lilly had driven to the edge of town and pulled off the road near the cemetery. The young woman in the passenger seat couldn't have looked more out of place in a car if she had tried. Putting the car in park and shutting off the engine, Lilly spoke first.

"What is it you want with my husband?"

Rosita shook her head and rubbed her stinging eyes, without a notion of how to explain anything to this woman. "*Martin*, he is…everything to me. I have loved no other in my life."

Lilly focused on her breathing, having made a deal with herself that she would not lose her temper. This sad young woman probably knew nothing about Martin's real life and probably hadn't even known that Lilly existed. "You are aware that we are married? Right?" she began. "For twenty years now. In other words, the man you say you love has been married to me since you were a child."

Rosita tried to rise above the tide of despair threatening to swamp her. Knowing this woman held the key to her ability to possibly ever see Martin again, she tried to make some sense of the day. "*Senora* Teebs? Yes? *Senora* Teebs, I cannot explain this to you, although I wish I could. The last thing I remember was seeing Martin and that *monstruo* Farber in Fort Sumner. When I saw that, I…." Rosita turned away toward the window, unable to finish, with her choking gasps filtering across the front seat. Lilly stared at her, this day still mostly incomprehensible to the older woman.

"I could not live with this on my soul, this...horror," Rosita continued. Lilly wasn't sure, but this episode must have been the reason that Martin instantly disliked Farber. After what she'd seen of him today, on this, at least, she could agree with Martin and Rosita: Carl Farber was a piece of crap. The worst dregs of humanity. "Anyway," Rosita added, "I did something so shameful that I should be cast to hell. I left our son to fend for himself!" With this, Rosita began wailing again, unable to face the memory of that day in 1881.

"Your son? Yours and Billy's?" Lilly asked.

"*Con Bilito*? *No, no…no, Senora* Teebs. My son - *Martin Teebs, Junior* - is named after his father." Rosita knew the news wouldn't be received well, but she had spoken the truth.

"What?" said Lilly weakly, as her own tears began to flow. "You and Martin have a child together? Where is he?"

The sadness of not knowing the answer to that question was beyond the scope of human pain. "I do not know. At that time, Junior was two years old. Now I am here in your time, and I do not know to where I go back. I'm lost here, I'm stranded here, and now I'm all alone." Her tears drained, Rosita just sat numbly in the seat, waiting to be interrogated further, or maybe asked to leave.

"Where...where did you come from today, Rosita?" Lilly asked the question that had been on her mind ever since Martin had been shot. "Were you pretending to be Trisha this whole time?"

"*Senora* Teebs, this makes no sense, I know. For the past three days, I feel I've been in bed, trying to awaken. As if I've been asleep for a long, long time; and each moment, I wake up just a bit more, but still I cannot rise. I understand this Trisha, and she is *not* me. Only today when *Martin* was shot did my heart beat fully to rise and join him here in *his* time."

Lilly wiped her eyes, trying to figure out what to do next. This was Martin's mess to clean up, but he wasn't here to man the broom. Her loyal, faithful husband had been screwing some nineteenth-century Mexican girl behind her back and had even fathered a kid with her. That this story seemed ridiculously impossible was beside the point. The obvious object of Martin's affection was sitting right here, two feet away from her. She was younger, prettier, and had given Martin the thing that Lilly never could - a child.

At first, Lilly fell victim to pitying Martin for all he'd missed out on, but then another emotion took over: rage. How dare he create another life, entirely separate from their own, with this young woman! How dare he dedicate even a portion of his mind and soul to someone other than Lilly, whom he had sworn to love until death do them part.

While at first she was tempted to feel sorry for Rosita, that idea flowed rapidly away; now Lilly just felt *used.*

"Martin is in the hospital, I'm going to see him n..."

"Take me, *por favor*?" begged Rosita, as she cut in. "Just so I can see he is all right?"

"*I'm* going to see him now," replied Lilly, finishing her sentence, "and *you* are not to see him, ever again! Do I make myself clear, *Rosita*! Find a way back to wherever the hell you came from and find your own man...preferably one who isn't already married! Now get out!!"

Rosita's heart sank, both at her inability to see Martin and at being on the receiving end of Lilly's wrath. With a silent tear coursed down her check, the broken young woman stepped out of the car. In anger, Lilly floored the accelerator, spraying up dirt and gravel in Rosita's direction. As the car's tires screeched out of sight, Rosita walked limply back to Trisha's house to try to determine what to do with her second-chance life, suddenly gone terribly astray.

Sunday – 5:30 pm

With Martin and Steve stabilized, both men were transferred to two of the few rooms available in the crowded hospital. As it was overflowing with Covid-19 patients, even Billy couldn't be admitted to the ICU, and he was set up in a room near Martin's, the best the hospital staff could manage. The Kid had received several units of blood transfused into his failing body and, at present, had two IV bags of saline dripping into his veins. While doctors were optimistic that he'd survive, the danger of one or more of his internal organs shutting down was a real and present threat. Heavily medicated, the young man was in and out of consciousness, occasionally calling for someone named 'Tibbs' or 'Tipsy,' which the hospital staff could not seem to understand.

Martin himself was on a pleasant cocktail of pain meds as he laid in his hospital bed, hearing the sounds of the overworked staff rushing back and forth, trying to keep up with a crushing burden of patient needs. With the lights off but plenty of late daylight still streaming into the room, Lilly arrived at the doorway and looked upon her husband. The drive here from Lincoln had been spent preparing for what she'd say to him, following her intense conversation with Rosita. With her blood initially boiling, she'd gradually recognized that a knock-down, drag-out confrontation while Martin was recovering from a gunshot wound was most probably not the best idea.

Lilly had thought about divorce for a good part of the drive. In fact, at one point, her better sense told her to point the car toward Albuquerque, fly back to New Jersey, and meet with the best divorce lawyer she could find the very next morning. However, as she ruminated on that plan, she realized that she'd have very little evidence to present. Would her divorce lawyer have to time travel, too, in order to verify Martin's infidelity? How would she prove that Martin had cheated on her with a woman who might disappear at any moment? Would Lilly herself be locked up in a looney bin for believing that her husband was banging some hottie who'd died a century or so before she was even born?

The risk of it all didn't seem worth it, at least not at the moment. Standing there in the doorway of a hospital room, Lilly decided that the best thing to do immediately was nothing. Play the faithful, concerned wife who just wanted her husband to be okay. As it was, the hospital staff only allowed her to visit because of the violent nature of the incident and to assure herself that her husband would recover. Covid protocols prevented almost everyone else from visiting, and Lilly was allowed a grand total of fifteen minutes to see Martin. After that, she was invited to sleep in her car; a friendly staff member would run out to tell her if her husband had died - and perhaps been raptured.

"Martin, it's me. Lilly," she said, as she approached him and touched his cheek.

Initially appearing to be asleep, he pushed open his eyes and offered a feeble smile. "Some show, huh! How'd it end?" he asked, either as a joke or to verify the unbelievable turn of events of which he'd been such an integral part.

Lilly touched her cool palm to his forehead to soothe him. "Don't worry about that right now. Right now, you need to rest and get better." Lilly watched Martin's steady breathing and tried to understand how the man who had faithfully (or so she had thought) been by her side for twenty years could have found love in the arms of a...a child? Was this some ridiculous time-traveling, mid-life crisis to him? What next? A convertible and a house at the beach (as if they could afford such things) - or maybe Martin would get an earring and a few tattoos? Whatever, she'd have to accept that the man she'd married was irrevocably changed, and Lilly would have to decide if *that* man could still be a suitable husband for her.

Martin weakly reached up with his right arm to hold Lilly's hand, an act that surprised her and caused her to pull away. Catching herself, she slipped her hand back in his and simply smiled at him. "Thanks for...you know, the...it's just that...." Martin smiled at something only he could see. "Man, that's so…," and then stopped. Whatever he was trying to say or convey to Lilly was lost. However, the trip he was on seemed to be a good one so she concluded her visit, knowing that at least, he'd be alive tomorrow, when the hospital staff had said she could come and pick him up.

"You rest now, Martin, I have to leave. I'll see you tomorrow," said Lilly and bent over to kiss him on the forehead with pursed lips. Martin just nodded, apparently indeed on a really good trip; and he closed his eyes, still smiling at some unseen happy image that existed just beyond where anyone else could see.

Sunday - 5:35 pm

"Trisha! Open up!" yelled Jane, pounding on the front door of the house where her friend was staying. "Open the damn door!" After a couple of minutes of silence, with no expectation of having her demand met, Jane - still bloody after the hit she took from Farber - prepared to break through a window, if need be, to find out what had happened to her friend.

Jane had spent the better part of an hour with the Lincoln sheriff, explaining what had occurred with Carl Farber immediately prior to his rampage. She truthfully told the lawman that she'd retrieved her gun and was on her way to kill Farber for his assault upon her when she suddenly saw him run from the courthouse, after she'd heard several gunshots and someone yelling he'd been hit. The sheriff asked her how she knew that Farber was the one who did the shooting, rather than someone looking to protect innocent lives.

"I didn't," was her only and chilling reply.

In the end, the sheriff confiscated her gun as evidence, took the rest of her statement, and allowed her to go, with a warning not to leave the area without first letting his office know. The case would be turned over to the district attorney to decide whether she'd be prosecuted.

Jane smiled and raised her chin, asking, "Prosecuted for what?"

The sheriff looked confused after her ten-minute confession, responding, "For shooting that school teacher."

Jane confidently countered, "Okay, then, show me the alleged victim."

The sheriff opened his mouth as if to say something else but finally shook his head and simply said, "Just don't go anywhere until this is all resolved." And he walked away.

Now Jane stood on the porch of the grand house, trying to figure out what the hell had happened with Farber and with Trisha. She'd seen her friend run toward Martin Teebs and also what had appeared to be an uncomfortable moment with his wife; but without being close enough to hear, she was in the dark about what had transpired between Lilly and Trisha. Just as she began looking for a rock to break one of the small front windows, the door silently opened; Trisha stood there, having obviously been crying for quite some time.

"Girl! Are you okay? The fuck happened out there?" questioned Jane, as she pushed her way in through the front door. "Did you see that shit with Farber?"

Trisha just stared, as if at a complete stranger, but the mention of Farber's name and the blood on the woman's face finally prompted her to speak: "That animal did this to you also?"

Something about the way Trisha spoke, the rhyme and rhythm of it was off, and it confused Jane.
"'Also'? What's with the way you're talking, babe?" she asked curiously.

"What is so wrong with the way I speak?" responded Rosita.

Jane just stared at her friend, unable to determine if this might be some sort of Candid Camera joke, or if perhaps the shock of the day's events had impacted her friend enough to give her an accent. Determining to ignore it for the moment, Jane answered the first question. "Yeah, that piece of shit did this to me. You were right all along, Trish. I should have stayed away from him! You believe that freak expected me to move to New Jersey with him?!"

In a heartbeat, Rosita understood what was wrong. This woman thought she was Trisha, not understanding that Trisha, at least in this moment, was no more. She reached out to pull Jane toward the bathroom. "Come now, let me clean this for you, *si? Ven aqui.*"

Unable to figure out the end game with this new accent, Jane just followed her friend into the bathroom to see what would come next. Staring at Trisha, Jane studied her closely. She looked like the same incredible beauty she'd always been - but something beside her accent was different. There was a different vibe to her, a…maturity? No. A sadness? Perhaps. A resignation to what had occurred today? That seemed to describe it as ably as anything else.

"What happened out there with Teebs's wife? That looked pretty uncomfortable," Jane inquired, while Rosita dabbed at her lip with a warm, wet washcloth.

"This woman hates me for what I've done, and I cannot say I blame her," said Rosita softly. Jane waited to see exactly what 'what I've done' meant, but Trisha didn't volunteer any further information.

"Did you screw him? Martin, I mean?" asked Jane, as she mugged at Trisha in the mirror.

Rosita cocked her head in confusion. "What is this 'screw' you speak of? *No entiendo.*"

"Look, *chica*, I get it…today was brutal, but who the hell are you? I mean, the Spanish, the accent, the shy little girl routine? Where'd my friend Trisha go?" demanded Jane, with some concern.

Rosita took a deep breath before answering. "She's gone, I believe. She went away during the fighting. I am all that is left."

Now Jane was truly worried. She remembered the exchange they'd had this morning in her car when Trisha had asked her, "Who am I?" This woman was having an existential crisis right here, and right now! Maybe she'd fallen in love with this Martin character, and the wife had slapped her back into her lane? Maybe she was digging on *Farber*, and that's the reason she'd told Jane to stay away? Hell, maybe she just took the first exit to Looney Town with the pressure of thousands of annoying tourists causing her to crack! Whatever it was, she wanted to shake it out of her friend so they could talk some real shit about how Jane put a 9 mm slug in Farber's chest, and the scumbag just vanished into thin air.

"Look, babe, you're gonna be okay. Whatever it is, we can fix it. You want this…um... Martin? You can get him. You want to teach a Rosetta Stone course in Spanish, I'm digging on it. Just please...be back the way you were, okay?"

Rosita dabbed the last bit of blood from Jane's face and smiled at her. "You pronounce my name incorrectly."

"What?" asked Jane, shaking her head. "What?"

Rosita actually laughed for a second and corrected her, "You say *Rosetta.* My name is *Rosita,* and my last name is no *Pena*, it's *Luna*."

Sunday – 8:30 pm

Martin flipped his legs over the edge of the bed and unsteadily gained his feet. Other than some pain that the drugs hadn't seen fit to mask completely, he actually felt pretty well, which he knew was a byproduct of modern pharmacology. Reaching over to his rolling IV tower, he padded softly out in the hallway to find Billy's room. A nurse had told him that, with the overcrowding, his friend was nearby and stable. While the hospital might be over capacity at the moment, the staff seemed to be enjoying a lull in the action; Martin could hear laughing voices filtering down the hall from the nurse's station.

Martin peeked into a few rooms, reading the names on the whiteboards, but didn't find a room for Billy the Kid. Suddenly laughing to himself, he wondered under just what name Billy would have been admitted - William Bonney? Kid Antrim? Henry McCarty? Oliver Roberts, or maybe John Miller? With the drugs tickling his cerebral cortex, Martin laughed out loud, so much so that he was worried the staff would come and shove him back into bed. Finally, about four doors up and across the hall, Martin found a name that could be a match: Kevin Barrow. He suspected that Billy must have still had Kevin's wallet in his pocket at the time of the shooting, and this afforded him access to medical care versus a hanging, had anyone realized who actually was in room M27.

Martin gently opened the door and slid in quietly so as not to arouse anyone, including Billy. There, on the bed, with a variety of tubes and wires connected to him, was none other than the prince of pistoleers, Billy the Kid. Someone, perhaps a nurse, must have been sitting with Billy because a chair had been pushed next to the bed. Martin carefully sat down and parked his IV next to himself.

As quiet as Martin had been, the young man stirred. "Who's that?" Billy asked, in a small, weak voice. "Somebody comin' to finish the job?"

Martin's mouth was dry, and he licked his lips before answering. "Regulators, let's mount up."

Billy's eyes closed a little tighter, and a grin spread across his face from cheek to cheek. "Still quoting that shit movie, huh, Teebsie?"

Martin patted the boy's arm to let him know where he was. "Good to see you, Billy. Not like this, of course, but, man, am I glad to see you!"

"Wish I could say the same, but I can't open my eyes right now. What's this weird feeling - like I'm floatin' or somethin'?" asked Billy, in wonderment.

"I think you're high, Billy. They must have you on some pretty good drugs for the pain. Enjoy the ride," chuckled Martin.

The grin slipped from Billy's face as his head rolled side to side on the pillow. "What's gone on, Teebsie? One minute I'm eighty damn years old, and then I see ya in that courthouse, and I'm young again. You do this?"

Martin gripped tighter on the boy's forearm before responding. "The truth is, I don't know. I mean, maybe? I might have had something to do with it, but I'm not sure how. This whole thing has got me twisted around, you know what I mean?"

"Clear as mud, Teebsie, just like always," said Billy, with the faintest of laughs, which descended into some painful coughing.

"Look," said Martin, "I live my whole life. You and I, well, you know what we've been through. Do you remember coming to see me in Sumner, when I gave you that pardon?"

"I do."

"Well, the very next day was my last on Earth - at least, that was the plan. After I went down to Rosita's grave, I just…I don't know…died."

"I was there, *amigo*."

"What!" exclaimed Martin. "Where?"

"I juss knew somethin' was gonna happen for ya, and I wanted to see it. Was standin' over the wall and seen it all."

Martin was touched that his friend would forgo heading back to his own time, just to see him off, "Thanks, Billy, I really appreciate that." The young man just nodded.

"So I wound up, well…dead, or I thought I was. Then I was back at the Patron place," recounted Martin, "and all of a sudden, everyone was there. I was back with Rosita and Junior!" Martin smiled widely at the memory. "My father was there, Lilly and that guy Roberts - a bunch of people."

"Was I there?" asked Billy directly.

"No…you weren't. Other than Rosita and Junior, everyone was from *this* time period.

Anyway, I started to choke on something…some food. Rosita was trying to save me, but she couldn't. The last thing I saw was Junior's crying eyes." Martin had to stop for a moment, the memory overpowering him. "And then, it got brighter and brighter, and it was *Lilly* knocking loose what I was choking on. Shit, Billy, when I came to, I was in Lincoln for the first time, back in 2021 - I mean, now - and that was just last week."

"You sure you ain't drunk somethin', Teebsie? If not, you want some of what they's givin' me?"

Martin could only laugh, which rescued him from the remaining tears he'd been saving up, thinking about Rosita and his son. "Thanks, but I'm on some pretty good stuff, too. Anyway. Last week, I go out in the town, and I meet you…I mean, Kevin, Trisha is Rosita, and Farber and Steve are themselves, but they don't remember anything. It's like somebody turned the dial on my life back four years in one fell swoop."

"Who'd you think done it? Farber, juss so's he could try us again? Maybe get away with it this time?" contemplated Billy.

"I don't think so. I thought about Steve, but he was always a pawn in this thing. The one person who could have done this, some way, was that writer, Sergio Bachaca."

"That's who old shithead shot 'tween the eyes, ain't it?" Martin was forced to laugh at the description of Farber as 'old shithead.'

"Yeah, he wrote that book I lost and you found. That book had *something*. Some meaning, some ability. I'm not sure what or how. When Bachaca heard it might have been in Magdalena, he sent Steve looking for it."

"I ain't sure that book is anything. Ya ever think you had the power to do all this shit? Damn, Teebsie, if *you* don't belong in Lincoln back in '78, then I ain't sure who does. Maybe this juss was your destiny?"

Martin pondered the boy's question for a moment. He wanted to agree, but a twenty-year marriage to Lilly prevented him. "I don't know, Billy. I have a life *here*, *now*. I'm married. And the thing is, Lilly hasn't done all of the stuff that I remember with Dallas and so on, at least not that I know of."

"You mean she ain't done it *yet*, right?"

"Huh?" asked Martin. "What do you mean?"

"Well, if she's juss here for the first time, then all that stuff ain't happened yet, but it might? She did ya dirty, Teebsie, and I remember standin' there when she found out another guy put a baby in her. You think she done changed that much, just 'cause you're goin' around on this again?"

Martin snorted. "So you want me to preemptively divorce my wife because she *might* do something, and so I can live back in 1878 with Rosita?"

"Yep," said Billy, straight out, "somethin' like that."

"I think that's enough for one night. Get some rest, and I'll come see you in the morning."

With that, Martin stood up, just as a giant shadow appeared in the doorway. A voice boomed off the vinyl floor and antiseptic walls. "Is this where the Lincoln County Regulators are meeting? Cause this time, I wanna come along for the ride!" With a hearty laugh, Steve stepped into the room and found himself a seat.

Sunday - 8:45 pm

"This is crazy. How in the hell do you expect me to believe in all of this?" asked Jane, with tons of questions clouding her eyes and her mind.

While picking through the rest of the extensive library after being thrown out of Lilly Teebs's life, Rosita had found the first editions of *Back to Billy* and *1877*, both written by someone named Michael Anthony Giudicissi. Rosita had a suspicion that Martin had actually written the books, but regardless, they told the story of her life from the time he'd bumped into her on the street until she….

The books were a testament to the fact that, somehow, her life had been reversed. According to Jane, Trisha was only twenty-four years old, which now made Rosita the same age as when she'd first met Martin. It was as if Junior, Fort Sumner, and her... demise...had never (or not yet) happened. The books spelled it out for Jane, and she continued to look back and forth at Rosita, trying to determine if either one of them was sane anymore. Jane's blood boiled when she reached the part describing Farber's brutal rape of Rosita - a fate Jane might have shared, had Carl not hated Billy Bonney more than he wanted to dominate her.

These were the things being revealed to Trisha that had her so down and so worried; she knew from her visions, or memory, or whatever it was, that Farber was a monster, and it would just take a tiny spark to set him off. "He's dead? You killed him?" queried Rosita.

Although Jane's shot was a bad one, in the lungs, and Farber had been struggling for breath, the man clearly wasn't dead when he'd grabbed that book and somehow disappeared. "I don't know. I got him pretty good, that prick. I hope so, but I don't know what happened to him."

"He's gone back," said Rosita eerily, "back to Fort Sumner. That is the only place that book could have taken him. He will be there…waiting." Rosita said it with such resignation in her voice that it made the hair on the back of Jane's neck stand up.

"It'll be different this time, Rosita."

"Why do you say this?" she questioned Jane, in return.

"Because last time that asshole knew you were there, and he surprised you. This time, the tables are turned…."

Sunday – 8:50 pm

"Listen, boys," began Steve, in his baritone voice, "if ya'll are plannin' to go skippin' through time again, you need to take me with you." Although the cowboy was grinning in the glow of Billy's monitors, he was dead serious.

“It doesn’t work that way, Steve. There’s no time-travel bus to get on - “destination 1878’! That’s just not how it happens,” objected Martin.
“Well, look, I’ll admit that crackpot Farber got me today, but I damn sure never expected he’d have the balls to pull off somethin’ like that. Shit, I thought he was a prissy little schoolteacher.”

Martin looked over at Billy, who still kept his eyes closed. “Let me ask you something, Steve, do you remember me now? Everything we went through? Any of it? All of it?”

“Shoot, hoss, when I got laid out by that damned .45, I remembered every damned thing. The real kick in the ass is that I remember you from, hell, four or five years in the future, and damned if we ain’t back here today. Now, explain to me how that happened!” Steve folded his arms and waited for clarification.

“Teebsie can’t figure it out. Probably that dead writer did it.” Billy spoke in a weak and tired voice.

“You’re tellin’ me, I get four more years of this shit?” asked Steve, permeated with a big laugh. “Then what happens? We do it all over again?!”

Martin was tired and didn’t have answers for any of Steve’s questions. “Look, let’s take this up tomorrow. Give Billy some time to rest. We’ve got to have a plan.”

“All right, all right,” said Steve, “let’s put it up for the night. I’ll see you boys in the morning. Now don’t go runnin’ off to another time without me tonight!” he said, laughing his way out the door.

Martin patted Billy’s arm one more time and quietly whispered, “Night, Billy.”

Billy finally pried one eye open as Martin’s shadow moved out of the door and whispered, “G’night...Dad.”

Sunday – 9 pm

"Look, you just hit these buttons to spell out the words you want, then you hit 'send,' and it goes right to him." Jane held out Trisha's iPhone for Rosita's examination as she explained the finer points of text messaging to the Belle of Lincoln County.

Astonished, Rosita asked, "How long do these words take to reach *Martin*? He's so far away, in Roswell, can they make it in one day?"

Jane laughed and rolled back on the floor, nearly spilling her third glass of wine. "One day, sister?! Like, instantly!" She snapped her fingers to emphasize the point. "You send it, he gets it...just like we're talking here."

Rosita's eyes went wide, almost in disbelief. In her short time in the present, she'd seen guns that didn't need to be reloaded after six shots, cars, tourists with the same weird clothes that *Martin* used to show up wearing, and now something called an 'iPhone,' which to her seemed like a visitor from another planet.

"*Esta bien*, I will put in the letters. What should I say?" giggled Rosita.

"Well, you could ask him how he is. Tell him you're thinking about him. Shit, tell him you love him if you want," said Jane, between sips of wine.

"I should first see if he is all right, *no*? That is most important."

Rosita typed out: Hello Martin. This is Rosita Luna. This woman Jane is helping with this eye phone and I want to know if you are all right?

Looking at the message, Jane howled in laughter, which only served to confuse Rosita more. "Why is this funny?" she asked.

"Girl, you sound like a lawyer. Ease up some. Here, give that to me, and let me fix it." Jane grabbed the phone and started quickly editing the message:

"Martin, it's me, Rosita. Jane's helping me learn to text, are you okay?" Then handed it back to Rosita. "There, what do you think of that?"

Rosita looked a little worried. “Will he know who I am? He cannot see me or hear my voice.”

Jane was tempted to tell her about FaceTime, but figured that she should start slow and text first. “He’ll know. Believe me, he’ll know. Just hit that little button there, and send it to him.”

Rosita hit the arrow to send the message and waited, staring at the screen. For almost a minute, she saw nothing, and then: “What is this? *Martin* has sent me three dots that move about the screen. What does this mean, Jane?”

Jane saw the indication that Martin was typing and slapped her knee so hard it hurt, as she descended into hysterical giggles once again.

“Why do you keep laughing at me!” Rosita snapped, unhappy at being part of a joke she didn’t understand.

“He didn’t send you any dots!” Jane said, putting her hands on Rosita’s shoulders to calm her down. “They mean he’s typing out a reply. Just wait, and whatever he says will be here in a second.”

Rosita waited, holding her breath. *Martin* could just as easily tell her to go away or that he didn’t recognize her - either of those, she thought, would kill her all over again. Then, with a loud chime, the return message arrived:

Is this really you? Rosita?

Yes, *mi amor*, it is me. Are you well?

I’m fine. Oh my God, Rosita. I can’t believe this is you.

Believe this, Martin, this is true.

Where are you now?

I am at the home of Trisha. You know this place?

I do, I was there early today with you…umm...her.

There is only me now, and Jane. She helps me.

I must see you. Can you come to the hospital?

In Roswell? It would take a day, *Martin*!

No, not in a car.

A car like Lilly has? I was in her car.

You were with Lilly?

Si

What's wrong?

She told me never to see you again, *Martin*.

I must see you. Can Jane drive you?

Jane has been drinking the wine. A lot.

Oh no, don't let her drive.

Does this car go by itself?

No! The person driving has to know what she's doing

Jane knows the car to drive

No, she's drunk! You'll both be killed.

I cannot drive the car, *Martin*

No, that would be dangerous. Please, come and see me tomorrow. Please?

I will ask Jane to drive the car tomorrow?

Yes, my love. Oh, Rosita, I've missed you terribly.

Martin

Yes?

What has happened to me, to us? Has our time gone back?

Yes, we're getting a second chance.

Are you there?

Rosita?

I'm here. My heart breaks for what I put you through.

No! It was my fault!

What I did was…

Rosita?

Yes, *Martin*?

I love you. Please get some rest and come to me tomorrow.

I love you, too, *mi amor*. Rest as an angel.

MONDAY 8 AM

Martin woke with a start, a large nurse standing over him while making notes on his chart. Seeing his eyes open, she smiled warmly. "Mr. Teebs, good morning. How did we sleep last night?"

Martin tried to think if he recollected anything about his sleep, but from the time he got back to his room and slid into bed, finished texting with Rosita, and closed his eyes, he had not a single memory. "Good, I guess, I don't remember a thing."

"Good, the drugs must have helped. Your doctor will be in sometime this morning, and we'll probably release you today."

"Umm, can I have a visitor before I go?" asked Martin, thinking of Rosita.

"No, sir, only one family member, and then only to admit or discharge. The new rules with Covid, you know. Don't worry, we'll let Mrs. Teebs know what time you'll be ready so she can come and pick you up."

"Great," said Martin, through a fake smile. Now he was trapped. Rosita couldn't come to see him, and by the time he was free to leave, he'd be in Lilly's care. It felt like Sumner in 1881, all over again. The woman he loved was so close, yet he just could not reach her. Still, he had other business to attend to, so he forced himself out of bed, took a leak, and pushed his IV down the hall to Billy's room.

"Damn, son! That money you and Wilson were passing was funnier than Chris Rock!" Steve bellowed. Billy laughed, too - mostly at the delivery as there was no way he could know who Chris Rock was. "Oh, hey, hoss, welcome to the land of the living," greeted Steve, as Martin pushed his way into the room.

"You guys are having too much fun. They'll throw you out of here if you're this healthy," Martin joked while looking at Billy, who looked incredibly better than he had the day before.

"Mornin', Teebsie!" exclaimed Billy. "You ever tasted apple sauce? They outta sell this stuff at John's store, it's so damn good." The young man poked his spoon back into the cup as if it were gold and let a small amount touch his tongue again.

Martin looked at Steve, who'd dressed himself in his hospital gown - which hit above his knees since he was so tall - plus his cowboy boots and his giant cowboy hat. "That's some outfit, Steve. Any chance I could take a picture?" grinned Martin.

Steve looked down at his white kneecaps and chuckled back at Martin. "Looks like we're wearing the same designer, hoss."

Martin sat in the chair still at Billy's bedside and got right to it. "Listen, Billy, I'm getting out of here today. You're not. We need a plan."

Billy licked the last vestiges of apple sauce from the spoon and pondered out loud, "Plan fer what, Teebsie? Ta kill that son of a bitch Farber?"

"Well, no, yes, no. Not yet. A plan to get you back to where you belong. Back to your time."

"Don't need no plan, you juss wait for me in Lincoln, and I'll git there once they toss me from this place. We'll get Rosie and go back together."

Martin looked at Steve and then at the floor, unable to face his friend. "I can't go back, Billy. I've got...Lilly, here. I can't just run away."

The thought that Teebs wouldn't be coming with him had never occurred to Billy. Here Martin was, the man who desperately wanted to be reunited with his dead lover, and he'd actually somehow made it possible...but now he wasn't going to do it? "But, Teebsie, the baby, the men Lilly was with, the whole thing...she did ya dirty. Don't ya remember?"

Martin grimaced a bit before answering. "The thing is, she hasn't done all of those things, Billy. All of *us* - you, me, Steve, even Rosita - remember everything that happened to us, but *Lilly* doesn't. To her, it never happened."

"How could that be? It did happen, didn't it? Or are we juss all crazy?" Billy asked seriously.

Martin just looked back at the ground and shook his head. "I don't know." After a few moments of silence, Martin continued. "Listen, Steve, take this book." Martin held out the now-signed, worn copy of Bachaca's book. "Hold onto it til Billy is released. Billy, get Rosita and use this to go back to whenever it was you're supposed to be. You know how to do it." Steve nodded his understanding. Billy just stared at Martin.

"And what'll you do, Teebsie?"

Martin drew a deep breath. "I'm going home. I can't live through all that again. I can't do it to Lilly. Hell, I sure can't make *Rosita* live through it again. History would have been better off if I'd never been a part of it," he sadly added.

"Says you," Billy frowned.

Martin stood up, grabbed his friend's hand, and shook it gently. "I had the honor of meeting the best pal I ever had - not once, but twice. I can go back and watch Young Guns and laugh at it all over again, Billy. I can read the history books and know exactly what they missed and how things *really* happened. For guys like me and Steve," said Martin, gesturing toward the big cowboy, "that's all we could ever ask for."

"I 'spose," responded Billy.

"Don't forget me, Billy, 'cause I sure as hell won't ever forget you." Martin smiled broadly.

Resigned to the fact that his friend was leaving, Billy just grinned and said, "You'd better git, Teebsie, or old Steve here'll start tellin' ya where they stuck Olinger in the ground and ain't nobody knows it but him!"

Martin sighed in Steve's direction as the big cowboy just grabbed the brim of his hat. Teebs turned to walk away. When he reached the door, he pivoted to speak once more. "Don't try to use that book to come and find me, Billy. You belong to history now… not to me, anymore." With that, the big man disappeared around the corner and out of sight. Steve narrowed his eyes as he saw him go, puzzled about what Martin Teebs had meant.

Monday – 8:15 am

Martin walked back into his room and noticed his phone's green notification letting him know that he'd received a text message. Opening it, he was greeted by a picture of Rosita, swathed in bedsheets, and smiling like she'd just seen God. The message along with it said: Jane took the picture and sent it to me. When will I see you, *mi amor*?

It hadn't been five minutes since Martin had decided that the past needed to stay just that…the past. He had trul y justified in his mind that Rosita would have been better off without him, and now he had the chance to prove it. The problem was, Martin wasn't sure exactly *how*. He loved the woman to the point of feeling physical pain when they were separated. Now, with her just up the road in his own time, in the town to which he'd shortly be returning, how could he *not* see her? Of course, he knew if he saw her, there was no way he could simply leave. Ghosting her was not an option; he cared for her far too much to not say goodbye. With no better choices at the present, Martin stalled for time.

"I'll be leaving here soon. Lilly will drive me. I'll text when I get back to Lincoln, my love," Martin wrote. None of it was a lie, yet he also didn't tell Rosita that texting her was as far as he currently planned on going. At a very minimum, his message bought him a couple of hours to try to figure out what to do.

Martin vaguely remembered Lilly visiting him in the hospital last night, and, of course, no words had been spoken about Rosita. He realized that the ride back to Lincoln would be uncomfortable. Someone had to say something, right? It's not like husband and wife could just go back to the *casita*, nurse Martin's gunshot wound, and then pick up and fly back to New Jersey the next day, like nothing had happened.

How would Lilly play the scene? Martin wondered. Would she be curious? Furious? Lay on the guilt trip? To the best of his knowledge, Lilly knew no details of her husband's life with Rosita, other than the fact that they had been lovers. She knew nothing about Junior, Martin's plans to stay in the past forever, or Rosita's untimely end. Lilly probably didn't know anything about what Farber had done, either. While Martin had learned from Rosita's messages that she and Lilly had talked, he remained unaware of the exact context or depth of their conversations. If only he knew what had been discussed, he would know how to prepare himself.

As it was, his wife had talked to his lover, and he had no idea what had been said. Martin Teebs was racing toward a crossroads in his life, and the driver was going to be none other than Lilly Teebs.

Monday – 9:30 am

"So you're feeling okay?" asked Lilly, through tightly pursed lips. She had just picked up her husband from the hospital upon his release, following a minor gunshot wound he'd received the day prior.

"Umm, yeah. My arm hurts, for sure, but other than that, I'm okay, Lil," Martin replied, turning back toward the road. Both people knew the conversation that was coming; it was just a matter of who was going to begin and where they'd start. After a couple of miles, Martin lost patience with waiting and blurted out, "I know you talked to Rosita yesterday. I'm sorry about all this, Lil."

Lilly was secretly happy that Martin had lobbed the first volley to her as she thought better of coming off like 'controlling bitch,' opting for 'jilted spouse' instead. "Sorry, huh? I'm not even sure where to begin, Martin. When you told me about this, this… dream, you said Rosita was *Billy's* girlfriend. Now I guess I know why you lied to me."

Martin could not deny anything. "You're right. The honest truth is, when I went out that night - after I was choking - I didn't know any of this. I had little pieces of the story, but not enough to really even remember it. Then I went for a walk; and all of a sudden, Rosita was there, running at me. It was only for a second, like a mirage, I guess. As she reached me, she disappeared. I swear, Lil, I thought I was just losing my mind. No way did I think any of this was real! In my Dream, I knew I was with her, but I didn't see any sense in making you upset over something that never happened...."

"But it did happen, right, Martin?"

Martin hung his head as he responded. "Yes, it did. I just didn't know it at the time."

"You slept with another woman, kept it from me, got her pregnant, and then came back to our bedroom to sleep with me? Have I got that right, Martin?" said Lilly, strangely calm and sounding detached.

"Well, there was more, but, yeah, that's about right."

"More? Oh, pray tell! How much more good news can I take?" Lilly queried sarcastically.

"It won't change anything, Lil," answered a dejected Martin.

"Here's the thing I can't figure out in all of this, Martin, " Lilly began. "If you were with this Rosita on and off for years, how did you get here to Lincoln? Did you time travel from New Jersey? How did it all work, and where was I while this was all going on? You got five years to do over again, and what did I get?"

Martin had reached his crossroad much sooner than he'd expected: only fifteen minutes into the drive back to the Patron House. It was time to either let Lilly know about her part in all of this, or bury it and keep lying for the rest of his life.

"Let me answer one at a time. First, no, I didn't time travel back to Billy and Rosita from New Jersey. It doesn't work like that. In fact, I'm not even that sure *how* it worked…it just seemed to happen.

"Second, how I got back here to do it is that I landed a new job at work in the sales department. We opened a new LA office, and I was the west coast regional sales rep. I traveled out this way quite a bit." Martin glanced over at Lilly to see if she was paying attention. Her eyes scanned back and forth from the road to Martin, with a look in them like she was hearing the rants of a crazy person. Martin in sales? Lilly said nothing, however, not wanting to give him a chance to bail out of their conversation.

"And the part about you…." Martin hesitated, still not sure what to do. He decided to just ask her: "Do you really want the whole truth about what happened with you over those years, Lil? I mean, it might be hard to hear."

Lilly shot him a death stare. "Oh, puleeze, Martin. You think anything you say now will be harder to hear than that you've been cheating on me?"

“Okay, then,” began Martin, as he sucked in a huge gulp of air, perhaps hoping he could release it all in one run-on sentence, thus quickly getting it over with. “Well, it started with you having sex with Dallas, right here in Lincoln, on our vacation...probably more than once. I found out later that he’d even flown to New York, while I was out of town, and came by our house. You had sex with him again, right there in our bed. Oh, I always meant to tell you that I hoped you washed the sheets before I got home.

Then, Billy came to our house one day while Farber - who’d raped Rosita while I was away, by the way - was there with his girlfriend Jane, but not the same Jane you know here. This woman was older and actually really nice, you two became friends. Anyhooo...we all had a big fight, and you walked into the guest room, while everyone started spilling the beans on each other.

Billy asked you to share a secret as you got a call from your doctor saying you were pregnant. And...it wasn’t by me, Lil! So, you and Dallas had a little boy named Austin - nice touch by the way: *Dallas, Austin* - I get it. And eventually, you left and moved to New Mexico, where you found out Dallas was good with his junk, but bad at relationships. So, you threw him out and bought the Patron House! But you went and changed the name to *Casa de Teebs*, which was a disaster, of course. You tried getting me back after all you’d done, but I wouldn’t go for that. Once I moved to Denver, you decided to sell the place; and I scraped up some money from my book deal and sold my loft to buy it from you, so I could lock it up forever, you know.

Then, you went back to New Jersey and wound up shacking up with some guy whose picture I put on the back of the three books I wrote. Billy told you that you seemed like a nice couple and suggested you give the guy a break.” Martin, completely out of breath, shook his head to get the blood flowing again and glanced at Lilly, who looked back at him with crazy eyes and her mouth wide open.

“You’re making all of that up!” she accused.

“Lil, you’ve heard about me and Rosita. That’s all the truth. There’s no reason for me to lie about you and your life. That’s all the truth, too,” said Martin, and then added, “Oh yeah, almost forgot…when I was dead for a few seconds, you and that Michael Roberts were there in the Patron House - dead, too, I suppose - with a bunch of other people, and you looked pretty happy."

Martin's missive was way too much for Lilly to take in on one shot. She stared out at the road for a few miles and then finally ventured, "I had a son? Austin, you say? If I had a son, Martin, where is he?"

For the first time since the conversation started, both Martin and Lilly had some true common ground. "I don't know, Lil. Probably where my son is. Wherever that is. Whenever that is. I can't figure it out. It's like all this stuff happened, but it didn't *really* happen, because here we are, back in 2021."

"What did he look like? Did he look like me?" Lilly asked sadly.

"He looked a lot like Dallas, Lil," Martin admitted. "Good-looking kid, and he seemed to be really happy."

A big tear escaped Lilly's right eye and plopped down on the thigh of her jeans. "We got divorced, Martin? Are you saying we're no longer married?"

The confusion that had plagued Martin since the previous week returned in full force. While worrying about Rosita, and Billy, and Bachaca's book, he never thought to analyze the mechanics of all that had happened. Now Lilly, the practical one, opened a can of worms that seemed to be crawling all over both of them.

"Lil, I don't know. I *think* we are married, since it's 2021, but I'm just not sure. This is the muddle that I've been dealing with for the past week. That's why I was acting so weird. Trying to figure all this out."

Lilly drove on, and Lincoln clawed its way nearer to them with each passing mile. Lilly pushed and prodded her brain to remember any of this, for any of this to be true, but to no avail. "So, Steve? Kevin, or Billy, or whatever? Do they remember everything that happened, too?"

Martin stared blankly out the window as he answered, "They do. Farber did. I do. You're the only one who doesn't, Lil."

"Why?" she snapped back.

A possibility that he hadn't considered before dawned on Martin. "Maybe *you're* the only one who can change your past, Lil? The rest of us have tried and failed - many times. Maybe yours isn't written in stone, for some reason."

As the car swung off on Route 380 just a few miles from Lincoln, Lilly asked the last remaining question on her mind. "Would you change yours if you could, Martin?"

Martin closed his eyes, and his head slumped, as if he needed to think about the answer. His evenly paced breathing didn't betray a single emotion, while the car urged its way toward the tiny town. He finally decided to speak. "Yes," he lied.

Monday – 10:30 am

The rental car glided to a stop in front of the same cemetery where Lilly had talked to Rosita. Martin cast a strange look at his wife, wondering if perhaps she intended to kill him and dump the body among his old friends. For Lilly's part, she couldn't go back to the *casita* with the enormous question still looming in both their minds: What next?

"Uhh, what are we doing, Lil?" Martin asked cautiously.

Lilly put the car in park and shifted on her seat to face him. After drawing a deep breath, she spoke. "I don't think you're crazy, Martin. I did, at first, but I don't anymore. I think that every single thing you told me is true, at least to you. I'm not sure about my part in any of this, since I can't remember it, but I'll believe what you told me." Martin looked at her without changing his expression, waiting for the fuse to burn down and the bomb to go off inside the tiny car.

"We can't go on like…*this*. If we're going to get on that plane tomorrow and head back to New Jersey, back to our home, back to the lives that we've built over the past twenty years, it has to be because that's what *you want*. No looking back, no regrets," she continued, "Do you understand what I'm saying?"

Once again, Martin felt as if he'd been dropped off by helicopter in the middle of a

minefield, afraid to move even one step in any direction. He quietly nodded yes, while still looking Lilly in her eyes.
"Today, I'm going to Ruidoso with Darlene and the ladies, just like I'd planned. I'm giving you a gift. I'm giving you a day with this...*Rosita*, to figure out what you want to do, and who you want to do it with. When I see you tonight, I want your answer, and I want it once and for all."

Martin didn't move a muscle. At any point, he expected to have Lilly break out into a malevolent grin, saying, "Gotcha!" But that didn't seem to be forthcoming. Finally, he just bobbed his head the slightest bit, unsure of what was supposed to happen next.

"She's still here, right?" asked Lilly. "I saw the messages on your phone while you were getting dressed. Where is she? I'll take you there." Martin looked out the windshield, numb, and pointed to the large house just up the road.

Monday – 10:40 am

Martin slowly headed up the brick pathway to Trisha's house while, behind him, he heard Lilly accelerate away. Like a kid being dropped off at school for the first time, Martin thought perhaps she'd wait to be sure it was the right house, or maybe for Martin to turn back with a 'thumbs up.' At that moment, Lilly apparently didn't care *what* her husband did, however; and so he was left alone, on this precarious walk between past and present.

That Lilly had looked at his phone messages worried Martin since he'd professed his love for Rosita as recently as last night. How would he be able to show up at the Patron House later today and tell Lilly that he'd realized he didn't even like the young woman? Casting such worries aside for the time being, Martin walked up and knocked firmly on the door. Upon hearing footsteps inside, he moved back a pace or two, not to seem too eager.

The door swung open, and there stood Jane, a crooked smirk on her face. Martin noticed the cut on her lip and mark on her cheek where Farber had hit her. "Marty McFly," she said, "how ya been?"

The ice broken, Martin smiled and followed her inside. "Did Farber do that to you?"

"Yeah, he did - but I paid him back. I guess you saw that," Jane retorted.

Martin hadn't known who'd shot Farber, everything having happened so quickly. "What, that was you? You shot him?" he asked, surprised.

"Yeah, hopefully killed him. Of course, the only way to find that out is to go wherever he ended up, but I guess you're the guy to tell me that, huh, Marty?"

Truthfully, Martin had no idea where Farber had gone, but thanks to the *Sunset in Sumner* book, he at least had his suspicions. "I'm really not sure, Jane. Can I please see Rosita? Is she here?" For a second, Martin panicked, thinking perhaps Rosita had been sucked back in time, and this conversation he was about to have with her might never happen.

"C'mon, lover boy, she's out back," Jane said, turning away and waving her hand for Martin to follow her.

Martin's body and mind sizzled with both anticipation and fear. He'd not been in Rosita's presence since that night in Fort Sumner, so many years ago - not withstanding the brief few seconds after he was shot, but didn't understand what was happening. As they exited the French doors leading from the kitchen to the back portal, he saw his lover, a beaming smile on her face, dressed in a loose-fitting sundress that undoubtedly belonged to Trisha.

At the first sight of her great love, Rosita bounded from the chair and yelled his name joyfully. "*Martin, mi amor*!" Flinging herself into his arms, she plastered his face and lips with kisses. Martin had rehearsed in his mind how he'd gently stop her, explaining they needed to talk; but in that instant, he lost all inhibitions and pulled her tightly to him, reveling in the touch of her body to his.

This…this was the moment he'd spent his entire life pining for, and in some second-chance miracle, it had arrived. "Oh, Rosita, how I've missed you," he said between kisses. "I begged for this day to come for…." Martin couldn't even answer how long he'd waited, so he stopped talking.

Jane stood in the doorway, amused. "Well, I kinda hoped this would go better than it has, but hey!" Martin turned his head, nodding his appreciation. "Well, if y'all are just gonna stand here and make out, then I guess there ain't anything else for me to do," she added.

Rosita let Martin go briefly and rushed to Jane. "*Gracias*, for everything you have done. I would have been lost here yesterday, without you," said the young woman, tightly hugging her friend.

"It's my pleasure, *chica*, and you remember how to send those texts, right? If you need me...." Jane responded.

"*Si, si*. I will send to you later," Rosita answered with a smile.

Before she left, Jane turned her attention to Martin. "Okay, now, you treat her right, understood? I only used one bullet on that creep Farber and got plenty left if you ever get outta line." Jane delivered the line half in jest; Teebs received it the same way.

Martin nodded to let her know that violence wouldn't be necessary and mouthed, "Thank you," before she turned to leave.

Burying her head against his chest, Rosita began crying as if the tears had been bottled inside her for a hundred years. "Oh, *Martin*, I have missed you more than you can know. I don't understand this 'time' we are in, but I won't let you go again, *si*? I will never let you go." Martin said nothing, breathing in her intoxicating scent and feeling her body press so firmly into his as if to become one. "*Te quiero, Martin Teebs, por siempre*."

"Let's sit, Rosita, so we can talk," Martin said, as he guided her to one of the striped chairs that must have come from a Home Depot or Lowes, or some other such place that Rosita couldn't even imagine. "It's been so hard without you, without Junior. I wanted to die without you." Martin could no longer hold back his own tears, and he cried heavily, dropping his face into his hands. Rosita reached out for him, pulling him to her breast, and stroked his hair, not saying a word. Finally, Martin was able to swallow hard and wipe enough of his tears away to continue. "How much do you...

remember...about us?" he asked, tentatively.

"*Martin*, when you were shot, I was there; and in that moment, I remembered it all," Rosita confessed, before adding, "the good *and* the bad."

The implication that she knew about her end, and Farber's violation of her, was plain for Martin to decipher. He looked straight at her, crying again, shaking his head over all that he'd put this incredible creature through. She put a smile on her face. "Oh, no! No, *Martin*, please do not weep. This is not a time for sadness. We are together again. As you say, we have a second chance. Please do not."

The distraught man breathed heavily, wondering how to respond. 'I'm sorry' wouldn't even come close to covering it, nor would 'I love you.' Martin's emotions and feelings were so far beyond those two extremes, they were seemingly immeasurable.

"Rosita," Martin began, "I'm so confused. I have so many questions. I don't even know where to start. May I ask you some things?"

"Anything, *Martin*."

"Where is Junior? Do you know about him? Do you remember him?"

Rosita smiled with the memory. "Of course I do, *Martin*! Our baby boy! I do not know what became of Junior after I passed. Do you?"

"Yes, he went to live with Billy and Maria."

The thought of that pleased Rosita, and she seemed happy. "But now, it seems we are *before* Junior has been born, *Martin*. I don't understand this, but I think this is true." If what Rosita said were true, Martin truly would be getting a new start.

Martin felt along his abdomen for the gruesome scar, a reminder of being gut-shot by Barney Mason in Fort Sumner; but, of course, it wasn't there. Time, it seemed, had truly been reversed. "Did you see me on the street here in Lincoln, just a few days ago? Did you run toward me, and then when we touched, you disappeared?" he asked, trying to fit more puzzle pieces together.

“The days have been strange, *Martin*, for me,” Rosita started. “I felt each day a little more alive, but still I could not join you. I could see you here in Lincoln, but you were just too far to reach. I wish I could help you understand, but I cannot.”

Martin hesitated to ask the next question on his mind for fear that he might get an answer. Finally, he buckled up his will power and inquired: “Last week, Rosita, I died, maybe only for a moment. I was choking. After everything went black, I found myself walking, here in Lincoln, and you came to me. Junior did, too. He was just a boy, maybe five years old? We went back to the Patron House, and it was full of people that I knew in my life. You guided me in to watch the television with Junior while you cooked for everyone. Does any of this seem real? Do you remember anything at all like this?”

“I gave you the *enchiladas*, *Martin*. Junior, he got startled and caused you to choke. Si, I was there. I had waited for so many years for you to come to me.”

“But where were we? Was I *dead*?” questioned Martin, not sure he wanted to know the answer.

“*Si, mi amor*, you had come to the other side. This is how it is. When you fell, I screamed for you because I knew you were being taken from me again. I’m sorry - I was being selfish.”

Martin let the weight of what Rosita had said rest on his slumping shoulders. “You mean, you weren’t trying to save me? You were trying to keep me from living?”

Rosita’s eyes misted over in sadness and embarrassment. She wanted to hide from the truth but understood she could not. “*Si, Martin*. For our *familia*, I wanted you by my side, as we always talked about.”

Martin had no idea how to feel. If what Rosita told him was true, he had died, and she had wanted him to stay that way. At first, this felt like a betrayal, but Martin thought back to where he’d come from to arrive on death’s door (and the Patron House). He’d been an old, broken man, who’d begged and prayed daily to be taken from this world so that he might meet Rosita in eternity. His wish seemed to have been granted, and the only thing for which Rosita was guilty was wanting to keep it that way. If all this was true, Martin wouldn't be getting a rewind on five years of his life, he'd be getting it on almost forty of them - right up through the moment he'd knelt in the old post cemetery in Sumner and carved Rosita's name on Billy's tombstone. His lover had waited thirty-five years in the next life for him. How could she be blamed for wanting him to stay there? Martin himself, once he became aware of what The Dream was, also wished he could have stayed. He resolved not to torture himself or Rosita any more with such thinking.

"You were right to try, Rosita, because that's what I wanted, too," Martin confessed. "I begged and prayed for it every day since I lost you. I went to your grave every day and talked to you, just to be close. I always wondered whether you heard me."

Rosita reached a hand out to softly touch Martin's cheek. "I heard every word, *Martin*. Every day and every word. I talked back to you, but you could not hear me."

Martin was stunned. Admittedly, he knew nothing about the afterlife, but he assumed that prayers and words to those who'd passed on were only to soothe the living. "I wrote you every day, my love, every single day. I kept journals of letters to you." Martin wished he had just one book to show her.

"Someday, I will read these, *Martin*, I am certain of it. I cannot wait."

Martin pulled Rosita onto his lap, wrapping his arms tightly around her waist. Had death come to claim him again, he wished only to die right here, as they sat together, never to be separated again. Regrettably, he knew that not to be true. "Please, Rosita, don't be upset with me."

She carefully turned her head as much as it could go, asking, "Why should I be upset with you? I am not, of course."

Martin buried his face into the back of her sundress and testified as if before a judge. "I'm married, Rosita, to Lilly. Not in the past, but right now. Right here. She's less than a mile away, getting ready to go to Ruidoso with some ladies, and she expects me to let her know tonight if I'll be with you or with her."

Anticipating Rosita to be angry or hurt, yell or scream, he got none. She slowly spun on his lap until she was straddling him, and she bent forward to kiss him deeply. Her hands went to the sides of his head, pulling him so close that he could not escape, even if he had wanted to.

Rhythmically, they rocked back and forth in the chair, lost in the passion they both felt. Over a hundred years of aching and loneliness welled up in each of the lovers as they pressed their bodies even tighter together. Martin could feel Rosita's breasts pushing into his chest. On his thighs, he felt the warmth between her legs. He felt the insistence of her movements drawing him nearer and nearer to the edge, the place he would go and could never come back from.

Easing her hands from his head, Rosita darted her tongue within his lips one last time and then pulled back, a deep and satisfied look on her face. She stared at him with dancing eyes and asked simply, "So, what will you tell her?"

Monday – 3 pm

Martin walked slowly out the front door of Rosita's house, having just spent hours in the near paradise of her presence. Although the thought of never leaving had occurred to him, he owed Lilly an explanation. While he stepped his way along the road toward the Patron House, he played a mental game of table tennis with his feelings and his decision. What he did and said in the next fifteen minutes would shape the rest of his life.

As he approached the main house, Darlene came out with a worried look on her face. "Martin, I've been waiting for you," she began.

Martin thought of all of the times in the past (well, past/future) that Darlene would have made advances on him, and he wondered why the current Darlene seemingly could not care less. In any event, the expression on her face didn't portend her making a pass at him this time, either. "What's wrong? Did something happen?" he asked.

"It's nothing," Darlene said firmly, as if to convince Martin - or maybe herself - "but we had a little accident on the way to class." Martin's heart skipped a beat, expecting to hear that Lilly had been seriously hurt, or worse. "Lilly's fine, she was just dizzy, so we brought her up to the *casita*, and Dallas and I have been checking on her all afternoon. Maybe a mild concussion, but we didn't want to take her all the way to Roswell - unless you think it's a good idea?"

Martin bolted toward the *casita* and up its steps. Once inside, he quickly climbed to the loft to find Lilly lying there, ice pack on her head. With a weary smile, she reassured him. "Hi, hon, I'm okay, don't worry," Lilly said sleepily.

"What happened?" Martin wanted to know. He was tinged with a touch of guilt for having spent the day with his lover while Lilly was hovering near death after a horrendous car crash - or so his guilty mind convinced him.

Lilly just laughed and sighed a little before telling him the tale. "So silly, nothing really. We were on our way to Ruidoso, the girls and I. I guess someone's horse had gotten out of the pasture, and it ran toward the road. Darlene swerved a little and sideswiped a car coming up on our right. I just bumped my head into the window, that's all. I was feeling a little dizzy, and they insisted on bringing me back here. I've been lying here ever since."

Martin breathed a deep sigh of relief that his wife was seemingly all right, aside from looking tired. All seemed fine. However, while Martin felt that now was not the time to discuss their future or his past, Lilly wasn't willing to wait. "Did you have a good time with Rosita?"

And there it is, thought Martin. Lilly not only addressed the gorilla in the room, but she dropped it right on Martin's back. "Lil, can we maybe talk about this later?" he suggested gently.

"Martin, I'm here. You're here. Rosita's right down the road. What better time are we going to get to talk?" Although the words were direct, Lilly didn't convey them in a tone that seemed to assume any specific outcome.

"Okay, then," said Martin, as he launched into his completely unrehearsed speech. "It was good to see her, Lil, I won't lie. It was something like you can't imagine because, although I guess she and I have this history, I can't say for certain that I ever met her in person. I mean, I did, I get that…but those memories seem almost - unreal." Lilly patiently looked at Martin, waiting for him to get to the point. "And, yes, there were a lot of emotions there. I can't lie. More than I expected, to be honest. I'm still trying to work out how to deal with those."

Lilly's calm voice cut through Martin's confusion. "What did you decide, Martin: her or me?"

Time's up, thought Martin. The clock had wound to midnight, and he didn't have an answer.

"This is the hardest thing I've ever had to do in my life, Lil. I didn't ask for any of this to happen, you know."

"Your answer, Martin?" Lilly repeated.

"My answer is: I don't know. I love you, I have since we first met. We've been together for half of my life. That should be it, right? That should make the decision, right there. I tell myself that's the right thing to do, but you don't control what you feel, Lil. Do you understand? I'm not in control of this." Martin spoke more quietly as if only talking to himself: "I'm not in control of *anything*."

Revealing virtually no emotion, Lilly stared at her husband of twenty years. She wondered what he was feeling this minute and what he expected her to say. When she did speak, it wasn't the voice of a woman scorned, but rather of one whose eyes had been opened. "That's it, then, Martin. If your choice isn't clearly to stay with me, then there is no choice to make. I won't be married to a man who considers me an afterthought. Go, get out. Go to your Rosita," Lilly said with scorn. "And don't let me see or hear from you again." With that, she rolled onto her side, adjusting the ice pack on her forehead.

"You didn't even let me finish," said Martin, incredulous at having been dumped by his own wife.

"You finished, Martin. Go tell Rosita the same bullshit you just told me about how you can't decide and see what *she* says," came the sharp retort.

"No!" Martin snapped, completely out of character. "I won't be dismissed like that! You think this is easy, Lil? You think everything I've been through hasn't brought me to the brink? *You're* the lucky one. You haven't been tormented by a lifetime of memories that make no sense. For you, today is the first day 'today' happened - for me, it's happening *again*. Do you have any concept of that? Can you even imagine it?"

Lilly looked at Martin defiantly, but didn't speak.

"All I'm asking for here is some time to figure this out. I never said you were an afterthought. *Never*. I can't imagine how difficult this has all been for you, but don't forget, I need to be able to forget your *sins*, too. I need to wash away from my mind the vision of you screwing Dallas in my bed. I need to forget that somewhere, on some other plane of reality, you have a son, and it's *not* with me. I need to somehow forget you buying this very place that we're in right now and turning it into some...Disneyland for rich tourists - and you put *my* name on it!"

Martin's admissions about her broke Lilly. Her self-righteous anger melted away. "You're right, Martin. At least, I think you are. I'm sorry to be so cold. Look, I'm leaving tomorrow. If you truly want to come home, I'll welcome you with open arms. We'll get through this. If you don't, I'll be incredibly sad, but I will understand. Take tonight for your decision. Please, though, sleep on the sofa. I would like to be alone, to think things through."

Martin sighed sadly and nodded his head. He spent the rest of the afternoon and early evening reading, checking on Lilly, and choking down what food they had available in the tiny *casita*. By 7 pm, he was no closer to making a decision. By 9 pm, he was hopeless and laid down on the couch, nearly in tears. In eight more hours, he'd need to wake up and break one woman's heart. There was no good solution to any of this, and Martin closed his eyes, praying that sleep would come and guide him to who it should be.

Monday – 9:15 pm

Martin lay silently on the sofa, hearing Lilly breathing in her sleep from the upstairs loft. The naked truth was that Martin was in love with two women. Experts would tell him it was impossible, but he felt a very strong bond with each of them. Each bond was different, yes, but nevertheless, it was there. He tried to envision the scales of justice in his mind, balancing his feelings for each woman to see which held the weight of love. Every single time he ran the equation in his brain, he came up with the same conclusion: Lilly was his wife, and he loved her greatly; but Rosita was the matching piece of his soul whom he could not live without.

Teebs had full recollection of every mistake he'd made the last time around, and he vowed not to repeat them. He wondered how he'd be able to stay in the past - or if it were even possible. It seemed to work for Farber, and Martin thought that by letting Lilly go, perhaps his connection with the modern world might very well go with it. If so, he could start the rest of his life in 1878 and die - hopefully many years later - a happy man.

Martin had been explicit with his instructions to Rosita. She must meet Billy, once he'd retrieved Bachaca's book from Steve; this time, she was to leave as soon as possible. Someday very soon, authorities were going to come looking for Trisha Davis and Kevin Barrow; however, all they'd find would be two people who looked exactly like them but who claimed to be from the 1800s. Martin couldn't bear the thought of Rosita being detained, scared, and alone like that. He told her, if he could not make the jump back in time, she was to go anyway. Rosita cried and protested greatly; but in the end, she'd understood that her position in 2021 was, at best, tenuous. Martin told Rosita he'd somehow find her, book or no book. They agreed on the plan just before Martin left to walk back to his wife.

In that moment, Martin had been sure of his decision; however, the second he'd heard Lilly had been hurt, his mind began to spin. Now he lay in the darkness, wondering what to do when the sun came up. Once he finally was able to relinquish his thoughts, sleep came and swallowed him into its inky blackness. Martin did not dream nor stir the entire night. His mind switched off, allowing him to rest deeply. When the alarm woke him the next morning, it was as if he'd been dead after choking on green-chile enchiladas.

TUESDAY 7 AM

Martin pushed his eyelids open after his extended slumber. He could see Lilly moving quickly around the *casita*, packing belongings and rolling suitcases near the door. None the worse for wear after her bump on the head, his wife moved with the purpose of a woman starting a new life, or maybe restarting an old one.

"You're awake," she said, in a more cheery voice than he'd expected. "I'm loading the car now. We have to be on the road in twenty minutes." After thinking for a moment, Lilly added, "That is, if you're coming?"

Martin just nodded at the 'you're awake' part and let Lilly figure out what it meant. As he rose from the sofa, he looked with dismay at the coffee pot. Lilly hadn't made any and apparently didn't plan to; she'd probably buy a cup of convenience-store coffee on the way to Albuquerque. He found his way to the bathroom and splashed some cold water on his face, took a leak, and brushed his teeth. Not knowing what decision Martin might have reached, his wife had simply left all of Martin's things where they lay. He picked out the last clean pants and shirt he had and stuffed the rest into his suitcase.

Lilly, still outside loading the car, never saw Martin bend over to inspect the trash can.

With all of his things now loaded into the suitcase, Martin wheeled it outside, still not sure where it would be heading. Lilly was nowhere to be seen, as she'd probably gone into the main house to check out. With the trunk closed, he simply left his bag near the back of the car and walked out to Lincoln's one road. Looking east, he could just see the mailbox that would be in front of Rosita's home. Looking west, he'd see the route that would snake through town and connect Lilly with I-25 north, taking her straight to Albuquerque and her flight back to Newark.

Martin had cautioned Rosita not to send anymore text messages since Lilly had been checking his phone. Nevertheless, he'd still had hope when he pulled it out of his pocket and pushed on the messages icon, even though already knowing there was nothing new. Standing there in the middle of the street, caught between two different worlds, he felt as lonely and torn as a man could feel. He wished that someone would just make the decision for him, sparing him the agony of saying goodbye to either woman.

With no savior forthcoming, he looked back toward Rosita's house and saw a pickup truck making its way in his direction. As it reached Rosita's, the vehicle slowed to a crawl and then stopped. Out from the driver's side jumped a big cowboy...Steve. He went around to the passenger side to help its occupant, and Martin saw Billy, his arm in a sling, stepping down.

Before he knew what he was doing, Martin began walking down the street to meet his friends. Seeing Teebs approach, Steve handed Billy something - Bachaca's book. Martin had cleared maybe half of the distance between them when a car horn blared behind him. Turning quickly, he realized it was Lilly, car running in the middle of the street and ready to go.

Martin heard his name being called from the other direction. "Teebsie!" Billy yelled and waved with his good arm.

Martin's immediate thought was to run to Lilly and ask for five minutes to say good-bye. That plan was dashed when she shouted across the distance, "Martin, I'm leaving. Are you coming?"

Teebs looked back to Billy and saw Rosita, hair flowing, dress billowing in the breeze, smiling as if to light the morning on her own, and calling his name: "*Martin! Martin!*"

The horrible reality of Martin's very existence was laid bare. He was the rope in a virtual tug-of-war game being played out on the Most Dangerous Street in America.

As his name was being called from both directions, Martin's world began to turn fuzzy. The sounds, though still there, became muffled and indistinct. He had retreated into his own cocoon where no one could touch him, regardless of how they tried. With one scene playing out in slow motion, he saw Rosita waving and calling to him. Steve's face cocking to the side and smiling, and Billy grinning and waving Bachaca's book at him. On Martin's other flank, the rental car horn blared again, and Lilly opened the driver's side door. He saw her drift to the trunk of the car and remove his big blue suitcase, placing it squarely in the middle of the road.

The warped and twisted sounds collided in his brain, the visions of both Lilly and Ros-ita almost too much for him to view. The microseconds ticked away in Teebs's mind as Billy began opening the book that would take him and Rosita back to…somewhere. Lilly returned to the car, slamming the driver's side door closed, and Martin heard the engine rev up. Billy found the page he wanted and opened the book, and he and Rosita began the slow process of fading from the present.

Unable to stand it all anymore, Martin took off at a full sprint toward his destiny.

SUNDAY 5 PM

"And we're on final approach to Newark Liberty International Airport. Would you please put up your tray tables and seat backs in preparation for landing? We'll be on the ground shortly."

Lilly sighed, having survived the long flight, wrapped up as she was in her tormented thoughts. She stared over at the empty seat next to her, wondering if it would ever again truly be filled.

"Sorry, Lil," said Martin, as he plopped down in the seat, "something I ate didn't agree with me. Must have been those green-chile enchiladas at the airport."

After he buckled himself in, Lilly reached out her hand to hold Martin's. "We're home, Martin. *Home*," she said, as if convincing Martin of something he didn't believe to be true. "I'm so glad you chose me - you chose *us*. This is a brand-new start for us. It's like, I guess, somehow the clock turned back, and we're getting a chance to do this part of our lives over again." Martin turned to Lilly and smiled, happy to soon be off of the plane and ready to puzzle out the next part of his life. She gripped his hand even more tightly as flight attendants buzzed back and forth, picking up trash and empty soda cans. "Tell me something good, Martin, tell me something exciting!"

Martin calmly looked at his wife, the one he had indeed chosen over his soulmate Rosita, and gazed in her eyes. "Something exciting, huh?" he asked rhetorically. "Okay, I know something. You had sex with Dallas Jones in our *casita* yesterday. How's that, Lil?"

Lilly's eyes went wide and her mouth nearly hit the floor at Martin's accusation. "What are you talking about? Why are you bringing that up now, Martin?"

"Well, Lil, you asked for something exciting, and that sure fits the bill. From the look of the condoms in the trash can, I'd say you two went at it, what, three times?" Lilly looked even more uncomfortable and shocked but said nothing.

"You remember it all, don't you, Lil?" asked Martin, in such a kind way that one would think he was asking his wife whether she wanted ketchup on her french fries.

Lilly breathed in hard before speaking, wondering if it was wise to say anything at all. "I didn't. Not at first. That knock on the head yesterday changed that. But yes, now I do remember it all, Martin. Every single bit." Martin just smiled patiently until Lilly wanted to confess the rest of the story. "When Dallas brought me up to the bed, I knew he was a dolt. I knew what I'd gone through with him in the past, but I also knew the way it felt when he was inside me. I wanted that feeling one more …okay, three more times. You had your great love with Rosita, I figured I, at least, deserved that."

Martin just laughed, having known about his wife's transgressions since early this morning. Finally, he conceded, "I'm sure you did deserve that, Lil. That's why I didn't say anything earlier."

"But if you knew, Martin, why are you here? Why did you choose *me*?" Lilly implored.

Martin composed his thoughts for a moment before answering. "If you'd had no memory of what your life became, Lil, things never would have worked out for us. You would always have held it against me that I had 'something' with Rosita, but you didn't really know if you had 'anything' with Dallas. You'd have had to take my word for it. We never would have lasted like that. When I saw the trash can this morning, I knew exactly what you'd done. I knew you had gotten it out of your system - now we can start over, equal - both guilty of the same sins, and both wanting to do better going forward. Anyway, that's the way I see it."

Lilly was stunned, but at least in her own mind, she had to agree with her husband. While she was ashamed of her actions of the previous day, those actions in some way had helped make things work out for her and Martin, and it really did seem like they both were committed to rekindling the love they shared for so many years. "Thank you for not holding it against me. Really. We've both made mistakes, but now let's move forward, okay? I love you, Martin Teebs. You're the only one I want."

Martin pulled Lilly in closely and kissed her lightly on the forehead as the plane touched down. If he said anything to her, it was lost in the screech of tires landing and engines struggling to hold the big bird back from the end of the runway.

In his final sprint toward his new life, Martin could only make one decision: the right one. Rosita Luna was the most incredible woman he'd ever known. However, Martin was betting that if he ran toward her and Billy, he'd wind up somehow jogging back and forth in time yet again, causing her more pain and, ultimately, ending in the same tragedy he'd witnessed in Maxwell's bedroom in July, 1881. As much as Martin loved Rosita, he knew he could not, would not put her through that agony again. Nor could he put himself through it. Although the ache of his decision tore at him like someone was peeling the skin from his flesh, he had to believe that misery would someday subside. Martin had understood, in those final few seconds, that sometimes the most loving thing you can do for someone is to simply…let her go.

6 MONTHS LATER

"Hi, Lil, I'm home!" announced Martin, as he entered the Teebs household. Smiling, Lilly came from the kitchen, having been working on dinner for the past thirty minutes. She noticed Martin held a grocery bag.

"What did you get, big boy?" she asked, peeking inside the rim of the bag.

Martin seemed almost embarrassed to answer. "Umm, chocolate fudge ripple ice cream?" he said, more as a question than an answer. "It was two-for-one at Shoopman's."

Lilly tilted her head to the side and frowned a little at Martin's dietary choice but said simply, "Okay, but go easy on these. I want you around for a *long* time, Martin Teebs!" She grabbed the bag and headed back to the kitchen, saying on her way out, "Dinner in fifteen minutes. I'm making your favorite: pot roast."

Martin smiled and danced upstairs to get changed, thrilled at the feast he was about to enjoy. Stripping off his pants, he grabbed his wallet, keys, and phone and tossed them on top of his dresser. As he opened a drawer to find a pair of shorts, his phone buzzed with a text message, most likely from Colin, his friend at work. He and Martin were planning a big bash to watch the NFL draft on the coming weekend, and Colin had volunteered to run to the grocery store after work to pick up some snacks. He was probably going to present Martin with the queso versus salsa question.

Tapping the appropriate icon, Martin's heart stopped, literally for a few moments, as he read the message from the contact in his phone labeled "T" for Trisha.

"*Martin*, I am with child. I need you, *mi amor,* please, I beg of you, come to me. I have waited. Come to me."

EPILOGUE

Carl Farber awakened to the gurgling, sucking sounds coming from both his mouth and the wound in his chest. Clutching a bloodstained copy of *Sunset in Sumner,* he came to exactly in the spot from which he'd disappeared: the dirt lot next to the Lincoln County courthouse. Farber writhed in pain, desperately trying to breathe in enough oxygen to sustain life. At first spotted by a man on horseback, Farber rolled toward the road, unable to stand, begging for aid.

"I need help!" he cried, sounding like he was under water. "I've been shot…I need help!" he called again and again.

Soon, a frantic crowd gathered around the man and put him on a wagon to move him to the clinic operated by the town's oldest doctor, Jules Riley. Riley had spent time in urology and appearance surgery in his past, prior to establishing his small clinic in the now-peaceful town of Lincoln, NM. When the horribly injured man was wheeled into the office, Riley was caught both by the severity of the wound, which seemed to be from a small caliber pistol, and by the man's face, which looked eerily familiar from a time and place that Riley could just not quite recall.

The doctor medicated the poor bastard with morphine while he cut off the man's bloody clothes, which looked like they might have been remnants from the town back when it was a wild and woolly war zone inhabited by the likes of Billy the Kid. Now, in 1901, Lincoln was just a spot on a map that people passed by on their way to somewhere else.

"Celsa! Come now!" the doctor shouted. "I need my surgical kit right away!"

Celsa Gomez ran into the other room to fetch the requested kit and bring it to Dr. Riley. "Send everyone else away, we need to try to save this man's life!" he barked at her upon her return.

While the few remaining patients filed out of the waiting room, Celsa wished she had a way to get a message to the young man she was supposed to have a date with tonight. Based on how bad a shape their emergency patient was in, there was no way she'd be able to make it home in time to dress and attend dinner with the guy she'd met in town. However, just as Riley was starting his surgery, a large, grinning individual burst through the door, hoping to speak to the woman he was to date that very evening.

“Junior!” Celsa cried in surprise, “We’re in the middle of a surgery here. You have to go, now!”

The young man - the spitting image of one Martin Teebs - bent over the dying man; Carl Farber’s eyes went bigger than the bloody mess of a hole in his chest. Somehow, he managed to fashion his upper lip into a sneer and uttered a single word, as the scalpel penetrated his flesh.

“You…”

The End

ABOUT THE AUTHOR

Michael Anthony Giudicissi is an author, screenwriter, and speaker from Albuquerque, NM. Michael hosts the internationally popular YouTube channel, "All Things Billy the Kid". In addition to the Back to Billy series, Michael has written a number of other books focused on personal growth, business, and sales.

Disclaimer: *Due to the shifting nature of fiction versus reality, we're unsure exactly who is currently writing these books. Clearly a fictional character named Martin Teebs is not writing them, but who is Martin Teebs, really? Recent reports point to the fact that a Martin Teebs might just exist after all. We're not clear on whether Michael Anthony Giudicissi is a real person, or perhaps Michael Roberts might be the driving force behind the manuscript. It's possible, as disagreeable as it may seem, that even Carl Farber could be at the helm of current and future Back to Billy stories. Anyone with any information on this vexing puzzle is encouraged to contact the "author" at the links below.*

To Contact the Author: billythekidridesagain@gmail.com

Books in the "Back to Billy" saga:

Back to Billy – 2nd Edition (Mankind Media, 2023)

1877 (Mankind Media 2021)

Sunset in Sumner (Mankind Media 2021)

Bonney and Teebs (Mankind Media 2021)

One Week in Lincoln (Mankind Media 2021)

4 Empty Graves (Mankind Media 2022)

Pieces of Us (Mankind Media 2023)

COMING SOON:

1950, Book 8 in the Back to Billy Saga (Mankind Media 2023)

Lightning Source UK Ltd.
Milton Keynes UK
UKHW040218240223
417572UK00001B/39